Plane *in* *the* Lake

PRAISE FOR THE TONY VALENTI THRILLERS

* A House on Liberty Street *

Turner hits the mark in a spellbinding, page-turning thriller featuring a worthy underdog hero and prose that tugs at the heartstrings. The author has a great sense of plot and timing. **IndieReader 4.5 Star Review**

Neil Turner unravels an ever-deepening drama that exposes the lengths one man will go to protect his family in *A House on Liberty Street*, a suspenseful and heartfelt thriller. Tapping into evocative themes of family, fatherhood, and second chances, this is a fast-paced read with a clever protagonist ducking and dodging in a classic pursuit of justice. The storytelling is casual but compelling, with memorable characters, intriguing dynamics, and an unpredictable case for readers to piece together. ...there are also touching moments of paternal wisdom and honesty that shine... *A House on Liberty Street* is a neatly penned thriller that will keep readers guessing to the very end. **Self-Publishing Review**

* Plane in the Lake *

Neil Turner's latest Tony Valenti thriller, *Plane in the Lake*, pits the no-nonsense lawyer and his fiery partner against entrenched power in this classic Chicago crime story. Lawyers and liars go hand in hand in the pearly offices of the city's underworld, as a well-to-do family's desperate attempt to cover up the truth behind their daughter's death spirals into something much more. As Valenti is faced with saving not only his firm but his family too, Turner skillfully wields an incisive pen that takes on the seemingly untouchable upper classes and shady crime families. With his trademark breezy style reminiscent of Dennis Lehane, Turner has produced another devourable thriller. **Self-Publishing Review** ★★★★½

Plane in the Lake is a satisfying blend of tense thriller and whodunit that calls into question and ultimately strengthens Tony Valenti's bonds with friends, family, and peers. The novel works on many different levels to involve readers in a puzzle that remains murky up to its surprise conclusion. It's a fine story that will keep readers (whether newcomers or prior fans of Tony's gritty streetwise style) thoroughly engrossed to the end. **D. Donovan, Senior Reviewer, Midwest Book Review**

* A Case of Betrayal *

In his third powerful Tony Valenti Thriller, *A Case of Betrayal*, author Neil Turner puts his charming and brilliant defense attorney back into the fray, where his loyalties to old friends will be tested against his passion for justice. Diving into tough subjects - from the deeply rooted racism in America to the struggles of single fatherhood - this installment stands out from other thrillers; there is real heart in this prose, as well as nuanced character development that keeps the read continually engaging. Packed with suspense, and a page turner from the start. **Self-Publishing Review ★★★★½**

---

* A Time for Reckoning *

"A character-driven thriller that fearlessly reveals the dark corners of human nature – misogyny, greed, violence, power, and control. Driven by strong dialogue, unpredictable twists, and more than a dash of colloquial country charm, this savagely honest novel is a stellar addition to the *Toni Valenti Thriller* series." Self-Publishing Review, **★★★★½**

* Scared Silent *

"A brutal and gritty novel of survival on the merciless streets of Chicago, *Scared Silent* is a gut-wrenching ride. Given the national spotlight being recently turned towards the desperate plight of the poor, this gripping story is not only expertly penned, but also timely and fearless." **Self-Publishing Review, ★★★★★**

Plane *in* *the* Lake

Neil Turner

First Edition

Published by Neil Turner Books, Canada 2021

CHAPTER ONE

W*hat a perfect morning to fly,* Megan Walton thinks as she watches a gas jockey pump fuel into the high-winged Cessna 210N she'll be piloting on a city sightseeing tour on this, the last morning of her life. The robin's-egg-blue aircraft, which is emblazoned with the scarlet Windy City Sky Tours logo, glistens in the September sunshine on the tarmac at the Chicago Executive Airport. Megan pops a stick of Juicy Fruit gum into her mouth and pockets the foil wrapper. The smell of the gum is a welcome antidote to the acrid odor of the avgas, especially with her stomach still roiling from last night's party. She'd woken up just after seven with a jack-hammer headache and not enough sleep, having gotten back into town from her cousin's Labor Day weekend wedding in St. Lucia a little after two o'clock this morning. What a party! Cousin Emerald's parents had chartered a Gulfstream G280 executive jet to fly select wedding guests to and from the Caribbean. Now, *there* was an aircraft, complete with a uniformed flight attendant who catered to Megan's every whim, be it for booze or eats. Someday, Megan plans to be flying Gulfstreams instead of a Cessna.

The mechanics Uncle Jonathan hired to service the Windy

1

City aircraft are working on a little plane beside hers. Megan meets their eyes and looks away without acknowledging them. She forgets their names, not that it matters. They're just hired help. Megan, a pretty twenty-three-year-old dressed in tight designer jeans and a form-fitting red company polo shirt, knows she looks good. Guys like these two, dressed in oil-stained coveralls and grimy baseball caps, can gawk at her all they want, but they'll never touch what they're pining after.

Megan tucks her long, glossy blond hair into a ponytail while she watches the refueler disconnect the fuel hose from the Cessna and wind it back onto his truck. As soon as he departs, she shepherds the four waiting guests toward the six-seat Windy City aircraft. Leading the way is a cute tyke of four or five wearing jeans, a miniature New York Yankees jersey, and little sneakers that light up with every step. His smiling mother is close behind as he bounds along with unbridled excitement. She's an elegant woman wearing a canary-yellow sundress and sandals. A single strand of pearls the size of marbles circles her throat. A beaming, well-dressed older couple, no doubt Grandma and Grandpa, bring up the rear.

After her customers climb into the passenger compartment, Megan shuts the door behind them, pulls the chunky, black-and-yellow rubber wheel chocks away from the tires, and tosses them aside. Then she walks around the nose of the plane, climbs into the pilot's seat, straps herself in, and fires up the single-piston-powered engine. The initial roar blasts a burst of blue smoke into the air before the engine settles into a pleasing purr, just as it should. As she releases the brakes and begins to roll toward a taxiway that leads to the runway, one of the mechanics starts running across the tarmac while frantically waving to her. She looks away. Whatever he wants can wait until she gets back. Megan just wants to get this flight over with so she can unwind a little and maybe sneak in a nap before her eleven o'clock tour.

Five minutes later she's flying into the sun, passing over Navy Pier and out over Lake Michigan, happy to let the rich bitch in the back narrate the sights for her kid and the old folks. It's not easy to keep the thirty-minute flights interesting, especially three or four times per day. Too bad the woman's high-pitched voice is so damned grating.

"Ferris wheel, Mommy!" the kid squeals.

Shut him up! Megan pleads silently.

"Fast boat, Mommy!" the little noise box shouts while a speedboat races beneath them.

Megan winces. It's going to be a long half hour. The pounding in her temples won't quit, not even after she downed a handful of Extra Strength Tylenol with the Venti-size Caramel Brulée Latte she'd scored at Starbucks on her way to work. A second cup rests in a cupholder tacked onto the armrest of her seat. *Probably shouldn't have had that second glass of champagne on the Gulfstream,* she thinks as her lips curl into a devilish grin. Or the third, fourth, and fifth glasses—hell, she's not sure the bubbly is completely out of her system even now. What the hell, it was a party flight. Thank God she's wearing a pair of Bvlgari sunglasses to keep the blinding sun out of her eyes… and to keep her bloodshot eyes out of sight. That was $600 well spent. She'd given herself an extra spritz of perfume to mask any hint of hangover seeping from her pores. The Juicy Fruit should mask any unwelcome odor escaping her curdling stomach.

The back seat falls blissfully quiet as Megan flies out over the lake at a height of 3,020 feet at a ground speed of eighty knots. That's a little too fast, so she eases back on the throttle. She plans to travel a couple of miles offshore before turning south to let her passengers ogle Chicago's iconic skyline for a few minutes. Then she'll loop around downtown on her way back to the airport.

"I wanna see the Ferris wheel again, Mommy!"

Jesus Christ! Shut the brat up already! Megan fumes as she glances in the mirror. The kid's seat belt is off and he's bouncing on the rear seat. Did she check that he was strapped in before they taxied? Screw it, she isn't gonna fight with them about it now… or tell them to shut the kid up. After all, they're apparently Very Important People—politicians or something. She's already forgotten the family name they seem to think is so impressive. Probably the types who will kick up a stink if Megan isn't the polite little lackey they're treating her as. She knows about people like this. Her mother, for example.

Megan had enrolled in the aviation associate degree program at Parkland College on a whim, mostly because the guy she was interested in at the time had done so and it looked like fun. Her affection for the boy fizzled soon enough, but her love for flying blossomed. After she graduated, her parents poured a small fortune into rental aircraft so Megan could build the hours she needed to get her commercial license. When Uncle Jonathan and his friends bought Windy City Sky Tours to mess around with, Mother had put the heat on her brother to give his favorite niece a job… *and when Mother wants something, Mother gets it.* It was turning out to be a good gig that kept Megan in pocket money for parties and shopping. The hours were reasonable and she was generally able to milk the family connection to avoid early-morning shifts, leaving her free to stay out late and party—the whole point of living at her age.

BAM!

"Mommy!" the little kid exclaims while a shudder passes through the aircraft.

The engine backfires again. What the hell?

"Miss?" the old guy in the back asks uncertainly.

Megan shrugs her shoulders nonchalantly and replies with an airy "Just a little backfire" to shut the guy up. Then

4

she digs into her foggy mind, struggling to remember what she knows about backfires. It's been forever since flight school and all the boring shit about stuff like this.

Megan's stomach lurches when the engine coughs and dies with a final convulsive shudder. *What the hell do I do now?*

From the back comes a screeching *"Mommeeee!"*

"That's enough, Pumpkin," the man in back tells his grandson in a soothing voice. "Let's get you strapped in."

"No, Grandpa!"

"Shush, sweetheart," he purrs to the kid. "Let the pilot do her job."

Bless you, Gramps, Megan thinks gratefully. Okay, so now what? She runs her eyes over the bank of gauges and dials on the khaki-colored instrument panel in front of her. Altitude 3,105 feet. Airspeed seventy-three knots. Okay. She has a little time to work things out.

The mother and kid start whimpering while Megan tries to organize her thoughts.

Restart? Yes. There's a checklist for that. Her eyes dart around the cockpit. Where the hell is it? There's plenty of crap tucked away here and there but no sign of the engine-restart checklist. Okay, then. How hard can it be? She fiddles to reset the fuel mixture, hopefully to the correct mix. Then she cranks the ignition switch and pushes the throttle forward. Nothing. She tweaks the fuel mix and tries again. Still nothing. Shit!

"Shouldn't we turn back, Miss?" the old guy asks.

Not a bad idea at all, Megan thinks as she gazes through the windscreen at the flat blue expanse of Lake Michigan stretching away into the distance. It's strange and unnerving to see the scimitar propeller blades locked into place at eleven, three, and seven o'clock. Something about their appearance bothers her, but whatever it is remains just out of reach. Whatever. It's probably just seeing them stopped in flight. She relaxes her death grip on the control wheel while struggling to recall something that might get her out of this mess. *At least I'm flying a Cessna,* she thinks. Cessnas glide pretty far. How far? They'd joked at school that a small aircraft would glide pretty much forever without power, but the 210N is bigger than the pissy little planes they'd trained on at school. It wouldn't glide forever, but she had time. They couldn't be more than a minute into the emergency.

"I'm scared, Mommy!"

"Turn back!" the woman in the back shouts. That sets the kid to wailing again.

Megan glances in the mirror at the kid's tear-stained face and his mother's enormous, panicked eyes, then tunes them out while she studies the airspeed and altitude indicators: 2,800 feet; sixty-eight knots? Already? What the hell was the sink rate of this damned plane? Megan tries to work out her next steps, but nothing comes to mind. She squeezes her eyes shut and fights to control the rapid, shallow breathing that presages one of her panic attacks. How the hell had she gotten herself into this mess? Flying was fun but she hadn't bargained on a morning like this. Her uncle greasing the palm of a pliable flight instructor had seemed like an inspired move when she struggled a bit to master the 210N rating qualifications, but it wasn't looking like such a good idea at the moment. Sure, she can fly well enough, but this is a bit more than she can handle with her limited experience—especially while severely hungover.

Fragments of her training finally float into her mind. She takes a deep, cleansing breath and lets it out slowly, taking stock of the situation and tapping the tips of her French-manicured fingernails on the edge of the wheel as she thinks. The first thing she needs to do is get the damned plane headed back toward Chicago. She's only what—a mile offshore? Maybe two?

"Miss?" the man in the back ventures. "Maybe we should radio for assistance?"

The radio can't help them now. It's up to her. "I've been

gathering my thoughts," she tells Grandpa in a bid to shut him up. Her eyes drift across the instrument panel. Fifty-eight knots, 2,200 feet? What the hell is going on? They aren't going anywhere if she keeps losing height and speed at this rate. The altimeter drops to 2,100 feet, and another knot bleeds off their airspeed in the time it takes her to process the thought. *Should* she radio for help? *And look like an ass?* No.

"Turning back now," she mutters over her shoulder as she banks the Cessna into a tight 180-degree left turn to get back to safety. If the damned plane isn't going to fly, she needs to get closer to shore before she sets it down in the water. She'll be okay then—she was on swim team in high school.

"Miss!"

"Mommy!"

Megan doesn't register the panicked chaos in the back seat as the wing loses lift and her aircraft drops nose first out of the turn. She's now fully absorbed in her own horror as the surface of Lake Michigan fills the windscreen of the plummeting Cessna.

Fuel starvation? Megan wonders as she finally starts to make sense out of what's happening. No fuel reaching the engine would explain things. *Did I bleed the tanks?* She doesn't remember, but she suddenly realizes that she didn't feather the prop after it shut down. That's what bothered her when she was looking at the blades. With the flat surface square against the wind instead of turned edge on, they'd been acting like a speed break. Then she notices the Gear Down indicator light glowing green by her right knee and the landing-gear handle locked in the down position. She even forgot to raise the landing gear after taking off. No wonder the damned plane was sinking like a stone when it should have been gliding. Her final mistake was not using the rudder to make a longer, flat turn back to shore to preserve lift under the wing.

Megan adds her own screams to those coming from the

backseat. She pins the wheel to her chest in a futile bid to defy the laws of gravity for the thirty seconds it takes the Windy City Sky Tours September eighth morning flight to complete its death dive. As they plunge into the cold depths of Lake Michigan, Megan finds the silence she's been craving over the final fifteen minutes of her young life.

CHAPTER TWO

"**D**amn it!" I mutter as I lose yet another game of computer solitaire in my executive office at the oh-so-very prestigious law firm of Brooks and Valenti, a fifty/fifty partnership I own with Penelope Brooks. I think more than a few people familiar with the firm refer to us as Brooks and Dum; maybe they think we're the country-and-western duo Brooks and *Dunn*? Whatever. I roll my faux leather executive chair across the bruised tile floor toward my office door, a classic wooden one with a frosted glass insert. A cheesy fake brass plaque glued on the outside surface announces that this is the office of one Tony Valenti, Partner.

"Any sign of my one o'clock?" I shout to our receptionist/legal assistant/paralegal/office mother, Joan Brooks. She's Penelope's mother, a homey former Midwestern farmwife with a biting sense of humor she generally keeps hidden behind a taciturn demeanor.

Joan shakes her head and scowls at me. "Decorum, young man! This is a law office."

That's right. Shouting is frowned upon in the hallowed halls of Brooks and Valenti.

"What she said!" Penelope hollers from the slightly larger

executive suite beside mine. Her office is twelve feet by twelve feet. Mine is twelve feet by eleven feet, six inches... and yes, I have measured. Her office is also quieter, not sharing a common wall with the kitchen of the Chinese restaurant next door.

I roll my chair back to my naturally distressed oak desk to start a new game.

We're not *really* the two-bit, low-rent law firm we appear to be in our current premises. We're on day sixty-three in our temporary 1960s-era strip-mall digs while a contractor completes renovations on our permanent offices in a slightly more upscale heritage building a few blocks away in down-town Cedar Heights, a small suburb tucked just beyond the southwest corner of Chicago. Low rent is the point of being shoehorned into this dump. Oddly enough, the place is growing on me. It fits us: Brooks and Valenti—Lawyers to Little People and Lost Causes.

I'm delightedly dragging my fourth king into place when a discreet knock on my door interrupts my progress. I glance up to find Mama Brooks standing in the doorway.

She says, "Your one o'clock appointment is here."

"Please inform Mr. Likens that I shall be with him presently."

"Certainly, Mr. Valenti," she replies in mock deference as she backs away.

I frown at my interrupted game—*I might have won this one, damn it!*—and unfold my lanky frame out of my chair. It would be extremely poor form to keep Mr. Likens waiting while I finish the game.

"How the hell are you, Billy?" I boom as I stride into the reception area, pluck my visitor off the ground, and give him a heartfelt hug while his feet dangle several inches off the floor. Billy is five foot eight or so of aircraft mechanic. I'm six foot five. I wrinkle my nose at the sickly-sweet scent of whatever new floral air freshener Joan has plugged in today to do battle with the cooking smells that permeate our office from our neighbor, The Golden Dragon. I prefer the smell of Chinese food to most of the scents Joan tries to smother it with.

"Put me down!" Billy whispers furiously. "You know I hate it when you do this."

"I can't help myself," I say with a laugh as I set him down. "You're just so darned cute!"

Billy, the baby brother of the probable love of my life, Melanie Likens, blushes like a little beef tomato. It looks adorable on his cherubic face, which still sports a little baby fat in the cheeks at forty-three or whatever age he is now. I've been picking him up since he was nine or ten years old. It's been pissing him off since he was eleven or twelve. His dark, curly hair echoes my own, albeit without the touch of gray I'm developing. That said, when his baseball cap is off—which isn't often—his mane has started to show the first hint of receding. He's dressed up for his visit. New blue jeans, a dark-blue Chicago Cubs windbreaker over a Cubs polo shirt, and hiking boots. His customary attire is ratty jeans or sweatpants, logoed T-shirts, and sneakers.

Something in the blue eyes set into his angelic face gives me pause. Real anger over being manhandled? Nope. I see worry on Billy's face. Maybe even fear. I wrap an arm around his shoulders and walk him into my office, where I close the door and wave him toward a worn chrome-and-fabric stacking chair positioned in front of my desk. We drop into our assigned seats and stare at each other.

"What's up?" I ask.

Billy doesn't seem to know where to begin.

"Have you had lunch yet?" I ask. "I haven't eaten."

"Too nervous to eat, but you go ahead," he mutters. Spoken like a true lunch-bucket guy who brings his midday meal to work every morning.

Me? I don't even own a lunch box. "We attorneys generally dine out with clients."

Billy looks at me uncertainly. My sparkling wit doesn't seem to be putting him at ease.

"Sorry for the jackass humor," I add with a frown.

He waves the apology aside.

"Seriously though, it's after one o'clock and I haven't eaten," I continue. "There's a sandwich place down the block. We can talk there if you don't mind."

He nods and gets to his feet, tucking a manila envelope into the pocket of his jacket. I hadn't noticed it. Maybe he's actually here on a legal matter? I figured he was just dropping by to bullshit for a bit. We've been getting together to do so every couple of months since I moved back to Cedar Heights a year ago.

We stick to small talk while briskly covering the two blocks to the imaginatively named The Sandwich Emporium, which is located in a converted 1920s-era bungalow. I open the door for Billy and inhale deeply of the yeasty aroma of freshly baked bread. I'm disappointed that the co-owner who usually greets guests is conspicuously absent. Maiko is a big part of the attraction of coming here. Day off, I guess. We cross the black-and-white checkerboard floor to a little counter topped with a very old-style cash register. After ordering a pair of eight-inch Italian grinder sandwiches, a couple of kosher dill pickles, and two glasses of whatever beer is on tap, we sit on a pair of unbalanced chairs at a wobbly Formica-topped table set against a wall. We talk about his kids while we wait for our food. I pick it up when it's ready, pay, and carry it back to the table.

When Billy pulls out his wallet, I hold up a hand, grin, and wave him off. "I can't accept, pal. If, as I suspect, you've come to avail yourself of my legal expertise, the cost of this meal will end up on your bill."

He shakes his head and chuckles. "You're in fine spirits

today. Working in a run-down noir law office seems to agree with you."

I cock an eyebrow. "Noir… that's good. We think of it as a dump. Noir is much better!"

His expression turns serious as he pulls the manila envelope out of his jacket pocket. "Actually, I *am* here for legal help."

I don't like the fear and worry radiating off my friend. I promised his sister before she died that I would keep an eye out for her baby brother. He'd run a little wild in his midteens but sorted himself out on the baseball diamond as one of the top junior ballplayers in Chicagoland. When his Major League Baseball dreams petered out, he settled down and started a family. My job is to make sure he doesn't backslide. I've always called him on Mel's birthday to keep in touch. Back in the days when I lived in Atlanta, I made a point of hooking up with Billy for lunch or a beer at least once a year when I was in Chicago. It sounds as if I'm about to be called upon to keep my promise to Mel.

"Tell you what, Billy. Let's eat and finish our beer, then I'm yours all afternoon to talk about whatever you've come to discuss. Okay?"

He nods, lays the envelope down alongside his paper plate, and says, "Fair enough." Then he digs into his sandwich with gusto.

I join in, downing a few mouthfuls of sandwich and quaffing half my beer before my eyes focus on Billy's envelope. It's addressed to his company, R & B Ramp Services, but it's the return address that horrifies me. The envelope is from Butterworth Cole, a prestigious legal behemoth with which Penelope and I have some complicated history. Butterworth Cole doesn't piss around with legal issues unless there's big money involved. Billy doesn't have big bucks. I can't imagine his partner, Rick Hogan, is any better off. Ergo, they're mixed up with someone who *can* afford the services of Butterworth Cole. I can't think of a way this spells anything but trouble.

A sense of foreboding suddenly curbs my appetite, but I make myself down another couple of bites while Billy polishes off his sandwich and pickle. Might as well let him enjoy the meal before we get down to business.

"Glad you made me eat," Billy says as he pushes his plate aside. He wipes his lips and chin with a couple of paper napkins. "That was good."

"Best sandwiches in Chicagoland!" I exclaim, purloining The Sandwich Emporium's tagline. Some of the sloppiest sandwiches, too. I've been to the dry cleaner a few times after spilling food and/or sauce on my suits and ties. I'm not always the tidiest guy when it comes to eating, but I've managed to get through today's lunch without a mishap.

Billy's expression sobers when he picks up the manila envelope, cracks open the flap, and pulls out a sheaf of papers that I, in all my glorious legal expertise, instantly recognize as lawsuit paperwork. I'm distressed to spot R & B Ramp Services among a laundry list of defendants. I look up to meet Billy's eyes and wait.

"Did you hear about the tour plane that crashed into Lake Michigan the morning after Labor Day?" he asks.

"Congressman's wife and parents?"

"He's actually a senator named Evan Milton, but yeah. His wife and son died. Parents, too."

The story swims into focus. A tour plane had inexplicably landed nose first in Lake Michigan. Nobody swam away. "R & B is involved?"

"We did their maintenance," he replies, then lifts a corner of the paperwork with his pinky finger. "This legal stuff is way over my head. Fortunately, Windy City's owners have plenty of money."

"Windy City? What's that?"

"The owners of the plane. They've set up a meeting with me and Rick to go over this thing."

"Who are these people?" I ask. "Where does their money come from? At $100 bucks per trip or whatever tour operators charge, I can't imagine anyone is getting rich from the air-tourism business."

"Windy City is owned by some rich kids who work at the Board of Trade. The air-tour gig is a sideline. I figure they want a tax write-off and access to their own plane whenever they want it. One of them goes to football games at his alma mater, another goes on weekend jaunts to shop."

Alarm bells are going off all over the place. "And these nice people are anxious to help you and Rick, huh?" Billy gives me an uncertain look as I fold the legal papers back into the manila envelope, pocket it, and get to my feet. "I'm glad you brought this to me. Let's go back to the office and kick it around with Penelope. She's the brains of our little operation."

We chat about our kids on the walk back to the office.

"I'll pay you for your time," Billy says while I hold the outside door open.

That's kind of funny, I think as he walks past a baby-blue copy-paper notice taped to the wall immediately beneath our firm's temporary sign. An excerpt from Emma Lazarus's poem "The New Colossus" that adorns the pedestal base of the Statue of Liberty is printed on the page:

Give me your tired, your poor,
Your huddled masses yearning to breathe free,
The wretched refuse of your teeming shore.
Send these, the homeless, tempest-tost to me.

That pretty much spells out the mission statement of Brooks and Valenti. The poor creatures referenced in the poem constitute far too much of our client base. Billy is a good fit for our firm—someone in no position to pay us anything near what a legal battle with Butterworth Cole is likely to cost.

"I mean it, we'll pay you for your time," Billy reiterates as we enter Joan's cramped reception area.

"Don't worry about it. We'll work something out," I say as I knock on my partner's open door and poke my head in.

"Work what out?" Penelope asks, then sits up straighter when she sees Billy easing in behind me. "Sorry, I didn't realize we had company." She smiles, gets to her feet, and extends a hand to Billy. "Penelope Brooks."

"Billy Likens," he says as they exchange a crisp handshake.

Penelope waves us into her visitor chairs and meets my gaze. "Business?"

I nod.

She points at the office door. "Get that?"

I reach back to push the door closed, then place the Butterworth Cole envelope into her outstretched hand without saying a word. We sit quietly while she reads. Penelope's a wholesome and athletic Kansas country girl with shoulder-length brown hair cut with bangs across her forehead. She stands barely above five feet tall and is a remarkable reproduction of her mother, right down to the hairstyle. She'd been drawn to the law by her admiration of a grandfather who was elected local judge after their family hardware store had been put out of business by Walmart coming to town. Penelope loved how he did the job—"armed with a bushel of common sense and integrity but not a law degree." He inspired her to go to law school. Penelope's mother had worked in her father's judge's chambers after the kids were in school, developing the skills she now employs on our behalf. Joan has been widowed for something over two years. Filling her empty days with us seems to be good therapy.

Penelope lifts her enormous chocolate eyes to us, bounces

her eyebrows, and whistles softly. "They're looking for quite a payout."

I'll say. Twenty million dollars is a fair chunk of change.

"I assume you're one of the defendants?" she asks Billy.

"R & B Ramp Services."

"Who are the rest of these folks?"

"Windy City Sky Tours owned the plane," he replies. "We serviced it."

"And the lawsuit names everyone else who might have touched the plane in passing any time over the past few years?" Penelope asks drolly.

"Pretty much," Billy replies with a chuckle.

She thinks for a moment. "What does the NTSB say?"

The National Transportation Safety Board investigates aviation accidents, among other things. It never ceases to amaze me that she knows things like this off the top of her head.

Billy shrugs. "They're investigating. It'll probably be a few months before they reach any conclusions."

Penelope leans back while her eyes drift to the ceiling. It's what she does when chasing a thought or a bit of information that's just out of reach. My eyes follow, and I watch with interest as a particularly large dust mote breaks free from an old fluorescent overhead light fixture and floats down to land on one of my shirt sleeves.

"Haven't they been giving public updates?" Penelope asks as I flick the speck of dust aside.

"Just the facts, madam," Billy says with a goofy little smile he flashes whenever he thinks he's being clever. In this case, he's parroting Dan Aykroyd's Detective Joe Friday in a 1980s motion-picture parody of the classic old television series *Dragnet.* How in hell Mel indulged Billy by watching that movie with him a thousand times is beyond me. I mean, the movie was okay, but how many times? But that was Mel— anything for her baby brother. His eyes cut to mine to make sure I didn't miss his witty moment. I reply with an indulgent eye roll.

Penelope's eyes pass between us before she purses her lips, drops her head, and continues reading. When she finishes, she tosses the paperwork on the desk. "They're fishing."

That they are. The lawsuit has no particular focus. Instead, it throws a wide blanket over every potential defendant they can think of and makes every conceivable claim of negligence and malfeasance... and then a few more.

"Butterworth Cole is staking its claim as lawyers for the plaintiffs," I tell Billy.

"What does that mean?"

"They're pissing on the case to mark it as their territory in hopes the family won't look elsewhere for representation."

"Don't lose any sleep over it for now," Penelope tells Billy.

"I'm plenty worried," he says with a frown. "How long will this last? A couple of months?"

"No," Penelope replies. "Cases like this last months, maybe even a year or more."

"But it's only been a month since the crash," Billy says. "They seem to be moving plenty fast."

"Like I said," I say. "They're marking their territory. With that accomplished, things will slow down. Butterworth Cole will drag things out as long as they can to milk their client for every possible billing hour."

Penelope tilts her head to the side and studies Billy. "How long have you been working with these Windy City people?"

"A little over a year now," he replies.

"Did you know the pilot?"

"Megan Walton. I was introduced when she started, but we didn't get to know her. The pilot turnover at Windy City is atrocious. As Rick says, 'If they paid their pilots more than a couple of bucks above the going hourly rate for flipping burgers, maybe they'd stay longer than a month or two.'"

"Who's Rick?" Penelope asks.

"Rick Hogan, my partner at R & B. He was never comfortable with Megan flying the Cessna and wondered if she was properly qualified. That question gnawed at me from the day she arrived, never more so than on that morning."

Penelope cocks an eyebrow. "Tell us about Megan."

Billy frowns. "She's Jonathan Walton's niece."

"Who's Jonathan Walton?" she asks.

"One of the Windy City owners. He seems to be the guy in charge."

Penelope nods. "Okay. So, back to Megan. Why was Rick concerned?"

"She barely looks—looked—old enough to have a driver's license. We wondered how she built enough flight hours to qualify for the gig at Windy City."

Penelope knits her eyebrows together. "She had her pilot's license, right?"

"Yeah, and she was rated for the 210."

"So, why were you concerned?"

"The 210 has retractable landing gear and other complexities that necessitate more than basic private piloting skills. It demands an aviator with experience, not someone who happens to look ravishing in aviator glasses and tight clothes."

Penelope's eyes narrow. "That sounds a little sexist."

Billy shrugs. "That's not how I meant it, Penelope. The family connection concerned me, and Megan was very much a 'look at me!' kind of gal—hard to take seriously. It was so typical of Windy City to exploit the looks of their employees to promote business. All their pilots look good—guys and gals. Anyway, the owners seem much more focused on appearances and marketing than safety. Even before the accident, we decided not to re-up the contract when it comes up for renewal."

"Why?" I ask.

"Too much trouble. I'm tired of fighting with the cheap bastards to spring for the money to keep their planes airworthy."

"How long had this Megan been around?" I ask Billy.

His brow furrows while he thinks. "Coupla months, maybe three?"

Not long, then. I follow up with "What happened that morning to concern you?"

"We were on the ramp next to her while she prepped the Cessna," Billy replies with a faraway look. "When she started to taxi, I realized that I hadn't seen her bleed the fuel tanks. Neither had Rick, so I ran after her, trying to get her attention so I could make sure she had done it. If she hadn't, we could do it before she took off."

"This might be a dumb question, but I don't know what bleeding the tanks means," Penelope says.

"You want to make sure you've worked any air bubbles out of the fuel tanks before flying," Billy explains. "The last thing a pilot needs is to have an air pocket block a fuel line in flight."

I think of air in the fuel lines of lawn mowers and such. "No gas gets to the engine?"

"That's right."

"How long does the problem last?" Penelope asks.

Billy meets her gaze. "Until the pilot manages to glide to a landing or the plane crashes."

Penelope winces. "Is that what you think happened?"

"Could be, but nobody knows," Billy replies. "I'm sure the NTSB will look into it." Then he taps a finger on the paperwork he brought in. "I don't get this lawsuit, guys. Shouldn't it wait until the NTSB finishes investigating?"

"Welcome into the pool with the legal sharks, pal," I mutter.

"This isn't exactly our area of expertise, Mr. Likens," Penelope says.

"Billy, please."

Penelope smiles. "Billy it is. Are you sure you want us to represent you in this matter? We could do a little research and recommend a firm with more experience in air accidents."

Billy looks at me and shakes his head. "Mel trusted you. I trust you. I watched your dad's trial and that business with the village where you saved Liberty Street from the wrecking ball. You folks are big time!" he concludes with a grin.

"Big time, my ass," I say with a chuckle. He's referring to the one and only criminal trial I've been involved in, and what was essentially a zoning battle with a village of several thousand people. Both had gotten a little press about a gazillion media cycles ago.

Penelope smiles at Billy. "Guess we've got a deal."

Bless her. No questions about billing, no equivocation whatsoever, just "How can we help?" This is why our firm's monthly billings generally cover the rent with just enough left over to keep the partners in mac and cheese.

Billy tells her about the Windy City invitation to drop by to discuss things, including a brief explanation of what he knows about the owners.

Penelope's eyes cut to mine. She doesn't seem to like the idea any more than I do. She cups her chin in her hand and taps the end of her index finger on the tip of her button nose while she ponders the situation, then says, "I don't like the idea of you meeting with the Windy City people."

"At least not by yourself," I add.

Penelope dons a half smile and shoots Billy a sideways glance. "Uh-oh. That's his 'Scheming Valenti' tone of voice."

I feign an indignant expression. "Me? A schemer? Maybe I plan ahead a little now and then. That's a crime?"

"Come on," Penelope says with a soft chuckle. "Out with it, partner. What have you got in mind?"

"An observant fly on the wall in that meeting might learn quite a bit."

Penelope's eyes twinkle. "Would this fly on the wall happen to go by the name of Tony Valenti?"

I wink at Billy. "Behold the legal and feminine intuition of my partner, Billy, my boy. You're in good hands."

Penelope may be smiling as she chuckles and shakes her head, but her eyes are wary as she looks at me.

"What?" I ask.

"You make for a pretty big fly."

She has a point. There aren't many flies my size buzzing around town, not even in a city the size of Chicago.

"You're pretty recognizable these days, too," Penelope adds.

I shrug. Since the aforementioned murder trial and village squabble ended, I may as well be the Invisible Man. All that was months and months ago—ancient history in today's media landscape. Besides, Billy's would-be benefactors are Board of Trade creatures. "I doubt those people watch much news beyond the market reports."

"But they *may* recognize you," she cautions.

"I doubt they'll shoot if they do."

Billy's eyes have been tracking between Penelope and me as we've batted our ideas back and forth. His expression lightens and his eyes settle on mine when understanding finally dawns. "You're coming with us?"

Well, that hopeful expression settles things, doesn't it? I can't say no to that face, which is so similar to Mel's. I reach over and squeeze his shoulder. "We can't be sending an innocent little Christian boy like you off to the Board of Trade Colosseum to face those Chicago Loop lions all by yourself, can we?"

Billy grins. Penelope looks mildly skeptical. I belatedly wonder what the hell I'm getting us into.

CHAPTER THREE

"I'm not sure about seeing these guys without lawyers," Oliver Franklin says uncertainly two days after Billy brought the lawsuit to Brooks and Valenti.

"Don't be a pussy," scoffs Jonathan Walton, one of Franklin's two partners in Franklin, Tyson, Walton Commodity Brokers, LLC. The trio also owns one hundred percent of Windy City Sky Tours. "We're dealing with blue-collar troglodytes with grease under their nails, Franklin," he adds. "That's why all three of us are here. If this meeting is ever questioned, it'll be our word against theirs."

Partner number three, Caitlyn Tyson, laughs in delight. "That's hardly even fair."

They're seated in the FTW corporate boardroom with Walton at the head of the conference table, as befits his status as their unofficial leader. Walton began life with a healthy leg up that he owed entirely to the family he was born into. His wealthy mother is a pillar of the Chicago philanthropic and fine-arts scenes, and his father is a prominent plastic surgeon whose services his handsome WASP son couldn't conceivably need. Jonathan Walton has never quite had to grow up; he still wears ball caps backward away from work and talks more like a college frat boy than a professional trader.

Walton taps his copy of the lawsuit paperwork. "*We're* not going to get stuck paying for this, Franklin. A case like this is *exactly* why Windy City is set up the way it is. We're golden."

Tyson, five foot nine of upper-crust sorority girl dabbling in the business world with a couple of decimal points worth of her family's fortune, reaches over to cover Franklin's hand with her own. "Jonathan's right. No lawyers today. We can string these R & B dopes along with the BS that we're all in this together, just business partners looking out for one another." She grins wickedly and adds, "We'll get our lawyers involved to screw over these bozos later. For now, let's learn what we can about what happened out there. These two probably have some insights into what went wrong."

"They sure as hell know more about it than we do," Walton agrees. "We can pass that along to our attorneys. That can't do anything but help us. The plan is to push hard to get this settled and put it behind us."

"Why?" Franklin asks. "The crash was only a month ago. Civil lawsuits drag on forever."

Walton shakes his head. "We hold all the cards here, pal. Lots of cash to spread around, top-shelf lawyers, motivated partners in AAA Avgas—"

"Partners who know how to be persuasive," Tyson cuts in with a grin.

Walton chuckles. "To put it mildly."

"Plus the access our wealth and social standing provide."

"Right," Walton agrees. "Hell, R & B probably doesn't even have a lawyer yet. So, we're going to use our advantages to bury those rubes—quickly and completely."

Franklin's eyes track between his partners while a tentative smile creeps across his face. "Okay, I see where you're going with this. You two are considerably more Machiavellian than me."

So we are, Walton thinks with a grin. Franklin, a thin, plain former prep school and college buddy of his, can supposedly trace his lineage back to Benjamin Franklin. Even he thinks that's most likely bullshit, but he's happy to take advantage of the story. Given that his family trades on that tenuous connection for their social standing in lieu of conspicuous wealth, Franklin tends to be the most cautious of the partners. He'd been a straight arrow at school, the guy who got the mercurial Walton out of a few scrapes with schools and the law. Walton and Tyson sometimes chaff at his timidity, but both recognize that it tempers their more reckless tendencies.

"It sucks to be down to a single airplane," Tyson grumbles. "Having a plane available for a weekend or two was a nice little perk."

"It *was* nice," Franklin adds with a wistful smile.

Walton frowns. That *does* suck. Taking their only remaining aircraft out of service for personal jaunts is out of the question. They discussed replacing the lost Cessna out of pocket, but Franklin had persuaded them to wait until the insurance company paid up. He argued that they were headed into the winter season and wouldn't need a second aircraft until spring. Left unsaid was the fact that it would be a struggle for him to come up with his third of the cost.

"I planned to use the Cessna for a shopping and clubbing trip to New York City next weekend," Tyson gripes. "Now I'll have to fly commercial."

Oh boo-hoo, Walton thinks. She can afford to charter a jet any time she wants to.

Now in full-on annoyed mode, Tyson glares at the polished, black-granite wall clock. Its brushed aluminum hands point to a couple of minutes past two o'clock.

"Where the hell are those damn mechanics?" she snaps. "I have things to do!"

"We're gonna be late," Billy complains to Rick and me as the Willis Tower elevator doors glide closed and he pushes the button for floor number sixty-seven.

"No big deal," I say as the elevator begins its ascent. "They're probably annoyed that the help is keeping them waiting. Having them a little off balance isn't going to hurt." In fact, I'd lingered over a cup of coffee at Dunkin' on West Adams Street until two o'clock sharp to ensure that we'd be five minutes late.

Billy meets my gaze and shoots me an easy smile. "If you say so. You're the lawyer."

"Don't mention that upstairs," I remind him with a grin as the elevator begins to slow. Brooks and Valenti hasn't formally taken on the case, so I have no obligation to tell our hosts that I'm an attorney.

"Man, these things are quick," Rick marvels as the elevator slows to a smooth stop and dings to announce our arrival.

It reminds me of the elevators at the former Sphinx Financial Tower in Atlanta, where I worked as a high-powered corporate attorney once upon a time. There are no elevators, of course—slow or fast—at the offices of Brook and Valenti, Strip Mall Attorneys at Law.

The elevator spills us out into a hardwood vestibule flanked by a pair of generous reception areas behind glass walls. We pick Door Number Two: Franklin, Tyson, Walton Commodity Brokers LLC. I hang back, allowing Billy and Rick to take the lead. Both are decked out in Haggar slacks, button-down long-sleeve shirts, and deck shoes. I've dressed down to a pair of jeans, a black-and-gray striped short-sleeve shirt, and a pair of loafers—all the better not to look lawyer-like. I hope to become part of the wallpaper when the meeting gets underway.

While Rick talks with the receptionist, I gaze around at the richly appointed reception area. My feet sink deeply into pile carpeting that threatens to swallow us whole. A burnished steel FTW logo stretches across the wall with the tagline Feeding the World just below it. Black-and-white photos of basic foodstuffs dot the walls—bushels of maize and soybeans, fields of grain. *Feeding the world, my ass,* I think as we're shuttled toward a meeting room. I've done some reading up on these folks. FTW is a commodity-trading firm that works to manipulate the futures market to drive up prices. There seems to be nothing that the world's bankers believe they shouldn't be free to exploit, including food staples. I imagine that in their perfect world, bankers would pocket a penny or two with every bite.

We're shown into a large conference room. The smarmy smiles our hosts paste on their faces as they greet us heighten my suspicions about why they've invited Billy and Rick for a visit. I continue to hang back while my friends shake hands with their so-called partners. Then they sit down in a pair of brown leather chairs at the opposite end of the polished conference table. I take a seat alongside Billy, who nods toward me and introduces me as his friend Tony, "who we brought along today as a third set of ears." I smile and nod at the jackals.

The gaze of the woman introduced as Caitlyn Tyson lingers on me for a long moment after her partners dismiss me as unimportant. "Do I know you?"

I shake my head. "I don't think so."

"You look familiar," she mutters as she continues to stare.

I'm tempted to say something—anything that might prevent my cover from being blown—but decide to keep my mouth shut. I shrug and look away.

Billy has the presence of mind to distract everyone. "Man, I'm so glad you guys called!" he gushes to our hosts. "Getting served with this lawsuit really shook us up."

Walton turns an oily smile on him. "Glad to help, buddy. We're all in this together."

Of course, you are! I think while intuiting that Walton appears to be the leader of this unholy trinity. The guy's got a streak of bullshit on him a mile long.

"Thanks, man," Billy says.

Tyson leans closer to smile at Billy and waves a hand toward the window, beyond which the expanse of Lake Michigan stretches away to the horizon. "So? What do you think happened out there?"

Billy turns his palms up. "No idea. The NTSB report should tell us."

The investigation will take at least two or three months. I advised Billy and Rick to keep their heads down as much as possible until the accident report is published. They've already been questioned by the NTSB Go Team and have turned over their maintenance records. Windy City doesn't need to know any of that. I suspect the only reason we're here today is to allow our hosts to pick Billy's and Rick's brains for ideas Windy City's lawyers can exploit to dodge responsibility for the crash and pin the blame on their R & B "buddies."

"Sure," Walton says agreeably to Billy. "But what do you guys think?"

"You're the experts," Tyson adds while all but batting her big eyelashes. "What do you think? Bad fuel? Pilot error?"

Her second guess draws a sharp look of disapproval from Walton. No surprise there. The pilot was his niece. It looks as if he intends to protect Megan... at least at this early stage. "Structural failure seems to be a possibility," he says, pointing the finger away from the pilot and squarely at R & B.

Yeah, yeah, you're all in this together.

Billy shrugs uncomfortably. Rick's eyes narrow as he says, "The maintenance was all current."

"It was supposed to be, anyway," Tyson says enigmatically, showing the first card the Windy City owners are likely to play in their bid to pin the blame on R & B.

Walton taps the lawsuit paperwork. "According to the plaintiff's lawyers, our plane fell out of the sky for no apparent reason, my friends. They contend this was almost certainly due to faulty maintenance—either mechanical failure or structural failure, both of which point directly at you guys, right?"

"That's bullshit," Rick mutters.

"That remains to be seen," Walton says as he sits forward and smiles at Billy. "That leaves you vulnerable, buddy. We can help. We'll have your back, but we have to work together to do so."

Billy's shoulders relax. Walton, apparently seeing him as R & B's potential weak link, is trying to lure him into the trap of trusting his so-called partners. It's time for me to enter the fray.

I lean in and smile at Walton. "Let's all remember that you folks are the lead defendant in this lawsuit."

My intervention surprises Walton, whose eyes cut to me before turning back to Billy. He looks like a predator whose prey has just escaped its grasp.

"There's a reason for that," I continue. "R & B is just an add-on defendant. Same with the fuel vendor and the airport." I pause and make eye contact in turn with Walton, Tyson, and Franklin. "You folks *do* get that, don't you?"

The Windy City three exchange glances. Walton's smugness has faltered, Franklin looks genuinely worried, and Tyson is once again eying me suspiciously.

"Sure, sure, but we're all vulnerable," Walton says as his eyes again settle on Billy. "We've got good lawyers, buddy. The best. The more we can tell them about possible causes for the accident, the better."

"And the sooner, the better," Franklin chimes in.

I think back to the video of the NTSB Go Team media briefings I watched this morning while I prepared for this meeting. I can still hear the flat recounting of the facts being delivered in the bureaucratic legalese so typical of government spokespersons. Based upon air traffic control radar, the established facts of the accident are: The Windy City Cessna was flying straight and level in an eastward direction at an altitude of 3,100 feet and a groundspeed of seventy-three knots when it began to lose speed and altitude beginning at 9:03:15 a.m. By 9:04:05 a.m., the airplane had descended to 2,800 feet and was traveling at sixty-eight knots. The NTSB had no opinion on whether the pilot was executing a planned descent, but nothing in the flight profile indicated otherwise. At least not for twenty-two more seconds, at which time the plane was traveling fifty-seven knots at an altitude of 2,100 feet. The final sentence of the briefing has stuck in my mind, perhaps because the dispassionate recitation of tragedy had been so utterly bereft of emotion. "At 09:04:27 the aircraft initiated an abrupt left turn, at which point the aircraft commenced a vertical descent. Radar contact was lost at 09:04:41."

"Billy and Rick were right earlier," I say. "The NTSB investigation will get to the bottom of what happened. Of course, that report can't be used in court, so anything that gets said at this stage could turn out to be a problem. It's probably best for all of us to sit back and let things play out."

Perhaps aware that I'm onto their scheme, Walton gives me a long, decidedly unfriendly look.

Tyson slams an open palm on the tabletop and explodes, "I *do* know you. You're a lawyer! You helped your father get away with murder!"

Recognition dawns on Franklin's face, as well. "You shot down Titan Development's plans in Cedar Heights, too, didn't you?"

Penelope apparently called things correctly.

Walton shoots to his feet and levels an accusing finger at me. "You didn't tell us you're a lawyer! That's unethical!" A sly smile curls his lips. "I'll have your balls for this. Kiss your law license goodbye, asshole."

I smile back. "As Billy told you off the top, I'm just here doing a favor for a friend. I haven't been retained to represent R & B."

Walton snorts and waves my comment aside. "I think it's time for you gentlemen to leave."

I lock eyes with him as I languidly get to my feet. "With partners like you folks, it's pretty clear that Billy and Rick will need their own lawyers."

Walton's color is up as he points at the door. "Get the fuck out!"

"Roger that," I answer back. "Fucking off now."

War has been declared.

CHAPTER FOUR

L ife is good. I'm in the kitchen two days after being chased out of the meeting with the Windy City assholes, up to my neck in preparations for a Sunday backyard dinner of Tony Valenti's Famous Burgers. Family occasions such as this are a big reason why my daughter, Brittany, and I came to the Valenti family home in Cedar Heights when we fled Atlanta last summer in the wake of my failed marriage to Brittany's mother. My mother may be gone now, having passed away a little over a year ago, but my father, Francesco—"Papa" to us—and my fifteen-year-old daughter are making up for lost time.

Papa is washing a batch of his prized homegrown tomatoes at the kitchen sink. "You want the tomatoes?" he asks Brittany.

"Those yucky things?"

"No?"

"I'm just kidding!" she exclaims as she eases closer to Papa. "I'd love a few of your tomatoes."

He gives her the stink eye as he pulls the bowl away from her. "No tomato for you! You have only the one chance when I ask!"

My father stands a couple of inches under six feet, has a wiry build, and tufts of thinning gray hair. The most prominent features on his olive-complexioned face are wild, bushy eyebrows over a pair of piercing hazel eyes. He talks and walks fast, always has. I recall oftentimes running to keep up with him when I was a kid. There's a fair amount of him in my features, although I keep my eyebrows carefully trimmed. I have his hazel eyes, but inherited Mama's lengthy eyelashes and a more rounded face in comparison to Papa's sharper features. You'd be hard pressed to find much family resemblance between my daughter and father. Brittany's lithe build, bright blue eyes, and striking good looks owe much to her mother.

As I turn away from yet another faux grandfather-granddaughter confrontation to survey my meal preparations—raw hamburger patties, German-style potato salad, and pasta salad—I see Papa wink and flip a tomato to Brittany. She catches it and pops it into her mouth in a single motion. What in hell makes these two think their fake dramas are so amusing is beyond me, but that might be because I'm neither young nor old enough understand the dynamic. Or maybe I'm just dense. What the hell, they seem to enjoy it.

I've prepared a dozen of my signature half-pound patties —two each for my father and myself, one for Brittany. The rest will find their way down Papa's gullet within a day or two. I pick up the platter of uncooked burgers and head for the door leading to our backyard while Papa smiles in anticipation. He came late to the burger party—burgers hadn't been a thing where he grew up in Calabria, Italy. He and Mama tended to favor Italian dishes in the years after he immigrated to the United States, yet Papa loves the damned things nowadays. It's a wonder he hasn't chained me to the grill for the entire summer. Deano, our plump fourteen-year-old black Labrador retriever, lumbers along in my wake, wagging his tail at the prospect of a stray bite to inhale.

"Hey, Ed," I say when I reach the beige flagstone patio.

Ed Stankowski is a retired Cedar Heights detective we've hired to provide a little security for Papa. After my father was acquitted of murder charges and our home was rescued from a predatory developer last year, he often faced harassment when he ventured out in public. The abuse had eventually followed him home. Hence the security.

Ed dips his chin in my direction. "Tony."

I lift the platter of patties. "We've got plenty of burgers if you want one."

Ed glances at his watch. "May as well. Jake's gonna be late picking me up."

"Again?" I ask with a wide-eyed chuckle.

"Yeah," he grumbles, but he's smiling as he does so. "Another big case, or so he says. He might just be out having a pre-brew brew, y'know? Maybe with one of those young women cops they've got nowadays."

I lift the lid on our Weber grill and start tossing patties on the rack. "Nah, Jake's a one-woman kinda guy, don't you think?"

Jake Plummer is the Cedar Heights PD homicide detective who was the lead investigator in Papa's case. To my immense surprise, Plummer turned out to be a good guy. He'd put me onto Ed when it became clear that Papa needed a little temporary security.

Ed laughs at my observation. "You're damned right. Jake has the good sense not to piss off his wife by chasing after young women. We senior citizens need people to care for us in our dotage. It's not as if the gals are interested in us old farts, anyway."

I soon have a veritable bonfire going on the grill. I'm using two spatulas to move the patties around in an almost futile bid to keep them out of the grease flares that always threaten to overwhelm me when I cook burgers. It's like playing whack-a-mole with continuous bursts of flame.

Ed watches with an amused smile. "Y'know you need a bigger grill for that many burgers, don't you?"

"Oh, I know," I reply dryly. I've been thinking that I might be able to get Papa to spring for a larger grill by telling him I could cook two dozen patties at a time on a bigger grate. My appeals for a grill manufactured within the past century have fallen on deaf ears. "Papa seems to think a Civil War-era grill is all we need."

"Lemme talk to the old coot and knock some sense into him."

I give Ed a skeptical look. "Good luck with the old coot."

His eyes stray around the backyard sanctuary my parents built over the years. Papa and Mama added plenty of Mediterranean flourishes, including a creamy four-foot-tall stucco fence that features a mural my late sister, Amy, painted the summer after she graduated from high school. A rock-and-rose garden rises in the middle of the yard. Papa's tomato plants line the north side of the fence. To the surprise of everyone—no one more than me—I managed *not* to kill Mama's prized rose bushes over the summer.

"Every time I come here, I find myself thinking about what a cool yard this is," Ed says. "Makes me wanna do something with my own place."

"Why don't you?"

"Too damn lazy," he says with a chuckle.

Papa eventually saunters out. Deano trots over to join him —another bloodhound hot on the scent of fresh meat. My father appears surprised but happy to discover that Ed is still here. They get along well, and I'm pleased that my retired father has someone to hang with. They're of an age, and Ed appears to enjoy the company as much as Papa does. He seems to be in no hurry to wind things up. It's not as if he's charging us much, so I'm happy to play along.

"Plummer, he late again?" Papa asks Ed in his fractured

English. After forty-plus years in the US, he still hasn't mastered the language.

Ed nods, then points at the grill, where I'm just visible within a blanket of smoke as I battle to keep from charring the burgers. "Your kid needs a bigger grill, Francesco. Stop being a cheap bastard and get him one!"

"Yes?" Papa asks him with an appraising glance my way.

Ed nods. Papa nods. There must be a generational wavelength at work here. I may be getting a new grill!

Papa wanders back into the house. Deano stares after him but isn't prepared to abandon his burger quest.

Jake Plummer lets himself into the backyard a minute later. The detective is in his mid-fifties, maybe five feet eight inches tall, is well on his way to bald, and is dressed in a nondescript gray suit that probably came off the rack at a department store. Cheap suits seem to be his detective uniform. "Ski!" he exclaims.

Ed turns to look at his friend. "Hi, you culturally insensitive son of a bitch!"

Plummer's frosty mustache twitches as he laughs. He swears that his use of "Ski" to refer to Ed is nothing more than commentary on his friend's rather prominent nose, whereas Ed insists it's a slur on his Polish ancestry.

Plummer makes a point of sniffing the air, which is still thick with smoke pouring out of the grill. "Smells pretty good out here."

"Good timing," I tell him as I start transferring the cooked burgers into a CorningWare serving dish. "Want one?"

Plummer takes another sniff and smiles. "Don't mind if I do."

"Would one of you guys mind poking your head inside to let everyone know that we're ready out here?" I ask.

When Ed nods and starts to stand, Plummer puts a hand on his shoulder to stop him. "Got something I need to talk to you two about without anyone else listening."

Ed settles back into his seat. I plop the lid on the Corning-Ware bowl and set it on the side shelf, where the heat from the grill will keep the burgers warm. Something in Plummer's demeanor puts me on edge.

"A pal of mine from Chicago PD intelligence dropped in on me this afternoon," he begins. "That's why I'm late."

Ed cocks an eyebrow. "And?"

"Some organized crime wise guy gave him a heads-up about a visitor from Italy who's in town putting out feelers about Francesco." Plummer studies me intensely. "Any idea what that's about?"

I might have an idea, but I need to think this through before answering.

Plummer pauses for a beat to let me answer before he continues, "My first thought was that this has to be bullshit, but then my guy told me a little bit about who this character is supposedly associated with. You familiar with an outfit in Italy named *Ndrangheta*, Tony?"

My sphincter muscle contracts. Yeah, I know who they are —mafioso on steroids.

"Those are some nasty bastards," Ed mutters.

Jake nods in agreement, then turns back to me. "No screwing around here. What's this about?"

How do I handle this? On his last night in jail during his murder trial, Papa had told me a horrible story about the rape and kidnapping of his sister from their hometown of Orsomarso in Italy when he was twenty years old. She was taken by members of the *Cosche*, a local offshoot of the national *Ndrangheta*. Papa had found her and killed the man who abducted her. He'd then spirited his sister and mother away to a monastery in a different Italian province before he fled to the United States with a price on his head. I tell Jake and Ed the story and end with a request to keep the information as confidential as they can. They both nod.

"So, you think we need to take this seriously?" Ed asks.

37

Plummer is looking at me as he nods. "Good call telling us about this, Tony. I get the feeling it was a tough call for you to make."

He's got that right. The story was meant for my ears only and I've respected Papa's confidence ever since. Much as I'd like to continue doing so, this is no longer about keeping a secret. If the *Ndrangheta* has finally caught up to Papa, he may not be the only person at risk.

"If you're worried about legal jeopardy in the US over what Francesco did, don't be," Plummer adds. "It happened ages ago and thousands of miles away. It's nothing I'm inclined to act on."

Ed weighs in. "The bastard deserved to be blown away."

"Ain't that the truth?" Plummer agrees. "Anyway, the question is: What are we gonna do about this?"

"Why is this coming back on Papa now?" I ask. "It's been almost fifty years."

Plummer purses his lips. "Francesco's trial was pretty big news. Maybe word got back to the wrong ears in Italy."

"Most likely to this Orsomarso place," Ed says. "I'll bet this is personal. Some old asshole from back in the day wanting to settle a score. An outfit like the *Ndrangheta* ain't likely to bother with shit like this, but if they did, they wouldn't have come fishing for information. They would've just sent someone to take Francesco out."

Plummer nods thoughtfully. "Ski's probably right."

"So, how do we play this?" Ed asks.

I haven't got a clue, but I think I know what I have to do next. "Papa needs to know. You guys decide what needs to be done, and we'll do it."

Ed appears skeptical. "You think Francesco will just go along with whatever we tell him to do?"

"Normally, I'd say no, but I'm not giving him a choice," I reply.

"He's probably gonna be pissed that you told us this story at all," Ed counters. "I doubt he'll be in any mood to play along."

I've been thinking this through as we've talked, and my nonnegotiable bottom line is already clear. "Papa's got a choice. He either does whatever you say needs to be done, or Brittany and I are out of here."

"Good call," Plummer says.

Ed nods. "Agreed."

Papa can rant and play the stern patriarch all he wants, but Brittany's safety comes first. I glance down at the burgers. "Let's go eat before these things congeal. Then I'll talk to Papa, and we'll go from there."

"Sounds good," Ed says. Plummer agrees.

I walk Papa to his bedroom after we eat and bring him up to speed. He's pissed at me for spilling the beans to Ed and Jake. I let him rant for thirty seconds and then put my foot down. "We're going to do whatever Ed and Jake suggest."

My father's face morphs into that of the stern father of my youth. "You no tell me what to do, Anthony."

I raise a hand to cut him off. "Here's the deal, Papa. It's either that, or I take Brittany somewhere safe. Tonight." That gets his attention. "Let's go. Jake and Ed are waiting in the backyard to talk with us."

My father blows out a long, lingering breath that seems to deflate him a little, then nods and gets to his feet.

"Boy talk," I tell Brittany glibly as we pass through the kitchen on our way to the backyard. "Back in a few minutes."

Plummer and Ed are in quiet conversation with their heads close together when Papa and I emerge from the house. Their eyes track from my father to me in silent question.

"Papa's on board," I announce.

"What we do?" Papa asks.

"We're having a little disagreement about that," Ed says,

getting the jump on Plummer, who appears annoyed to be beaten to the punch. "I suspect you're gonna agree with my plan, Francesco."

"Tell me this plan," Papa orders him.

"We've got a little group who call ourselves the fossils," Ed says. "We're a bunch of retired old cops who sometimes dust ourselves off to take on a security job. I'll talk to a few of the guys tonight. Hell, this will be a little welcome excitement for the old bastards. Checkers, darts, and dominoes can only fill so many hours in a day. We'll have guys here round the clock starting tomorrow morning while Jake tries to figure things out."

Plummer shakes his head and turns to me. "I'd sooner see you folks go somewhere for a week or two while I investigate."

"Nah, we can manage things here," Ed says confidently.

Plummer sighs. He's skeptical. Worried. Should I be?

"I no run away!" Papa proclaims in an outburst of machismo.

Plummer meets my eye. "Sounds like we'll have to dynamite Francesco's ass out of here if we want him to go."

I spread my hands and suggest, "Maybe we should."

"I no go!" Papa reiterates.

Ed, damn him, reassures Papa that he and the fossils can handle things.

Plummer shuffles close and whispers, "I'll expedite things, Tony—put out more feelers tonight to try to get to the bottom of this. If the threat seems real, we need to get your asses out of this house until we neutralize whoever the hell is gunning for Francesco."

"Agreed."

And so, against our better judgment, we surrender to Papa's and Ed's display of aging testosterone. For now.

The detectives stick around for dessert. I feel a little naked after they depart. Ed's fossils won't be here until tomorrow, which leaves only me to protect Brittany and Papa. The gun Papa purchased and used last year is long gone, trashed after he was acquitted of murder in the shooting it was used in. Looks as if I'll be staying up tonight with only 911 on speed dial to defend us.

CHAPTER FIVE

I pull my car to the curb in front of Pat O'Toole's Humboldt Park home a week later. Pat's an old high school classmate who re-entered my life in the midst of last year's turmoil. She's a local reporter for the *Chicago Tribune* newspaper. Pat had been steadfast throughout Papa's ordeal, even during a period when we had a falling-out. Our victory in the battle over the redevelopment plan for Liberty Street owed a great deal to her reporting. After a few bumps along the way, we've settled into a comfortable friendship with undertones of more.

Pat suggested going for a little run in the park, so I'm decked out in a pair of fraying royal blue cotton shorts, a graying Marquette University T-shirt, and a pair of severely scuffed Nike cross-trainers—an outfit that indicates how little I get out to jog, let alone run. She wants to discuss her concerns about our upcoming lunch meeting with an aviation journalist who contacted me about the Windy City crash. She meets me at the door.

"All good on the home front?" she asks. Pat knows that Ed Stankowski has stepped up Papa's security but doesn't know the details.

"Ed and a couple of buddies are on duty," I reply. "So far, so good."

Pat holds the door open and lets me in, then sits me at the breakfast counter with a sunshine yellow, smiley-face mug of steaming coffee. The mouth-watering aroma of bacon lingers in the air. Alas, I've come too late to partake.

"Tell me a little more about Stankowski," she says.

"Ed's an old detective who was pensioned off after he was shot in the leg during a domestic dispute. He says he's too young to call it a day, so he keeps his hand in with security jobs, like babysitting Papa."

"And the fossils?" she asks with a quizzical smile.

"Bunch of other retired cops looking for things to do."

"What's really going on, Valenti?"

"You know Papa's been hassled a bit since the trial," I reply. "We're just playing it safe."

Pat senses that something more is up, something to worry about. The fear on her face hits me hard. She'd been shot in our kitchen ten months ago when the son of Papa's shooting victim sprayed the back of our house with bullets from a .22-caliber handgun. The bricks still bear the scars from the slugs. Pat lost an eye.

"You're a crappy liar, Valenti," she says. "The drama around your father died down a while ago. Now there's suddenly a bunch of retired cops babysitting him. What's up?"

I shrug.

"So, don't tell me what's going on," she says irritably before spinning her laptop around to face me. "Read this while I get changed."

A *Chicago Sun-Times* article is open on the screen. The headline reads:

Milton Crash: Maintenance and Fuel Vendors Under Microscope

I do a slow burn as I read the article, the gist of which is

43

that the NTSB investigation is focusing on tainted fuel and/or shoddy maintenance as likely causes of the crash. Or so the *Sun-Times* reporter's unnamed sources tell her. The writer goes on at some length to establish that the fuel vendor at the airport, AAA Avgas, has reputed ties to organized crime. I resist the urge to slam down my coffee mug as I finish reading, limiting myself instead to an angry, "Son of a bitch!"

"Quite a smear job, huh?" Pat asks as she slides onto the black fabric barstool next to mine, plants her elbows on the butcher-block countertop, and rests her chin on the knuckles of her clasped hands.

I look at her in surprise, not having heard her come back downstairs. "No shit. Where did"—I scroll back to the top of the article for the reporter's byline—"Sandy Irving get this crap?"

Pat purses her lips and lifts a shoulder. "That's a good question. Maybe Ben Larose can shed a little light on that."

Larose is the aviation writer we're meeting for lunch. I stab a finger at the laptop. "You think he's the source for this?"

"I doubt it."

I lean back and look up at the ten-foot ceiling. "Billy Likens assures me they did nothing wrong."

Pat shrugs as she slides off her barstool. "He's your client, of course, but to play devil's advocate for a moment, what if that's not true?"

"It *is* a good question," I allow, but when Billy's angelic face appears in my mind's eye, I just can't buy it. "I don't think Billy's lying."

"Fair enough," Pat says, then pauses to give me a long look. "That name rings a bell. Billy Likens, as in Melanie Likens's little brother?"

"That's him."

"Did you and Mel stay in touch after school?" she asks.

After I nod, she frowns. "I heard she died. Hard to imagine… she was always so full of life."

Until she wasn't, I think morosely. Mel's death had devastated me. The topic of Mel is a dark place I try not to visit.

Pat rests a hand on the counter, reaches back to grab the toe of a white-and-orange Asics running shoe, and pulls her foot up to her butt to stretch her quadriceps muscles. She's clad in form-fitting, jet-black spandex, whereas I'm dressed in what might be euphemistically called shabby chic or, perhaps more accurately, like some bozo trapped in an athletic wear time warp. Frankly, it's a little embarrassing. Things are about to get worse.

She glances up at an antique wall clock with a different breed of bird pictured for every hour. "C'mon, Valenti. Limber up and let's get moving. We can talk about the Milton crash and Ben Larose while we run."

My eyes track up to the clock. Eight thirteen. She's right, we do need to get moving. I've got a prospective client meeting in just over two hours. While Pat goes through an elaborate prerun routine, I do a couple of stretches, polish off my coffee, and admire the main floor of Pat's house. Lots of hardwood, plenty of sunshine pouring in through oversized windows, tasteful minimalist leather and wood furnishings, several nice pieces of art, and a fascinating collection of bric-a-brac she's brought home from her extensive travels through Africa, Asia, Europe, and, well… everywhere. There's a tenant in a self-contained basement apartment. Upstairs, the second floor contains a remodeled master bedroom with an ensuite bathroom, a guest room, and a home office. A painting studio fills the converted attic space. It's a great house.

Pat finishes a couple of stretches on the floor, bounces up, and pulls her shoulder-length red hair into a ponytail that she stuffs through the back of a Chicago Blackhawks ball cap. She waves me along as she jogs to the front door.

"We'll start easy," she assures me as we cross Division Street to enter Humboldt Park in the crisp mid-October morning air. The park is a 207-acre gem, one in a series of elegant West Side urban parks developed by William Le Baron Jenney in the 1870s.

I focus on my stride as we head deeper into the park along a cracked ribbon of tree-lined asphalt. Pat's "easy pace" has me sweating inside a minute. At five foot ten, she has a long, loping stride that eats up a lot of real estate with every step. In high school, she'd been mockingly called "Stick," a reference to her tall, slender frame and lack of curves. Understanding that it hurt her more than she let on, I did what I could to shut the assholes down, but it *was* high school, and I had limited success. Still, she noticed, appreciated it, and we became friends, although she wasn't welcome among the crowd of cool kids I ran with.

"The full trail is about two miles," she says conversationally after we've covered a couple of hundred more yards.

"Okay," I wheeze. "I've never understood the point of running."

Pat cocks an eyebrow my way. "No?"

"What's the point if a scary monster isn't chasing you?"

She shoots me a bemused sideways glance. "You're such a doofus."

"I've been called worse."

"I'm a little surprised the Milton crash didn't get much attention after the initial feeding frenzy," she says a moment later as she coasts along.

"Why's that?"

"Senator Milton qualifies as something of a celebrity these days, right? Potential presidential run, all of that."

I chug along beside her and nod while focusing on my somewhat ragged breathing. My legs may be limbering up a bit. Or maybe I'm simply going numb below the waist. Either way, I'm hopeful that the worst is over. By silent agreement, she talks, I listen.

"The NTSB has pulled out all the stops for precisely that reason," Pat continues. "Feed the media beast, satisfy the clamoring politicians."

She's right. The Windy City Sky Tours Cessna has been retrieved from the bottom of Lake Michigan. The investigation seems to be moving quickly.

"It's kind of sad how little mention is made of the victims," Pat mutters. "Lots of talk about the forty-three-year-old junior senator with higher-office aspirations and how this might impact his political career. What about Tiffany?"

When I don't reply, she throws her hands up in exasperation. "See what I mean? Tiffany Walton, his thirty-two-year-old wife who won't turn thirty-three. Then there's Cameron, all of four years old, and let's not forget Cameron's apparently doting grandparents, dead in their mid-sixties. This isn't just about politics and money."

This is one of the reasons Pat is such a great reporter. She's interested in people. She shines a light on how the news affects the people touched by events. She's got a big heart— one that currently seems to be pumping a lot more oxygen to her body than mine is.

"I'm not terribly familiar with how the NTSB works, but I'm told leaks like what we saw in the paper are extremely rare," she continues. "So rare, in fact, that leaks generally originate from people working in some other facet of an investigation."

"I've… heard… that… too," I manage to gasp. The truth is that I don't really know what I should be doing at this point in an aviation accident case. I'm still trying to get up to speed. The NTSB does have what seems to be a well-deserved reputation for playing things close to the vest.

Pat asks, "*Is* Billy Likens in trouble?"

The question surprises me. I slow to a walk to catch my

breath, hopefully enough to carry on a bit of a conversation. "Why do you ask?"

Pat isn't even breathing hard as she jogs circles around me while I suck in as much life-sustaining air as I can. She grabs my sleeve and tugs until I start running again, then answers my question. "Sandy Irving has good sources in law enforcement circles, which makes me wonder if she's getting her information from the police. My understanding is that the NTSB only brings in law enforcement when there's a suspicion of possible criminal activity."

That's a disturbing possibility. Billy and Rick have talked with the NTSB and turned over all their records, but they haven't spoken with law enforcement. Not that I know of, anyway. I push the thought aside, ignore my burning thighs, and work to keep up while wheezing out an answer. "They haven't... talked... to... the cops."

"Let's pick up the pace," Pat suggests over her shoulder as she surges ahead.

Is she kidding? I'm a jogger of sorts; she's a runner. There *is* a difference. I belatedly recall that Pat was the queen of cross-country running in high school and has apparently completed a couple of full marathons and a bunch of half marathons. "You. Can. Keep. This. Up. All. Day. Can't. You?" I shout at her back as I fall behind.

She turns back to circle behind me and comes alongside wearing a smirk. "Not *all* day, Chubby, but I can go for a good while yet—especially at this pedestrian pace of yours."

We've finally rounded the north end of the park and are heading south when it first occurs to me that Pat may be out to kill me. She's loping along effortlessly with plenty of bounce in her step. I'm plodding along on legs of stone. We're now running into a middling breeze, which feels good but may well arrest my forward progress before much longer.

"Back to Ben Larose," Pat says.

"Yeah," I gasp hoarsely.

"He mentioned vendors, said he has some info about them, right?"

I nod.

"Why talk to you about that?"

"You. Tell. Me."

"Maybe Irving's source reached out to Ben and he's fishing for more information?"

They're good questions. I'm in no condition to speak, so I nod in reply and wonder why Larose would want to compare notes with me. Maybe Pat's right to be skeptical of the guy's motives.

"I'm not sure I want to be seen with him around our newsroom," she says. The meeting is set for noon at the *Tribune*. She suggests meeting Larose at my office instead.

"No way," I reply flatly. How can I expect Larose to take me seriously if he sees our office? Strip-mall lawyers going up against Butterworth Cole? Right. "Someplace... neutral."

"Ideas?" she asks as we start to round a lagoon.

I wave her off.

"When we stop?" she asks with an amused lilt in her voice.

I nod gratefully. We pass tall stands of wild grass and a mixture of yellow and blue wildflowers that hug the shore of the lagoon. The imposing Humboldt Park Fieldhouse Gymnasium is at the water's edge on the far side. I admire the graceful sweep of its base, a low ribbon of concrete dotted with arches along its length. Several stories of brown brick tower above it. Twin turrets capped with greened bronze roofs anchor the two wings running out from the center block. This would be an enjoyable jog if Pat weren't bent on breaking the Humboldt Park land speed record. Maybe we can stop and admire things for an hour or two while I catch my breath?

"So?" she prompts as we slow on the approach to North Humboldt Drive, a city street that bisects the park from north to south. She continues to run in place after I lumber to a stop beside her. "What have you got in mind for someplace neutral to meet for lunch?"

"The Sandwich Emporium?"

"Great idea! I haven't been there in months!" she exclaims with a smile. "I'll meet you at eleven forty-five."

The walk light comes on, and Pat trots across the street with me in her wake. She eventually stops in the parking lot outside the Boat Pavilion and looks back at me with abject pity. Having lost my forward momentum waiting to cross the street, I can't coax my legs back into action. I stagger up and stop with my hands on my knees. My head sinks almost as low while I struggle to inhale a thimbleful of precious air.

"Poor Valenti," she says in a sing-song voice as she runs in place.

I sink to my haunches and look up. Her eyes are tracking a pair of Spandex-clad mothers who breeze by, chattering away while they effortlessly push tank-sized baby strollers with a single hand each. Pat's eyes drop to mine, then cut away to the running mommies as a grin spreads across her face. "I've got a stroller like that at the house to push my niece around when she visits. I could nip home for it and push *you* around for a bit if you feel up to it?"

She's lucky that she's a girl… and that I can't catch her.

I'm a sopping bucket of sweat when we arrive outside Pat's house ten minutes later. I'd originally planned to make a pit stop at home to shower and shave before going to the office, but no way am I going to soil the leather seat of my Porsche Panamera with the river of sweat currently streaming off me. "I've got a set of sweats in the car. Mind if I change here?"

Pat wrinkles her nose. "All right. Try not to drip all over the house."

I grab a gym bag out of the back seat and follow her inside.

She points toward the main-floor bathroom. "Knock yourself out, Valenti. I'm gonna run upstairs to change."

More running?

The bathroom is off an alcove between the kitchen and living room. I push the door most of the way closed behind me and start to strip by pushing my shorts down around my ankles. While I try to kick them off, I attempt to multitask by pulling my shirt over my head, where it promptly gets stuck around my shoulders. I hate it when this happens, yet never seem to learn that a thoroughly soaked shirt doesn't come off easily. Shouldn't garments slide right off when a person is slick with sweat? *Oh shit*, I think as my feet get hopelessly tangled and I begin to topple sideways, unable to free a hand to break my fall. My head glances off the corner of the sink vanity as I crash to the floor in a pathetic heap of tangled limbs.

"Are you okay?" Pat asks anxiously when she rushes in a moment later.

"Yeah," I mutter in embarrassment as she works the shirt the rest of the way over my head. With my arms free, I quickly yank the shorts over my feet and squirm into my waiting sweatpants. In addition to being found in my jockey shorts helpless as a baby, it occurs to me that I probably smell like rancid locker room socks. Pat grabs the hand towel off the rack and starts running it under cold water. When I touch above my eye, my finger comes away with a smear of blood.

"Stay down there where I can reach you," she says when I start to stand, putting a hand on my shoulder and dabbing the cold cloth to my forehead. Her eyes go wide when they settle on the shoulder her hand is resting upon. "What happened here?"

She's staring at a patch of puckered red scar tissue running across the back of my shoulder and down to the shoulder blade. It's a couple of inches wide and five inches long.

"Just a little cooking incident," I reply.

She narrows her eyes. "On your back?"

In a fit of temper during our marriage, my ex-wife, Michelle, had clobbered me upside the head with a frying pan full of bacon grease. The grease spilled down my shoulder and back, scalding me before we could rip off my shirt. Thankfully, I emerged with my love of bacon intact. "Long story," I mutter without elaborating.

When it's clear that I've said all I'm going to, Pat mutters, "Okay," drawing the word out while handing me the top of my sweat suit.

I quickly pull it on and zip up. She's uncharacteristically quiet while I gather up my running clothes and stuff them into a plastic Jewel shopping bag. "See you at lunch," I say as I steal away with my secret.

I'm the first to arrive at The Sandwich Emporium a couple of hours later, where six or seven people are already tucking into their lunches. Maiko Campbell, who runs the joint with her husband, Brian, looks up when I push the door open and the bell above it tinkles. As I do every visit, I inhale deeply and savor the yeasty air. Deano, our aging black lab, would suffer olfactory overload here… and love every minute.

"Tony-*san*!" Maiko exclaims happily as her round face bursts into an enormous smile. Maiko's short body is as rotund as her face, which is framed by a jet-black pixie hair-cut. It's a face and smile that could light up even the darkest dungeon.

"Hello, Maiko," I reply with an answering smile. I've never seen anyone respond to Maiko's greeting with anything *but* a smile. She's a delightful force of nature. "Missed you when I was here a week or two ago."

She smiles. "Of course you did!"

"Tony," her husband, Brian, grumbles as he looks up from behind a modest sandwich-assembly table and wipes a hand on his apron before lifting it an inch or two in greeting. He's as taciturn as Maiko is effervescent. They met while he was stationed with the United States Navy Seventh Fleet in Yokosuka Japan. He had the good sense to marry her and bring her home to Cedar Heights.

Maiko points at my forehead. "You made someone mad?"

"Such touching concern," I retort lightly. "I met a grumpy sink."

Apparently not inclined to pursue the details of my assault at the hands of Pat's washbasin, Maiko slides behind the cash register. "What will you have today?"

I lift my eyes to the wall-mounted menu behind her that lists the standard sandwich shop fare in black-plastic lettering on a white background. Under that is a slate chalkboard where Maiko writes the daily special in a big splash of brightly colored chalk. The Sandwich Emporium Daily Special is an institution. Maiko shops at several local grocery wholesalers every morning, where she buys whatever happens to be on sale. She and Brian create daily specials from whatever she brings home, which makes for some highly unusual sandwiches. "Shouldn't the prices be lower if you get everything on sale?" I'd once asked her playfully. That had gotten me a good-humored slap on the arm but no deals on sandwiches.

"I'm meeting a couple of people," I tell her. "I'll order when they get here."

"Oh!" she exclaims. "You wanna use our private dining room?"

I stare back at her in slack-jawed surprise. "You have one?"

"Downstairs in our apartment. Ha ha ha!" This cracks her up to the point at which she has tears in her eyes as she slaps her palms on her thighs.

It's not that funny, but her laughter is infectious, so I find myself chuckling right along with her. Hell, even Brian cracks a smile, albeit a very weak one.

"How many guests?" Maiko asks while wiping a final tear from the corner of her eye.

"Two."

"Plus you?"

"Yup."

"Two plus you equals three, Tony-*san*," she says with a twinkle in her eye. "I hope you don't help that beautiful daughter of yours with her math homework."

In a battle of wits, she'd take me down ninety-nine times out of a hundred—*if* I got lucky once.

"You wait here while I fix you a nice table in back," she says before bustling away toward the rear of the restaurant.

A "nice table in back" is a little table crammed into a cubbyhole by the back door. It's as private as things get at The Sandwich Emporium. God help her and Brian if a fire inspector ever happens by while diners are wedged into the shop's only emergency exit. It's where she stashes Penelope and me when we visit on Thursdays for our weekly working lunch. How she plans to squeeze a third chair in there is beyond me. She returns a minute or two later, just in time to hear the door chime tinkle again when Pat walks in. Pat has exchanged the running gear for jeans and a powder-blue polo shirt. I've changed, too, of course, into a lawyer suit. I left the suit jacket and tie hanging on the back of my office door, where they're safe from eating mishaps.

"Miss O'Toole!" Maiko squeals with delight. Her eyes soften when she asks, "Are you okay?"

Pat smiles and nods, looking mildly annoyed as she does. Continuing to be asked what she calls "the health question" the better part of a year after her shooting is testing her patience. "I know people mean well, but enough already!" she told me, following that up with "like I need constant reminders of the shooting every time I manage to put it out of mind."

Time to change the subject. "So, what the hell is The Sour

Kraut?" I ask Maiko with a pointed glance at the daily special chalkboard.

"Ah," she says as her smile returns to full wattage. "German sausage with a lemon compote. Sour. Kraut. Get it?"

Maiko stares at me expectantly, waiting for the laugh she's sure is coming. I battle to keep a grin at bay and sternly point out, "You know that's culturally insensitive?"

Maiko's hand shoots to her mouth as her eyes pop wide open, and she asks innocently, "Does that make me a bad person?"

So much for keeping a straight face. I laugh and roll my eyes. "Probably not."

"Definitely not," Pat says with an easy smile. "Sandwiches don't have feelings."

The bell tinkles when the door opens again. Pat nods at the new arrival and takes a step forward with her hand extended. "Ben."

Ben Larose is not what I expected, sterling judge of unseen characters that I am. Having heard that he's a pilot as well as an aviation writer, I was expecting a gung-ho, once-upon-a-time fighter jock. Why, I don't know. I guess we all have our unwitting prejudices and misconceptions about all manner of things. Larose is as tall as I am but might weigh no more than one of my legs, and I'm not exactly bulky. The arms dangling out of the short sleeves of his sky-blue, plaid button-down shirt look like two wisps of straw. A prominent Adam's apple protrudes like a bird's beak out of a neck that barely looks substantial enough to support the weight of his head. Larose's face looks as emaciated as the rest of him: sunken eyes, hollow cheeks, sliver of chin, all crowned with a mop of tousled shoulder-length straw hair. His face sports thick stubble that suggests he could grow a full beard within hours. He turns to me after greeting Pat and reaches for my hand. His blue-gray eyes sparkle with intelligence as an engaging smile appears. We exchange greetings before he announces that he needs a bathroom break.

"What do you think?" Pat asks when he's out of earshot.

"I've been drawing this guy since high school!"

The blank look she gives me slowly morphs into a grin and a chuckle. Pat's a talented artist; in fact, one of her paintings hangs over the fireplace mantel at our house. I can't paint for shit, but I have a rare gift for drawing stick people. I've kept Pat and others amused many a time over coffee with my little creations.

She touches a fingertip to the bandage on my forehead with an amused smile. "How's it feel?"

"Like I got hit with a sink."

"I'm happy to report that the sink escaped the encounter unscathed," she assures me with exaggerated relief.

As soon as Larose reappears, Maiko bustles over and shoos us toward our freshly prepared private table. It sports a crisp, black plasticized tablecloth, utensils wrapped in designer paper napkins stuffed into a water glass in the center of the table, and a set of salt and pepper shakers in the shape of two swans. A trio of sweating water glasses completes the picture. *It's a good thing Pat and Larose take up about as much lateral space as a pair of broomsticks,* I think as Maiko shoehorns us into our seats.

"Three daily specials?" she says with a stubby pencil poised above an order pad.

Pat and I nod. Larose glances at us, shrugs, and says, "Sure."

Maiko favors him with a motherly smile and departs.

"I take it you two are friends?" Larose asks.

Pat replies, "We worked together on our high school newspaper and have done a little investigative work together lately."

Larose's brow furrows when he looks at me. "I thought you were a lawyer?"

"Oh, he is," Pat says. "Valenti couldn't cut it as a newspaperman."

Maiko swoops in with our sandwiches, three unordered glasses of draft beer, and a pile of extra paper napkins. The sandwiches smell great. The beer smells better.

"I, uh, don't drink," Larose informs Maiko as she turns to go.

She glances back over her shoulder. "You do today!"

He laughs and nudges his glass across the table until it sits between Pat and me. I get the sense that he's perpetually entertained by the world around him, as if the absurdity of life is a source of unbridled amusement.

We tuck into our Sour Kraut sandwiches, pausing frequently to grab one of a quickly diminishing supply of paper napkins to wipe our chins. Larose narrates a quick recap of his life and times between bites: private pilot license at eighteen; journalism degree at twenty-three; commercial flying license at twenty-four; three years trying to break into aviation journalism while building up flying hours... "neither of which paid for shit." He holds up his sandwich, takes a bite, and mutters, "Good stuff!" around a mouthful.

He's right. Maiko and Brian have managed to slap together yet another bargain-bin gastronomical marvel.

I push my empty paper plate aside and reach for Larose's untouched beer. "Let's cut to the chase," I suggest after drinking off a long draft of brew. "What are we doing here?"

"Did you read the *Sun-Times* this morning?" he asks.

I nod and lean in closer while we lock eyes. "Did you have anything to do with that?"

His eyes cut to Pat. "Really? You thought that?"

Pat shrugs. "I don't know what to think, Ben. I don't know you all that well."

His tone, which carried an edge when he fired his question at Pat, softens. "True enough, but remember that I called Tony before this morning's paper came out."

"Which doesn't exactly exonerate you," I point out while tapping my middle finger on the table to punctuate my words. "The story didn't materialize out of thin air overnight."

Larose smiles as his eyes turn to Pat. "Ah, he *is* a lawyer."

Pat chuckles as a return smile lifts the corners of her lips. "For better or worse, that he is."

The good humor fades when Larose turns back to me. "Cutting to the chase, then. I started hearing last week about some of what we read this morning. That's not the type of thing anyone at the NTSB puts out."

"And?" I prompt.

"I made a couple of calls. My NTSB contacts are pissed. They claim Irving didn't get her information from them."

"Law enforcement?"

"My first thought, as well," Larose mutters with a hint of approval for my insight.

I flip a thumb at Pat. "The thought occurred to her."

"Sandy Irving," Pat explains in reference to the *Sun-Times* reporter after hastily swallowing a bite of sandwich. "She's tight with the police."

Larose nods thoughtfully. "Yeah, she is. Here's the thing, though. My NTSB sources say they haven't called in the police, at least not to this point."

I sink back in my seat and blow out a lengthy breath. "Good to know, I suppose."

"If not the police or the NTSB, who is Sandy Irving talking to?" Pat asks.

"I hoped you might have some ideas," Larose mutters. "Nothing pisses me off more than some asshole trying to use me to push a false narrative."

Pat nods sympathetically. I nod as well, but a little guiltily. As a lawyer, I'm well schooled in the art of pushing false narratives. Shame on me. Probably best not to mention that just now.

Larose scowls and continues, "I got a phone call last week from some guy who took great pleasure in identifying himself as an anonymous source with knowledge of the matter."

Pat laughs softly. "God, don't you just love asses like that?"

No need to get personal, I think dryly.

Larose snorts. "Give me a normal source instead of some wide-eyed amateur playing Deep Throat to my Woodward and Bernstein."

I look at the reporters in confusion. Who are we talking about?

Pat seems to intuit my unspoken question. She gives me a sympathetic look and pats my hand. "The source and reporters who broke Watergate," she informs me while sharing a disbelieving look with Larose.

I'm apparently some sort of news-history ignoramus. Never mind that Watergate happened in the early 1970s, when I was in diapers.

We fall silent. I run the *Sun-Times* article through my mind while they polish off their sandwiches and push their plates aside, then ponder Irving's source. I suspect Pat and Larose are doing likewise. I'm first to take a stab at connecting the dots. "Could it be the owners of Windy City Sky Tours trying to get a narrative out there to taint Billy and Rick?"

"Billy and Rick?" Larose asks.

"R & B Ramp Services," Pat answers. "Windy City's maintenance vendor. Also Tony's clients."

Larose nods his understanding. "Irving was also peddling the possibility of bad fuel. Her source wants the fuel vendor to look bad, too."

"Yeah, but it's pretty common knowledge that AAA Avgas is all mobbed up," I say. "They hardly need to be tainted in the public eye, do they?"

"No, they don't," Larose agrees thoughtfully while Maiko swoops in and clears the table. We decline her offer of dessert.

"I think Billy and Rick were the primary targets of Irving's story," I mutter angrily after Maiko walks away. "It really pisses me off that she put Billy and Rick in bed with Avgas."

"Pretty clever ploy to paint your guys as common crooks," Pat says when her eye settles on me. "Who might want to do that?"

The pieces of the puzzle settle firmly into place. "My money is on the bastards at Windy City." Sooner or later, it's a sure bet that Billy and Rick are going to find themselves in court against their Windy City pals, who have just fired the opening salvo in what promises to be a nasty battle to shape public opinion.

CHAPTER SIX

While we're having lunch, Francesco Valenti pokes his head out the back door of his Liberty Street home. "Coffee?" he asks Ed Stankowski.

Ed shoots a look to his fossil partner for the day, Max Maxwell, who is a granite block of retired Chicago PD sergeant with a graying military brush cut. Max is seated on the opposite side of the patio from Ed. They both wear jeans and short-sleeve, police-department-logoed golf shirts with well-worn leather shoulder holsters holding Glock pistols.

"Coffee?" Ed asks.

"Nah, just makes me hafta piss," Max grumbles.

Ed smiles at Francesco and holds up a single finger. "Just one, pal. Thanks."

"The guy makes a hell of a sandwich!" Max says after Francesco disappears back into the house. It's his first day here. Sharing his sunflower seeds with Deano has made him a fast canine friend. The dog is lounging in the grass a couple of feet away from Max, patiently waiting for his new pal to toss another sunflower seed his way.

They've just finished paninis piled high with every Italian cold cut known to mankind, compliments of Francesco, who has insisted on feeding the fossils lunch every day. He'd gotten downright pissy the one time a fossil brought a sandwich from home.

"Seems like a nice enough guy, too," Max adds.

Ed belches and slaps his stomach. "Yeah, he's good people. We've been able to shoot the shit quite a bit over the past week. Interesting guy."

Max frowns and digs a hand into his ever-present bag of Spitz sunflower seeds, causing Deano to go on point. "Seems strange to be talking that way about a guy who killed a cop, don't it?"

Ed has no qualms about being in Francesco's corner. He'd initially been a little conflicted about protecting a cop killer, but Jake Plummer considers Francesco's exoneration a righteous acquittal, and Jake's word is gold with Ed. The story about how Francesco had rescued his sister and put down the sack of shit who raped and kidnapped her also earned him some serious props with the retired detective. Taking down a mobster face-to-face to save a loved one at age twenty or thereabouts took some balls. *Too bad Jake won't let me share that story with the fossils,* Ed thinks. The guys would appreciate what Francesco did and would feel better about being here.

He looks Max in the eye. "Andrew O'Reilly was a sad excuse for a cop."

"Can't argue that point," Max mutters.

Their heads snap toward the crack of splintering wood at the back of the yard. The old cops are still frozen in place when a figure wearing a black balaclava steps around the corner of the garage.

The man—*it's gotta be a man judging by the gait and build,* Ed thinks as his mental synapses fire to register the deadly risk they're facing—looks around the yard, his eyes following the arc traced by a handgun thrust ahead of him in a two-fisted hold. The turning head stops at Ed. The gun follows. Ed is reaching for the pistol in his shoulder holster as the intruder's gun barrel settles on him. *People weren't shitting me. That gun barrel looks ten feet wide.*

A streaking Deano shoots past the rose garden and launches himself at the attacker. The dog's jaws clamp shut on the shooter's biceps in the same instant the man pulls the trigger—a fraction of a second too late. Ed spins around with the impact of the bullet and topples off the edge of the patio into a rose bush while a bolt of fire rockets up his arm. The crack of more gunfire permeates into his brain, accompanied by the fierce snarling of Deano. The shooting stops in the same moment that the dog's growl is abruptly cut off. It's replaced with a pitiable whimper before the back gate slams shut.

When the yard falls silent, Ed is face down in the dirt, gritting his teeth and squeezing his burning biceps with his good hand.

"Max!" he cries out frantically as his eyes track across the patio. A battered pair of Reebok cross-trainers stop a couple of feet away from Ed's eyes a moment later. *I hope to hell those belong to Max.*

"Hang in there, brother," Max says as he kneels down and pushes his face in front of Ed's. "Just the arm wound?"

"Just?" Ed moans through clenched teeth.

"That's it?" Max asks sharply as his eyes lift to survey the yard.

Ed finally gets it. Max isn't about to piss around with a nonlethal wound while the threat of an active shooter persists, no matter how much the damn thing hurts. Ed nods and waves Max away.

"What happen? I hear the shots!" Francesco shouts as he bursts through the back door. His wild eyes quickly lock on Ed. "You are shot?"

No kidding. Ed shoots a disbelieving look at Francesco and shouts, "Get back inside, you dopey old son of a bitch!"

Max gets up in Francesco's face and bodily shoves him toward the door. "Get your ass back in there and call 911!"

"Now!" Ed adds while Max's eyes sweep the yard with his Glock at the ready.

Given something useful to do, Francesco seems to get a grip on his initial panic. He nods and hustles back inside.

"Did you get the bastard?" Ed asks when Max returns and kneels at his side.

Max's eyes continue to sweep the yard. "Don't know. Didn't wanna hit the dog, and the garage blocked my line of sight to the gate, so I only had a split second to shoot after Deano dropped out of sight."

Speaking of which, Ed thinks as he struggles to sit upright and casts his eyes around the yard in search of Deano. "Oh shit," he mutters disconsolately when he spots an inert mass of black fur just inside the back gate.

Max's eyes track Ed's. "Damn!" he growls before he gets to his feet and marches toward the back of the yard, pistol leading the way in a two-fisted grip. Given the murderous expression etched on his face, Ed suspects Max is hoping a target pops into view.

They both startle when the back door slams open again and Francesco pokes his head out. He's got a telephone jammed tight to his ear. "The police! They come!"

Ed twists around to face Francesco. "Perfect. Now stay the hell inside before someone shoots your ass off!"

Thankfully, Francesco only glances Max's way before he goes inside. It wouldn't do to have him rushing over to Deano before the scene is secured. Ed scooches his ass back around so he can see Max, who is standing stock-still by the back gate. The stucco fence along the sides and front of the yard is only four feet tall. The back fences along the alley are a full six feet, so between those and the garage, the yard has privacy from the alley and, at the moment, that means protection. *Stay in the yard*, Ed silently urges his partner. While it's unlikely that their assailant is lurking in the alley, the smart move is for Max to remain where he is and wait for the cavalry to arrive. As Ed watches, Max backs away from the gate and kneels beside the dog. Ed can't bring himself to ask how Deano is; he's acutely aware that the old dog probably just saved his life. No way was the shooter gonna miss a kill shot from twenty feet with that cannon.

After a thirty-second inspection, Max looks up and meets Ed's gaze. "No blood, but he's hurt. The bastard must have kicked the shit out of him on his way out."

Ed squeezes his eyes shut as sirens in the distance announce that help is on the way. *Better than being shot... unless the bastard pumped a bullet into Deano that stopped his heart instantly before he could bleed out. Is there some sort of 911 for dogs?* He slips his belt off and ties it around his arm to stem the flow of blood while Max paces back and forth by the back gate.

Sirens begin converging on the scene a minute later. Ed waves his good arm to get Max's attention as the first sirens die and car doors slam on the street out front. "Get the vet's number from Francesco and get Deano some help."

Max nods as he walks briskly toward the gate at the front of the yard and shouts, "We're in the backyard! Scene is clear! Retired police officer down!"

"We're coming in," a tense voice calls back. "Hands where we can see them."

"Understood," Max replies calmly.

Ed manages to stagger to his feet and get one hand on top of his head before a pair of Cedar Heights PD officers march into the yard. Their guns linger on Ed and Max for a long moment before the older of the two cops says, "I know these two."

Ed recognizes Marty Zeller. Good cop. Good guy to have around in a crisis. "Yard's clear," he tells Zeller. "Shooter went out the back gate."

The cops nod but sweep the rest of the yard and the garage, anyway.

"You okay, brother?" Max asks while they wait.

The wound burns like hell and throbs with every beat of Ed's heart, but it isn't debilitating. "Sure. Hurts like a bitch, though."

Max nods, then goes inside to get the number for Deano's vet.

"What the hell's going on, Ed?" the older cop says as they walk back.

"I'm doing just great, Zeller. Thanks for asking."

A police cruiser with siren wailing skids to a stop in the alley behind the garage.

Zeller takes a few steps toward the back fence, identifies himself, and announces, "Yard and garage have been cleared. The shooter left through the back gate."

"Got it. We'll hold here."

More sirens scream down Liberty Street and die out front. More car doors slam shut. "If the bastard's still anywhere in the neighborhood, he's screwed now," Max mutters as he returns.

Zeller walks back, takes a good long look at Ed's arm, and then locks eyes with him. "Doesn't hurt too much?"

Ed nods. *Hell, now that he mentions it, it doesn't feel too bad. Good sign? Bad sign?*

Zeller herds Ed to one of the Adirondack chairs and all but shoves him into it. "Could be going numb, or you could be going into shock."

"Sit down," Max snaps when Ed resists.

A uniformed policewoman walks up. "There's an injured dog?"

Zeller nods toward the back gate. "Down there."

"I'll take care of it," she says with a concerned glance as she starts toward the back of the yard.

Max calls her back and hands her a Post-it note. "The

dog's named Deano, and he just saved our asses. This is the number for his vet."

She nods solemnly and hurries away.

"What the hell went down here?" Zeller asks.

Max gives him a quick recap, ending with "All over in less than a minute."

"Did anyone go after the shooter?"

"This old wreck?" Ed snorts with a sideways glance at Max. "Hell, he'd probably give himself a heart attack if he tried to walk fast for more than a block."

Zeller looks at a glowering Max and chuckles.

"No point, anyway," Ed adds. "He wouldn't catch a young buck like that."

Zeller's eyes snap back to Ed. "Did you get a good look at the shooter? Enough to put it on the air?"

Max nods. "Let's see. The back fence is six feet tall, so let's call the guy around six foot?" he asks Ed, who studies the fence and gate and then nods.

"Kinda stocky," Max adds. Ed nods again.

"Definitely a man?" Zeller asks.

"Yeah," Ed replies. "That was my first impression. The build. How he moved. Probably young, too. Pretty agile."

Max nods. "Absolutely."

A cop pushes the back gate open. "There's a little blood on the gate and a few drops leading away. Is it from anyone in there?"

Max's eyes light up. "I got the son of a bitch!"

"The blood's not from anyone in here," Zeller shouts back. He turns back to Max and Ed. "Anything else you can tell me about the shooter?"

"Black pants," Ed says.

"Dark hoodie, too," Max adds.

"Anything else? Hair? Skin?"

Ed shakes his head. "Balaclava."

"Gloves, too," Max mutters. "No idea what color his skin is."

"It's a start," Zeller says before turning away and calling in what they have. He ends on a hopeful note. "Possible gunshot wound, as well."

"I hope they find him bleeding out somewhere," Max mutters before he turns and stalks toward the back door. "What kind of cocksucker hurts a dog?"

Don't forget that he shot your partner, too, Ed thinks with a painful chuckle. The laugh dies on his lips when his eyes settle on the limp lump of fur at the feet of the distraught policewoman standing by the back gate.

CHAPTER SEVEN

I t's a little after nine o'clock the next morning when I pull into our driveway after a night at the animal hospital. My fifteen-year-old daughter, Brittany, her eyes puffy and red from crying most of the time we spent sitting beside a comatose Deano after the vet finished examining and treating him, insisted on remaining at the dog's bedside while I came home.

Papa's frantic call after the shooting had cut short our lunch with Ben Larose, sending Pat and me racing home as fast as my Porsche could take us. After being assured by the paramedics hovering over Ed that he was okay—other than having been shot—we'd hopped back in the car and chased the police cruiser taking Deano to the nearest animal hospital.

As near as the vet can guess, the shooter pistol-whipped Deano once across the face and had also landed one or more vicious kicks to the dog's midsection with a heavy boot. Bad, yeah, but I'm grateful the bastard didn't simply put a bullet into our mutt. Assuming there's no underlying organ damage that has yet to reveal itself, Deano should recover in anywhere from a few weeks to a month or two. The vet suspects he's got a doggy concussion, as well. I doubt any of it will curb his appetite.

I take a deep breath after I shut off the car and work my stiff neck around to produce a satisfying crack. Then I hustle through the rain to the front porch and take refuge with a pair of Ed Stankowski's fellow fossils.

"How's the pooch?" the white-haired one asks. I'll be damned if I can remember the names of these guys. Hell, they're *all* white haired or well on their way to being so… if they have any hair at all.

I tell them what I know, prompting a few caustic remarks leveled at the kind of scum who hurts animals. I'm mildly amused when neither castigates the guy for shooting Ed.

"How is Deano?" Papa asks anxiously as soon as I step inside. He looks haunted, not unlike the near catatonic state he'd lapsed into during the days after the shooting last year. He's once again overcome with guilt. For Ed? Deano? Both?

I rest a hand on his shoulder and squeeze. "Stop blaming yourself, Papa. This isn't your fault." When his eyes meet mine, I realize that nothing I can say will convince him of that. "Deano's doing as well as can be expected."

"I will pray," Papa announces solemnly when I finish.

What the hell? Papa hasn't prayed since my sister, Amy, died during a covert US Army operation in Colombia sixteen years ago.

"Plummer and Ed are here," Papa tells me before he heads toward the back of the house.

"Ed?" I ask in surprise as I follow. I knew Jake Plummer was coming by; he'd called last night to tell me that we need to talk.

Papa nods. "Plummer, he say Ed stupid to come."

"He might be right."

Papa's nostrils flare. "You no make Ed joke!"

"Just kidding around," I assure him as I walk through the

kitchen and open the back door. "Come on, Papa. Let's hear what they have to say."

We find Plummer and Ed lounging on a pair of pastel Adirondack chairs tucked under the extended retractable awning. Ed's bandaged arm is in a sling, and he looks a little pale. To my surprise, his partner from yesterday, Max, is also here, standing off to one side. I met Max for the first time in our yard after the shooting. He seems to be a formidable old bugger.

"How's Deano?" Ed asks immediately. "He gonna pull through?"

"Looks like he should."

Ed sighs in relief. "Who woulda thought the lazy old mutt had a mean streak?"

I smile tightly and turn to Plummer. "Did they catch the bastard yet?"

He looks decidedly unhappy when he shakes his head no.

"Any leads?"

He shakes his head again and mutters, "Not yet."

Shit. I don't like the idea of staying here while somebody is targeting Papa. At least I had Brittany spend last night at Pat's house. She's at school today, and this morning I told her to go to Pat's after school. I don't understand my father's insistence on staying here. There's the fatalistic streak in him that revealed itself last year during his trial when he seemed resigned to whatever destiny awaited him. He may feel like his time will be up whenever fate decrees, but why tempt it? Not to mention that there are other people's lives at stake this time. He's a stubborn old cuss, true, but this just seems so out of character. There has to be a way to talk some sense into him.

"We just arrived," Max says. "We're about to compare notes and kick some ideas around."

"Don't let me stop you," I say, perching myself on the arm of an empty chair while I wait.

"The crime scene folks collected the blood from the back gate," Plummer begins. "They'll test that against the DNA database. They also recovered the slug that nicked Ed, and they'll test that for a ballistics match."

"Nicked?" Ed mutters. "Painful damned nick, Jake."

"Shell casings?" I ask, thinking back to Pat's shooting earlier this year. Spent shell casings had helped the police track down the guy who shot her.

"Afraid not," Plummer replies.

"Doesn't sound like there's much to go on," I observe glumly.

"Let us work our magic," Ed says with a wink. "We old bastards still have a few tricks up our sleeves."

Plummer shoots an amused glance Ed's way before taking in everyone with a sweep of his eyes. "Now that we've had some time to reflect, let's talk about what happened yesterday. Ed? Max?"

Max takes the lead. "The guy knew what he was looking for. He walked into the yard and immediately had a look around, then looked right at me and moved on as if I wasn't here. He locked in on Ed as soon he saw him. No hesitation at all."

"That's right, the guy had zero interest in Max," Ed says. A smile plays on his lips when he adds, "Maybe it was a woman, after all? They ain't *never* interested in Max."

Max shoots Ed the bird. "Why did the guy go straight for Ed?"

Plummer's eyes twinkle. "Maybe he knows Ski and was trying to do the world a favor?"

The schoolyard taunts, while mildly amusing, surprise me. This is professional detective work?

"My point is that the shooter definitely targeted Ed," Max continues with a hint of impatience. "Leaving aside the smart-ass bullshit, let's think that through. It's important."

"No doubt about it," Ed agrees.

I look from Ed to Papa and back again. "You know, at a glance, Ed and Papa bear a resemblance. Maybe the shooter mistook Ed for Papa?"

Max purses his lips and nods thoughtfully while he processes the possibility. Papa blanches, perhaps at the suggestion Ed may have taken a bullet intended for him.

Plummer points at Ed and chuckles. "But the nose, man. Dead giveaway! Nobody sees that honker and mistakes the profile for anyone but Ski!"

"Screw you, Jake," Ed shoots back, but there's a smile on his face when he does.

Cop humor, I suppose. Kinda beyond me. "Children!" I admonish them. "Let's focus on the problem, shall we?"

Three sets of bemused eyes settle on me before Ed says, "Sorry, man. This is how cops deal with stuff that makes us piss our pants."

Plummer nods before he pushes himself off his Adirondack chair and takes a step away from it. "Whoever was here yesterday certainly wasn't *Ndrangheta*."

"How do you figure that?" I ask.

"Too many mistakes. If *they'd* sent one of their guys after Francesco, he'd be dead by now."

"Agreed," Ed mutters as he and Max nod.

Plummer continues, "Dollars to doughnuts this is the work of some local shitbag from Francesco's hometown trying to settle a personal score."

Papa's mouth twists in fury as he spits out the words, "*Cosche* filth!"

"But didn't you say it was a young guy?" I ask in confusion.

"The shooter was," Jake replies.

Ed carries the ball from there. "Pulling on that string, we've got some old son of a bitch from Calabria hiring a local punk to do his dirty work. Why?"

"Too old to do it himself?" Max suggests. "Too infirm?"

"Possibly," Plummer says. "Or maybe he just doesn't want to get his hands dirty, especially on foreign soil, where his buddies don't own the cops and judges."

"Will he try again?" I ask Plummer.

"*There's* the question, folks," he says as he cuts his eyes to mine.

Max steps a little closer. "If so, he won't be sending the punk from yesterday. The little shit targeted the wrong guy and got himself shot doing so. Totally balled-up job. It's one and done for that boy, fellas."

"Especially if you winged him good," Ed adds.

"From your lips to God's ear," Plummer mutters.

"So, maybe the old bastard from Italy decides he needs to do this himself to get it done right?" Ed says.

"Maybe he thinks the kid got Papa yesterday," I interject. "The news reports didn't have Ed's name."

"True, just that some old guy got shot," Max says thoughtfully.

The rain is now pouring down so hard that we can hardly see the back fence. With the talk of someone taking another shot at Papa or Ed or whomever they're after, I can't help worrying about what might lurk beyond the veil of water.

Plummer starts to pace around the perimeter of the awning while he talks. "Could be, I suppose, but the news reports made it clear that the victim was treated and released. Whoever's behind this has gotta know that."

"Hurts like a bitch," Ed mutters to eye rolls from the other detectives.

"For Christ's sake give it a rest, Ed!" Max grumbles. "Swear to God, I ain't never heard anyone bellyaching and carrying on so much about a pissy little scratch."

I'm trying to work out if Max's outburst was real or feigned when Plummer walks to within three feet of my father and plants himself with his hands on his hips.

"You need to get the hell out of here until we get a handle

on this, Francesco. These guys seem to be in a hurry. Hell, I only caught wind of this a week ago, and they've already struck twice."

I turn to meet Papa's eyes. "Jake's right."

My father dismisses me with a flick of his wrist, then locks eyes with Plummer and resolutely replies, "No!"

Plummer stands his ground. "It's folly to assume the threat isn't real. There's no shame in playing things smart."

Papa glowers back at him. His obstinance is starting to piss me off. He's not the only person living here.

Plummer levels a finger at Ed. "You want to risk *this* happening to someone else, Francesco?"

I look Papa in the eye. "Or worse?"

He glares at me for a heartbeat before stomping off into the house, slamming the door behind him.

"What the hell is that?" Plummer asks angrily. "He's staying?"

I turn my palms up. "Damned if I know."

"Talk some sense into him."

"I'll try after he cools down a bit, Jake."

"Don't *try*," he snaps. "Get him the hell out of here... and if he's too pigheaded to go, at least get yourself and Brittany out."

I inform him that I've temporarily moved Brittany in with Pat.

"You should go, too," Plummer suggests.

After they leave, I head for Papa's room and rap on the door. "Ed and Jake are gone. You and I need to talk."

Silence.

I raise my voice. "We need to talk right now, Papa."

After a long moment, the door opens and Papa stares back at me. Between the stomping off into the house, the slamming of the door, and the reluctance to open his bedroom door, I'm reminded of dealing with a petulant teenager.

I meet his angry gaze with one of my own. "Jake is right. It's time to go somewhere else for a few days."

"I no go."

"Ed's already been shot. Are you trying to get someone killed?"

"No."

I brace my hands on either side of the doorframe and lean my face closer to his. "Well, you're going to, and it's not going to be me or Brittany, damn it."

"I no run away from *Cosche* filth!"

"Enough with the old-country macho bullshit, Papa! Nobody's going to think you're less of a man if you use a little common sense in the face of danger."

"I no go! Ed, he think they can keep me safe here."

Damned Ed! I slap a hand on the doorframe. "Brittany isn't coming back until this is over with."

The agony in his eyes challenges my decision, but I stand firm. "I'm not putting Brittany at risk no matter what you or Ed or anyone else says, Papa. Period."

CHAPTER EIGHT

It's Friday evening of an eventful week that started with Ed's shooting. With Papa's pigheaded refusal to move out of his house, I've moved Brittany in with Pat for the time being. Deano will follow when he's released from the animal hospital tomorrow. Which leaves me. Pissed as I am with Papa for putting others at risk by insisting on staying here because of some macho "I not run away" bullshit, I don't feel right leaving him on his own, so I'm splitting my time between home and Pat's place. To Jake Plummer's disgust, Ed and the fossils seem to have no more sense than Papa—or maybe they share his prehistoric testosterone. In their eyes, Ed's shooting has made this personal, and they're determined to see things through. As much as possible, they have one or two guys stationed in the backyard and one on the front porch, with another retired cop in the house with Papa. They're running short this evening, so I'm sticking around, not that I'll be much help if anything goes down. There's one fossil in the backyard, and Ed Stankowski is inside with Papa. Max Maxwell will be here around seven o'clock, as soon as his grandson's third birthday party wraps up. A fourth fossil will join them shortly.

Pat and I are hanging out on the front porch awaiting the arrival of Ben Larose so we can conclude our interrupted Monday lunch meeting. She glances at her watch. "Where the heck is Ben? I have to pick up Brittany from volleyball at seven thirty."

"Where was her game?" I ask.

"Some prep school way the hell and gone up in Winnetka. She was griping about having to travel all over Chicago to play."

"Yeah?"

"Yeah," Pat says with a smile. "Such is the life of the varsity volleyball player."

"It's a tough life," I agree sarcastically.

Pat frowns. "She's right, though. They do travel all over the place to play."

"She's the one who insisted on going to private school." If anyone deserves sympathy about things school related, it's me. Brittany is attending Hyde Park College Preparatory High School, which is costing me almost $20,000 in annual tuition—twenty grand that her mother should be paying.

"That's the price of having her here with you instead of over in Brussels with her mother, Valenti."

"I know."

She smiles. "So quit griping about it."

She's right. I went through hell when Brittany went to live with her mother last year. Maker's Mark bourbon and I had grown close in those months... much too close. Brittany had left for a number of reasons, one of which had been a refusal to return to St. Aloysius High School after a brief suspension following an uncharacteristic blowup with a teacher. She'd had a number of run-ins with teachers and students in the wake of Papa's shooting incident. If the price of having her back in Cedar Heights is astronomical tuition, it's a cost I'm willing to bear. Still, a guy can bitch a little about his kid's hit on his pocketbook now and then, right?

We can see into the living room from where we stand. Papa is parked on his venerable La-Z-Boy recliner, and Ed has settled into Mama's old easy chair while they watch a dated rerun of *The Rockford Files* television show. Along with *Kojak* and *Columbo,* Papa has a thing for old cop and private-eye shows—yet another thing he and Stankowski have bonded over. I don't know about Ed, but Papa has watched every episode of the shows enough times that he can probably recite the dialogue word for word. He claims that he learned English from watching TV. That may be, but I don't recall any of his favorite TV dicks speaking broken English.

Pat's brow furrows. "Shouldn't Ed be at home resting?"

"He's a tough old bird."

"Dumb old bird, if you ask me," she mutters with a wondering shake of her head. "Have the cops figured out who shot him?"

"Nope. We're starting to wonder if maybe they took their shot and moved on."

An elderly gentleman is strolling past with the help of a cane. He peers up at the house as he goes. Pat studies the old-timer on the sidewalk for a moment, then smiles at him and lifts a hand to wave at him in greeting. He doesn't seem to notice.

"Who's that?" she asks.

I've been back in Cedar Heights for over a year now, and I'm still meeting the new crop of neighbors. "I don't recognize him. He looks like he belongs around here, though, doesn't he? Probably someone's grandfather."

"It's only been a few days, Tony," she says when she turns back to me and picks up the thread of our conversation. "If some guy is still after your father for something that happened almost fifty years ago, what makes you think he'll walk away five days after he finds him?"

It's a good point that's been nagging at me, as well. "I wish Papa would close the damned blinds."

Pat glances back at the expansive front-room window. With darkness falling and the living-room lights on, Papa and Ed are totally exposed to the street. Papa refuses to move the wall-mounted, fifty-five-inch television—"I no make more holes in the wall!"—and he isn't about to rearrange the living-room furniture, which is placed exactly where Mama thought it should be. I think of the old guy looking inside as he wandered by. Anyone on the sidewalk has a front-row seat to whatever is going on in our living room.

"Yeah, they should close them," Pat agrees as we watch them.

Papa's eyes drift to the portrait of Mama that hangs on the wall between the front door and picture window. I often find my father sitting and gazing at Mama's picture or the trinkets and mementos she scattered around the living room, occasionally doing so with her rosary beads in hand when he thinks no one is watching. He's not a demonstrative man, but I know the loss of his wife of forty-seven years still tears at his heart every day he's forced to live without her.

"He misses her, huh?" Pat asks.

"He sure does."

"Maybe he doesn't want to leave the house and all those memories behind, even for a few days."

I hadn't thought of that. Maybe that has something to do with his determination to stay here. God, but grief is a complicated mess.

We watch a Cedar Heights PD cruiser approach and wave back to the pair of officers who lift their hands in greeting as they coast by. It's a relief to know they're coming by fairly regularly. Jake Plummer has warned us that the frequency of patrols will likely dwindle as the days pass.

Pat and I chat and watch every car that comes down the street as we wait. Liberty Street is two long blocks of post–World War II brick bungalows that end at Independence Park. Almost every lot features a stately old oak, elm, or ash tree that towers high overhead, creating a canopy above the street. Over the years, the mostly Italian immigrants who settled here have added flourishes to infuse both the bland tract houses and the neighborhood with splashes of personality.

"So, anything new with this lawsuit business?" Pat asks.

"They seem to be in an unusual hurry," I reply. "They've sent a raft of requests for discovery and want to schedule depositions next week."

"What's the rush?"

I shrug. "Good question."

Larose finally arrives at six-fifty, twenty minutes late. "Traffic was a bitch," he informs us.

We're distracted by the deep rumble of an approaching car. A muscular Carousel Red 1969 Pontiac GTO Judge eases to the curb in front of the house and parks behind Pat's aging Hyundai Sonata. The GTO has been fully restored with twin hood scoops, fat Mickey Thompson street tires, and a functional rear spoiler. I know the details not because I know a damned thing about cars, but because Max had waxed poetic for fifteen minutes about what three years of detailed work in his backyard garage had wrought. I seldom hear him string more than five or six words together in a single go. It's amusing and touching to see the guy get so emotional about having lovingly restored his father's old wheels.

"That'll be Max," I announce as the car falls silent and the door pops open. Max climbs out and locks the door with a key. I guess they didn't do power locks back in '69.

"Nice wheels," Larose says admiringly when Max trudges up the front steps.

"Thanks," Max mutters as he eases into one of the two lawn chairs squeezed into the far corner of the porch. He plunks a thermos down next to the chair.

"You're early," I note.

"Even a grandfather can only take so much of screaming three-year-olds," he grumbles, then adds with a sardonic grin, "so when Ed told me you were standing guard out here, I thought I'd best get my ass in gear."

"Good call," I say before giving his shoulder a squeeze. Then I lead Pat and Larose inside, meet Papa's gaze, and tilt my head at the front window. "If you're going to insist on watching TV with all the lights on at night, at least close the curtains. "

Papa's nostrils flare. "I like to see the outside."

"You two look like a couple of ducks in a shooting gallery," I retort.

Ed nods. "Point taken."

Papa shoots a scowl Ed's way.

"Thanks, Ed," I say while closing the drapes. "Good to know one of you has a little common sense."

Papa's scowl swings to me before I turn away and lead my guests to the kitchen, where Larose, Pat, and I settle around the maple table. I pour myself a bourbon. My guests settle for soft drinks.

Larose gazes around at the hand-built ceiling cornices, doors, and doorframes, as well as the ceramic tile floor and countertop. "The village tried to condemn *this* place last year?" he asks in disbelief.

I nod. "Go figure, huh?"

"What's the world coming to?"

Pat takes a pointed look at her watch. "Let's get to it, guys. I've got thirty minutes, tops."

"Did you get a chance to ask your clients about the stuff I mentioned?" Larose asks me.

He called on Tuesday with a few questions. I touched base with Billy and Rick to get the answers he's after, but I have a few questions for him before I share Bill's and Rick's replies. I don't want him writing an article that quotes my clients.

"I did," I reply. "Tell me what you plan to do with the information."

"I'm not entirely sure. I've been poking around a bit, learning what I can about what happened."

"Working on a story?" Pat asks him.

"At some point, assuming I'm able to cobble together enough to write something that offers a reasonably factual account of what happened."

"Why not just wait and do a story on the NTSB report?" I ask.

His eyes drift to the window for a long moment before they settle back on mine. "That's a good question," he says thoughtfully. Then his lips tighten, his brow furrows, and his voice hardens. "I guess I'm offended by the idea of someone like Megan Walton flying a Cessna 210 with paying passengers aboard. Someone needs to look into that and ask some tough questions about how it happened."

"She wasn't qualified?" Pat asks in surprise as she plants her elbows on the table, settles her chin on her knuckles, and waits for Larose's reply.

He frowns. "Technically, she had the requisite flight hours and was rated on the 210N."

"But?" Pat prompts.

"As a practical matter, I very much doubt that she was *really* qualified. She had the bare minimum number of hours."

"So she *was* qualified and yet *not* qualified?" Pat asks uncertainly.

I'm as confused as Pat. How could Megan Walton be both?

"The Cessna 210 isn't a simple aircraft to fly," Larose mutters. "You'd like anyone flying one to have had some high-quality instruction, plus cockpit time with someone who knows what he or she is doing. There's a big difference between simply being rated on a 210 and knowing the aircraft well enough to get out of a jam when something goes wrong. Putting a greenhorn in the cockpit with paying passengers is criminally negligent."

"Is that what happened?" I ask, wondering how Larose could possibly be sure if that was so.

He leans back in his seat and sighs. "I've got a lot of contacts in aviation, Tony. Lots of good sources, especially when they speak off the record. I was able to gather some interesting details about Megan Walton's piloting career."

"And?" Pat asks.

"Her flight instructor for the 210 is a pretty sketchy character," Larose replies with a look of distaste.

"How sketchy?" I ask after draining the last of my bourbon. Man, that went down quickly.

Anger flares in Larose's eyes when he replies, "He's somehow managed to skate by more than a few times when people have raised concerns. Rumors of kickbacks have dogged him for years. No reputable flight-training outfit will touch the guy, but he manages to get by on his own. Given how much money is behind Windy City Sky Tours and the Walton family, hiring him makes absolutely no sense. There are way better choices readily available. The Waltons could have hired anyone they wanted."

"Why is this character still in business?" Pat asks.

Larose turns his palms up. "Why are so many sketchy people able to make a living? Some are con artists, some make a go of it by sacrificing quality by bidding low, others are simply willing to deliver whatever results people are willing to pay for, ethics be damned. I suspect that's what happened with Megan."

"That seems like a pretty risky proposition for Windy City to undertake," I suggest.

"Yeah, well, from what I've learned about Jonathan Walton, it sounds like he's been buying his way out of trouble his whole life," Larose says.

I think back on the time I spent with Walton the day I visited his office with Billy and Rick. "He's certainly an arrogant bastard. I guess I can see him pulling a stunt like that."

"Especially if you know anything about his sister," Pat adds.

"I've heard a thing or two about her," Larose says. "By all accounts, the woman is hell on wheels. Not someone you want to cross."

"You're talking about Megan's mother, right?" I ask.

He nods. "I talked to a guy who runs in their social circles. According to him, if Megan's mother told Jonathan to give Megan a job, he'd make it happen one way or another. These are the kind of people who think the rules the rest of us play by don't apply to them."

"Money does talk," I grumble.

"Which brings us back to the flight instructor," Larose says. "He wouldn't jeopardize a fat payday by pushing back against a client's demands. That would require some integrity."

I've heard enough to feel as if Larose isn't going to betray our trust regarding Billy and Rick, but decide to lay down some ground rules, anyway. "Whatever Billy and Rick say can't be quoted in your article."

When he gives me a questioning look, I explain that I don't want anything on record that might come back to haunt my clients at trial.

He drains his can of 7Up and sets it aside. "Fair enough. I'm more interested in the Megan Walton angle, anyway."

"Glad to hear it," I say. "I put your questions to Billy and Rick. To your first point, they swear everything that needed to be done to that aircraft was completed. To quote Billy directly, they did so 'despite the assholes at Windy City dragging their feet at every turn before coughing up the money to keep the maintenance current.' Billy and Rick claim everything is properly documented. They're confident it will be crystal clear to the NTSB and anyone else who investigates that the fault for whatever happened isn't theirs."

Larose gives me a skeptical look. "That's some touching faith in the integrity of the system."

"The NTSB is rock solid, aren't they?" Pat asks.

"*They* are, yeah," Larose replies.

The NTSB will play things straight; that's not his concern. He just doesn't share Billy's touching faith that the legal system will invariably work as it should. I've seen the law subverted by the rich and powerful often enough to share his skepticism. "It's everyone else we have to worry about," I mutter.

Larose points a finger at me and says, "Bingo."

We spend a few more minutes discussing the accident before Pat tells us that she needs to leave if she's going to be on time to collect Brittany. I gather their empty soda cans and dump them in the recycling bin after they depart, making a mental note to chat with Penelope about using Larose as an expert witness when this eventually goes to trial. Then I go to the living room to visit with Papa and Ed. I'm bidding them good night when my phone rings. To my dismay, the name of my ex-wife, Michelle Rice, pops up on the caller ID. I briefly consider ignoring the call, then reluctantly give in. She'll just keep calling until she wears me down, anyway. I walk into the kitchen to take the call.

"Another shooting at that damned house!" she exclaims in lieu of a greeting. "You may as well be living in one of those Black neighborhoods, for Christ's sake."

Despite being fully aware that attempting to reason with her when she's worked herself into this state is a waste of breath, I try, anyway. "We've got secur—"

"This is not acceptable, Tony!"

"Calm down."

"I will *not* calm down!" she shouts. "I won't have my daughter living in a shooting gallery!"

I'm trying to work out a non-incendiary response when I realize that she's said everything she intended to and has ended the call. Our next contact will most likely be through the Rice family's formidable army of lawyers. A shaft of fear worms its way into my heart when I realize that another contest for custody of my daughter is probably brewing. It's hardly a stretch to imagine a family court accepting the argument that Brittany isn't safe in the Valenti family home. Yes, she's parked at Pat's house for the moment, but this isn't a battle about temporary arrangements. It will determine what country Brittany is going to live in—and with which parent.

CHAPTER NINE

"**W**here *is* she?" Brittany asks in exasperation while we stare out the living-room window on a dreary Monday afternoon three days later. We're waiting for Pat to pick up Brittany and drop her off at a friend's house.

I smile inwardly as I watch my daughter bouncing impatiently from foot to foot. Her hand shoots up to the short, spiky bottled-blond hair that has replaced the lustrous auburn hair she was born with. The hairdo seems to be a little touch of rebellion. If so, it's the only touch of teenage revolution I've seen from her. I can live with that.

"Gawd, this is so lame," she gripes twenty seconds later. *Gawd* is pronounced with a hint of Georgia drawl that she picked up while living in Atlanta for the first fourteen years of her life. She's never sounded like a native Southerner—not with parents who hail from Chicago and Connecticut—but it's there, particularly when she's agitated. When you're fifteen years old, I guess losing a couple of minutes with your friends is a big deal.

As for me, I've enjoyed the morning and am in no hurry for it to end. It's the first time we've spent at home together since I moved her in with Pat a week ago. Pat dropped her off a couple of hours ago while she went to the office to tie up some loose ends on a story. She was due back at noon. It's now seven minutes after.

"Relax!" I say with a laugh. "She'll be along shortly."

My daughter gives me an exasperated look, the type reserved for old people who can't possibly understand the travails of youth. She announced earlier that she was going to walk to her friend's house. Before Ed's shooting, I would have been fine with that. Not now.

Pat's Sonata squeals to a stop at the curb two minutes later. I walk onto the front porch and lean against the wood railing while Brittany rushes down the steps and races to the street. Pat's barely out of the car before Brittany is on her as if she hasn't seen her for, well, a lot longer than two hours.

"Sorry," Pat says as they stroll up the sidewalk to the porch. "I was doing an interview for a story. It took a little longer than expected."

"That's okay!" Brittany says brightly.

Really?

Pat drops her keys into a colorful handbag the size of a small suitcase and meets my gaze while she climbs the porch steps. "You're driving, Valenti. Mind eating on the run? We're going to be late as it is."

"Are we going somewhere?" I ask while my daughter scoops up a backpack from the floor just inside the door.

Pat nods at me, then asks Brittany, "You all set?"

"Yup!"

I collect my car keys from the entry-hall table. Brittany is already through the door.

Pat's now the one bouncing from foot to foot while she holds the screen door open. "Get a move on, Chubby. Chop, chop."

"Where are we going in such a hurry?" I ask while I secure the dead bolt on the front door.

"I'll tell you about it on the way," she calls over her

shoulder as she bounds down the steps to the Porsche and yanks the passenger door open. Brittany is already clambering into the back seat on the other side.

"So, where are you guys going?" Brittany asks after I back out of the driveway and put the car in gear for the five-minute drive.

"Lunch first," Pat replies. "Subway or something?"

Brittany shakes her head. "Not me. I'm eating at Jocelyn's."

"There's a Quiznos on Cicero," I say as we near the end of the block. "Does that work?"

"Quiznos. Subway. There's a difference?" Brittany cracks.

I chuckle before responding, "Millions of advertising dollars swear there is."

Pat groans. "Don't get me started on advertising."

"So? Where are you guys going this afternoon?" Brittany asks again.

"I help rehab houses in Lawndale on Monday afternoons," Pat replies.

I recall her mentioning it. I wonder what I'll be doing.

"The paintbrush!" Brittany exclaims.

Pat laughs and nods. "Yes, the paintbrush."

"The Paintbrush" hangs on the wall in Pat's home painting studio. It was presented to her by the Reverend Alvin Jakes at the conclusion of the first Lawndale rehab project she worked on. It's engraved with her name, the address of the house, and the date of completion.

"You're taking Dad to Lawndale?" Brittany asks as I pull away from the stop sign at the end of Liberty Street.

"Yup. Something to keep his mind off everything else that's going on."

Brittany frowns. "Is it safe? Isn't that one of those inner-city neighborhoods?"

I can all but hear her mother's sneering characterization of "colored communities."

Pat sighs heavily. "I hate that inner-city tag. Lawndale is a west-side neighborhood that has suffered through some tough times, kiddo. Almost every employer there pulled out after the riots in the late 1960s. That left most folks out of work. *That's* what put Lawndale into a death spiral. Reverend Jakes and others have been working to turn it back into a safe and vibrant community."

"Pat's been telling that story in the *Tribune* for years now," I add. "Reverend Jakes told me that they probably couldn't have kept their funding flowing without her help."

"I've played a very small role," Pat scoffs.

"Riiight," I retort with a sidelong glance at her. She won a local reporting Pulitzer Prize for one of her stories about Lawndale. The paintbrush suggests she's played a more practical role, as well.

"Are there gangs and stuff?" Brittany asks.

"There's crime," Pat allows. "But not as much as there used to be."

"You're safe, though, right?"

Pat turns in her seat to make eye contact with Brittany. "It's not like I'm out wandering the streets at night or dealing drugs. I'm working with people in the community, so I'm cool with the locals."

"How did you first get involved?" I ask.

Pat smiles at the memory. "I did a story about a church named Calvary New Life that works in the community. Reverend Jakes's church, as a matter of fact. One thing led to another, and next thing I knew, I had a hammer in my hand."

"Like, what do you do there?" Brittany asks.

"We fix up old houses so families can move in. That's how they reclaim the neighborhoods. The families and church work together to chase the troublemakers out. It works well."

"Sounds cool," Brittany says as I ease the car to a stop in front of Jocelyn's house.

Pat shifts her gaze to me. "Assuming your old man finally

knows one end of a hammer from the other, we're going to put him to work."

"One end has a big clawlike thing, right?" I ask.

Pat chuckles. "There might be hope for you yet. You, too!" she adds to my daughter.

"Yeah. Right!" Brittany laughs as she pushes the rear door open and hops out.

"Don't forget that we're picking up Deano this afternoon!" Pat shouts after her.

Brittany replies with a thumbs-up and an enormous grin.

"Quiznos?" I ask Pat after Jocelyn lets Brittany in.

"Sure. Music?"

Dinosaur that I am, I still load discs into the Porsche's CD player. I browse the collection and select one I think she might like. Pat settles back into the supple leather seat and closes her eyes while she listens. We drive the next couple of miles without speaking. About halfway through a track called *Tattoo'd Lady*, she starts rummaging in the glove box and comes up with an empty CD case.

"Is this what we're listening to?"

"You bet." Rory Gallagher. *Tattoo*. For my money, his best album, showcasing the eclectic range of his musical influences.

"This is great! How come I've never heard of this guy?"

"He was a lot bigger in Europe than he ever was here," I reply.

"How come?"

"He refused to release singles, never whored himself to a record label. Plus, he died years ago when he was only forty-seven."

Pat frowns. "That's too bad. How did you hear about him?"

"Amy." The crown jewel of my sister's meager estate had been her prized record collection. More so than whatever was on the radio when I was in my adolescence and early teens, hers was the music I grew up on. I've still got her LP records, which have been safely tucked away for years and replaced with CDs.

"God, I *love* that song!" Pat exclaims as she hits replay, dials the volume higher, and settles back to listen for the rest of the drive to Quiznos.

"Drive-through?" I ask while turning into the parking lot. This is the only Quiznos I know of that has a drive-through.

Her eyes don't open. "Perfect."

I ease into line behind a single car. Guess nobody expects to find a drive-through Quiznos.

"Nine-inch meatball," Pat tells me before I ask.

I've never tried one, so I place an order for two meatball subs. Sandwiches and sodas in hand a few minutes later, we pull into an empty spot in the parking lot and let Rory serenade us while we eat. The sub tastes every bit as good as its savory aroma promised.

"That was good," I say happily when I finish, ball up my napkins in the wrapper, and toss it all at the garbage bin outside the car window. I miss.

Pat hands me a napkin and points to a spot on her chin. "You missed a spot, Valenti."

I wipe the tomato sauce off, collect Pat's waste, and climb out of the car to stuff everything into the trash container. Then we set out for Lawndale.

"How's it going with Britts at your place?" I ask after we turn north on Cicero.

Pat groans. "What's with the superhero movies, for God's sake?"

Brittany is in a superhero movie phase.

"I'm enjoying the break from them," I reply with a laugh.

"She's been coming up to the studio and sketching while I paint," Pat says. "She's pretty good."

"Yeah, she is."

"Turn left here," Pat tells me after a fifteen-minute drive. "Pull in behind the pickup truck."

We're outside a tiny old bungalow sitting in the middle of perhaps the most woebegone excuse for a lawn I've ever seen. The siding has been stripped off the house, and it's being swathed in white Tyvek HomeWrap. New white-vinyl windows wrapped in cardboard and plastic are stacked beneath a gaping hole in the wall where the largest of them will go. A couple of guys are on the roof laying a fresh layer of shingles.

"How y'all doing, Pat?" one shouts down with a big grin.

"Good, Pete. You?"

"Outstanding!" he replies before he greets me with a friendly nod. "Hey, man."

I smile back and return the greeting.

A diminutive, rail-thin Black man with a close-cropped head of graying hair steps through the front door and bounds down the steps as we come up the sidewalk. The smile his face splits into reminds me of why I love this man to bits. Reverend Alvin Jakes came into my life after Pat was shot last year. He stuck around to offer his support during my father's trial as well as throughout the ordeal of Titan Development's attempt to bulldoze our neighborhood. He wraps Pat in a bear hug. His eyes twinkle mischievously when he looks at me over her shoulder and asks, "Is this the new recruit?"

Pat steps out of the embrace. "I warned you that he may not be of much use."

"She's been talking about me again, has she?" I ask.

The reverend grins, then grasps my arm and tugs me toward the house. "Yessir, but you're still welcome."

"Thanks," I mutter while shooting a sideways stink eye at Pat.

"Uh-huh," he says. His eyes drift heavenward when he adds, "We appreciate every one of God's children that He sends to help with His work here."

"Once you see me with a hammer in hand, you may question His wisdom," I say.

He wraps an arm around my shoulder. "It sure is good to see you again, Tony. All is well?"

I nod. Something in his eyes telegraphs his knowledge of recent events around our house, but he doesn't broach the topic. I'm grateful.

"What are you gonna have us doing?" Pat asks.

Jakes winks at me. "Considering Tony's hammer handicap, I think you two should do some painting." He looks me up and down. "Did you bring any old clothes?"

I shake my head.

"We oughtta have something you can slip on over those nice uptown threads."

"They've got a ton of old stuff you can throw on," Pat adds.

Jakes squeezes my shoulder as he turns back to the house. "Pat knows where to find 'em."

She takes my arm and leads me inside. More effusive greetings welcome us to Lawndale before Pat heads to the basement with me in tow, pulls a pair of well-worn but clean coveralls from a wire strung between two crosshatched ceiling beams, and tosses them to me—all the while chattering with a couple of guys who are busy hanging drywall. I pull on the coveralls. Now protected against unruly splatters of paint, we make our way back upstairs. After a brief tutorial by Pat, we begin slopping paint on the walls of a bedroom.

"I hear there's been some action on the lawsuit front," she says.

"Yup. Now that they've had time to sniff out where the money is, Butterworth Cole has amended the lawsuit to add the principals of Windy City and Megan Walton's estate as defendants."

"Plenty of money in the Walton family," she says with a healthy measure of distaste.

"Not a Walton family fan?" I ask.

She frowns. "I was assigned to help a cub reporter cover Jonathan's society wedding a few years ago and to write a profile on the Walton family. Not a nice group of people. I don't get the public fascination with people like them."

"The whole celebrity thing, I guess. Nothing new in that. It's been going on for decades."

"I suppose. It just seems worse now."

"Can't argue with that," I say. "Maybe it's that old saw about people who are famous for nothing more than being famous? They seem to be breeding like rabbits these days."

"Yeah, I suppose," she grumbles.

We paint in silence for the next couple of minutes.

"Nice work," she says with a snort when I slop a giant glop of paint on the floor. "We'll be putting carpet in, Valenti. No need to paint the floorboards."

"Thanks for letting me know."

"Anyway, back to the Waltons," she says. "It might be worthwhile for you to know a little more about them."

"Shoot."

"Lillian Walton is a staple of the Chicago philanthropic and fine-arts scenes—a true matriarch of Chicago society. Young Jonathan married well, to a wife in the mold of his mother. Mind you," Pat continues with a sardonic smile, "there's just a whiff of distaste amongst the true hoity-toity when it comes to the social standing of his wife."

"Why?"

"For starters, she doesn't come from old money. There also seems to be some doubt that her grandfather came by his money honestly in the age of the robber barons. Anyway, between his mother's and wife's fortunes, Jonathan is a lucrative target for a lawsuit."

"Sounds like it," I say while dipping my paint brush into the can and carefully working off excess paint so as not to soil any other forbidden surfaces.

"Megan's mother, Annabelle—an absolute rich bitch if ever there was one—is Jonathan's sister. Annabelle's husband's grandfather made a killing during the Prohibition era, sometimes literally, if the rumors are true. Not that the family talks about *that*. Megan had a huge trust fund that's just waiting to be picked over in a lawsuit if she's found to be at fault for the crash. Her mother is apparently apoplectic about the possibility of even a penny of that money ending up in the pockets of 'a dirty damned politician' like Senator Evan Walton."

"Apoplectic?" I say with a chuckle.

"Writer word," she replies sheepishly.

"Nice to be hanging out with such an erudite painting partner."

She smiles. "Screw you, Valenti."

The Walton nonsense reminds me of the Rice family bullshit I suffered through during my marriage. They all sound like peas in a pod. As if defending Billy Likens isn't motivation enough, inflicting a stinging defeat on the Waltons would be satisfying as hell. We return to our painting.

"Who's going to live here?" I ask after several minutes, during which I managed to roll paint onto a section of wall without spilling a drop. At this rate, the good reverend is going to be begging me to return.

"Shit!" Pat exclaims when *she* misses the paint tray while reloading her roller, adding a nice dash of paint to the floor.

"Carpet's coming," I remind her with a nasty grin.

"Screw you again," she mutters while hooking a thumb at her glass eye. "At least I have the excuse of compromised depth perception with this damned thing."

I immediately regret my smart-assed remark. Pat seldom mentions the eye, but I know the depth-perception issue challenges her on a regular basis, especially as it affects her personal painting.

She shrugs it off and gets back to work while she answers

my question about who will live here. "They'll find a family that needs a home and is willing to do the hard work needed to rebuild and reclaim the neighborhood. Folks have to be in for the long haul and be willing to face down the punks and druggies."

"Not a job for the faint of heart. Jakes and his people sell the houses to these folks?"

"Whenever possible. The project needs the money to move on to the next house."

"What if the family can't get a mortgage?"

"Reverend Jakes has recruited a couple of community banks to get involved. New Calvary will take out a mortgage if they have to, then rent the house back to the family on a rent-to-own basis until the homeowners can get their own financing."

We paint and chatter for another half hour before Pat lays her brush aside. I pause in midstroke and realize that she's finished two walls in the time it's taken me to do about ninety percent of one.

She looks at her watch. "You go ahead and finish that wall while I start cleaning up. We need to get you home before Brittany calls."

I think about Pat as I finish. I came to understand last year just how deeply immersed she is in Chicago and have developed a deep appreciation of who she is. Despite having been raised in the same neighborhoods and attended the same schools, I've somehow managed to get through the first few decades of my life without contributing ten percent of what she's done. For all the social climbing I've done, hers has been far and away the richer life. With that lesson learned, I've been playing catch-up—not that I'll ever come close to matching her accomplishments. At least I'm now in the game.

"Have you and Penelope developed a sense about how vulnerable Billy Likens and his partner are?" Pat asks once we're in the car and on our way back to Liberty Street.

My thoughts turn to the NTSB investigation and the lawsuit that R & B Ramp Services is caught up in. "Sort of. There are so many moving parts to this thing. It's like trying to sort out a giant jigsaw puzzle with a couple of thousand scattered pieces. Papa's trial last year was like a ten-piece toddler's puzzle in comparison."

Pat snorts at my analogy.

"Really," I insist. "I'm so over my head with this thing that it frightens me."

"You're not up to the challenge?" she asks sharply as we coast to a stop at a red light.

"I promised Mel I would look out for Billy, but I'm not sure how to do so in this case. I can't stand the thought of letting them down."

Pat turns sideways in her seat. "Look at me," she commands. I do. "This sounds an awful lot like what I heard from you last year, Tony—the whole 'I'm not good enough, I'm going to get Papa executed' crap you were spewing before you went to trial and got him acquitted. Why is it so hard for you to accept that you're smart and capable?"

I gaze back at her angry face and shrug. Over the years, my older brother, my ex-wife, former business colleagues, and a string of disillusioned girlfriends have all attested to what a worthless piece of shit I am. I've always had a tough time arguing against what seems like a mountain of evidence. I *do* try, but it's a constant struggle, and I'm sometimes prone to backsliding at the merest hint that they had me pegged correctly.

The honk of a horn behind me interrupts our staredown. I glance up to see that the light has turned green. Cicero Avenue may be clear ahead, but I'm in no doubt that the lawsuit littering the road ahead will severely test my limited legal skills. Penelope is probably going to have to bail me out if we hope to save Billy's and Rick's asses in court.

CHAPTER TEN

I'm sitting at the kitchen table with Papa and Ed Stankowski shortly after ten o'clock the following evening when I start nodding off and decide it's time for bed. I drain my glass of bourbon and get to my feet. "Bedtime for me, gentlemen." I fix them with a pointed look and add, "Stay in the house tonight, you two."

Ed smirks at me and lifts his damaged left arm in its sling, reaches inside with his good hand, and produces his pistol. "I'm right-handed. I'll be fine if anything goes down."

Officer Marty Zeller, who quietly told me that he'd driven here at the end of his shift after being told Ed was here tonight, turns a questioning gaze on me.

"I found these two sitting on the front porch with a couple of beers last night," I tell him over my shoulder as I rinse my glass.

Zeller rolls his eyes. "Even if you had two good hands, Ed, the two of you sitting out there is dumb as hell—especially only a week after you got yourself shot. Tony's right. Stay inside. I'll personally drag your asses back into the house if I catch you out there."

Ed doesn't argue.

Papa's another story. "You no tell me what to do at my home!"

Zeller ignores my father. "Get your head out of your ass, Ed."

Ed glares at him. The 'head up his ass' crack was apparently going a little too far. Cantankerous old buggers that he and Papa are, they'll probably take an entire case of Moretti outside and guzzle the whole thing before the sun rises.

I should have crawled into bed the moment I got home from work this afternoon. The evening began with my father demanding that I bring Deano home from Pat's house, where he's still recuperating. I continue to refuse, reasoning that Deano is safe there. Apparently, the Deano argument isn't finished.

Papa looks up at me after I put my glass into the dishwasher. "Deano, he come home tomorrow."

"I'm done arguing with you," I retort as I head for my room. I'm asleep almost before my head hits the pillow.

A popping noise interrupts my sleep three hours later, the same sound I'd heard the night Pat was shot before my eyes. The sound of feet pounding through the living room brings me fully awake.

"Call 911!" Zeller calls out from the front of the house as more gunfire erupts outside. "Damn!" he shouts while I scramble out from under the covers and grab my cell phone.

I'm connecting with the emergency operator when I reach the living room and follow Zeller's voice onto the front porch. The smell of gunpowder hangs in the heavy night air.

"What the hell were you two thinking?" Zeller is yelling at a stunned Papa while I give the 911 operator our address.

Zeller steps past Papa and bends down. Ed Stankowski is crumpled in the corner of the porch. "Ed?" Zeller pleads. "Ed!"

"Ed's hit?" an approaching voice asks out of the darkness in the front yard.

"Bad," Zeller mutters. "You put down the bastard who shot him?"

"Yeah," Max says as he arrives at the porch rail and stares in horror at his wounded friend, whose breathing is distressingly labored. Max slams a meaty fist into the railing. "I told the stupid bastards to get inside when I heard them out here a little while ago."

"I sorry," Papa murmurs as he gawks at his bloodied friend.

"A lot of good that does Ed now," Max snarls at him.

I inform the operator that a retired cop has been shot, then send Papa inside to get a blanket. Zeller reaches over the rail, squeezes Max's shoulder, and points into the yard. "You're sure that guy's down?"

The second mention of a guy down registers in my discombobulated mind. My eyes follow Max as he walks to a body sprawled in the grass halfway between the sidewalk and our porch. The glow from the streetlights reflects off a sheen of blood on the torso. With his gun pointed at the head of the prone figure, Max none too gently prods a leg with his foot. When he gets no reaction, he bends down and presses his fingers to the victim's neck. After rolling the man face-down, he slaps a pair of cuffs on the guy and turns him onto his side facing the house. Max pauses for a long moment with his head hanging low, then straightens up and walks back toward us. His footsteps leave imprints in the dew on the grass. "Son of a bitch is still alive."

I tell 911 about the second shooting victim as Papa delivers an old picnic blanket to Zeller and then sits on the top step while Max and Zeller do what they can for Ed.

Zeller's hands are slick with blood when he gets to his feet and grabs the cell phone out of my hand to speak with the 911 operator. "Where's that damned ambulance?" he demands as the sound of approaching sirens grows steadily closer. His next words chill me. "Ed's been shot in the chest. He's coughing up blood and is struggling like hell to breathe. His heart's racing a mile a minute. I think we're losing him. What the hell should we do until the paramedics arrive?"

Zeller listens with a grim expression, then slaps the bloodied phone back in my hand and squats down to resume working on Ed.

Papa stares up at me. The haunted expression is back in his eyes when he gestures toward the body in the yard. "The man, he come for me. He walk on sidewalk and see us, look only at me when he take gun out of jacket and point it. Ed, he jump in front of me and try to shoot the man. He get shot!"

Papa's starting to go into shock. I pull him into an embrace and hold his frail shoulders tightly as he begins to sob. Then I take him back inside, settle him in his La-Z-Boy, cover him in a fuzzy blue blanket Mama had used to warm her legs, and pour him a glass of grappa. I make my way back to the porch as the first emergency vehicles arrive. At Max's direction, the initial team of paramedics hurries to the porch and starts working feverishly on Ed. A second ambulance arrives within the minute. Max directs those paramedics to the second shooting victim. When a uniformed officer shines a powerful flashlight on the casualty in the front yard, I recognize the old man who had walked past the house while Pat and I were waiting for Ben Larose four nights ago. Should I have done something when I noticed him staring at the house? Granted, he hadn't seemed threatening, but still. What had I said? "He looks like he belongs?" Right.

When a third ambulance arrives, I send its paramedics inside to check on Papa.

"Shit! We're losing him," one of the paramedics working on Ed exclaims.

"We need to get him to the hospital," his partner mutters grimly.

After they wrestle Ed onto the gurney, hustle him out to their waiting ambulance, and race away to the hospital, Zeller slumps onto the top step and watches the second team of paramedics as they work on Ed's shooter. "Damn it," he says dejectedly as his eyes meet mine. "I fell asleep at the kitchen table. How could I?"

He'd told me earlier that he started work at six o'clock yesterday morning. I look at him sympathetically. "How long have you been awake now?"

He shrugs and disconsolately murmurs, "No excuse."

"What the hell were they doing out there?" I ask angrily.

Zeller shrugs. "Beautiful night for a beer on the porch. For some reason, neither one of them seemed to think anything bad was likely to happen."

"Why? Ed got shot here a few days ago!"

He shakes his head forlornly. "Sometimes we cops get to feeling a little invulnerable. Maybe Ed figured he could handle any risk that popped up."

"Like I say, he just got shot. How in hell could he think that?"

"He was still on painkillers, Tony. Add a beer or two. Impaired judgment?"

"Damned costly error in judgment," I mutter.

We're ordered out of the house while detectives and crime-scene technicians pore over every inch of the porch and yard. A long night lies ahead while we anxiously await word from the hospital.

CHAPTER ELEVEN

My nose follows the smell of freshly brewed coffee when I wake up just after seven o'clock in the morning, two hours after I'd fallen into an exhausted sleep on the sofa in Pat's office after the ordeal of Ed's shooting. I stifle a yawn and run my hands through my unruly hair as I come downstairs into the kitchen, tug my sweatpants straight, and give Pat a grateful nod as she pours me a cup of coffee.

"Good morning," she says. Then she points at the kitchen table. "Sit, before you fall down."

"Morning," I mumble.

She's fully dressed and made up, at least as much as Pat is ever made up. As she walks over and slides the coffee in front of me, I wonder if she's been to bed since we straggled in just after three in the morning. We'd let Brittany sleep through the night in the second-floor guest room that she's claimed as her own. I'm not sure where Pat stashed my father.

I lift the coffee to my lips. "Thanks."

"Uh-huh," she murmurs in Chicago's approximation of "you're welcome." She looks down at me with concern and rests a hand on my shoulder. "How are you?"

Shell-shocked. Confused. Frightened. Pissed at Papa and

Ed. I shrug and turn my hands up helplessly, then steer the conversation elsewhere as Pat settles into the chair beside mine.

"Papa?" I ask.

She tilts her head toward the living room. "Crashed on the couch. Still sleeping."

"Brittany?"

"She'll be down shortly. I heard her hitting the shower a few minutes ago." Pat's eye settles on me. "I haven't told her what happened."

I get it. I'm the parent. Still, I'm not looking forward to telling Brittany about the latest gunplay on Liberty Street. It turns out that I don't have to. My daughter bursts into the kitchen a minute later in tears, throws herself into my arms, and exclaims, "You're okay!"

I hold her close. "I am. Papa is, too."

She smells of soap and shampoo, some sort of citrusy scent. She sobs against my chest a moment longer while her damp hair wets my shirt. Then she turns her eyes up to mine. "I just saw the morning news. They said two people were shot?"

"Ed Stankowski and the guy who attacked them."

Her startled eyes ask the obvious follow-up question.

I guide her onto the chair beside mine before I answer, "Ed's in the hospital. It's bad. We're hoping for the best."

"Why?" Brittany sobs disconsolately while Pat deposits a steaming mug of coffee in front of her.

There's really no satisfactory answer to that, so I wrap an arm around my daughter's shoulders and hug her to me for a long minute.

"I'm so afraid for Papa," she murmurs into my shoulder before she sits back and gulps down a shot of coffee.

"We all are, honey."

Pat putters at the counter while we sit silently, then returns with a big bowl of communal fruit. We pick at it. A stack of buttered toast grows cold beside it. Pat finally breaks the oppressive silence in an effort to get our minds off Ed.

"Sandy Irving broke a new story in the *Sun-Times* this morning about the Milton crash."

"What's that about?" I ask.

"Windy City has filed a lawsuit against its insurance company for denying their claim to replace the aircraft. Ben Larose told me yesterday that the NTSB released the plane wreckage to the insurer a couple of weeks ago. He's figured all along that pilot error is the most likely outcome of the investigation, so the denied claim didn't surprise him. His guess is that the insurance company is probably suggesting that Windy City was negligent in putting Megan Walton at the controls of the aircraft."

My thoughts turn to how this might affect the R & B case and conclude that it should help us.

Pat glances at the clock and turns to Brittany. "Bobby should be here in fifteen minutes, kiddo. Are you ready to go?"

Brittany nods.

"Lunch made?" Pat asks her.

"I'll buy something at the caf."

I meet her gaze. "You don't have to go to school today."

"Seeing Bobby will help, Dad."

Ah, yes. The boyfriend. There used to be a time when Daddy was the Soother in Chief. I miss those days. The ringing doorbell interrupts my pity party.

Brittany scoots to the front door and returns a minute later with a somber Jake Plummer in tow. Jake's rumpled charcoal suit, red eyes, and the stubble on his face suggest he hasn't been to sleep. Papa, awakened by the doorbell, stumbles along in their wake and veers off to the bathroom.

Fearing bad news, I capture Jake's eye. "Ed?"

He wearily shakes his head. "He didn't make it."

We're still sitting in stunned silence when Papa wanders

back from the bathroom wearing worn pajama bottoms and a fraying sleeveless T-shirt. He's rubbing sleep out of his eyes when it registers that something is terribly wrong.

"Ed?" he asks with a frightened tremor in his voice.

I break the bad news. It sends a visible jolt of pain through my father, who sags onto a stool at the breakfast bar and buries his face in his hands while a wretched groan erupts from the depths of his being. An uncomfortable silence settles over us as Papa struggles to rein in his emotions. When he does, he looks up at Jake. "We go home now?"

The glower Jake turns on him doesn't contain a trace of empathy. "This is now a homicide investigation, Mr. Valenti. Your house is a crime scene until further notice."

"Until when, Jake?" I ask. "Later today? Tomorrow?"

He shoots a flinty gaze my way. "Until I decide it isn't."

The lawyer in me wants to argue, but Papa beats me to it. "After I shoot O'Reilly, you let Anthony go back next day."

Jake's angry eyes lock on Papa's for a long moment before he turns his attention to me. "As I was saying a moment ago, Ed's shooting is now an active homicide investigation. We'll require formal statements from you and Francesco today. Make your way to the station after lunch and ask for me or my partner—Francesco at one o'clock and you at two. Got it?"

"I go back to my home," Papa insists stubbornly. "They no chase me away!"

Jake steps up to the breakfast bar, braces his hands on the countertop, and leans across until his merciless face is no more than two feet from Papa's. His voice is pure ice when he growls, "Ed Stankowski was a good friend of mine, Mr. Valenti. I'm *not* going to conduct another homicide investigation at your damned house just because you want to keep thumping your chest and pronouncing yourself unafraid."

Papa stares back at him wordlessly.

"Got it?" Jake presses. "Get the hell out of that house.

Whoever is after you has now failed twice with a single shooter. If they come back, it will be with a small army. We're *not* looking out for you another goddamned day."

Papa is shocked by the outburst. So am I, although I quickly realize that I probably shouldn't be. Jake is right. Papa needs to be elsewhere. But where? I don't want to put Pat and Brittany at risk by stashing him at Pat's place. A hotel? That hardly seems secure. Where the hell in the limited options we have available will he be safe?

CHAPTER TWELVE

As if Ed Stankowski dying yesterday hadn't already cast enough of a pall over my morning, Billy Likens called with news that the FBI has invited him and Rick Hogan in for "a chat" today. Right. Like the FBI invites people in to shoot the breeze. Something potentially unwelcome is afoot. I'd gotten the contact information for the agent who phoned Billy, then gave the woman a call to let her know that either I'd be joining the party or there would be no party at all.

So, here we are late in the afternoon at the FBI Field Office on Roosevelt Road in downtown Chicago. Compared with the interview rooms at Cedar Heights PD, the room they've deposited us in isn't too bad—still Spartan, but a little larger and with somewhat newer institutional furniture. It also smells clean, a nice change from the lingering sweat and fear that have seeped into every corner of the Cedar Heights PD interrogation chamber. Yet it's still depressingly drab. I'm not pleased to be here and am in a pissy mood.

The vibe Agents Johnson and King are throwing off isn't improving my disposition. Johnson is big and burly, with a pug face that looks as if maybe he's gone a few rounds too many in the boxing ring with other big, burly guys who had better boxing skills. King is a lithe Black woman with close-cropped hair and a simmering anger that threatens to explode at any moment. They're seated across the table from my clients. I'm seated a little off to one side of Billy. One end of the table is pushed up tightly against the eggshell-white wall.

Ed Stankowski's face keeps popping into my head, which prompts an overwhelming sense of regret, responsibility, and fury. *Compartmentalize, Valenti.* Whatever is going down here requires my undivided attention. There'll be time to resume mourning Ed at the end of our FBI visit.

"So, the aircraft," Agent King says to Rick after the preliminaries are out of the way. "What can you tell us about it?"

Rick, who has arrived dressed in his work overalls, stares back at her in confusion.

The stone-faced agent studies Rick as if he's perhaps a little on the dull side. "Make? Model? What do you know?"

Why in hell is the agent testing Rick's knowledge of the aircraft? If King is trying to knock us off balance right from the get-go, she's off to a good start.

Rick sounds a little annoyed when he answers, "Cessna 210N. Built in 1979. Continental 10-520L fuel-injected engine that puts out three hundred horsepower or so. Purchased by Windy City Sky Tours for one hundred and forty-five thousand dollars."

The agent's eyes shift to Billy, who tossed on a pair of faded blue jeans and a red plaid shirt before hopping in the car with Rick. "That sound about right to you?"

"It does," Billy agrees.

King's steely eyes pass between Billy and Rick. "Were there any engine issues that you're aware of?"

"None," Rick replies in the same moment that Billy shakes his head and says, "Nope."

Her eyes narrow. "Structural deficiencies?"

Billy is shaking his head and preparing to reply when I

reach over and clamp my hand on his forearm. "Don't answer."

I lock eyes with Agent King. "This isn't an 'information session,' Agent King. You're conducting an interrogation without Mirandizing my clients."

She gazes back impassively and doesn't deny it.

"This is beneath the FBI," I say while glaring at the agents.

Instead of backing off, Johnson poses a question to Rick that comes right out of left field. "Tell us about the circumstances leading up to your liver transplant, Mr. Hogan."

This smells like a setup. Rick was away from work for a few months earlier in the year for the surgery. I mimic a zipping motion across my lips, hold my hands up in a timeout gesture, and turn to the agents. "I need a minute with my clients."

"Sure," Johnson says agreeably. "We'll step out."

"No," I reply sharply. "*We'll* step out, thank you. While we're gone, I suggest you revisit the FBI manual to refresh your understanding of Miranda rights."

Once we're out in the hallway, safely away from any recording devices that might be running inside the interview room, I look up and down the hallway of closed doors before I turn to Rick. "Is there something I should know? Drinking issues they're going to unearth?"

"Nothing that isn't bullshit," Billy retorts angrily.

Rick's flinty eyes narrow. "What the hell does that mean, Tony?"

"I'm just doing my job and trying to figure out what the hell is going on here, guys," I reply while holding my hands up in a peacemaking gesture. I tilt my head back toward the interview room. "Those two are gnawing at a bone someone has tossed their way. Worse, they're not affording you your basic legal rights. So far as I know, that's not the FBI's usual style. I'll deal with that later. For now, I need to know if there's something to what they're digging into. Is there?"

Rick and Billy exchange a glance that sets off alarm bells.

"Out with it," I say firmly. "There can be no surprises."

"Our insurance company heard allegations from someone suggesting that Rick's liver transplant was the result of alcoholism," Billy says. "Our policy just came up for renewal and they canceled it. They told us that Rick's supposed drinking is evidence of poor character and that we were negligent by hiding it from them."

"Anything to it?" I ask Rick.

He shakes his head. I hold his gaze for a long moment to satisfy myself that I'm getting the truth. He stares back resolutely. So what is this about? I roll several possibilities through my mind. If the insurance company is claiming that it canceled because of a fraudulent application that didn't disclose alcoholism, I can imagine the insurer trying to skirt liability claims arising from a legal claim of responsibility for the crash. These guys will be royally screwed if that scenario plays out. Where will Penelope and I get the money to go after the insurance company if it comes to that? It would cost many thousands of dollars to take on the insurer, and these two probably don't have more than a few thousand lying around between them—if that. The color drains from their faces when I explain the possibility of their being found liable without insurance coverage. I cross my arms over my chest. "True or not, why the hell didn't you tell me about this?"

"Because it's BS!" Billy shoots back.

"And who might have put that bug in the insurance company's ear?" I ask. "Did you ask yourselves that?"

Their blank expressions are answer enough.

"Figure it out," I suggest. Then I wait.

"The insurance company knew about the transplant," Rick finally says. "We made a claim on our key man disability policy for the time I was off. The same company holds all of our company policies."

"Yet they didn't question things when you made the claim?" I ask.

They shake their heads.

"Which suggests someone tipped them off to the alcoholism possibility fairly recently. Who might do that?"

They exchange a bewildered look.

Windy City, that's who. I drop my shoulders and sigh heavily. "Okay, let's set that aside and see what else our FBI friends have on their minds. Don't answer a single question unless I give you the okay. Understood?"

They nod before I lead them back to the interview room.

My eyes cover both agents when we resume our seats. "Miranda?" I ask pointedly.

After King belatedly reads Rick and Billy their rights, I place my hands on the table and eyeball the agents. "Nothing said to this point counts for shit. Whatever recording you're making of this better make note of that. Understood?"

Agent Johnson nods reluctantly.

"All right, then," I continue. "We're done with the transplant topic. What else is on your minds?"

Johnson turns his attention to Billy. "The subject aircraft was due for a hundred-hour inspection in August. Was that done and, if so, when?"

"Go ahead," I tell Billy.

"I don't have an exact date off the top of my head, but it was done around the middle of the month," he replies.

"You sure about that?" the agent asks with a hint of skepticism.

Billy looks confused by the line of questioning. "Yeah."

The agents remain silent, as if they're feeding Billy plenty of rope to tie around his neck if he's so inclined.

"We gave a copy of the inspection report to the NTSB," he tells them.

"Yeah, we've seen it," King says dismissively. "What

about a billing statement to Windy City Sky Tours for the work?"

If they've seen the paperwork, why are they questioning it?

Billy and Rick exchange a look. I recall Ben Larose mentioning that an NTSB briefing mentioned a wing strut showing signs of failure, but hadn't the spokesman also said they were unable to determine if the strut had failed before the plane hit the water? I probably should have explored that in more depth when Larose first told us about it. If I had, I might be better prepared for what I'm hearing now. I don't like where this seems to be leading, but I want to know exactly where the FBI is going with this line of questioning. I decide to let it play out and nod at Billy to answer.

"We sent one," he says.

"Have you got a copy of their payment?" King asks.

Billy frowns and looks to me. I nod again. There's a note of exasperation in his voice when he replies, "No, we always have to chase them for payment."

"We're lucky if they pay any sooner than sixty days," Rick adds. "As if we can afford to float credit to a bunch of millionaires on a regular basis."

My mind has shot ahead during this exchange. Is someone suggesting R & B is guilty of fraudulent record keeping? Is that why the FBI was called in? The questioning is suggestive of neglect or worse. My clients either said something to the NTSB investigators that raised suspicions, or someone else has fed them information that has. Billy and Rick are naive enough to blindly trust their business partners to do the right thing, because it wouldn't occur to them to do otherwise, but it's looking as if someone has buried a knife deeply into their backs. The most likely culprits are the principals of Windy City and/or AAA Avgas, undoubtedly counseled by lawyers every bit as ethically challenged as they are. Unfortunately for my clients, they're represented by a lawyer who doesn't know his ass from a hole in the ground when it comes to countering legal chicanery on this scale.

The FBI agents exchange a look that suggests they have whatever they were after. I decide it's time to terminate our little chat and get out of here before one of us says—or neglects to say—something that might come back to haunt us. The agents look smug as they see us out.

The ramifications of the past half hour unnerve me. The prospect of Rick and Billy being found liable for millions of dollars in a lawsuit was a daunting-enough prospect. The added concern of not having insurance coverage to cover the cost has come as an unwelcome shock. That said, at the end of the day, the case is all about money. The threat of Billy and Rick facing criminal charges in the deaths of five people is a problem of a whole other magnitude. Is that where the FBI is heading?

CHAPTER THIRTEEN

The morning after being grilled by the FBI, Billy joins Penelope and I in our conference room to be deposed by an attorney named Andrea Wisnowski. Wisnowski is representing Windy City Sky Tours in its lawsuit against R & B Ramp Services, an action that seeks to pin sole blame for the September eighth crash on R & B. AAA Avgas's silent, brooding lawyer, Luigi Mafioso or some such, is in the lobby with Wisnowski. He's joined her case as a second plaintiff against Billy and Rick. So, our codefendants in the initial court action, Windy City and AAA Avgas, are now suing us. Something smells foul in this tangle of lawsuits and lawyers, but I can't yet put my finger on it. Wisnowski and Luigi plan to depose Billy's partner, Rick Hogan, after lunch.

Billy leans close. "Is this going to be like yesterday?" he asks me nervously. He'd been thoroughly shaken when we left the FBI building yesterday.

"Nowhere near as intense," I assure him. "Some of the same topics may come up, though. Just tell the truth again."

Penelope nods. "This is exploratory, Billy. They'll be looking for anything they think they can exploit."

"What if I screw up and give them something?"

"Do you think you did anything wrong, Billy?" Penelope asks.

"No."

She smiles reassuringly. "So, don't worry. Just do as Tony said. Keep telling the truth and we'll be okay."

"If you say so," Billy says uncertainly.

Of course, the truth is highly malleable in legal matters—not that I'm going to burden our client with that inconvenient truth this morning. He may find out how that works in due course, but he doesn't need to hear it today.

"Showtime," I say with a wink at Billy, then pat his shoulder on my way to wave our guests in.

Wisnowski, a humorless, petite woman, has brought along a court reporter of her choosing. It's an unusual and insulting move, suggesting that our law firm can't be trusted to provide a competent or impartial reporter, but we didn't bother to contest the matter. We stood our ground by insisting on hosting the deposition, so I suppose turnabout is fair play in the never-ending one upmanship between lawyers.

We set up, Billy is sworn in, and the fun begins.

Wisnowski adjusts a pair of designer eyeglasses on her prominent nose, then locks her narrow brown eyes on Billy. Luigi lounges in a seat at the end of the table, continuing his brooding performance from the lobby. It occurs to me that he's here to act as a little muscle to back up Wisnowski, a play to intimidate us—a reminder that AAA Avgas is reputed to be a front company for the mob.

The initial questioning about Billy's training and experience underscores that he's a decidedly blue-collar guy. He tells Wisnowski that he went to work as an apprentice bus mechanic with PACE (the Chicago suburban transit agency) out of high school, then attended the City Colleges of Chicago at night to learn how to repair and maintain aircraft.

"Did you graduate?" Wisnowski asks.

"Of course," Billy replies indignantly. "I wouldn't be doing what we do if I hadn't."

She cocks an eyebrow. "That's right. We'd like to see your transcripts."

Billy looks annoyed and I'm about to object when Penelope coolly interjects, "We can do that."

"We'd like them in a timely manner," Wisnowski brusquely informs Penelope. "Close of business next Friday is acceptable. That holds true for all documentation I request today."

"Is that so?" Penelope responds tartly. "We'll see what we can do."

"And will inform you of our progress in due course," I add. Who does the woman think she is?

"I presume you will reciprocate with prompt delivery of any materials we request," Penelope says.

"We'll do what we can, Miss Brooks," Wisnowski retorts. "We have numerous cases on the go at any given time."

"With plenty of eager little lawyer beavers, interns, and other gophers to help," I respond.

"Do you have other active cases?" Wisnowski asks with a smirk.

"Actually, we do," I reply. "But, we promise that our wee little firm will try its best."

"And no more than you deliver in return," Penelope adds.

Wisnowski ignores us and turns back to Billy. "Tell us what you did after aircraft school."

"I served an apprenticeship and picked up several years of experience before me and Rick started R & B Ramp Services."

"And here we are," I say. "Let's talk about matters that are relevant to the case."

Wisnowski shoots me an annoyed glance, then focuses on Billy again. "Tell us about the morning of September eighth, Mr. Likens. You prepared the Windy City aircraft for flight?"

"No," Billy replies.

Wisnowski's eyes widen in surprise. "You have the maintenance contract for Windy City?"

I cut off Billy's reply. "I'd like a moment with our client."

"I see no need for—" Wisnowski begins.

"I wasn't asking for your permission," I interject as I get to my feet, gesture at Billy and Penelope to follow, and lead them to the door, where I pause to look back at Wisnowski. I point at Luigi. "Perhaps you can ask your co-counsel about the quality of the fuel they pumped that morning."

I head for my office with Billy and Penelope in tow. Penelope closes the door after we enter, then leans her back against it.

"What's up?" she asks.

"After the grilling the FBI gave Billy and Rick, I'm not comfortable having them answer questions about anything more than we discussed in that meeting."

Penelope cups her chin in her hand and taps the tip of her nose with her index finger. "Why?"

"Someone's angling to place the blame for the crash on them," I reply before turning to Billy. "Just to be sure that I understand things properly, the pilot is ultimately responsible for flight preparation?"

He nods. "That's right. It's up to the pilot to complete a final visual inspection, make sure the plane is properly prepped, and fueling is completed properly—all the checklist material. None of that is on us."

"You don't want Billy to answer any questions about what went on with the aircraft that morning?" Penelope asks me.

"That's right," I reply. "If we get into that topic, I think it opens the door to a claim that Billy and Rick had some degree of responsibility to correct any oversights they observed."

"Like Megan not bleeding the fuel tanks?" Billy asks.

"Exactly," I reply. "If the NTSB asks, then you answer, of course, but let's not hand any potential ammunition to these people."

"I think you're on point, partner," Penelope says.

I rest a hand on Billy's shoulder. "You're doing fine in there, pal." I look at Penelope. "If Wisnowski goes down the same path the FBI did, that means they share a source, or—even worse—that the FBI and these folks are talking."

She nods gravely. Then we go back to the conference room. To our dismay, Wisnowski promptly asks about the one-hundred-hour inspection *and* Rick's transplant.

CHAPTER FOURTEEN

The autumn wind is biting late the following Monday morning as we leave Ed Stankowski's funeral mass at St. Aloysius Church. It's an ill wind that portends even more heartache. Breaking somewhat with the Catholic Church custom of burial within two to three days of death, the burial was postponed an extra day to accommodate an autopsy and then again to avoid either a Halloween or Sunday service. In a further rupture from tradition, Ed's widow eschewed a full-blown police funeral. Max told me that she remains bitter about the force casting Ed aside, railing, "Now they want to pay tribute? Why? To assuage their guilt about discarding him, or just to pretend they care?"

I'm with Papa, Brittany, and Pat. Brittany's boyfriend, Bobby Harland, is also here at her request, and she's leaning on him for support. I feel a little stab of irrational jealously; that used to be my job. Bobby and I have barely spoken... this is hardly a social occasion, let alone the time or place to get to know someone. As I watch Brittany and him together, I wonder what I don't know about her life these days. A stupid thought, I know, but the topic of Brittany is a loaded one today. No sooner had I finished breakfast this morning than I was served with papers from my ex-wife. Michelle is taking me to court, seeking full custody of our daughter. This morning has been difficult enough for everyone as it is, so I haven't mentioned Michelle's bullshit to anyone. Breaking the news after dinner tonight or waiting until tomorrow will be plenty soon enough.

The church service brought back unwelcome memories of Mama's elaborate funeral mass last summer in this very church. Ed, a Polish Catholic, had gotten the full treatment as well, including a vigil and service at the funeral home last night. We'd stayed away. Given Jake Plummer's current hostility to Papa and reasoning that he might not be the only one of Ed's buddies feeling that way, it seemed the prudent thing to do. Pat went and spoke to Ed's widow to pass along our condolences and appreciation for all Ed had done and ultimately sacrificed to keep Papa safe. Mrs. Stankowski was very gracious, offered her thanks, and extended her apologies for any grief we've taken from Ed's buddies. She told Pat that she wants to speak with Papa and me today.

So, we're hanging around on the sidewalk twenty yards from the church entrance in case she still wants to. Mindful of Jake Plummer's wrath, we're doing our best to keep out of his way while remaining available.

Mrs. Stankowski emerges from the church into the sunlight with Max Maxwell and looks around. When Max points to us, she pats his arm and starts in our direction. Mrs. Stankowski is a fine-looking woman, a little taller than Ed's modest height. She's dressed in a calf-length black dress under an open slate-gray wool overcoat with a matching veiled pillbox hat that rests atop graying shoulder-length hair.

"Thanks for waiting," she says in a crisp New England accent as she walks up to us.

I introduce myself, Pat, Brittany, and Bobby, leaving Papa for last.

"Ed was very fond of you," she tells Papa after greeting

him with a brief lean-in hug. "He told me last week that he didn't mind getting shot for you, Francesco… not that he was happy about it," she adds with the trace of a smile. "He enjoyed spending time at your home and probably would have come even if he didn't have the security work for an excuse."

Papa is overcome with emotion to the point at which he can't speak. His eyes fill with gratitude and a few tears.

Mrs. Stankowski turns to me. "I'm sorry about Jake Plummer. Max told me he's been hard on you. Jake's real upset, but he shouldn't be taking it out on you people."

I wave the apology aside. "We understand. I know Jake's a good guy."

She nods. "I'm happy to hear that."

This leads to an awkward moment. All that needs to be said has been said.

Mrs. Stankowski wears a sad smile when she touches Papa's arm and says, "Okay, then. God bless you folks."

We intend to go straight home. Papa has been attracting hostile stares from a few of Ed's buddies. Like Plummer, they're pissed at Papa for being outside with Ed that night and incensed at him for putting people at risk by refusing to move out of the house. Thankfully, the fossils who had been at our home with Ed have largely been supportive. Most made a point of stopping by to have a word or two, which seems to have meant a lot to Papa. Having belatedly realized that Jake's anger is plenty justified, my father has been wallowing in guilt since the morning Ed died.

Max hurries across the lawn and intercepts us as we make our way toward my car for the drive back to Liberty Street. "You folks coming to the cemetery?"

I shake my head no.

"Yes, you are," he says. "Stick around afterward. Jake wants to talk to you."

I wonder why. Speaking of the unexplained, Jake's a pall-bearer. Max isn't. I ask why, adding, "You guys were pretty tight, right?"

"Sure, but Ed and Jake go *way* back. I was never CHPD, so I only got to know Ed over the last coupla years. Anyway, stick around after they bury Ed, okay?" After I nod, he gives Papa a reassuring pat on the shoulder.

We pile into the Porsche and head for the cemetery.

Mrs. Stankowski stands proud and erect at the windblown graveside twenty minutes later, setting aside the crushing grief she must feel while she honors the man she married but won't get to enjoy retirement with. They'd come heartbreak-ingly close. I remember Ed mentioning that she's retiring from her teaching position after the school year. "Then we'll be a couple of old tumbleweeds blowing around the country," he'd happily told me.

I wipe away a tear as the priest begins the brief Catholic graveside service and have shed many more by the time Ed's body is committed to the earth. Everything about this day transports me back to Mama's funeral, so I'm mourning for two.

As the mourners straggle away in groups big and small, we edge away from the grave site and linger under some trees. I admire the fall foliage as the leaves perish in vibrant shades of red, orange, and gold. My eyes are drawn down to the mound of dirt beside the pit that now holds Ed's coffin, then once again range over the breathtaking show being put on by the dying leaves. The tragedy of Ed's life being snuffed out is thrown into bitterly stark relief. He deserved to exit at the end of a long, well-earned retirement, just as the leaves around us are going out in style at the natural end of their life cycle.

Jake and Max find us five minutes later. Jake looks as if he hasn't been to bed since the night of Ed's murder.

He begins by touching Papa's arm. "Sorry if I was hard on you, Francesco. Ed's wife gave me hell when she heard about it."

Papa nods.

"Make no mistake, though, you need to get your ass out of that house."

Papa nods again.

Jake switches gears. "The bastard who shot Ed is still in grave condition, but we were able to speak with him briefly."

Max's expression leaves little doubt that he wishes the guy wasn't doing even that well. I'm totally in sync with his thinking. Mind you, we'd all like to hear everything the guy can tell us. Then he's free to croak.

"We've done some digging on the guy," Jake continues. "He's not from Italy, after all. He's from Toledo and is connected to the Luciano family's operations there, though he's pretty much retired now. It turns out that his family traces their roots back to Calabria and the *Cosche* assholes there."

Papa's eyes switch from sorrow to rage in an instant, but he holds his tongue.

Jake gives him a moment to say something, then moves on. "We were right. Some sorry old bastard from over there is behind this."

"That name—Luciano," I say to Jake. "Wasn't there a Mafia bigwig named Luciano?"

He nods. "Lucky Luciano."

That sounds pretty damned scary. "Are these his people?"

He shakes his head. "Nah, Lucky operated in New York City way back—eighty, maybe a hundred years ago. This bunch today just share a name with him. They might be twentieth cousins, fifty times removed or some bullshit. Definitely not as powerful or scary as old Lucky used to be."

"Good to know," I say in relief. "So, Jake, what do we know about this guy who's after Papa?"

His lips tighten into an angry straight line that suggests frustration. "The line between Italian law enforcement and *Ndrangheta* gets a little murky at times, so I had Interpol do a little poking around Calabria to smoke out this fucker." His eyes shoot to Brittany and Pat. "Sorry about the language, ladies."

Brittany, who has been plucking leaves off the oak tree we're standing beneath, is now absently picking one apart. She waves the apology aside and hisses, "They *are* fuckers."

I feel Bobby Harland's eyes on me when I don't react. I won't correct Brittany for saying what we're all thinking. When my eyes meet Bobby's, I offer him the slightest nod. He responds with the ghost of a smile. Damned if I don't like this kid.

"Anyway, until we work this out, Francesco needs to make himself scarce," Jake concludes.

"We're working on a plan for that," I inform him.

His eyes cut to mine. He spins his hand in a "come on" motion and waits for me to explain.

"We're thinking we might spirit Papa away to stay with his sister in Italy."

Jake's brow furrows as he absorbs the news. "Italy?"

"Who's gonna look for him there?" I reply. "Plus, he'll be with people we can trust."

"I guess there's some twisted logic in that," he allows after he thinks for a minute, but he's clearly skeptical.

Max jerks a thumb at Jake and addresses Papa. "I hear this guy told you that you're on your own now?"

Papa nods.

Max shoots Jake a pissed-off look. "Well, he don't speak for all of us, Francesco. You're moving your ass out of your house, right?"

Papa nods.

"Good move," Max says before he turns to me. "Tell me about this plan of yours."

I explain our nascent plan, such as it is.

"I kinda like that," Max says. "When do we leave?"

We?

CHAPTER FIFTEEN

P apa and I arrive at Cedar Heights Police Department headquarters shortly after eight o'clock three evenings later to execute our hastily arranged escape plan for Papa. In an echo of the September evening when my father shot a man a year ago, we're ensconced in the Spartan reception area while someone fetches Detective Plummer. Once again, he leads us to the last in a row of metal desks that have seen better days and seats us in a pair of folding chairs placed in front of it. It's déjà vu all over again, including the stench of charred coffee. At least Papa isn't behind bars tonight, although he's not exactly a free man—not with a death sentence hanging over his head yet again. This one seems more threatening. Instead of the prospect of due process in a courtroom, this threat could end at any moment with a bullet to the head.

Jake's eyes look like a shattered windshield with the cracks rimmed in red. I've never seen him wearier. Trying to track down his friend's killer of is taking one hell of a toll on him. "I'm still not sure what to make of this caper of yours, but I'm glad Max is going along for the ride," he says.

Caper? I think with an inner smile. Who uses that word nowadays?

Max arrives while I'm trying to come up with a suitable response. Like Papa and me, he's dressed all in black and has a matching ski cap in hand. He looks us over, nods in approval, shakes hands all around, and faces Papa when he's done. "Your timing sucks, Francesco."

My father's response is a blank look.

Max sits his ass on the corner of Jake's desk. "Oktoberfest is over, and it's too early for the Christmas markets. You wanna take me on any more European adventures, you gotta plan better is all I'm saying."

Jake shakes his head with a bemused expression, then slaps a hand on his desk. "I'm coming with you as far as Bolingbrook."

Bolingbrook?

"No need," Max counters.

"Shut up, Max," Jake says. "I arranged the rides and I'm tagging along."

I can see that Max is pleased to have him along when he nods at Jake. So am I, even if his presence underscores the danger threatening Papa. I'm grateful that Jake stepped up to manage logistics after we told what we had in mind. Unsurprisingly, he had plenty of good ideas, not all of which he's shared with me.

Jake's desk phone rings before I can ask why we're going to Bolingbrook. He listens briefly and then says, "Right. We'll be right down." He hangs up, pushes back from his desk, and gets to his feet. "Suit up, folks."

Max pulls his ski cap on low over his forehead, so Papa and I do likewise. Then we troop out of the squad room after Jake, who leads us down a back stairwell.

"The fewer people who see us leave, the better," he explains while he peers through a peephole in a door that must lead into the rear parking lot. Apparently satisfied with what he sees, he pushes the door open and motions us out.

Max leads and ducks into a Cedar Heights PD black-and-white cruiser. Papa and I pile in behind him, then Jake hops into the front passenger seat, slaps a hand on the dashboard, and says, "Let's go."

As we zip out of the parking lot, Jake tells the driver that we're going to a bookstore and gives him the address on Berwyn. He told us upstairs that we'll be switching vehicles. News of a bookstore stop comes as a surprise.

"We gonna score some girly magazines?" Max asks.

Jake snorts. "It's a bookstore, Max, not the kinda place that sells *your* style of reading material."

Max shrugs. "Whatever."

"Do you know Zack Menzies?" Jake asks him.

"Sure," Max replies, then does a double take. "Oh! This is *his* bookstore?"

"Yup."

"Always wanted to visit."

"You won't be browsing the shelves tonight," Jake says. "We'll be going in the front door, hustling through the mysteries and police procedurals, then straight past the thriller section and out the back door."

Max chuckles. "What? No romance section? No classic literature? *No sports?*"

"Maybe a sports book or two," Jake allows. Then he turns to Papa and me. "Zack's another old cop. Bought himself a little bookshop when they pensioned him off."

The cruiser zooms along the damp streets without regard to posted speed limits, slicing through a steady drizzle and the haze wafting off the pavement as it evaporates. How is it that nights like this seem to swallow all light? It's like driving without headlights.

"And here we are," Jake says ten minutes later when the cruiser coasts to a stop under a streetlight. Zack's Used Books is a little storefront establishment in a well-weathered block of them. A Closed sign hangs in the door window.

"There's an unmarked panel van waiting in the alley out back," Jake tells us before he opens the door. "Heads down and follow me. Don't stop, don't look around. Getting in and out of here is our riskiest move." He hops out, takes a quick look up and down the street, then yanks the cruiser's back door open. "Let's go!"

I swallow and follow him across the sidewalk. A silent man in a fedora and raincoat stands beside the front door and swings it open for us. This is even more noir than the Brooks and Valenti temporary offices.

"Thanks, Zack," Jake says without slowing. He leads us through the narrow aisles of the darkened store, which is illuminated by a handful of recessed lights with dimmers dialed almost all the way off. Either that, or Menzies found a bunch of two-watt light bulbs somewhere. The only sound breaking the ghostly silence is the squelching of our rubber soles on the polished hardwood floor. Tall shelves crammed with dusty-smelling books tower above us on either side, teetering ever so slightly as we hurry past them. The prospect of being buried beneath hundreds of books puts an extra pop in my step. I'm right on Jake's tail when he steps into an alcove that houses another exterior door.

"Move your ass, Francesco," Max grumbles from behind us.

Jake has a half smile on his face when his eyes meet mine. "Right into the van out there. Keep your head down. No stopping to gawk." Then he peers through another peephole, shoves the crash bar to open the door, and waves us out.

With his warning that this is the riskiest part of the trip fresh in my mind, I hustle across the four-foot gap between the building and the waiting vehicle. When I plant my feet to stop outside the van's open side door, my shoes slide on the slick pavement. "Shit!" I cry out as I crack my shin on the rocker panel and crash facedown on the van's grimy, smelly floor.

Max rolls me deeper inside as he enters behind me. "Smooth move," he says with a smirk.

I'm on my back with both hands clutching my skinned shin when the door slams shut and the driver stabs the gas, throwing me backward to smack my head on the steel of the wheel well. Great. The wound on my forehead from Pat's bathroom has almost healed; let's start a new one on the back of my head.

Max shakes his head as he watches, then turns to Jake. "Maybe we should drop Tony off at Loyola Emergency along the way so he'll be in good hands when he really hurts himself."

"Up yours, Max," I mutter through clenched teeth, even though my leg feels as if it could use the ministrations of Loyola's Level One Trauma Center staff right about now.

My cursing prompts a deeper laugh from Max. "We'll turn you into a potty-mouthed old bastard like the rest of us yet!"

I work myself into a sitting position with my back braced against the van's side panel and look around in the dim light. If the outside of this thing is in as poor shape as the grubby interior, our wheels won't attract any attention. The roaring road noise bleeding through the bare steel floor and shell of the van make me long for the cathedrallike hush inside my Porsche.

"Did we get away clean?" I ask Jake.

"Yeah. I had uniforms stationed at both ends of the alley to make sure no one saw us pile in here. We should be good."

I roll my pant leg up and frown at the angry two-inch gash on my shin. Max smirks before he looks away. I follow his gaze to Papa, whose eyes are glittering with excitement. At least one of us seems to be enjoying our little caper.

"Is fun!" Papa exclaims when he catches me looking.

"First time I've heard a target talking about how much fun

it is to be out dodging bullets," Max mutters with a dark chuckle.

Papa and Max will be on a flight to Europe by morning, but I'm not yet privy to the logistical details of their departure. In fact, I don't even know what airport they'll be leaving from. This whole production is an eye-opening glimpse into a darker cloak-and-dagger world than I've never experienced. When I travel, I simply catch a cab or drive myself to the airport.

"What next?" I ask Jake a few minutes later, after the van accelerates up a ramp and settles into a steady pace. We're obviously on a highway, most likely Interstate 290 or I-55.

"We're on our way to the airport. If anyone's tracking Francesco, it's most likely a Mickey Mouse operation using cars and shoe leather. They won't be prepared to track an aircraft."

"Are they leaving from O'Hare or Midway?" I ask, referring to Chicago's two major airports.

"Neither. They're flying out of Clow."

So, now I know why we're going to Bolingbrook.

Jake turns to Max. "I'm looking forward to seeing this place."

"Nothing to write home about," Max says with a chuckle. "Damnedest little 'international' airport I've ever seen."

I've heard about the place from Billy Likens and am intrigued. Clow International Airport is a general aviation facility in the far-southwest suburb of Bolingbrook, around thirty miles away from downtown Chicago. The man who founded it as a grass strip in the 1950s, Oliver Boyd Clow, managed to bring a little fun to the staid world of airport nomenclature by attaching *International* to the name of the field. I smile as I recall Billy telling me that Clow had said his airfield was named on a lark that bordered on the ridiculous. He had that right. I wonder how many—if any—of the little aircraft flying in and out of Clow have the range to reach the

Canadian border in a single hop, let alone wing their way across oceans to Europe and beyond.

"We'll be monitoring the comings and goings at the airport to make sure nobody gets a good look at what's going on," Jake says as he turns back to me. "From Clow, our boys are off to Minneapolis."

"We'll be flying KLM from there to Amsterdam," Max says.

"Minneapolis?" I ask.

Jake nods. "Yup. The Luciano clan might have eyes at the Chicago airports. Their reach doesn't extend to Minnesota."

Makes sense, but I was expecting to be home within the next hour or so after seeing Papa and Max off. "Guess I won't be spending the evening at home, after all," I grumble. "Hell, I'll be lucky to be back by morning."

Jake's eyes cut to me. "You're going to Minneapolis? That isn't in the plan."

"I'm going to see Papa off," I announce firmly. Jake considers arguing for a long moment, then lets it go.

"The more the merrier," Max quips before he outlines their travel plans beyond Amsterdam. "We'll be traveling south by train through Germany with stops in Hannover and Munich on the way to Innsbruck, Austria. Francesco's nephew will pick us up there, then it's an eight-hour drive to Francesco's sister's place."

"They can travel in the EU without passports after they clear customs in Amsterdam, so tracking them after that won't be easy," Jake explains.

Papa's sister has been safely tucked away in the town of Penne in Italy's Abruzzo province since she fled Orsomarso some fifty years ago. We're hopeful Papa can also fly under the radar there.

Buried in the back of the van as we've bounced and jostled our way along since leaving the expressway, we haven't seen much other than streetlights and the occasional building flash past. The first visual clue to our arrival at Clow comes when we pass through a pair of large sliding doors and find ourselves inside an aircraft hangar. Who knew there were hangars at Clow?

We tumble out of the van and find ourselves standing beside a gleaming white, high-winged airplane. It's bigger than I imagined Jake's "puddle jumper" would be, although it's small by airline standards. The hangar isn't expansive, either—maybe twenty feet wide by thirty feet long, and twenty or so feet tall. Only about one in three of the overhead lights is switched on. The place smells of airport—whiffs of grease and oil overlaid with the sharp stench of aviation gasoline. My eyes settle on the aircraft. It looks familiar. The first inkling of why is a stylized red-and-blue Cessna decal that is mounted on the lower half of the fuselage just forward of the pilot's door. Beside that sits an emblem that reminds me of a Roman soldier's helmet.

"What?" Max asks when he sees me staring.

It can't be. I shake my head. "Nothing. Where are the suitcases?"

"Already on board," Jake replies. "We shipped them ahead. Wouldn't do to have Francesco and Max seen hauling luggage around, would it?"

"Good point," I reply. He seems to have thought of everything. Maybe he even knows what kind of aircraft this is. I point and warily ask, "Is this a Cessna 210?"

"Pretty sure it is."

A kid comes around the front of the aircraft, smiles at us, and gives Jake a quick half hug. There's a slight family resemblance there, something in the chin and cheekbones. But whereas Jake is a little on the short side and balding, the newcomer is tall and gangly with mussed black hair covering his ears. He's wearing blue jeans, a button-down, western-style, long-sleeve shirt and a pair of beaten-up Nike sneakers that may have been white at some point in the distant past.

Think castles, knights on white chargers, lots of kings and queens in charge of the Western world—that far back.

"Is this thing a Cessna 210?" Jake asks the youngster.

"Yup. A Centurion."

Holy shit. Given what happened to the only other Cessna 210 I know anything about, I'm not sure how I feel about flying in this thing. "Does it fly?" I ask in a lame attempt at humor.

The kid gives me an odd look before he leads us around the airplane and opens the door leading into the rear passenger compartment. I follow Papa and Max inside and glance up to greet our pilot, but the left front seat is empty. I glance back outside and see Jake talking with the kid.

He slaps the youngster on the shoulder. "Thanks, Tony. I owe you one."

"I'd say you owe me several!" the kid counters with a grin.

"Jake's nephew, Tony," Max explains when he sees me watching. "We'll call him Tony Junior for tonight."

Jake pokes his head inside while we strap in, Papa and me in the rearmost seat looking forward and Max in a seat that backs onto the pilot's seat and faces us. Our knees are maybe three or four feet apart.

"Have a good trip, guys," Jake says as he shakes hands all around. "Good luck," he adds pointedly to Papa and Max before he turns and walks away.

Tony Junior speaks briefly with another man who is wearing the type of coveralls Billy Likens and Rick Hogan wear on the job. Junior then climbs into the pilot's seat and starts flicking a bewildering array of knobs and switches and dials while the mechanic waits.

I take advantage of the opportunity to examine my surroundings. There are windows on either side of us with a pretty good view outside, the roof is close overhead, and the black floor is made from the same type of material I'm accustomed to seeing under my feet in jetways when I board or exit real airplanes. The seats are leather, or a pretty decent imitation thereof. I'm reminded of piling into the cavernous back of our old Pontiac station wagon as kids when we went on road trips... and I'm going to fly how many feet high in this thing?

My eyes snap forward when the kid pulls his seat belt and shoulder strap snug, fires up the engine, and glances over his shoulder. "Everyone strapped in back there?"

"You're our pilot?" I blurt as the engine roars to life.

"He's older than he looks," Max assures me while Tony Junior nods and smiles at me.

Older than he looks, huh? So, he's what? Sixteen? Megan Walton could have been his mother!

After the engine settles into a steady purr, I try to console myself with the reassuring knowledge that he at least knows where the on switch is.

Junior shoots a cheerful thumbs-up to the ramp hand outside, who promptly disappears beneath the aircraft and emerges dragging the black-and-yellow rubber thingies that kept the plane from rolling away. He walks across the floor to push the hangar doors aside. Then, before I have a chance to leap out of the aircraft, we're on our way out into the night.

"Next stop, Minneapolis-Saint Paul!" Junior announces happily as we taxi away from safety. "I'd like to thank you for flying with us this evening on Plummer's Put-Put Airlines."

Papa pays no attention to our pilot's patter, Max dutifully chuckles, and I look around for the nearest barf bag. Then we're clawing our way into the black sky at fifteen or twenty miles per hour and bouncing along as if we're hitting atmospheric potholes every five or six feet. Or so it seems... I hope to hell we're going faster than that.

"Looks like we got away cleanly," Max says with satisfaction. "Nobody got shot, anyway."

"Yeah, that's a relief," I reply dryly. I'm surrounded on a

death flight by comedians. Not exactly how I imagined going out.

Just under five white-knuckle hours later, we're back on blessed terra firma, rolling past blue taxiway lights until we reach the general aviation apron. An airport pickup truck awaits us. I clamber out of the plane ahead of Max and Papa and resist the urge to kiss the ground. Then I help schlep their bags to the back of the pickup. The smell of approaching snow is in the air as a fuel truck pulls up alongside the Cessna. I hope to hell we're on our way before the white shit arrives.

After a quick hug and goodbye, Papa climbs into the front cab of the pickup with Max. Tony Junior supervises the refueling while I watch the rear lights of the vehicle carrying Papa and Max disappear toward the main terminal building in the distance. I say a silent prayer for their safekeeping. Then I add a quick one for my own safety. When I turn back to our aircraft, I find young Tony grinning at me.

"Ready to do it again?" he asks. The little shit knows exactly what I'm thinking.

I nod, wondering if Max and Papa are in any greater jeopardy than I am. At least they'll be flying in a great big airplane with a grown-up at the controls.

CHAPTER SIXTEEN

The shakes from last night's aerial adventure to Minneapolis are subsiding by the time Penelope and I depart for our weekly partner luncheon at The Sandwich Emporium. We're still shoehorned into our strip-mall offices while we await completion of the future law offices of Brooks and Valenti on this, day ninety-three of what our general contractor had confidently assured us would be a ninety-day project. As I recall, he'd scoffed at the possibility that they'd take the whole ninety days to get the work done. I stopped by our future digs on the way in this morning. To my admittedly unpracticed eye, things seem to be maybe fifty percent along.

Maiko Campbell looks up when the tinkle of the door chime announces our arrival. She breaks into one of those smiles that casts light into black holes. "Tony-*san*! Penelope!"

"That's us," Penelope replies with an answering smile. The combined wattage of these two smiling is probably as dangerous as looking directly at a solar eclipse.

My eyes immediately travel to the chalkboard and today's eagerly anticipated daily special creation, then drop back to Maiko, over to Brian Campbell, and back to the chalkboard. "Corned beef on rye?"

"Complain to the wholesalers!" Maiko gripes. "No good sales this morning, Tony-*san*. Even the corned beef wasn't such a good deal."

"This is disappointing," I mutter dramatically. "Guess I'll have the corned beef on rye. Mind you," I add with a sideways glance at Penelope, "we could have gotten that at any old deli counter for half the price."

Penelope smiles at Maiko. "I happen to *like* corned beef on rye. I'll take one…. without the side of whining."

Maiko winks at her. "Coming right up. Go, sit down. Your usual table is ready."

We make our way to the back and settle in at our little table, set for two today instead of the trio of place settings Maiko had squeezed in when Pat O'Toole and Ben Larose joined me a couple of weeks ago. I make a show of breathing in the sweet aroma of Brian's baking bread and licking my lips. "I'm starving."

"What happened to all the complaining about corned beef?" Penelope asks.

I shrug.

She eyes me for a long moment. "You look tired, partner. Late night?"

"Something like that," I reply. Jake ordered us not to mention last night's escapade to anyone, even wives and partners—at least not until Papa and Max arrive safely.

Penelope gives me an indulgent look and shakes her head. "You read my notes?"

The FBI's interrogation of our R & B Ramp Services clients had shaken us badly, prompting Penelope to dig more deeply into the peculiarities of aviation lawsuits. The result is a detailed briefing paper to guide our planning. We also sent off an indignant pro forma complaint to the FBI about their agents attempting to interrogate our clients without first reading them their Miranda rights. I imagine it's now under careful review by the shredding department.

I nod in reply to Penelope's briefing-notes question while tearing the paper away from the tip of the straw sitting at my place setting.

"Don't!" Penelope warns as I lift the open end of the straw to my lips and blow, shooting the tube of paper across the table. "You're such a child!" she exclaims with a laugh after she ducks out of the way.

I beam back at her.

She straightens up and dons her serious lawyer face. "Let's get back to work."

"Do we have to?"

"Yes!" she retorts with mock exasperation. At least I think it's mock. "I talked to Ben Larose yesterday. I think you're right about tagging him as an expert witness."

"Yeah?"

She nods. "For a couple of reasons."

"Such as?"

"He knows his stuff. I also trust that he's on the side of the angels."

I bounce my eyebrows. "That's us?"

She does the adorable little nose twitch that signals when she's amused. "Of course. Well, me, anyway."

I smile back. How is it that this woman doesn't have a significant other? I've never seen her with anyone other than her roommate, Becky Seguin. Oh well. None of my business. Back to the matter at hand. "What did Larose have to say?"

"Based on what I told him about the FBI interview, he agrees that the FBI—and possibly the NTSB—must have concerns about the hundred-hour inspection that should have been completed in August."

"That *was* completed in August," I counter. "Billy showed us the paperwork and invoice."

She thoughtfully taps a finger on her nose with her chin in her hand. "I know, and yet they're zeroing in on that. There's something there."

Damn. She has to be right. Why else would the FBI be so interested in the topic? "What does it tell us that Wisnowski dug into the same topic?"

"And Rick's transplant," Penelope grumbles. "You were right. It suggests that there's some level of coordination happening between her and the FBI. That's concerning."

"It scares the hell out of me," I say. "Why is the FBI dancing to their tune? I've never thought of them as party to garden-variety corruption like this."

"No, and I wouldn't be too quick to come to that conclusion," Penelope says. "The FBI and Wisnowski may be dancing to a tune being played by a third party."

"Windy City?"

"That's one possibility," she replies. "So is Butterworth Cole."

"Speaking of which, have you spoken with Randall Lennox's pal there?"

She shakes her head, "Still exchanging voicemails."

"Let's not forget the Luciano family," I suggest.

"Time will tell, of course."

"It always does, doesn't it?"

Penelope smiles ruefully. "Hopefully, we'll figure things out before we get steamrolled."

"You're supposed to be showing me the bright side of things, you know," I remind her.

"It's not all doom and gloom, partner."

Maiko bustles over while I sigh in relief. "Corned beef on rye for Miss Brooks," she announces with a flourish as she places a paper plate in front of Penelope. Then she smiles at me and deposits a second plate under my nose. "And for Tony-*san*, who does not like a simple sandwich, we have a true daily special! Corned beef on raisin!"

I burst into laughter when I look down to see a slab of corned beef squeezed between two slices of raisin toast.

"You deserve that, Tony," Penelope laughs. "Well done, Maiko!"

I smile up at Maiko. "I'll bet it tastes good!"

She wrinkles her nose. "If nothing else, perhaps you'll learn not to complain about the food here."

"Go ahead," Penelope urges with a pointed look at my sandwich while Maiko scoots away to collect our beverages.

However this tastes, I will rave about it, I decide as I lift the thing to my mouth and take a healthy bite. I smile around it as I chew. Maiko returns and cocks an eyebrow at me while she slides a pair of iced teas in front of us—we have a strict no-alcohol rule during Brooks and Valenti professional meetings. "This *will* be a thing," I announce after swallowing and wiping my chin with a paper napkin. It actually isn't bad. It isn't great, either, although wild horses couldn't drag that admission out of me in my current company.

Maiko tilts her head and nods, as if she's come to a decision. "We'll call it the Valenti Vomit."

Penelope's face twists into a revolted grimace. "Pee-yew!"

Maiko smiles and walks away.

"Getting back to not-so-gross topics, the FBI zeroed right in on the invoice for that inspection," Penelope muses between bites.

"Yeah," I mutter around a mouthful of Valenti Vomit. "Let's explore that."

She nods, swallows, and sets her sandwich down on her plate before touching a corner of napkin to her lips. She's somehow managing to eat her sandwich without smearing grease all over her face. I, on the other hand, am doing a fair imitation of a one-year-old face-painting himself with a slice of birthday cake. *How does she do it?* I wonder with a guilty look at the pile of grease-soaked napkins that is growing alongside my plate.

"Did you ask Larose what's included in the hundred-hour inspection?" I ask.

"I did. It's pretty thorough. A lot of mechanical checks, testing and examining the electrical systems, plus—and I found this interesting—they inspect the airframe for structural integrity. Rust, cracks, and the like."

"Hmmm," I murmur while I swallow and wipe my chin. "But didn't the NTSB seem to be focused on engine failure?"

"I went back and reread the transcripts of all of the NTSB public statements so far, then went through them over the phone with Ben. There *is* a single mention of a wing-strut failure that they left open."

"Left open?"

"For further review," she replies before taking a sip of her iced tea. "They didn't make a determination of whether or not the strut failed before or after impact."

"Oh. That sounds ominous."

"Not necessarily. Ben says it's entirely possible that the strut may have been subjected to stress in flight that exceeded its ultimate tensile strength."

"In English," I request before popping the last bite of corned beef and raisin toast into my mouth.

"In layman's terms, the plane wasn't designed to dive at a hundred fifty-plus miles per hour while the pilot fought the controls, causing the plane to twist and turn as it fell. Structural failure is a definite risk under those stresses. Ben can't imagine that the NTSB will be able to determine what actually happened, and certainly won't be in any position to make a definitive determination that the accident was the result of in-flight structural failure."

"Thereby clearing Billy and Rick of responsibility for the crash," I conclude happily.

"That might be a little too definitive," she warns. "In Ben's words, a plane failing under those circumstances is on no one unless the pilot deliberately flew the aircraft beyond its design tolerances."

"Stunt flying and such?" I ask.

"Exactly."

"So, what's the FBI up to?"

"Good question," she replies with her eyebrows knitted together. "Let's not forget the mention of Rick's liver."

"Yeah," I mutter while pushing my empty plate aside. "That was a bit of a surprise. That said, you know how anal cops can be when it comes to drugs and booze—unless they're the ones partaking."

"True, but it still concerns me."

"I can't see how that fits into the crash narrative. Can you?"

Penelope turns her palms up. "All I know is that there's something in that paperwork that we need to be aware of."

I hold up a finger, dig my cell phone out of my pocket, and place a call to Billy.

After we exchange greetings, he informs me, "I planned to call you in an hour or two when things quiet down a little." Then he floors me with a bombshell we definitely weren't expecting at this point. "Some guy came by after lunch and served us with a lawsuit from Windy City."

"Jesus, Billy! You should have called right away!"

Penelope's eyes grow large at my outburst.

"Yeah, well, we're trying to keep our heads above water here," he snaps back.

The fact that we're pissed with one another doesn't sit well with me. Billy and I have never been at odds before. Maybe we shouldn't have taken this damned case.

"Penelope's here," I tell him. "I'm putting the call on speaker."

"Hi, Billy," she says pleasantly—ever the diplomat to soften the harsher edges of her partner.

"Hey, Penelope," he says. "Sounds like I messed up, huh?"

Her eyes shoot daggers at me. "No worries, Billy. Tony's one of those Mediterranean hotheads."

Billy laughs softly.

"What's going on?" Penelope asks. She drops her head back, looks up at the ceiling, and blows out a long breath after he tells her. "Did you read it?"

"Real quick. We're busy as hell here this afternoon."

"And?" I prompt.

"Me and Rick tried to sort through all the legal mumbo jumbo. Best we can figure is that they're claiming we didn't complete the hundred-hour inspection in August."

"But you told us you did," I counter.

"Because we did," Billy shoots back.

"Tony's just thinking out loud," Penelope says with a poisonous glance my way. "He *isn't* questioning what you told us. We're all a little upset about this."

She's right, of course. Before I can put my foot in my mouth again, Penelope asks Billy to fax a copy of the paperwork to her. She and Billy agree that he and Rick will come to our office for a meeting on Monday.

At the end of the workday, I make a one-hour stop at home to turn on some lights, start a load of laundry, and walk around a lot to make the place look occupied. The plan is to keep Papa's escape a secret for as long as possible. We hope to buy enough time for he and Max to reach their destination before anyone starts looking for them. After tossing the wet towels into the dryer so it will vent plenty of steam outside, I set several timers to turn lights on and off at preset intervals. The whole charade is designed to trick anyone who might be watching into thinking Papa's in the house. He is, to the best of my knowledge, currently on a train with Max somewhere in Germany or in my cousin's car in Austria or Italy—hopefully without any of the *Ndrangheta* or *Cosche* assholes any the wiser. I'll feel better when Max lets us know they've arrived safely at Papa's sister's house. When I finish, I set out for Pat's house.

"Who pissed in your Corn Flakes?" she asks with a smile

after I've grumped my way through our initial greetings and the obligatory "How was your day?" query.

The old high school line prompts a grudging grin of my own. "Who thought up that dumbass expression?"

"The world floats on a sea of stupid sayings," she replies with a nonchalant shrug. She's got a point.

"Where's Britts?" I ask.

"Upstairs in the midst of the shower-and-hair ritual."

I know Brittany has plans tonight and so won't be joining us for dinner, but she's been a little cagey about what those plans are. I mention this to Pat and ask, "What's the mystery?"

"No mystery. Just boyfriend stuff."

"Argh."

Pat greets my little outburst with a look of exasperation. "She'll tell you all about this stuff as soon as you stop saying dumb crap like that, Valenti."

After we perch ourselves on a pair of barstools at the breakfast counter, I explain how Windy City Sky Tours shit in my Corn Flakes today by filing a lawsuit against Billy and Rick. Her sunny disposition evaporates before I conclude, "The only upside is that it took my mind off Michelle's latest stunt."

Mention of my ex-wife never sits well with Pat. Is that simply because Michelle is a bitch, or is there something more lurking beneath the surface of my complicated relationship with Pat? Having now admitted to a mutual high school attraction that neither of us had acted on, we've danced a little do-si-do square dance around each other for the past several months. It's something we're going to have to come to terms with sometime soon. But not today.

"What's Michelle up to now?" she asks.

"I was served with a court order stating that, as Brittany's guardian, I'm to ensure that she doesn't come within a thousand yards of Forty-Seven Liberty Street."

Pat tilts her head to one side and frowns. "Lots of legal papers flying around today, huh? Actually, I can't blame her for doing that. It's a pretty good idea."

"I suppose. Of course, we're way ahead of her. Your place is many thousands of yards from Liberty Street."

Pat smiles. "True."

"How's it going with her here?"

"Pretty good. We talked before school this morning about the prospect of her going to live with her mother again. I guess Michelle pitched the idea over the phone last weekend."

My entire being sags: face, slumping shoulders, plummeting spirits. Even my eyes follow until I'm staring down into my lap.

Pat reaches over to touch my arm. "You'll be happy to hear that Brittany says she isn't interested."

I look up. "Really?"

"Really."

"Did she say why?"

Pat crosses her legs and pulls her coffee mug closer, tapping her fingernails on the rim while she considers her answer.

"Well?" I ask impatiently. "It's a simple enough question."

"If you'll shut up long enough to let me talk, I'll tell you."

I drag my thumb and index finger across my lips in a zipping motion.

Her eye dances. "How frigging cool would it be to actually sew a zipper on that yap of yours?"

I give her the mock stink eye.

"It's mostly girlfriend talk, but I can tell you a little," she says. "Brittany doesn't like her mother's boyfriend and wasn't thrilled to be left alone in Brussels as much as she was last year. She *did* like the other kids and getting around Europe a bit." She smiles. "Bobby the boyfriend also factors into wanting to stay in Cedar Heights."

I restrain myself from uttering another "argh" or anything else similarly "stupid."

Pat grins in approval of my impressive show of restraint. "There may be hope for you yet, Valenti."

"Thanks."

She pauses and rests her chin on the backs of her knuckles in a show of deep thought, then smiles brightly. "Oh, and Brittany *may* have mentioned something along the lines of enjoying life in Cedar Heights with her boorish old man."

"You didn't have to tell him *that!*" Brittany protests as she sweeps into the kitchen, plants a kiss on each of our cheeks, then settles a hip on the side of the counter while she eyes Pat suspiciously. "What else have you told him?"

"Nothing much," Pat replies with a laugh. "When's Bobby coming?"

Brittany's face lights up as her eyes cut to the clock on the microwave. "Any time now."

I give her a stern look and say, "This boyfriend of yours better be a good kid."

Pat chucks me on the arm. "This is *exactly* the kind of dumb shit you say that keeps Brittany from trying to talk to you as if you're an adult."

A smile plays on my daughter's lips as she points at Pat. "What she said."

Well, color me infantile. I'm spared further humiliation when the doorbell rings.

"Bring him in here," Pat orders Brittany, who looks skeptical when she turns her eyes to me.

"To borrow Pat's words, can we please do this without you saying any dumb shit, Dad?"

"I'm actually going to meet the beefcake?" dies on my lips. I nod instead. I do so solemnly. I do so under pain of death if I'm properly interpreting Pat's warning stare.

While I had a glimpse of him and we exchanged a few words at Ed's funeral, this is my first up-close-and-personal encounter with Brittany's boyfriend. Bobby Harland is a bitter disappointment. He's close to six feet tall. Well put together. Open smile. Good-looking kid. Why couldn't Brittany pick a spindly, acne-faced boy with zero sex appeal but an appealing personality? Yeah, I know that's insensitive. A couple of minutes of small talk reveals that he has the personality thing going for him, too. Uh-oh. While he tells me that he's impressed with the volleyball highlights from my college glory days that my daughter has shown him on YouTube— *I'm on YouTube?*—Pat smirks.

Brittany draws all eyes when she hefts a solid wooden rolling pin and fixes her sights on Bobby. "Pat told me an interesting story about this."

"Yeah?" he asks with a smile.

She starts slapping the rolling pin into her palm with a steady rhythm. "Tell him, Pat."

Pat chuckles. "That rolling pin belonged to my grandmother. She always claimed it was how she kept Grandpa in line."

"My grandmother had one just like it," Brittany tells Bobby. "Right, Dad?"

I like how she's thinking. "That's right."

Brittany's eyes settle on Bobby while she asks me, "And it's mine now?"

"Why, yes. Yes, it is."

"Ah, young love," Pat says with a sigh when the door closes after Brittany and Bobby leave.

"I'll bring the rolling pin by tomorrow," I tell her with a grin. The goofy talk has been a welcome bit of levity at the end of a trying week. Of course, the glow of young love hangs a light on the fact that any kind of romantic relationship between Pat and me is going exactly nowhere. Yet the world continues to turn.

Over the next two days, Penelope and Ben Larose compare notes and we all kick around ideas about what the

Windy City lawsuit against Billy and Rick really portends. Having decided that the truth is on our side, we end up feeling fairly optimistic. Jake calls on Saturday with the happy news that Max and Papa have safely arrived at their destination in Italy. Dinner at Pat's house with Brittany and Bobby that night goes well; no rolling pins needed, although I did remember to take ours and made sure Bobby got a good look at it.

The renewed glow of puppy love and happy thoughts lasts all of thirty minutes after dinner. That's when I get home.

CHAPTER SEVENTEEN

Did I close the blinds? I wonder after hopping out of the Porsche in the driveway. I honestly can't remember, so I shrug the concern aside and let my mind drift back to dinner at Pat's. As I unlock the front door while recalling the adoring —hungry?—looks passing between Brittany and Bobby across the dinner table, I make a mental note to develop an intimidating paternal warning scowl before my next Bobby encounter. Then I step inside with a smile and pull the door closed behind me. I've shrugged halfway out of my Gore-Tex jacket when the floor lamp in the living room snaps on.

"Good evening, Mr. Valenti."

I spin around to the pool of light spilling over Papa's La-Z-Boy recliner and find myself staring at a big, buff stranger who is settled in comfortably with his legs crossed. A massive hand is wrapped around one of Mama's special-occasion crystal tumblers. It's filled with amber liquid and rests lightly on the arm of the chair. The intruder is dressed in a pair of tan Dockers slacks, a wine-colored, short-sleeve polo shirt, and brown loafers—an outfit not unlike my own. Mind you, unlike mine, his outfit is drawn tautly over mountains of muscle. His forearms are covered in a mane of black hair, and a tuft of hair bulges out of the open collar of his shirt. Even the backs of his knuckles are a little furry. The guy fairly reeks of testosterone. His eyes settle on mine while he offers me a half smile that is utterly bereft of warmth. His hooded eyes are equally chilly as he appraises me. The only hair on his polished head is a pair of menacing bushy black eyebrows. Yet the tone of his gravelly voice is almost warm when he invites me to "have a seat."

"Who the hell are you, and what are you doing in our home?" I demand.

He doesn't appear to be the least bit alarmed to be facing down an angry six foot five inch man when he lifts his glass as if he's about to offer a toast. "Decent bourbon. Pour yourself a glass and join me."

It's not a suggestion. Something in the man's demeanor warns against doing anything other than exactly what he's told me to do. So, as ridiculous as it seems, I pour two inches of Maker's Mark into the tumbler he's thoughtfully left on the table with the bourbon bottle. Then I prepare to have a chat with a man who looks like some sort of gangster. A little dart of fear pricks my heart when we lock eyes after I settle into Mama's well-worn easy chair. I stare at his Mediterranean olive skin, prominent nose, and full, sensual lips that suggest Italian ancestry not unlike my own. There's an effortless confidence wafting off this guy, whoever the hell he is.

"Let's talk about your father," he says with a smug smile.

I steel myself in anticipation of being told that Papa and Max have walked into an Italian buzz saw a few thousand miles from where we sit.

"I couldn't help noticing that he isn't here," the intruder says conversationally. "Only a single toothbrush in the bathroom, along with one lonely razor and a single bath towel. You haven't moved out, have you?"

He knows damned well that I haven't. I don't respond.

"Where is Francesco?" he asks.

154

"I don't know. He left last week."

"Really?"

"Really," I ape.

His eyes narrow, and a soft chuckle escapes his lips. "Your instinct to cover for Francesco is admirable, yet pointless, Mr. Valenti."

I choose to remain mute while a shaft of worry wiggles down my spine at the easy familiarity with which he refers to Papa as Francesco.

"So, you're playing your cards close to your vest while you think things through," he says with a note of approval. "I see how you were successful in court during Francesco's trial and at the village hall when you kept your neighborhood intact. Bravo to that, by the way. I was impressed. Very few people get the better of Titan Developments."

Like I give a damn what you think, pal, I think, feeling a little cockier now that I suspect that Papa and Max are safe.

"The situation you find yourself in this evening isn't as simple as you probably believe it to be, Mr. Valenti."

What situation? I force myself to settle back in Mama's chair and cross an ankle over my knee in an effort to match his nonchalant manner.

He appears mildly amused by my play. "Aren't you curious to know how your predicament isn't quite what you think?"

"I can do without the cat-and-mouse bullshit. I figure you'll eventually get to the point."

"Ah, a man who likes to cut to the chase," he retorts in a mocking tone. His voice hardens as he continues, "There are two interests to be served where you are concerned, Mr. Valenti."

I silently wait for him to continue.

"The first is the obvious concern that someone is anxious to see your father draw his final breath as soon as possible."

There's a news flash, I think, but dare not say.

"The business with your father from the old country isn't our chief concern, though."

He looks as if he expects a response. I stay silent.

"It may surprise you to learn that we have a keen interest in the lawsuit that our friends Windy City Sky Tours City and AAA Avgas has just filed against your client," he continues.

His friends? What the hell?

"You see, Mr. Valenti, R & B Ramp Services must be found to be at fault for that unfortunate incident over Lake Michigan."

I drop my foot to the floor and lean forward with my elbows braced on my knees to lock eyes with the intruder. His connection to AAA Avgas cements my earlier suspicion that this guy is Mafia. By all accounts, AAA Avgas is a wholly owned holding of the Luciano criminal empire. "You, whoever you are, are colluding with Windy City against my client?"

"Now, now, Mr. Valenti. Let's be civilized about this, shall we?"

The Luciano family civilized? Right. I wave an open hand between him and me. "You find this civilized? Me and you having a nice chat in my home, which you've just broken into?"

His eyes flash. "You really don't want to antagonize me, Mr. Valenti."

Screw that. "You're here on behalf of the Luciano family, aren't you? What the hell's your name, anyway?"

The eyes flash again, this time dangerously. He ignores my question about the Luciano family. His voice takes on a harsh edge when he replies, "You can call me Joe."

Right. "Joe," I parrot with dripping sarcasm. Jesus. Two days ago, Penelope and I were lamenting having the FBI working against us in concert with a bunch of rich shits and one of Chicago's preeminent law firms. Now we have the

Mafia lining up against us, as well? What next? China? Russia? Aliens from outer space?

Joe uncrosses his strapping legs and adopts my aggressive pose so that our noses are two feet apart. I stare into his dead eyes and battle the instinct to back off… and the sudden urge to wet my pants.

"Your clients were offered an opportunity to work with Windy City on this, weren't they?" he asks.

I don't reply.

"So they've made their choice. Or perhaps you made it for them, and this is where you now find yourselves. Perhaps that should serve as a lesson to you, Mr. Valenti. Never mind little old me," he says as he settles back into his seat. "Worry about those Windy City motherfuckers. Man, in some respects we're choirboys in comparison. At least we have some scruples and a sense of honor in our own way—even if people like you fail to appreciate it."

I can't even begin to formulate a response, at least not one that won't antagonize this guy.

"You and your partner are going to ensure that your client is found responsible for the crash of the Windy City tour plane, and soon. Time is of the essence."

"The hell we will," I retort. "Your so-called friends were at fault, and we aim to prove it."

His eyes narrow. "At what cost, Mr. Valenti?"

What does that even mean? I lean back, realizing that this explains why Wisnowski seems to be in an unseemly hurry to move her case along.

"Where is your father?" he asks sharply.

"I already told you what I know."

"If you'll excuse the harshness of the term, Mr. Valenti, I believe you've just told me to go screw myself."

Like I'm going to confirm that. Good guess, though.

He drops all pretense of civility. "That isn't a wise decision. Why not make it easy on yourself and just tell me where

Francesco is?" When I don't reply, he continues, "We'll find him if we want to, Mr. Valenti. You know that. I'm here tonight to ascertain how cooperative a man you can be."

Bullshit.

"I must say that I'm disappointed with you so far," Joe continues. "You don't wish to disappoint people like me, Mr. Valenti. It's not healthy."

The menace that has lurked just below the courteous veneer of the last few minutes is now in the open. What do I do now? There's no telling what this guy might pull next. If I were to venture a guess, I suspect it will be painful. I meet his dead gaze. Well, screw him. They don't have a clue where Papa is and have no idea how to go about tracking him down. If they did, "Joe" wouldn't be here. I stare him down for a long, intensely unnerving moment before forcing a conversational tone into my voice. "Well, Joe, you obviously don't know my father."

A sinister smile spreads over his face. "You probably don't want me to, Mr. Valenti."

He's got that right.

"Papa has always gone his own way," I say. "The guy who raped his sister found that out the hard way, didn't he?"

Joe frowns. "We do not approve of what was done to your aunt."

His sanctimonious bullshit rubs me the wrong way. I mean, these people are killers, drug peddlers, pimps, and worse. Stashing Brittany at Pat's has never seemed more prudent. There's more to fear in this world than the wrath of my ex-wife.

"How touching, coming from a choirboy like you," I retort.

Joe purses his lips and gives his head a slow shake while he digests my insult. His cold eyes bore into mine. "Have it your way, Mr. Valenti. I'm afraid you'll have to live with the responsibility for what happens next."

CHAPTER EIGHTEEN

My drinking companion the next evening after I kick off the work week is a decided improvement on Joe. For starters, I know and like Billy Likens. He called a couple of days ago to suggest bonding over a bottle. Perhaps he's as disturbed as I have been to find us sniping at each other over all the legal bullshit for the past month. With the menace of Joe's visit fresh in my mind, I resisted Billy's offer to host our little get-together. I don't want to put his family—wife, Shelly; seventeen-year-old daughter, Melanie; nine-year-old son Kenny; and possibly twenty-five-year-old son Craig, if he happens to be visiting—at risk. Nor did I feel comfortable dragging Billy himself into the line of fire by having him over to our house. In an inspired moment, I suggested meeting at the Cuff & Billy Club, a cop bar within spitting distance of the Cook County Courthouse. I don't imagine that Luciano family thugs are welcome here, and that's whom I hope to avoid tonight. The place is a bit of a dive—think of a roadside greasy spoon, wipe a damp washcloth around here and there, and you've got the Cuff & Billy Club. It even smells like an overripe kitchen rag. We're seated at a little table for two in a dimly lit back corner. The noise generated by the boisterous, well-lubricated crowd affords us plenty of privacy. I push thoughts of Joe aside, determined as I am to spend the evening mending fences with Billy.

We begin the evening chatting about sports, Billy's passion. He's a rabid Chicago Cubs baseball fan. Mel had led him astray from the Likens family tradition of being South-side blue-collar White Sox baseball fans. In the winter he's a Blackhawks hockey fanatic and plays recreational pickup hockey. He's not just a sports fan, though; he's also a relief pitcher in the thirty-plus Chicago Central Baseball League, and he's damned good. Billy turned down baseball scholarship offers so he could go to work after he knocked up Shelly with Craig when they were eighteen. He's also into rocks; a rock hound and a rock climber when he isn't digging them up. He's allowed to take the kids rock hounding, but rock climbing is forbidden by Shelly—not even on the twenty-foot hill in their neighborhood park, "lest they also lose their minds and start risking their necks hanging off the sides of mountains." He's a fun guy to hang with.

My eyes stray to his hands while he gripes about the Hawks blowing a three-goal lead in the third period of last night's game before losing in overtime. At Shelly's insistence, Billy's hands are surprisingly clean for a mechanic's, at least when he's not working—"don't be touching the kids with filthy hands and leaving oil stains on their clothes!"

Billy steers our conversation to the topic we'd agreed to take a break from tonight. "That FBI stuff is eating at me, Tony. We didn't do anything wrong."

I relate the conversations I've had with Penelope and Ben Larose, complete with our conclusion that the NTSB can't make a solid case for structural failure. "Larose doesn't think they'll even try. The most likely scenario is that Windy City and/or AAA Avgas is casting aspersions to try to pin the blame on you in civil court. They're probably whispering BS in the investigator's ears to get the FBI sniffing around."

"Why?" Billy asks in exasperation.

Joe's visit last night offered a disturbingly stark explanation of why, but it's not something to be shared with Billy. Or is it? Doesn't he have a right to know everything about a situation that has the potential to destroy his livelihood? I decide to park that consideration until I've had time to think it through. Which prompts me to realize that I need to have a discussion with Penelope about what I learned during Joe's visit. What a mess. I tell Billy that we think something might be amiss with the paperwork about the hundred-hour inspection.

"How can that be when we've given the NTSB the paper trail for the work?"

"We're looking into it, pal. More to come. Now, let's get back to our agreement not to screw up our night by obsessing over this shit."

He gives me a rueful smile and apologizes.

"No worries," I say while waving to get our server's attention. When I do, I order another bourbon for me, a Miller Lite for Billy, and ask for more peanuts. Dry-roasted, generously salted peanuts... one of my gastronomical weaknesses. I hope to eventually be reincarnated as a cow so I can laze away the days with an endless supply of salt licks. Until then, I make do with peanuts and potato chips.

"So, what's up with your father and all the crap around your place?" he asks. "Real sorry to hear about the cop who got shot, man."

I give him a drastically abridged version of the story, leaving out the lurid details of Papa killing his sister's rapist and his recent flight to Italy.

Billy isn't quite buying the bare-bones tale I've spun, but he lets it go after I deflect a couple more questions. "How

161

about you, Tony? You've been divorced awhile now, huh? Any women in your life?"

There's a topic that won't take long to cover. I turn my glass of bourbon this way and that to catch the light. I definitely don't want to start wallowing in that misery over a few drinks. Morose Tony is definitely *not* Fun Tony. "Well, there's Brittany," I reply lightly. "A handful by any measure."

Billy lifts an eyebrow in surprise. "Really? I've always gotten the impression that she's a good kid. Troubles?"

I shake my head. Aside from her mother's threat to steal her away from me again, things are good on the Brittany front. "Not from her. More crap from her mother. She filed for custody again."

"Oh, shit."

"Yeah. Michelle and her parents have invited us to a little get-together later this week to discuss custody 'without the unpleasantness of going to court.'"

"That sounds hopeful."

"Hah!" I sneer. "I'm being given an opportunity to surrender gracefully."

"Why would you?"

"Because that's the way of the universe according to Prescott Rice the Third: You got. I want. You give or I take... and break you into a thousand little pieces in the process."

Billy frowns. "They sound like nice folks."

A bitter laugh escapes me. "Anyway."

"But things are good between you and Brittany, right?"

I guess I'm about to find out. Things *seem* okay, but they often do just before the broken relationship roof falls in on me.

"We've got a seventeen-year-old, man," Billy says. "Feel free to talk things through. I may have a useful insight or two."

"Nah, you were right. Britts is a good kid. I was just thinking about the BS with her mother."

"I'm glad you got her back from Europe."

Let's hope she doesn't go right back. Crap, I'm in danger of starting to wallow in it all. I shrug, probably looking as miserable as I feel while doing so.

"Okay," Billy says with a tight smile. "No more Brittany talk."

"Thanks." I pop a handful of peanuts into my mouth and signal our server for more.

"How about Pat O'Toole?" he asks, opening yet another raw topic. "You two seem to get along."

"Yeah, we do, but she's not interested in me that way."

"Which sounds like you're interested in her 'that' way?"

Am I? The distance she insists on imposing between us is starting to wear on me. Anyway, it's not a topic to bore Billy with. I decide to steer the conversation to his late sister. Mel's death had devastated me. I know it still haunts Billy, yet remembering her together seems to help both of us to shoulder the loss without sinking too deeply into melancholy. There are plenty of happy memories to sustain us, and we invariably get a few laughs out of remembering her wacky antics.

"Have you heard from any of Mel's friends lately?" I ask.

He nods. "You know how people loved Mel. I still hear from a few of them now and then, and we get lots of Christmas cards. I ran into Pete Livingston at a ball game last summer, and we shot the shit over a couple of beers."

I smile. Pete was a wild one who ran with our crowd. "How's Pete?"

"Good. Still doing his firefighter shit, still telling cornball jokes, still stuck in adolescence. He was telling me about a time he and Mel and some other nuts drank a little too much and tried to paddle a dinghy by hand all the way across Lake Michigan in the middle of the night. I can't believe they didn't kill themselves!"

"When I think about some of the dumb stuff we did, I'm

surprised we didn't kill ourselves several times over. That night we got it into our heads that we wanted to see Michigan," I say with a chuckle.

Billy grins. "You were there?"

I nod. "Pete's folks were out of town, so he suggested using his dad's 'little boat,' which turned out to be an inflatable Zodiac with an outboard motor—*not* exactly a dinghy. We didn't have a trailer hitch to take the whole thing, so we took the motor off and strapped the boat to the top of someone's car—I forget whose. Anyway, Dipshit Livingston forgot to load the paddles, which we didn't realize until we put the damned thing in the water. Mel, in particular, was disappointed about not getting to go to Michigan."

"All her fault, huh?" Billy asks with a chuckle.

"Not entirely, but she was a babe, and no guy wanted to let her down."

Billy laughs. "I still thought of girls as being gross back in those days—*especially* Big Sis."

Mel was anything but gross. While not drop dead gorgeous in any traditional sense of the word, she was vivacious and inherently appealing. Everyone wanted to get close to her all through school. The glue of the special bond between her and me had been the abuse we suffered at home —mine at the fists and feet of my older brother 'Fearsome' Frankie, and Mel's at the hands of her father, who was a twisted bastard of a child sexual abuser with his eldest daughter. Mel had suspected the truth about my brother by watching him interact with me at school and around the neighborhood. Her suspicions were confirmed one day when she arrived at our house while Frankie was pounding the crap out of me on the other side of the screen door. That particular beating had left me with a six-stitch scar on my right cheekbone that resurfaced when I tanned for years afterward. Things crystallized for me after school one day when she begged me not to go to volleyball practice and leave her alone in the house with her father. The fear in her eyes and her evident relief when her mother arrived sent my mind back to a number of other times when she'd exhibited uncharacteristic skittishness. Looking back on them, I'd realized that her father featured in every instance. She tearfully admitted to the truth when I pressed her for a definitive answer. Neither of us whispered a word of it to anyone else; we were friends, confidants, and a two-person, mutual-support network. I sometimes wonder if either of us would have made it through our teens without the other to lean on and love. Although the sexual tension between us was electric and we walked right up to the precipice of a full-blown relationship more times than I could count, the idea of going there and having it go sour terrified us, so we always backed away. The prospect of losing our best friend and one-person, emotional-support network was too terrifying to contemplate.

I pick up the story of the Lake Michigan escapade for Billy. "Anyway, we've got three sixteen- or seventeen-year-old boys spewing testosterone and the apple of our eyes is in distress, so, dumbasses that we were, someone came up with the bright idea of paddling across. The notion actually scared the crap out of us, but once it was out there, none of us were turning back. I mean, who wanted to risk looking like a chicken in front of the girls?"

"I guess no one thought about how stupid they'd look as bloated corpses washing ashore?" Billy asks with a wink.

"Hell no!" I chortle while flagging our server for another round. This time I order myself two bourbons.

"Pete said you didn't make it to Michigan. What happened?"

"We washed ashore on the Indiana sand dunes."

My mind turns inward to memories of Mel while we wait for the drinks. We spent years apart while Mel chased happiness around the globe in an unending string of bad relationships, each of which I think she hoped would erase the stain of her father. None ever could, of course, but I was always a safe home base when she came back to lick her wounds. If I hadn't been married to Michelle, something more might have developed between us on one of those early homecomings.

"Here you go, gentlemen," the waitress says as she plunks our drinks down. She adds another bowl of peanuts and grins at me. "You might wanna go easy on those, sir. The manager's gonna start charging you by the pound pretty soon."

Melancholy sets in somewhere in the middle of my fourth bourbon when Billy heads off to the bathroom and my thoughts turn to Pat. A series of bad relationships through my time in law school left me wondering if my older brother wasn't right about how worthless and dog-faced I am. I've never forgotten his telling me that I was one of those guys the girls all snickered at and said "eew!" about when I passed by. Sure enough, I came to feel as if I wasn't worth anyone's emotional investment. I still feel that way at times… and this is why I shouldn't drink too much.

"Penny for your thoughts," Billy says as he slips back into his seat.

"Just thinking about Pat. She talks a good game to explain why she isn't ready to commit to any more than friendship."

"Such as?"

"She's happy with her life and career, she doesn't need someone else to 'complete her.' She's committed to work, family, Lawndale, and painting. She's not sure she has time in her life for more. It all makes sense on one level, but I suspect it's more likely a way for her to keep me at arm's length without rejecting me outright. It stings, but I get it and accept it. I appreciate that she's trying hard not to hurt me, but it's still rejection."

"That's a lot of self-trash talk, man," Billy says softly when I finish and upend my glass.

"Yeah, well, at some point I had to come to terms with the reality that I'm simply not good enough."

"Good enough for what?"

"People. Friendship. Relationships. Just not cut out for it, I guess."

"Mel would slap you around something fierce if she heard this, Tony."

I smile the saddest of smiles and start in on my second glass of bourbon. "Yeah, she would. Nobody ever had a fiercer protector than I had in her."

"She had someone just as committed to protecting her."

I stare back into his eyes, wondering if he's ever figured out what his father did to Mel. She'd always protected Billy from that knowledge and had sworn me to secrecy, as well. "Sometimes I wonder if the reason Mel and I never went all in on our relationship wasn't something similar to the situation with Pat."

Billy shakes his head while giving me an incredulous look. "Nah, she loved you with her whole being, Tony. You two should have been together. Hell, you were meant for one another, whatever the hurdles. She knew that at the end."

Or maybe that was an act of pity on her part. By the time Mel and I finally found ourselves free of other entanglements after Michelle and I separated briefly for the first time when Brittany was only three and Mel had limped home from Australia after a particularly painful breakup, time was running out on us. We had three months together before cancer claimed her. I remember telling her how completely broken I felt during her last few days. I've often clung to her response. As she so often did, she found the right words in a song lyric. This one came from Leonard Cohen's song "Anthem" about how there is a crack in everything, but instead of lamenting the crack, he suggests that this is how the light gets in. I've always found the idea to be a profoundly positive way to find the light within the darkness.

Billy drinks off the last of his beer, then leans in closer and locks my gaze in his. "She *did* know you were the one, Tony. She told me that the biggest mistake of her life was not to roll the dice with you way back when, because she *knew* you would never, ever have let her down."

I nod and admit, "Yeah, I guess I do know that at some level." But would she have turned away from me if she'd rolled those dice? Everyone else has.

Billy rests his hand on my arm and leans even closer. "You're real messed up in the relationship department, my friend. Don't let Pat or your ex-wife or anybody else tear you down. You've told me more than once that my sister was the best person you've ever known."

I nod.

"You've told me that she knew more about people than anyone, right?"

I nod again.

"I've also heard you swear that Mel was the most honest person on the face of the earth… past, present, and future."

I smile at that. It *was* quite a pronouncement—one I believe to this day.

"We both made promises to Mel at the end," Billy says. "Mine was to make sure you never lose sight of her love for you. I guess she knew you had this morose streak in you, so I understand tonight exactly why she tagged me to keep an eye out."

"Thanks, pal."

"Can I give you a bit of advice?"

I twirl my hand in a "bring it on" motion.

"Get back on the horse, buddy. You've got to know a woman or two. Take someone out on the town, live a little."

Maybe he's right. Lord knows I can use a distraction from the ugliness that's swirling all around me. Maybe it's time to set aside my feelings for Pat and stop mooning over lost causes. Being her friend isn't the worst thing in the world. Maybe it's time to dip a toe in the water and see if maybe Mel was onto something. My thoughts track immediately to a former co-worker I ran into at the courthouse a few weeks ago. Note to self: call her.

CHAPTER NINETEEN

Jonathan Walton sighs inwardly as he and his partners ascend to their office in a Willis Tower elevator. Caitlyn Tyson is on the verge of one of her eruptions—narrowed eyes, lips drawn tightly, fidgeting from foot to foot while she impatiently flips her hair away from her face. Oliver Franklin simply looks worried. What's new?

They're on their way back to the office after meeting with their lawyers at Caitlyn's insistence. Someone from her family is filling her head full of shit supposedly gleaned from a source within the Justice Department. She wants to have legal advice in hand if it turns out to be true. The story is that the FBI is investigating Megan Walton's training and qualifications or some damned thing.

"Just relax, guys," he says impatiently when they're safely in his office and out of earshot of anyone else. "It's all under control."

"Yeah?" Caitlyn says in a challenging, grating tone.

Walton nods, then walks over to a compact conference table that sits beside a floor-to-ceiling window with a magnificent lake view. He drops into his usual seat and waves his partners into theirs.

"We're good on this R & B inspection angle?" Franklin asks.

"Oh yeah," Walton replies with a chuckle. "Those two are toast."

"You're sure that can't blow back on us?"

The guy can't get enough reassurance, Walton thinks with disdain.

"What's this shit you're spinning about doctored documents?" Caitlyn asks suspiciously. "R & B *did* do that inspection. We can't just magically undo it."

"They can't prove it," Walton replies smugly before a laugh escapes him. "Such a little pissant company those guys run. They use a typewriter! Can you believe it?"

"And that matters why?" Caitlyn asks in a caustically bitchy tone that amuses Walton—except when it's directed at him. Which has been happening a little too often lately. Fault lines are beginning to appear in their little band of brothers… and a sister.

"Let me tell you how that matters," he retorts. "Not only do they use a typewriter, they use carbon copies, Caits."

She throws up her hands in exasperation. "So?"

"Old shit like that is ripe to be messed with. Our Avgas friends dug up some ancient fart in a Mafia retirement home or someplace who knows how to forge and dummy up that stuff."

"They did, huh?" Caitlyn asks with a Cheshire Cat grin. She relaxes back into her seat and crosses her legs. Mount Caitlyn is temporarily dormant.

She knows what's coming, Walton thinks as he shoots her an answering grin. "The guy made the R & B carbon copy look like the original date was September ninth and that R & B did an amateurish job of trying to backdate it to August twenty-third."

"What's the point?" Franklin asks.

Walton winks. "It makes it look like they sent the paperwork *after* the crash, right?"

Franklin nods.

"And then tried to backdate it."

A slow smile spreads across Franklin's face. "As if they hadn't done the work, then panicked after the accident and cooked up some paperwork to suggest that they did."

"Exactly," Walton says with an answering smile. "And then realized they screwed up with the date and tried to fix it."

"August twenty-third was the actual date they sent the invoice, right?" Caitlyn asks.

Walton nods.

"What about our copy?" Franklin asks. "The NTSB took it."

"Yup," Walton replies airily. "No worries, dude. The Luciano guys substituted a new copy dated September ninth."

Franklin's eyes widen. "Right in the NTSB's files?"

Walton smirks and nods.

"How?" Caitlyn asks in a tone somewhere between skepticism and admiration.

"How the hell would I know? That's the Luciano family's area of expertise."

Caitlyn whips out her cell phone and stares at the calendar. "But August twenty-third was a Sunday."

Walton bursts out laughing. "I know, right? That's suspicious right there. Who the hell sends out invoices on a Sunday? Accounting departments are all at home, for Christ's sake!"

"Little pissant companies," Franklin replies. "That's who does weekend billing from their home office."

"Well, okay," Walton allows after a beat. "You got me on that one, dude. That's not really the point, anyway."

"Then what is?"

Walton sits straighter and slaps a hand on the table. His patience with Franklin's Nervous Nellie routine is wearing thin. "The *point* is that R & B is twisting in the wind."

"It all sounds maybe a little too clever by half, Johnny boy," Caitlyn says.

"It sounds perfect," Walton shoots back.

"Lorraine didn't seem too thrilled that Avgas is in the clear," Caitlyn says after a beat, referring to the senior lawyer of the group they'd just met with.

"No biggie," Walton scoffs. "Remember that Avgas is our partner in this."

"They're mobsters," Caitlyn shoots back. "Ours is a marriage of convenience. What's their motivation to stay close to us now?"

Walton slumps back in his seat. "Really, Caits? We know where the bodies are buried. They don't dare cross us."

"They *bury* bodies," Franklin says anxiously. "Don't antagonize them."

Oliver has a point there, Walton realizes. "So, we don't antagonize them. They don't antagonize us. R & B takes the fall, and we're all good."

Franklin stares back. "Do you honestly believe we're not going to take some sort of hit on this?"

"Windy City might have to kick in some cash, but *we* won't. That's the beauty of how the company is set up. Nobody can come after us personally. Our insurance company pays up on whatever we get tagged with."

"Our insurance rates would skyrocket," Franklin says.

"We just wind the whole thing up for a tax loss and move on if the rates get prohibitive, pal. It's not like flying tours are a big deal for us."

Franklin's expression argues otherwise. The Windy City revenue *does* matter to him. Walton often forgets what a pauper the guy is.

"Don't worry," he reassures Franklin. "We'll hook you up with another cash cow."

"It still bothers me that Lorraine is concerned about whether or not we will be able to pin all the blame on R & B," Caitlyn mutters.

Franklin sighs. "To be honest, it kind of bugs me that we're screwing those guys over."

"Jesus, dude!" Walton explodes.

"They do good work for us."

"Well, yeah, but that's beside the point," Walton argues. "We're talking big bucks here."

"No room for sentiment," Caitlyn agrees.

Walton appreciates her support and smiles at her. "As for Lorraine, Caits, remember that she gets paid to worry about shit whether it's a realistic threat or not. She'd worry about liability risks posed by the quality of the toilet paper in our public washroom if she thought she could turn it into billable hours."

Caitlyn chuckles.

Walton looks from one partner to the other and decides that it's well past time to sum things up and be done with the worrywart routine. "The key is that the accident wasn't foreseeable *by* us and that whatever went wrong was out of our control. Bad gas? Nothing we could have foreseen, and we sure as hell didn't pump the gas. It's all good."

"But *we* chose the vendor," Franklin counters.

Walton feels an almost overpowering urge to rip Franklin's nervous head off his skinny neck. "No, we didn't. *We* didn't choose anyone. Our aviation consultant did. We've got more layers of insulation between us and liability than a walrus has between itself and the Arctic Ocean. Relax, dude. *Nothing* was foreseeable from our vantage point."

Caitlyn uncrosses her legs and eases forward. "So, the big three potential causes. Bad fuel. Structural failure due to shoddy maintenance." She's ticking off each of her points by popping up a finger as she goes. She pauses for a beat, then thrusts out a third finger. "Pilot error."

Walton, who had been nodding along, hops off her blame train right there. "That's my niece you're talking about, Caits. She's off-limits."

"She was flying the damn plane," Caitlyn retorts.

Walton rises halfway out of his seat and leans across the table toward her. "We will *not* throw Megs under the bus!"

"Someone else might," Franklin replies calmly. "Then what?"

"Not our concern," Walton replies as he settles back into his seat. "*We* won't hang Megs out to dry. If the NTSB does… well, nothing I can do to prevent that, but my sister will crush my balls in a vise if she ever thinks we're smearing her daughter."

Franklin nods. "Fair enough. We're still sheltered if that happens?"

Walton smiles and nods. "Correct. Not foreseeable. Not under our control. See how simple things are?"

Caitlyn sits back in her seat, recrosses her legs, and taps her fingernails on the arms of her chair. "You keep repeating that mantra, Johnny Boy. Not under our control, not foreseeable."

"It's what makes us golden," Walton replies curtly. He hates it when she spouts the Johnny Boy shit. It never leads anywhere pleasant. It doesn't this time, either.

Caitlyn eases forward. "So, hypothetically, if there was anything untoward in Megan's hiring—maybe a sketchy Cessna 210 rating—where do we stand?"

Oh shit, Walton thinks. "Where's that coming from, Caits?"

"I told you earlier, Johnny Boy. The Justice Department."

"That's just people tossing a hypothetical out, Caits. Relax."

Her eyes narrow as she sits farther forward and rests her

175

elbows on the table. "And if there *is* something to the idea that your niece shouldn't have been at the controls?"

Walton doesn't reply. That could be a problem but probably won't be. He's been assured by their lawyers that their corporate structure is airtight. *It should be for the small fortune the bastards sucked out of us for that work.*

"Isn't that why our insurance company denied our claim for the plane?" Franklin asks.

"Sure," Walton replies. "But you knew they were going to look for a way to deny the claim. Besides, it was for what, 100K and change? Petty cash, dude. Anyway, I sorted that— out of my own pocket, by the way. The records are sealed."

"Sealed from the cops?" Caitlyn asks acerbically. "Give me a break! A court order in a criminal trial will open that can of worms in a heartbeat."

"Look, guys," Walton says in a tone intended to placate his partners and dial things down. "We hired that particular instructor for a reason. His ass is also in a crack if this goes sour. It's all good."

"You're a damned fool, Johnny Boy," Caitlyn hisses. "You paid off that instructor to make sure Megan passed so you could hire her, didn't you?"

Walton sits rock-still until the urge to smack the bitch passes. Then he shakes his head and reminds her in a strained voice, "I got his name from the consultant, too."

"How?" Caitlyn shoots back, like a dog with a bone. "Did you ask him to recommend someone precious Megan could blow for her rating?"

Walton manages, barely, to keep his cool. After all, there was no provable quid pro quo in the hiring or bribing of the instructor—it was a cash deal. "My mantra again, Caits," he mutters. "Not foreseeable. Not within our control."

"To hell with your mantra!" Franklin snaps. "*You* hired that instructor. *You* took Megan on as a pilot. If someone can show that you had *any* inkling this instructor is sketchy and/or that you even suspected Megan wasn't one hundred percent qualified to fly with paying customers, we're screwed, so let's quit talking like we couldn't foresee or control that."

Caitlyn fixes a poisonous scowl on Walton. "Oliver and I couldn't foresee or control that, but you sure as hell could, you asshole."

"Any half-assed lawyer could drive a bus through that defense," Franklin adds.

Walton starts to shake his head and open his mouth to argue the point. Caitlyn doesn't give him the chance.

"Show me some daylight between the company and that scenario, you moron!" she shouts.

"I can't believe you did that, Jonathan," Franklin says with disgust. "You assured us Megan was fully up to speed in the Cessna. Hell, you even told us she was qualified by that university flight school."

"I implied no such thing," Walton replies lamely.

"I had no idea you'd hired someone to shoehorn her into our pilot's seat," Franklin mutters. "What the hell were you thinking?"

"He wasn't thinking," Caitlyn sneers. "He was pussy-whipped by his precious sister, to use that disgusting term he's so fond of."

Walton jumps to his feet and slams a fist on the table. "Fuck you!" he snarls before he marches out of his own office. Sometimes he hates his overbearing shrew of a sister. Caitlyn, too. He backtracks to the office door and glares at his partners. "It's a good thing for you two that I'm always at least one step ahead of the wolves you see nipping at our heels all the damn time!" Then he slams the door and stalks away to the conference room, bangs that door shut behind him, and starts scheming anew.

CHAPTER TWENTY

We're in Cook County Circuit Court the next morning with Judge Ngo on the bench. He, like Wisnowski, is a Butterworth Cole alumni. He did a stint in the State's Attorney's office on his way to the bench, so we know whose side of the fence he'll be on. I did a little research on him: grandson of Vietnamese refugees who reportedly disowned him after he used community contacts to railroad a couple of Vietnamese college students for a drug crime they were eventually proven innocent of when it was revealed that Ngo bent more than a few rules to get the conviction—not that he faced any disciplinary consequences for having done so. Big surprise there. So, let's see, it's now R & B Ramp Services, represented by Brooks and Valenti, versus Chicago high society, big business, legal sharks, the Feds, the Mafia, and now the Cook County court system.

Court is called to order, with Wisnowski appearing on behalf of Windy City. We've agreed that Penelope will speak for us today. Aside from the fact that she prepared and filed our motion, I'm an exhausted wreck, wracked with guilt about Ed Stankowski and Papa's plight—not to mention my burgeoning fear of Joe and what's going to happen when I tell

Penelope about his existence and demands. The weight of it all is crushing.

Ngo peers down at us. "You've filed a motion asking the court to intervene in discovery, Miss Brooks. I won't pretend to be pleased to find you in my courtroom at this early stage of proceedings. Now, why on earth are you in a hurry to drag people into depositions?"

"This lawsuit is proceeding quite quickly, Your Honor, driven by plaintiff's counsel. We allowed Miss Wisnowski to depose our clients two weeks ago, on the understanding that they would make their clients available to us for depositions on or before November tenth. They've cancelled three appointments and are now refusing to schedule any depositions at all."

"Perhaps the attorneys for the plaintiff have more patience that you, Miss Brooks. This action is only a few weeks old. Attempting to enlist the assistance of the court at this time is premature, to say the least."

I can sense barely constrained anger radiating off my partner even as she remains outwardly calm. "As I mentioned, Judge, the attorneys for the plaintiff have been pushing this case forward. Now that they have what they want, they refuse to reciprocate in discovery."

Ngo's eyes are alight with amusement. "They're not playing fair, huh?" he asks in an almost mocking tone.

Asshole.

"They are not keeping their commitments, Your Honor."

"Feeling played, Counselor?" he asks.

I notice Wisnowski covering a grin with her hand. Bitch.

Penelope doesn't take the bait to get into an argument with the judge. She waits patiently. He doesn't appear to be pleased when she allows the awkward silence to drag out.

"What do you want this court to do, Miss Brooks?" he eventually asks.

"Our motion speaks to that, Your Honor. We're asking the

court to establish a discovery schedule that allows all parties to prepare for trial. Opposing counsel has intimated that they wish to go to trial before the end of the calendar year. To be prepared for that trial date, we will need to receive our discovery materials as soon as possible."

"You want me to referee, do you?" Ngo asks.

It's a good thing Penelope is speaking for us. If not, I'm sure I would have said something by now that would have prompted Judge Asshole to hold me in contempt and toss my butt in jail.

Instead of answering the judge's question, Penelope dares to ask one of her own. "Are you entertaining the idea of an early trial date, as proposed by the attorneys for the plaintiff?"

Ngo's eyes narrow. "I asked you a question, Miss Brooks," he snaps.

"Yes, you did, Your Honor," Penelope says. "To answer, I'm asking for clarification of your intentions."

Ngo glares down at her. "Yes, Counselor. I think an early trial date is a good idea."

"Shall we nail down a discovery schedule then, Your Honor?"

He shakes his head no. "Why don't we give you folks a couple of weeks to work things out among yourselves," he says with a smile at Wisnowski, who smiles back.

The fix is in," I grumble to Penelope as we leave the courthouse.

"Like hell," she mutters angrily.

It doesn't take much to set me off cursing. To push Penelope there is an accomplishment.

And woe to anyone who does.

CHAPTER TWENTY-ONE

I t's Friday morning, the day after our encounter with Judge Ngo. I'm standing at the window of my sixth-floor room in the Radisson Hotel Old Town Alexandria watching the Potomac River slog southward. The sludge-colored water, relentlessly dredging the bedrock of the river channel by a handful of millimeters each year, is doing so at breakneck speed compared with the progress of the hands crawling around the face of my Rolex. It's been six hours since I awoke at four thirty-seven this morning, plenty of time to stew about lawsuits, a Mafia asshole named Joe, and if Papa is safe. Wasting time dealing with crap from my ex-wife and her blowhard father is an unwelcome intrusion. I've been cautioning myself all week to hold my temper over lunch. I know myself; I'm likely to have a short fuse in the face of what I know will be one provocation after another. It's how the Rice family operates. We're meeting Michelle and her parents for lunch in a little more than an hour. Alexandria was deemed a neutral location for today's upcoming duel. Brittany and I flew in last night to avoid flight delays from a weather system tracking up the Eastern Seaboard.

I've only seen Michelle once in passing since she walked

out of our Atlanta home over a year ago with a suitcase in each hand. Her goal today is to rip our daughter out of my life. She'll have a fight on her hands to do so, but I'd be a fool to underestimate her determination to win. My goal for today's meeting is to get a sense of the lay of the land on which she and her father intend to fight this battle. I'm anxious to get on with it. I'm also scared to death of doing so.

Brittany is on the phone with Pat, checking in on the recuperating Deano. Why people insist on talking to dogs on the phone is beyond me; I've seen the bewilderment or simple disinterest of dogs when people do it. I suppose it makes *us* feel better. I pass the time revisiting an article about the restoration of Old Town Alexandria in a guidebook thoughtfully placed in my hotel room by the Alexandria Convention and Visitors Association.

"What did Deano have to say?" I ask when Brittany ends the call.

She replies by sticking out her tongue.

I'm going stir-crazy and we have time to do a little exploring before lunch. "Do you mind walking?" I ask.

Brittany is looking forward to seeing her mother and grandparents but isn't thrilled with their determination to revisit the child custody arrangements. I let her know that they want to do so, without revealing the specific details of her mother's custody suit. I doubt they care what she thinks. If they did, they would have discussed it with her. They would have invited her along today, too. I do care what she thinks about this and spent hours debating the merits of bringing her along. I know that the Rice family will be unhappy that I have, so I've tried to figure out how I can position this to satisfy them. Talk about an exercise in futility; I've seldom if ever done anything to Prescott Rice's satisfaction. I finally fell back on a pithy idea I'd stumbled across in a fortune cookie or something: "If you repeatedly hit yourself over the head with a baseball bat, you will feel better when you stop." Dealing with Michelle and her father is no different, so I stopped agonizing over what they'd think about my bringing Brittany and—voila!—I felt better instantly.

Once outside, we turn left on North Fairfax Street and find ourselves marching straight into the teeth of a raw wind whipping off the water. Hunched against the howling tempest, we start toward the center of Old Town Alexandria. Cobblestone streets cut between rows of restored colonial architecture. Too much of this suffers from an effort to achieve a certain patriotic colonial charm calculated to reel in tourists by the thousands. The presence of pizza parlors and coffee shops flanked by modern retail outlets and kitschy antique shops sounds a false note. Yet there's no disputing the rarity of the architectural masterpieces dotting the landscape— solid-brick buildings decorated with chunky ornamental accents and trim uniformly painted white. The buildings press close, set back a foot or two at most from the narrow brick sidewalk. Steps jut out from front doors to further impinge on the walkway.

When Brittany slips her arm through mine, I glance at her and wince at the sight of her rosy cheeks and runny nose. She dabs at her nose with a gloved hand and grins. "*Great* idea to get out and enjoy the outdoors, Dad!"

I grin back and shrug in a "What can I say?" gesture, then cut west in search of succor from the wind along tree-lined residential streets. The charm the business denizens of Alexandria have striven so hard to fabricate elsewhere is evident on these blocks. There's a timeless elegance here, something solid that isn't found in suburbs such as the Wildercliff development we had inhabited in Atlanta and others like it scattered from sea to shining sea.

I enjoy the ambience of the buildings for several blocks, then square my shoulders and head for King Street. The guidebook trumpets this strip as the "heart" of Old Town. When we turn the corner onto North Royal Street, my eyes settle immediately on Gadsby's Tavern and Museum, a pair of conjoined classic red-brick Georgian colonial structures. Gadsby's isn't exactly neutral ground; it's a Rice family favorite. We occasionally had dinner in the restaurant here in happier times, surrounded by period furnishings and colonial-garbed servers recalling the days when the storied building's tables were graced by the likes of George Washington, Thomas Jefferson, and Ben Franklin.

We linger along the final block to kill the last few minutes before the Rices are due to arrive, pausing to gaze in the windows of a glass gallery before meandering back to wait on the sidewalk outside the restaurant. Our eyes impatiently roam between the ends of the block and the streets beyond—we're both anxious to get out of the cold. At least I thought both of us were. Brittany ducks into the shelter of a doorway and unzips her coat. Is she nuts? No, just a teenager, a species seemingly impervious to the cold to judge by their willingness to challenge winter in running shoes and T-shirts. I glance up to see that we're standing outside a Banana Republic store and smile at the irony of this store taking root directly across the river from Washington, DC, beside the watering hole of the Founding Fathers. *Look at what's become of us, guys!*

A block-long Mercedes sedan with Connecticut plates finally eases to a stop in front of Gadsby's. The rear door swings open and a perfectly turned ankle appears, cradled within a burgundy leather shoe. A full head of immaculately coifed raven hair rising above the door announces that Michelle has arrived, doing so in all her impeccably arranged splendor. She glances up, spots me, and tosses a quick smile my way before ducking her head back into the car, presumably to speak with her father, Prescott M.F. Rice III. She re-emerges onto the sidewalk a second later, this time with a chic tan coat draped over the sleeve of a form-fitting, cream knee-length dress. Michelle possesses what I've always considered a uniquely extraordinary beauty. To this day, I don't quite know how to describe it—it's some ineffable combination of sultry sexiness overlaid with sophistication and elegance.

It won't do to fall under Michelle's sway, so I force my thoughts back to the matter at hand. We're here for one of two reasons. The Rices are convinced that their legal position with regard to custody is unassailable, in which case they plan to impress the hopelessness of my position upon me to prompt a bloodless surrender (thereby avoiding any public unpleasantness). The alternative is that they're not at all confident of prevailing over me in court, in which case they'll go on the offensive, blustering and threatening in an effort to intimidate me into a premature surrender (thereby also avoiding any public unpleasantness). In short, lunch today is a Rice power play. The story that we're all here to facilitate an equitable resolution between friends is a smoke screen that doesn't fool me for a second. Prescott Rice and his daughter play to win and won't quit until they do. I have no intention of yielding.

Brittany emerges from the recessed doorway and hurries toward her mother. Michelle's ironclad control falters for a microsecond when she sees her, but the moment passes quickly, probably without Brittany noticing a thing. They share a chaste embrace. Brittany has combed the spikes out of her hair, so the new color and short cut attract no more than a raised brow when her mother eyes the new hairdo. Then Michelle holds Brittany out at arm's length to conduct a fashion inspection. Our daughter is dressed for the occasion of a Rice family gathering, looking positively cultured this morning in a pair of platinum slacks and a pumpkin cardigan over a pale-tangerine silk blouse. She even sports a pair of burnished gold hoop earrings. A faint sheen of coral adds a touch of color to her lips. She's very much her mother's daughter today, not an encouraging omen given the reason we're gathering here—especially not on Friday the thirteenth.

Michelle meets my eyes after the inspection and smiles.

Her shoulders rise in the vaguest suggestion of approval, the gesture performed with exquisite grace. "Mother and Father will be joining us after they park the car. They thought we might wish to have a few minutes together."

So you can use your charms to soften me up? I shrug.

Michelle pastes a distant smile on her face and glides toward Gadsby's door, leaving us to follow in her wake.

I vigorously rub my hands together to restore circulation while we wait to be seated. "How are your parents?" I ask Michelle.

She accepts the peace offering with equanimity. "You know Mother and Father, always complaining about being harried, but otherwise they're well, thank you."

The tension between us is palpable, at least to me. Brittany seems oblivious to it as she tells her mother the latest school and Bobby Harland news. Our daughter looks embarrassed when she says, "Too much coffee this morning. Where's the bathroom?"

I direct her to the hostess for directions.

"What is *she* doing here?" Michelle hisses as soon as Brittany leaves.

"This is her life that you're screwing with, Michelle. She should have a say in her future. Given all the BS you've been filling her head with, I thought it might be instructive for her to be a party to what you and your father are up to." Then I shut up before I say something I might regret.

"You better not have told her about the custody lawsuit."

I don't answer. Brittany knows the current terms of custody, which were set by family court in Chicago. I have temporary custody while Michelle lives overseas. Michelle pays $2,500 in monthly child support. She's also on the hook for tuition and school-related expenses for as long as Brittany is in school, including four years of undergrad and three years of postgraduate studies if she goes to university. Michelle is contesting the private high school tuition from the settlement, arguing that the provisions of the original ruling only apply to postsecondary education. She makes it sound as if she can't afford to help on her Coca-Cola executive vice-president salary, prodigious bonuses, or her multimillion-dollar Rice family trust fund. Prescott Rice had threatened me with all manner of professional destruction if I didn't cave in to their demands during round one. I hadn't. Prescott was infuriated to discover that my lowly life as a lawyer in private practice has put me beyond the reach of his usual machinations to threaten careers, but I'm sure he's still working whatever angles he can to screw me over.

We wait in uncomfortable silence until Brittany returns. She appears a little pissed for some reason when she looks at Michelle, so we wait in awkward silence until our table is ready.

"This way," says a young lady wearing a bright smile and a period costume consisting of a full paisley skirt and a frilly white blouse. A sleeveless blue vest tops the ensemble, laced tightly enough to thrust her ample bosom dramatically upward.

We fall in behind her with Michelle in the lead, followed by Brittany, and finally me bringing up the rear. We settle around a table for six beside an impressive fireplace framed to the ceiling in mahogany or some similarly dark and exotic wood carved by a long-forgotten craftsman of surpassing skill. The wooden table and chairs are colonial, of course, and the table is set with period pieces. The walls of the room are sky blue. It's almost too warm in the heavy air near the fireplace, but that's okay with me. I'm still trying to thaw out.

Michelle has seated Brittany at her side, directly across the table from me on what I assume is meant to be the Rice side of the table.

"This place is how I expected Europe to look," Brittany says with a laugh.

A waiter also dressed in period garb appears like magic

and slides a breadboard onto our table. A loaf of the Sally Lunn bread I remember fondly from past visits rests atop the wood, as if welcoming me back.

"May I get you folks something to drink?" he asks.

I opt for a mug of Irish coffee that I can warm my hands on. After giving the waiter a thorough grilling about the contents of Gadsby's wine cellar, Michelle orders a glass of a French white wine and alerts our waiter to the imminent arrival of two more guests. Brittany loyally requests Coca-Cola, earning a smile from her mother. The server leaves behind a trio of menus and three glasses of ice water. I pull the bread platter close, then cut and distribute slices onto our bread plates.

Our daughter's eyes go wide when a strolling violinist enters the room and merrily bursts into a sprightly rendition of "Greensleeves." I've never heard the piece played quite this up tempo.

Brittany, who has a few years of piano instruction under her belt, laughs after several bars. "'What Child Is This' done in four-four time? Cool!"

Michelle is quick to correct her. "Actually, the tune is called 'Greensleeves,' honey. It's one of those things you often see identified in song credits or sheet music as a traditional arrangement. They used to slap lyrics to whatever piece of music they felt fit the words. Someone obviously thought this tune was a good fit for the 'What Child Is This?' lyric."

"No way!" Brittany exclaims.

"Tell me more about school," Michelle says imperiously as she takes control of our get-together.

I savor my heavily buttered bread and study my daughter and ex-wife while they discuss Hyde Park Prep School. The years have added a studied grace and maturity to the natural blessings bestowed upon Michelle. With the judicious use of makeup, she's learned to tease her high, finely chiseled cheekbones into even more refined prominence. Her eyes are a pair of blue orbs in a hue just this side of the Hope diamond, framed by gracefully curling ebony lashes. Many a time I've looked at her and never seen beyond those eyes. Brittany shares most of Michelle's facial features but lacks the exotic flourishes that set Michelle off from other women. The more subdued effect is better suited to Brittany's unadorned character.

Michelle finds my eyes on her and smiles a smile I haven't seen in a long, long time. Despite myself, I feel the blood coursing through my veins a trifle faster than it was a moment ago. Damn her.

"Tell me about the new job, Tony," she orders.

"Nothing much to tell," I reply while setting down my bread. "We're just a couple of lowly lawyers trying to see that everyday folks get a fair shake."

"I don't suppose that pays very well," she muses with a half smile. It's always about the money with Michelle.

"After expenses, I probably make about as much as a public defender."

Her jaw actually drops. The daughter of Prescott Rice locks eyes with me to determine if I'm being serious. After all, we're talking chump change in the Rice paddy. Then she leans a few inches toward me, the subtle movement just enough to suggest an increasing level of intimacy. "Perhaps it wouldn't be fair for you to pay child support."

Spoken as if she's already won custody. Not surprising, coming from someone who is accustomed to having her way. I bite back the prideful retort that I don't need or want her charity. The truth is that I do. Rather than say something I'll regret, I pop another bite of bread into my mouth.

"What are you doing the rest of today?" Michelle asks after the server delivers our drinks. I've noticed her consulting her watch and the mental day timer that resides in her head to regulate the minutes and hours of her existence, no doubt wondering where Mommy and Daddy Rice are.

189

"No plans," I reply while wrapping my hands around my big blue mug and slurping a little Baileys off the top.

"When do you fly back to Chicago?"

"Nine o'clock," I reply as circulation finally returns to my fingers. Amputation due to frostbite might yet be avoided.

"Mother and Father were thinking we'd spend the afternoon and evening at the house."

"The house" is one of the coveted Georgetown brownstones within walking distance of Saint Matthew's Cathedral, the Rices' DC stand-in for New York City's Saint Patrick's Cathedral. Each church is *the* house of worship for Catholics who matter in its respective power center.

"All of us?" I ask.

Michelle looks embarrassed.

"That would have surprised me," I admit. Not that I have any interest in visiting with the Rice family.

"How would you feel about the three of us hanging out until you go?" Michelle asks.

I cock an eyebrow in surprise. "No Georgetown?"

She smiles. "No Georgetown."

Brittany seems to be enjoying the fact that her parents are being civil. It's been a long time since she's had a chance to hang out with the two of us. For her benefit, I smile back at Michelle. "I'd like that."

"I saw a news report about Hank Fraser's testimony," Michelle says while her eyes linger on me. "The man's turned out to be every bit the snake I pegged him for." She's referring to my former boss at Sphinx Financial, who is on trial for fraud relating to the financial shenanigans that precipitated the fall of the firm. Even I've been shocked by how brazen some of Fraser's scheming and scams were. Michelle had proven a far quicker study of him than I was. While initially charmed by his easy manner and solicitousness (hadn't we all been?), she'd begun warning me that Sphinx was hurtling down the tracks toward derailment even before the first whispers of alarm began to circulate within investment and banking circles.

"You're right," I admit, grudgingly acknowledging to myself that I'd been willfully ignorant in matters related to Sphinx—all too happy to grasp the brass ring Fraser dangled before my nose. I scrambled up the corporate ladder to dive into the muck of privilege and obscene perks we'd all happily wallowed in like swine rollicking in sewage. Many of us were still skimming along atop a sea of drowning shareholders when the good ship Sphinx finally turned turtle and precipitously plunged beneath the waves.

"I knew Fraser would hang you out to dry to save his own skin," Michelle adds. "Who knows what other mischief that man is capable of?"

Is she warning me that Sphinx may yet come back to bite me on the ass once again? I was eventually cleared of wrongdoing by separate Congressional and SEC investigations, but the stench of Sphinx continues to trail behind me.

"What do you mean?" I ask.

She gives me a knowing smile above the rim of her wineglass as she takes a sip. "You can be a little naive at times."

"Me?" I ask facetiously. It's no secret that I was a babe in the woods at the time of Sphinx. Probably still am, I suppose.

She smiles, but it fades quickly. "I hadn't trusted Fraser for a long time before things went sour. You knew that. Your association with that man frightened me."

"And I wouldn't listen to you."

"Things could have been so different," she says softly, perhaps even wistfully. "I was so angry with you for not listening, for not seeing what was happening."

"Angrier than I realized."

She nods. "Which only made me madder."

Is it possible I was once again so absorbed in what was happening to *me* that I made myself unavailable to those around me? My mind tracks to Papa and Mama. Do I count this failure number three? Four? Five? Will I ever be there for a person I love when he or she needs me to be?

"I'm sorry, Michelle."

Her appraising eyes burrow deeply into my soul before her hand slides across the table to squeeze mine. "Maybe I wasn't as supportive as I could have been."

I turn my hand over in hers and give hers a return hug. The spell is broken within seconds when a voice from the fringe of the dining room thunders, "Michelle!"

I wince when heads throughout the room turn as one toward the assault on the tranquil atmosphere we've been enjoying. A heavy hand cuffs my shoulder seconds later.

Prescott M.F. Rice III, the self-proclaimed "Oracle of Vesey Street"—where he once ruled the roost at an investment bank with world headquarters in Manhattan's World Financial Center—steps into my field of view. Rice made his bones as a young Wall Street investment banker with the takeover and pillaging of a venerable old company whose time had come and gone. With the support and connivance of institutional investors, he had swooped in and plucked control of the company from the bewildered family before they knew what hit them. The sycophant business press had breathlessly marveled at the naked chicanery as Rice stripped the company of assets, saddled it with a mountain of debt, and peddled it back to investors in a public offering. This "radical" new business strategy was actually nothing more than typical corporate bullshit iconography: produce a steaming pile of shit, slap the moniker "Daisy Fresh" on refreshed packaging, and then turn the marketing shysters loose on an unsuspecting public. The same scam also worked well on the mortgage-backed securities and similarly toxic financial derivatives Rice peddled in the new century. He escaped the 2008 financial crisis unscathed, but left a trail of heartbreak and financial ruin in his wake. What a great guy.

"Tony!" he booms, thrusting a meaty paw to within a few

inches of my chest and holding it there until I rise to shake it. My ex-father-in-law is a man of privilege whose years of overindulgence have left him with an overstuffed belly and sagging jowls.

"Hello, Prescott," I say.

"Haven't seen you in a while, boy."

So, "boy" replaces "son," which served as a substitute for Tony when I was married to his daughter. I like it no better—especially coming from a racist bastard who's never been shy about denigrating the worth of Black folks. We both know how low a blow he thinks he just landed.

With my fuse already smoldering, I wisely turn to an aristocratic woman who is, as always, impeccably dressed and coiffed, a trait she passed along to her daughter. Unlike Michelle, however, this woman of sophisticated appearance and stately bearing has the brains of a gnat. Also unlike her daughter, Evelyn Prescott is the type of vapid woman who revels in the trivialities and moral squalor of being the trophy wife of a rich and powerful blowhard.

"Hello, Evelyn," I say, my words colored with the affection I nonetheless feel for this woman, who has unfailingly treated me well through the years. Perhaps there's also an element of pity and compassion inherent in my feelings, something akin to what one feels for an especially abused pet.

Evelyn steps forward to hug the outer edges of my shoulders ever so lightly with her manicured fingertips while blowing a kiss just wide of my cheek. "It's *so* nice to see you, Tony."

"Evelyn's been a little concerned with all the troubles you've gotten yourself into," Prescott gloats with a smug grin. The bastard's undoubtedly enjoying every unkind word about me that he's able to lap up. Is it any wonder so many people quietly use his middle initials when referring to him? Or to describe him? Motherfucker, indeed. And to think that I'd once been one of the brainwashed business types who bought into the iconography about men like this. Hell, I'd even aspired to emulate them. Being up close and personal with Prescott Rice disabused me of the notion that there was anything to admire in such men.

"Nice to see you, too, Evelyn," I say as she settles into the chair next to mine.

Prescott bullies his daughter aside so he can sit next to his granddaughter and confront me face-to-face across the table. It also places him in the center of the group, the position he always aspires to and feels entitled to. While he grills Brittany about her life, I study him and wonder what stew of aberrant pathologies produced such a creature. He's got every material thing anyone could ever possibly need, and enough spare change hanging around to purchase it all over again two or three or even four times. Yet he still works, still loves to see his name in print, still loves—perhaps more than all the other perks and privileges combined—to strike fear into the hearts of people of lesser station. He retired from the firm three years ago to do the bidding of it and its brethren in the halls and backrooms of Congress. I've often thought he enjoys this bullying best of all. As formidable as Michelle can be, this man is my most dangerous adversary today. I make a point to avoid his gaze and only half listen, which allows me to tamp down my temper.

"We'd best order," Michelle says, picking up her menu to underscore the point.

My eyes land on the prime-rib-sandwich listing as soon as my menu falls open, prompting me to close it in almost the same motion.

Daddy Rice turns to me after we place our orders. "Let's get down to business." He shoots a sideways glance at his wife. "Take Brittany and go powder your noses or something for a few minutes. I'll send Michelle to fetch you when it's time to come back."

I shake my head slowly. "I know what game you're playing, Prescott. I'm not playing along."

Brittany surprises everyone by cutting in with an emphatic, "I'm staying for this."

Michelle spins to Evelyn while her father nears detonation. As if Brittany hadn't uttered a word, she says, "There are some nice shops on King Street, Mother. Why don't you take Brittany and pick out a nice outfit or two?"

Evelyn's somewhat confused countenance brightens immediately. She reaches for Brittany's hand. "Doesn't that sound marvelous, sweetheart?"

Brittany yanks her hand back, then glares in turn at her grandfather and her mother. "You two want to play hardball? I saw the legal papers you sent to Dad."

I'm as stunned as everyone else is by this pronouncement.

"I also heard what you said to Dad when I was on my way to the bathroom," she hisses at her mother. "'What is *she* doing here?'"

The color drains from Michelle's face.

Brittany turns fully to her. "*You* left us, Mom, and now you start whining about wanting me back. *Why?* I was a latchkey kid in Brussels last year."

Michelle's initial shock is morphing into an angry scowl.

Brittany doesn't let up. "Dad's been my rock, my actual full-time parent. How dare you pretend that you care about me more than he does. How *dare* you suggest that he's an unfit parent! You want to go to court on this?"

For one of the few times in my life, I witness Michelle struck mute.

Brittany then turns on Prescott Rice and berates him in a tone I'll bet he hasn't heard in decades. "I *will* speak to the judge if this goes to court, Grandpa. I'll tell them who my real parent is."

He flashes her a scornful look. "You're just a child who

doesn't understand these things. Nor do you realize the risk you take by defying us, young lady."

"Is that a threat?" Brittany shoots back.

"Of course not, honey," Michelle cuts in. The stony glare Daddy Rice has fixed on his granddaughter says otherwise.

"The hell it isn't!" Brittany explodes with a quick sideways glance at her mother. Then she meets her grandfather's smoldering eyes. "I know bullying when I see it."

Daddy Rice turns a baleful look on Michelle. "Get a grip on your daughter! I will not be spoken to this way."

Michelle grabs Brittany's arm. "That's enough out of you!"

Brittany throws off her mother's hand. "What's the statute of limitations for assault, Mom?"

Michelle's eyes go wide. "What?"

"The frying-pan incident?"

Michelle replies with an uncomfortable laugh and waves a hand dismissively. "My goodness, Brittany. You know that was an accident."

"I'm not an idiot, Mother," Brittany retorts in a tone that makes *mother* sound like an epithet. "I was there. I *saw* what happened. That wasn't an accident."

"Of course, it was. The frying pan was a little greasy. It slipped."

Brittany does an eye roll. "*Riiight.* Come on, Mom. Why don't you just admit that you had one of your temper tantrums and attacked Dad?"

Prescott Rice has heard enough. "Stop, goddamn it!" he shouts while pounding a fist on the table.

I'm surprised none of the bouncing tableware topples to the floor. Michelle and especially Evelyn are mortified when the stares of our fellow diners settle on Daddy Rice, who doesn't notice at all.

"Even *if* Tony is determined to try to make something out of this story, it isn't happening," he proclaims.

"*If* I wanted to make something of it?" I retort. "If I'd

wanted to make something of it, I would have done so when it happened."

He carries on as if I haven't spoken. "There are no witnesses to what happened, anyway."

"What about me?" Brittany shoots back indignantly.

Rice's tone is dismissive when he replies, "You're a child. Your father has poisoned your mind against your mother. We're talking about his word against Michelle's in a court of law, for God's sake. A serial liar who should be in jail for his time at Sphinx! *His* word against *my* daughter's?" he says after leveling a finger at me. A harsh laugh escapes him as he sneers and mockingly challenges me to "Bring it on."

I ignore him and lock eyes with Michelle. "You didn't tell Daddy about my visit to the hospital?"

"High drama!" Rice exclaims as he slams a fist on the table again and turns his malicious eyes on me. "Angling to get a piece of my fortune by faking an injury? Hell, even for you, boy, that's pathetic."

"That's right," I shoot back. "I faked thirteen stitches and a third-degree grease burn."

His eyes widen a smidgen. I guess Michelle didn't give him all the details. I'm happy to.

"The ER doctor didn't buy our little story about how the frying pan slipped," I continue. "She wasn't fooled. She referred the matter to the police and recommended a battery complaint. They talked to me, you know. I'm sure there's a record." *How would throwing that out in court square with avoiding any public unpleasantness, asshole?*

The potential embarrassment of my going public with this tale lands on Daddy Rice and his daughter like a sucker punch. I can all but hear the gears grinding in their minds as they seek a way to turn this to their advantage. Good luck with that. Rice throws his napkin down, stands, and commands his wife and daughter to follow as he stalks out of Gadsby's.

I look on Brittany with wonder. Who needs a temper when he has a daughter who can rip into people the way Brittany just did? Makes sense, I suppose—her parents both know a thing or two about losing their shit.

"Guess we won, huh?" Brittany says with a sheepish grin.

I smile back. "What were you doing reading through that lawsuit?"

"You should be careful where you leave things. You're not mad at me, are you?"

I slap my hand over hers and squeeze. "Of course not. Thanks for sticking with me."

"No worries," she says breezily.

It's a nice sentiment, but I know better than not to worry about her future. Especially with the Rice family gunning for me. Not that she needs to waste time worrying about her future. That's my job.

"Just stay the hell out of my stuff," I say gruffly, making sure to temper the admonishment with a wink.

CHAPTER TWENTY-TWO

I *should have done this a long time ago,* I think the next evening as Trish Pangborne sashays away from our intimate table for two at Cité, "Elegant Dining at the Top of Lake Point Tower," which is on the seventieth floor of an exclusive condominium tower along the lakefront. The restaurant had been Trish's idea, and it's a great choice—especially at our window table. She had tactfully declined the first table the hostess had brought us to, pointing down at the bright lights and the Ferris wheel of Navy Pier as she protested, "Oh, please, not a Navy Pier view." She'd then wrinkled her nose in distaste as she touched the woman's arm and stage-whispered, "There's nothing romantic in *that* view, is there?"

I've taken Billy Likens's advice and climbed back on the horse by asking Trish out to dinner. It's turning out to do be a good night for having done so; blowing off a little steam on the Rice family yesterday seems to have done me good, as did having had Brittany's unflinching support. There's still plenty to fret about, of course, but I've been able to push past it so far this evening. All seems to be well in Italy, and it's now been a week since Joe showed up in Papa's La-Z-Boy. The initial shock has passed, although Joe is certainly still a concern. The lawsuit crap, well, it's a lawsuit. It can wait until after the weekend. It's Saturday night and I intend to enjoy it with a lovely woman.

I take the liberty of ordering a second glass of wine for each of us when our server returns. Wine is one of the many things I know crap about, but Trish has selected something from somewhere in Germany... or maybe France? From some river in Europe that starts with the letter *R*, anyway. Then I sit back and enjoy the view framed by the floor-to-ceiling windows while I await Trish's return. Our table looks down on the sweep of Lake Shore Drive curving away south across the Chicago River with the skyline rising above it. The mirrored interior walls reflect the blue-and-gold accent lighting and the outside view back onto the glass, casting a decidedly soft and romantic ambience on the crisp, white linen tablecloth and intimate candlelight that flickers from within a low crystal holder. Even the polished stainless-steel utensils that reflect the lighting seem to have been chosen to complement the mellow mood.

I'm enjoying spending time with someone who's completely removed from my current routines and stressors. Joe's visit is a week in the rearview mirror, all appears to be copacetic in Italy, and I got through Friday the thirteenth not only unscathed, but with something of a victory over Prescott Rice. I'm in a good place tonight.

Trish is an attorney who works at Fleiss Lansky, a big corporate law firm where I plied my trade for a few months last year. They fired me because they didn't like the optics of my defending an alleged murderer (my father) while also waging a very public battle to save our neighborhood from the wrecking ball. Fleiss Lansky also played a big role in funding the startup of our law firm. Penelope negotiated a substantial settlement after filing a wrongful-dismissal lawsuit on my behalf. The law firm is, of course, where Trish and I met. She made no secret of her interest in me, and I certainly took notice of her. Who wouldn't? Trish is an alluring woman in her mid- to late thirties, petite, with lustrous wheat hair that hangs to the middle of her back. Her almond-shaped hazel eyes are mesmerizing, especially with the candlelight flickering in them. Tonight she's wearing a silky, deep-blue, knee-length dress that suggests rather than advertises the subtle curves beneath it. A delicate gold necklace is draped around her throat, and diamond earrings dangle an inch or so beneath her earlobes. Her glistening hair picks up highlights from the lighting as it bounces gently on her shoulders. She glides back from the washroom, enjoying my stare every step of the way. As she sits down, I'm struck by the realization that her face bears a resemblance to that of Melanie Likens. Interesting… and not a bad problem to have.

Small talk isn't one of my fortes, but Trish is easygoing and has graciously overlooked more than a few of my malapropisms. After she settles back into her seat and meets my gaze with a warm smile, I show off my stellar conversational skills by noting that her surname isn't a common one. "You're my first Pangborne. Is that your married name?"

"I wasn't bringing any of my ex along when I left," she says while reaching across the table to touch her fingertips to the back of my hand. A playful smile plays on her lips. "You're my first Valenti."

The touch is electric. How did I resist Trish all the time I was at Fleiss Lansky?

My phone comes to life and vibrates on the table. I should have turned the damned thing off, or at least silenced it. "Sorry," I mutter while reaching to power it off. A reference to Brittany in the text message from Pat that has just arrived stays my hand.

Is B there?

I assume Pat means at 47 Liberty Street. Why would she think that? I glance up at Trish. "Babysitter. Mind if I make a quick call?"

Trish smiles and shakes her head. "Of course not."

Pat picks up on the first ring and asks, "Is she with you?"

"No. What's up?"

"Probably nothing. She went to drama rehearsal at Jocelyn's house with Bobby. They've done it a few times now. He walks her home afterward. They've never been late before."

"I assume you've called?"

"A few times after I sent several texts. Straight to voicemail."

The ignored calls and voicemails aren't surprising—kids don't talk on or answer their phones. The unanswered texts, however, are out of character. I force the memory of Brittany and Bobby exchanging longing looks across the dinner table last week out of my mind. Well, I try to. "That's odd for her."

"Yeah, but listen to us," Pat says with an uncertain laugh. "It's hardly after nine on Saturday night. I'm sure they'll be along soon." She's probably right.

I say, "Have her text me as soon as she gets home."

"One of us will. Hearing your voice seems to have settled my nerves. Thanks for calling."

"Uh-huh."

"What are you up to?" she asks.

I look up and find Trish's concerned eyes on mine. Well, isn't this awkward? "I'm out for dinner with a friend," I reply in a tone I hope doesn't invite further inquiry, then wonder why. Pat has made it clear that she's not interested. Trish *is* interested. I've got nothing to hide and nothing to feel guilty about. Mel made it clear that even I deserve happiness.

"Oh!" Pat says in surprise. "I'll let you go."

Trish's eyes are still on mine when I disconnect, silence the phone, and jam it into my rear pants pocket.

"Everything okay?" she asks.

"Yup. My daughter's just a little late getting home."

Trish cocks her head to one side. "Your babysitter doesn't know you're out for dinner?"

"Long story," I reply without mentioning shootings, custody battles, or any of the other complications I could cite to explain why my daughter isn't living with me at the moment.

She accepts the explanation with a nod and then fixes me with an amused expression. "Isn't your daughter fifteen or sixteen?"

"Fifteen," I reply.

She laughs a deep smoky laugh that stirs something inside of me, then injects a little note of challenge in her voice when she asks, "What time did *you* get to stay out until on Saturdays when you were her age?"

I must sound like the ultimate parental ogre. "Midnight, maybe?"

Trish leans back in her seat and pastes a mock scowl on her face. "She's a girl, so she can't stay out?"

I chuckle and shake my head. "It's not like that! The babysitter's a little skittish, that's all." *For many good reasons,* I don't add.

Trish covers my hand with hers. "Just teasing you a little, Tony. She's a lucky girl to have a father who cares so much." Something in her tone and deep in her eyes makes me wonder if maybe her father wasn't all he should have been to his daughter.

Supper is excellent—the food and especially the company. We're polishing off cherries jubilee for two when Trish leans closer and smiles. "I'm really enjoying this, Tony."

"Then I guess we both are," I say with an answering smile.

Her eyes continue to hold mine. "No need for the evening to end yet. We can have coffee or a nightcap at my place."

"That sounds perfect," I reply while a little thrill passes through me. It's been a long time since I've felt the ache of anticipation when a woman looks at me the way Trish is doing right now. I signal to the waiter and mimic signing a check.

"Where to?" I ask as we leave the table two minutes later.

She takes my hand in hers. "Just to the elevators and down to the fifty-third floor."

She stands close and smiles up at me while the elevator takes us down seventeen floors. Her perfume is a very subtle and appealing fragrance, dabbed on so lightly that it's only noticeable at close quarters. We step off the elevator and saunter along a carpeted hallway to the door of her condominium. She lets us in and flicks a light switch, powering on a pair of wall sconces that cast little pools of intimate yellow light on the ceiling. The light reveals a sprawling living room with floor-to-ceiling windows that follow the rounded contours of the building. They say this building is oriented to afford every suite its own unobstructed view of Lake Michigan. It seems to be true.

My eyes stray back to Trish when she asks, "You like?" She's posed like a game-show hostess displaying a prize while she awaits my verdict with a smile playing on her lips. Is she asking about the living room? The view of the lake? Or her?

"Yes," I reply while holding her gaze. It's the correct answer to all three possibilities.

She glides close and eases up on her toes to plant a kiss on my cheek. "Thanks. I'm glad you're here."

"Glad to be here," I reply as she lingers with her shoulder brushing up against me.

She smiles and steps away. "Drink?"

"Bourbon?"

"I'll join you," she purrs before she steps over to a bar, takes two crystal tumblers off a shelf, and fills them from a bottle of Knob Creek bourbon. It's a brand I used to indulge in back when I was pulling down a corporate lawyer's ransom. She hands one drink to me, and we touch glasses before taking a sip. It's spicy, sweet, and smooth as melted butter, a definite step up from my usual Maker's Mark bourbon—which comes as a surprise after I'd convinced myself that I can't tell the difference between it and premium bourbon. Maybe being with Trish just makes everything better.

"To good friends and good times," she says while peering up at me over the rim of her glass.

"Indeed," I reply hoarsely to the promise in her eyes.

Her eyes linger on mine for a long moment before she smiles and sets her drink down on a nearby glass coffee table. "I'm going to go freshen up a bit. Back in a minute," she says over her shoulder as she sways away.

My imagination edges into overdrive as I watch her slip into what appears to be a bedroom no more than fifteen or twenty feet away. I settle at one end of a supple wine-colored fabric sofa, pull my phone out from where it's digging into my butt, and give in to a niggling voice that has been nagging at the back of my mind even as thoughts of Trish fill my head. I'm surprised to see a couple of new text messages and a missed call from Pat. Nothing from Brittany. The red voice-mail icon is flashing. Shit. I can't not check in. Hopefully, Trish won't walk back in while I do.

Pat's voice is filled with worry when I listen to her voice-mail. It's thirty-five minutes old. "Why aren't you answering? Having both of you out of reach is making me crazy."

Which means she still hasn't heard from Brittany. I scroll through the text messages. Same story. The most recent one was sent ten minutes ago. Not good. I think of my date "freshening up" only several feet away. *Why now with the Brittany drama?* I wonder as Trish emerges.

"What's the matter?" she asks as she settles close beside me on the sofa with her warm thigh touching mine.

"Brittany still hasn't been heard from."

"Hmmm." She lifts my wrist and looks at the face of my Rolex watch. "You're worried," she says when her eyes come back to mine. Hers are soft and warm. Concerned... with maybe just a hint of the disappointment I feel lurking beneath the worry.

I nod, taking note that she hasn't returned in a slinky nightgown or a robe with nothing beneath it. Whatever "freshening up" entailed isn't obvious, not that she needed to do anything to improve on how lovely she looks tonight.

Trish's hand slides from my watch to my hand and squeezes reassuringly. "Call."

Our eyes telegraph a mutual hope that the call will put the matter of the missing Brittany to bed for tonight.

"Tony!" Pat exclaims in relief. "Is she there?"

I again assume she means our house on Liberty Street. "I'm not home," I remind her.

Pat is silent for a moment before she blurts, "Where the hell are you, then?"

"With a friend."

"She's still not answering her phone or my text messages," Pat anxiously announces after a beat. "Did you know that your land line is out of service?"

"We don't have it anymore, Pat. I got rid of it when we gave Papa Britt's old phone."

"Oh. I called Bobby's parents, and he isn't answering, either."

What are those two up to? Drugs? An accident? Who knows what other trouble kids get themselves into nowadays?

"Maybe she needs you and went to the house to see you," Pat says impatiently. "I thought you'd check after we spoke earlier."

I probably should have. I swallow a little bubble of guilt. What if Brittany went home and ran into one of Joe's boys, or Joe himself? "I'll go now," I announce, and wince at the disappointment that seeps into Trish's eyes.

She lays her head on my shoulder after I end the call and looks up at me. "Maybe I'll come with?"

There's no time to explain the many ways in which that's a bad idea. I lift Trish's chin with a fingertip and look into her eyes. "Any other time that would be a wonderful idea, just not tonight. There's some dangerous stuff going on around our place that I won't expose you to. Lame as this sounds, can I have a rain check?"

She gives me an ineffably sad smile and nods.

Does she think I'm bullshitting her? I take her face in both hands. "I promise you, Trish. I hate that this is happening tonight. It's just… complicated, and I don't have time to explain."

I can tell that she wants to believe, but there's hurt somewhere in the depths of her eyes that won't let her.

I cradle her face gently. "Did you see the news about the retired cop who was shot and killed in Cedar Heights a couple of weeks ago?"

She nods with a look of confusion, as if to ask what on earth that has to do with us tonight. "I heard something, but you know I don't follow the news."

I'd forgotten. "That happened at our house, Trish. It's not over yet."

Her eyes pop wide open. "Oh my God!" she exclaims as she pulls away, bounces to her feet, and pulls me up after her. "Your daughter could be in danger?"

I nod.

She throws her arms around my neck and holds me close with her frightened body quivering against mine for a long moment. God forgive me in the circumstance, but I feel every contour of her lithe form pressing against me.

"Go!" she orders when she pulls back. "Please be careful, Tony. Call with any news. Any time," she adds as she pushes me out the door.

CHAPTER TWENTY-THREE

Detective Jake Plummer, bless his heart, has answered my panicked plea for help the following morning. Brittany still hasn't been heard from, nor has Bobby Harland. They were last seen departing the drama meeting just after seven o'clock last night. After I finally got home to find neither Brittany nor any indication that she'd been there, Pat had called the cops to file a missing person report.

I watch from inside a busy Dunkin' near Cedar Heights PD headquarters as Jake exits his unmarked police car and hustles inside. Cops and others mill about, coming and going in a cacophony of conversations and shouted orders. The scents of baking, coffee, and fast-food cooking compete for olfactory supremacy.

"Coffee?" he mouths after he gets into the order line.

I shake my head and point at the cup sitting in front of me, my tenth or twentieth of the interminable night and morning. I fidget nervously until Jake finally slips into the molded plastic seat on the opposite side of my table for two. He arrives with a tall coffee and—what else for a cop?—two doughnuts.

"Yeah, yeah," he sighs when he catches me looking. "A cop and his doughnuts."

I don't reply, just sit and watch him getting organized with sugar and creamers and napkins. He chatters while he does. "Still bugs me that the corporate dicks who run this joint dropped the word Donut to change the name to Dunkin'," he continues without waiting for an answer. "It's a doughnut shop! I don't even wanna think about how much this boondoggle costs me every time I buy a doughnut. Supposed to appeal to younger customers or some such bullshit. Read somewhere that they kept the pink-and-orange color scheme to reassure old farts like me that I'm still welcome. Bunch of corporate doublespeak, if you ask me. I swear to God, we should be sending young cops to the overblown ego-stoking productions these corporate executives indulge in to herald the latest and greatest BS they're peddling. Great way to teach rookies how to spot someone spouting a line of horseshit. Good practice for the interrogation room."

I've got other things on my mind. "Thanks for coming, Jake."

"No problem," he says before he bites off half a doughnut in a single go. He chews and swallows. "Max is back from Italy. Says he could happily live in that little Italian village Francesco is holed up in. He stuck around for a few extra days to make sure everything seemed to be okay and fell in love with the place."

Jake's detective game face slides into place when he looks up from his doughnut and finds me sitting mute and disinterested in his news. "What's up?"

I fill him in on the events of last night and conclude, "They're still missing."

Jake pushes the doughnuts and coffee aside, plunks his notebook on the table, and starts scribbling while he walks me through the story and wrangles every conceivable detail he can think of out of me.

"What's the word from patrol?" he asks when I finish.

"Not a thing," I reply bitterly.

"Which is why you called me. They gave you the story that a person has to be missing for twenty-four hours before they'll do anything, huh?"

I nod. "Seems like bullshit when we're talking about a couple of kids."

"Yeah, it is."

"I know missing kids isn't really your thing," I say by way of apology. I don't really mean it. I want his help.

"It isn't until it is," he mutters, then winces for having said that to a parent who's still clinging to hope. "Sorry."

I shrug it off. Sort of.

"You've been in touch with this Bobby's parents, right?" he asks while looking down at his notes.

"Pat has. They're scared shitless, too. He's a good kid."

Jake's eyes rise to mine. "Let's hope so. How well do you know this kid?"

"Not well," I admit, "but—"

"If cops had a dime for every time we've heard that about some prick who abuses a woman or worse," he interjects. Then his face falls again. "Jesus, I'm sorry I put it that way."

As if I don't already have enough scary ideas bouncing around my skull about what may have befallen Brittany, that somehow hadn't yet occurred to me. I grow more incensed as the idea begins to fester, but my anger isn't directed at Jake. "The asshole cops we talked to last night and this morning chalked it up to a couple of kids out for the night with their raging teenage hormones taking their natural course. You know where they were going with that."

Jake nods. "They may be right."

"Damn it—"

He cuts me off with a raised hand. "It's a possibility, Tony, but only one of several. The guys Pat spoke with *should* have considered the not-so-innocent explanations, especially once their minds turned over the sexual possibilities."

"Such as only Bobby's hormones getting out of control."

"Yeah," he mutters while he gathers up the half doughnut and inhales it. He wraps the second doughnut in a napkin and jams it into one of his suit-jacket pockets as he stands and grabs his coffee. "Let's go."

"Where?" I ask as I scramble to my feet.

"Down to the station to make sure a missing person report gets filed and worked. It's time to get this show on the road."

We take his car, which smells much like the inside of Dunkin'. While he peels out of the parking lot, he orders me to call Bobby's parents to make sure they've filed a missing person report on their son. "Give them my name and number and tell their local cops to call me if they need a kick in the ass to get to work on it."

I'm still on the phone with Mr. Harland when we park behind Cedar Heights PD headquarters. Jake taps his fingers impatiently on the steering wheel while I finish my call. He flings the car door open when I end the conversation, then waves me out. We march inside and go straight to the front desk. "Busy morning?" he asks a cop sitting behind a ballistic glass partition that separates him from the lobby.

"Pretty quiet, Detective Plummer," the guy replies airily.

"Hrumph," Jake mutters as we continue deeper into the building in search of the watch commander. We find him at a desk, sitting amid a mountain of paper, a half-filled paper coffee cup, and a half-empty polycarbonate package of grocery-store miniature cinnamon doughnuts.

"I hear it's a quiet morning around here, huh?" Jake asks.

The sergeant appears pleased about it when he smiles and nods.

"Quiet night, too?" Jake continues. "Night shift didn't leave anything pressing for you guys to work?"

"Nope."

Jake angrily relates what he knows about the disappearance of Brittany and Bobby. "This case better not end up on my desk because you guys have been diddling the dog while a couple of kids are unaccounted for."

The sergeant's nostrils flare. "I didn't know," he retorts indignantly.

Jake is stone-faced as he stares back. After giving the sergeant a moment to think things through, he asks, "You were unaware that these kids are missing, or you're just incurious?" His tone makes clear that he considers neither answer acceptable.

The sergeant finally looks a little chagrined.

Jake tilts his head my way. "Meet Tony Valenti, the father of the missing girl. Perhaps one of your not-so-busy people can find a few minutes to help Mr. Valenti locate his daughter?"

After muttering a half-assed apology, the sergeant gets to work. I furnish more information and email him a recent picture of Brittany.

"What about Brittany's mother?" Jake asks after we finish and walk to the squad room and settle at his desk.

My shoulders sag at the mention of Michelle. "What about her?"

"Has she heard from Brittany?"

"If so, I would have heard from her."

"You haven't called?"

I shake my head. "She's angling for full custody. If something bad has happened, she won't know any more than I do, but she'll complicate things for everyone. I'll call if and when I have news."

Jake doesn't look convinced, but doesn't argue. I'm not entirely sure I'm doing the right thing where Michelle is concerned, but I honestly can't see how involving her will help things. If Brittany and Bobby have sneaked off to be together, there'll be plenty of time to bring Michelle into the mix once the dust settles. If something else is going on, Michelle (and inevitably her father) will go on the warpath to use our daughter's misfortune to slam me and advance her argument for full custody. Maybe I'm being selfish, I don't know, but this seems like the right approach at the moment.

I sit at Jake's desk and drink coffee while he works and the shift supervisor does whatever it is he needs to do. Jake has said a couple of times now that it would be very unusual for two kids the age of Brittany and Bobby to be plucked off the street by persons unknown, so, while he doesn't discount my concern, he's leaning toward them turning up with some sort of teenage misadventure story to explain their disappearance. Hearing about Joe would change that in a heartbeat if I could tell Jake about the son of a bitch, but I don't dare risk it. Maybe I should have. Maybe I should. Jesus, but this has me screwed up. I've been berating myself for the last week for not having the presence of mind to bag up Joe's bourbon glass. Mind you, it was likely my own bourbon intake that had dulled my mental synapses enough that the idea didn't occur to me. One thing is for sure; if he comes back, I'll try to keep my head out of my ass on that score.

The desk sergeant calls an hour later to inform Jake that the missing person report is done and circulating.

It's time for me to go. "Thanks, Jake."

"Uh-huh. That's what we're *supposed* to be here for," he mutters angrily. "You get back to the house and hold tight. I asked the watch commander to have a patrol car roll by periodically."

"Thanks." Do I mention Joe? I feel immensely guilty that I'm holding out on Jake. He's trustworthy and would probably know how to keep things on the q.t., but imagining Joe's reaction to my telling the cops about our visit has me spooked. For some reason—quite possibly simple stupidity— I decide not to.

Jake peers up at me. "You got a gun yet?"

I shake my head no.

"Right, the famous Valenti firearm prohibition shtick," he scoffs. "Get yourself a damn gun, Tony."

I wish I had a gun when I walk into my living room and again find Joe camped out in Papa's La-Z-Boy. He's brought a couple of friends this morning. Big friends—even larger than himself. Maybe the gun isn't such a good idea. I'm pretty sure I know who would come out on the wrong end of a shootout at the Valenti Corral.

"Where have you been?" Joe asks while he points at Mama's chair. "We've been here for a couple of hours."

"Just a little visit with the Cedar Heights PD," I reply, figuring I might as well get that on the table right away.

Joe's eyes narrow. "I hope you didn't mention our little get-together?"

I shake my head no as I sit and again wonder why I hadn't. At the moment, it seems like an especially dumb move—even for me.

Joe smiles. "Glad to hear that, Mr. Valenti. It's too late for cops now, anyway."

An icicle of fear gnaws its way into my heart. Why would he say that? There's only one reason that immediately comes to mind. I'm on my feet in a heartbeat, towering above Joe. "If anything happens to her—"

"*Sit*, Mr. Valenti!" he snaps as he pulls a handgun out of his lap and waves it lazily in my direction. The goons, who have been hanging back in the corners of the room, take a couple of steps in my direction.

Me with a gun seems even more ill advised. Having one would have just gotten me shot.

"Sit," Joe repeats firmly as he stares up at me with the gun now centered squarely on my chest.

I sink back into my seat and glare at the son of a bitch who seems to have orchestrated my daughter's disappearance.

"That's better," Joe says easily while the goons melt back into their corners. Then he settles back in the seat, folds his arms across his chest, and examines me for a long moment. "Did you file a missing person report?"

I decide to tell part of the truth and hope he's none the wiser. "Not personally. A friend did so last night without me knowing. Bobby Harland's parents have filed one, as well."

Joe's scowl lets me know that he doesn't like this revelation. "Meaning their faces will be plastered on every milk carton in Chicagoland within a day or two."

I don't think they do the milk-carton thing anymore, but there's no point mentioning it. I shrug. "Nothing I could do to prevent that."

He considers that for several seconds. "Perhaps not. You will *not* breathe a word about this to the police. Understood?"

I don't reply immediately as the possibility of telling Jake about Joe plays through my mind. My eyes roam over the living room tables, hoping to spy a glass Joe might have touched. Nothing, damn it. I'll at least throw a blanket over the La-Z-Boy after he leaves. Maybe the cops will find a fingerprint or two, or maybe some lint or whatever else they collect at crime scenes.

"Understood?" Joe repeats harshly.

The menace in his tone gets my full attention. I nod.

He switches back to conversational mode. "We should discuss a few things, Mr. Valenti."

Things that will undoubtedly involve the well-being of my father and daughter. I swallow and do what I can to tamp down the terror in my voice when I ask, "What things?"

"The whereabouts of your father, for one thing."

"I already told you that I don't know where he is."

He cocks an eyebrow. "And you haven't heard from him?"

"No."

His skeptical expression calls bullshit on me, but he doesn't pursue it. Bigger fish to fry? A slow smile creeps over his face. "That daughter of yours is a lovely girl. It would be a shame if something untoward were to happen to her."

"You son of a bitch," I snarl with my hands locked on the armrests of my chair to hold me in place. He's three, four feet away—I can probably get my hands around his neck before he can lift his gun. My threatening tone prompts movement in the periphery of my vision as Joe's goombahs go on point. "Where is she?"

Joe taunts me with a mocking smile. "Now, now, Mr. Valenti. You *know* I can't tell you that. Rest assured that Brittany is safe... for the moment. Comfortable even, especially locked away in a bedroom with that beefcake boyfriend of hers."

This is the first time he's explicitly acknowledged that he has Brittany and Bobby. *I should have seen this coming,* I think as the final moments of his visit last week play through my memory: "Have it your way, Mr. Valenti. I'm afraid you'll have to live with the responsibility for what happens next." This is all my fault.

"The boyfriend was a bit of an unwelcome complication," Joe continues. "But he might prove useful in keeping Brittany under control." He shoots a grin at the goons and adds, "Couple of good-looking fifteen-year-olds with raging hormones thrown together in a tough spot they might not get out of. It's a good bet that Bobby's keeping Brittany's mind off her troubles by fucking her brains out, huh?"

"Are you trying to provoke me?" I growl through clenched teeth while the goons chuckle.

Joe waves the notion aside.

"Just shoot me and be done with it if that's what you're here to do," I say.

Joe purses his lips and shakes his head. "It *may* yet come to that, Mr. Valenti—for all of you—but I've come today to make a point or two."

I glare at him wordlessly while my imagination plays out a scene of my caving his head in with Papa's floor lamp.

Something lurking in Joe's amused eyes suggests that he knows I'm thinking tough-guy thoughts. He doesn't look worried. "So, no cops, Mr. Valenti."

How many times is he going to tell me that?

"We *will* know if you talk to any cops," he warns me with a pointed look.

The bastards probably *do* have eyes and ears within the local police forces. Hell, Jake was worried about just that possibility the night we spirited Papa and Max out of the country. Joe seems to be waiting for an answer when my mind returns to the present. I nod curtly.

He dips his head in acknowledgment. "Are you ready to tell us where Francesco is?"

When I realize that he's leading up to exchanging my daughter's safety for my father's whereabouts, I stare back at him with as pure a hatred as I've ever felt toward a human being—not that this animal is anything more than a feral beast. What the hell do I do now?

Joe rests his elbows on his knees and eases closer. "The other thing we discussed last week was your legal work for R & B Ramp Services. Don't allow yourself to lose sight of your obligations in that matter, Mr. Valenti. The well-being of your daughter depends on it, yet we understand that you and your partner are not cooperating with our people."

"Your people?"

"The lawyers who represent our friends, Mr. Valenti. Your performance in court last week doesn't inspire confidence. It' time for you to work with our folks to arrive at a settlement."

I trust you've given some thought to how you can assure me that our mutual interests are aligned in that matter?"

Yeah, I've given this some thought, but not in the way he wants. I'm trying to figure a way out of this mess. Unsuccessfully. The leverage this guy has over me is like being squeezed in a vise. I nod dejectedly.

"Well?" Joe asks. "Ready to play ball?"

Am I? My daughter's life is at immediate risk. At least I hope it is. I've only got this asshole's word that she's even alive. My father's life will probably be forfeit if I reveal his whereabouts. The ruination of Billy Likens's future is assured if I play along. I can't betray any of them. I stare back implacably at Joe. I need to play for time while I figure out a way to turn the tables on this worthless piece of shit.

Joe frowns. "You're a hardheaded son of a gun, aren't you? Not necessarily a quality I disapprove of, but stupid when you hold no cards, Mr. Valenti."

My stomach is digesting itself while I stare back at him in the forlorn hope that he doesn't smell the fear emanating off me like steam in a sauna. Of course, he smells it. All predators play on and exploit the fear of their prey.

Joe slaps his thighs and gets to his feet, then fixes me with a long, intense stare. "You're playing a dangerous game with other people's lives."

Don't I know it.

"Let's go, boys," he says to his gorillas, who obediently follow him to the front door. Joe pauses with his hand on the doorknob and looks back at me. "The clock is ticking, Mr. Valenti. I'll expect to hear the answers I want within forty-eight hours."

And then? I wonder while an overpowering wave of gloom rolls over me.

CHAPTER TWENTY-FOUR

I t's Monday when I wake up the next morning. Brittany has now been missing going on two days, and I'm twenty-four hours into the forty-eight hours Joe has given me to fold. I tossed and turned all night, wrestling with the impossible conundrum I'm in. I'd be surprised if I managed even a single solid hour of sleep. I gulp down a cup of coffee and a banana before leaving for work.

"Tony?" Penelope asks an hour later, after I zone out on her yet again.

I'm not sure why I'm here. It may be because it offers a potential distraction, as if anything has a hope of seriously distracting me from the nightmare unfolding around me. Or maybe I'm trying to keep up appearances so that I don't arouse suspicions that there's more amiss than "simply" a missing daughter. I'm too fried to even know what I think much of the time.

Penelope walks around her desk and settles into the visitor's chair beside mine. She takes my hand in hers and gazes intently into my bloodshot, scratchy eyes. "You don't need to be here, Tony. Mom and I can hold the fort for a few days."

The unspoken end of the phrase is implicit in the river of

empathy flowing through Penelope's eyes and touch... *until you find Brittany.*

Tears well up in my eyes and a sob escapes me when Penelope reaches her arms around me and pulls my head to her shoulder. She doesn't say a word, correctly judging that nothing she can say will soothe me as much as her simple gesture of humanity. We sit like this for a couple of minutes before I ease out of her arms, wipe my nose on a Kleenex that has magically appeared in my hand from hers, and smile sadly. "Thanks."

She pats my hand. "Any time, partner."

We sit quietly for several seconds while she waits for me to make the next move.

"Let's go through this stuff again," I suggest. It's been a busy couple of days on the R & B front. My muddled mind is having a hard time assembling it all into a coherent narrative. "You don't mind?"

"Not at all," she replies. "Let me top up my coffee. You want one?"

I nod. "Please."

I pull a print copy of yesterday's *Chicago Sun-Times* in front of me and scan through Sandy Irving's latest "bomb-shell" story about the investigation into "the Tragic Milton Crash" while I wait for Penelope to return. This time Irving's been fed a tidbit that "structural failure cannot be ruled out." She's also been cleverly served a scoop that "a mandatory inspection that might have revealed structural deficiencies in a failed wing strut may not have been completed by R & B Ramp Services. Authorities are investigating allegations that records pertaining to the alleged non-inspection may have been falsified."

"What bullshit," I grumble. "We've seen the damned invoice for the work."

Penelope nods. "Windy City never paid that invoice, you know."

"They didn't?"

"Billy told me that Walton says they aren't paying for work that wasn't done."

"But it *was* done!"

Penelope nods. "Smells of a set-up, doesn't it?"

Jesus. How many blind alleys are we going to wander into by the time this nightmare ends?

"But how?" I ask. "We've seen the invoice."

"The question is: What are the FBI and NTSB looking at? Sandy Irving suggested that there may be falsified paper-work. If so, who doctored it?"

"And how," I mutter.

She nods.

I fold the paper closed and launch it at Penelope's trash can as she circles back to her desk chair after setting a steaming cup of coffee in front of me. "I hope this Irving bitch is being well compensated for spreading bullshit."

Penelope frowns. "Nice as it would be to catch her with her hand in the cookie jar, I doubt any money is changing hands. Sandy Irving strikes me as one of those ambitious people who doesn't let scruples get in the way of getting her byline on a sensational story."

The characterization echoes Pat's scathing accusation that her cross-town rival "lacks even the most basic respect for journalistic ethics."

I sink back in my seat and attempt to organize my thoughts. "What's the point?"

"Of Irving's story?" Penelope asks as her eyes drift to the newspaper on the floor about two feet wide of the garbage pail.

"Yeah. What's the point of that article? Who's her source? What's their game?"

She shrugs. "If I had to guess, I'd say someone is laying groundwork for a future trial."

My mind drifts away to Brittany. Where is she? Which

leads me to thoughts of Joe. Is he behind Sandy Irving's stories? If so, is he expecting a reaction from me? Am I doing or failing to do something that's putting Brittany in more jeopardy, assuming she's even alive? God, this is torture.

Joan Brooks pokes her head in. "Ben Larose is here, honey."

"Thanks," Penelope says to her mother. Then she glances at me. "Ready?"

I nod.

Joan gives me a soft-eyed look dripping with empathy before she backs out. Like mother, like daughter.

Larose enters. After the initial greetings are dispensed with, he stands awkwardly and meets my gaze. Then he shrugs as if he's at a loss for words. "Sorry, Tony," he finally mutters uncertainly. What else is there to say to a father who doesn't know if his daughter is dead or alive?

I nod. The topic of Brittany is quietly set aside.

"Any more news on the fuel sample?" Penelope asks after Larose settles into the second guest chair beside mine. It's a tight squeeze, two sets of long legs wedged into a space more suitable to the limbs of grade school kids.

He shakes his head.

I have a vague recollection about something to do with a missing fuel sample. I ask him to fill me in on the details.

He shoots a concerned sideways glance at Penelope. I get it. He's wondering, "How can he not know all about this?"

She gives him an almost imperceptible nod and graciously says, "I'd like to hear it again, too."

Larose nods and turns back to me. "The NTSB recovered an uncontaminated fuel sample from the engine block of the Cessna."

I nod. This much I know.

"The sample they sent for testing went missing sometime in the past week or two," he continues. "The original thinking was that it had been misplaced in the lab and would turn up when they had a good look around."

"It hasn't?"

Larose shakes his head with a disturbed expression. "Not only that, but a second sample they held back from testing for just that eventuality is also nowhere to be found."

"Casting doubt on the misplaced-fuel scenario," Penelope adds.

"Correct," he agrees with furrowed brow. "This kind of stuff simply *doesn't* happen during an NTSB investigation."

Apparently, it does, I think before asking, "Do they at least have the test results?"

Larose nods, but his expression remains troubled.

"The rumor is that the test results indicated that the fuel was contaminated," Penelope says. "The problem for us is that nobody *but* the NTSB can utilize those test results."

That's right. NTSB reports cannot be presented as evidence in a court of law, damn it.

"Contaminated with what?" I ask.

"Nothing nefarious," Larose replies. "It sounds like there was water in it. The contamination was fairly minor, so it may or may not have been a contributing factor. That's what makes the loss of the backup sample so devastating. Without test results, there's no way to hold AAA Avgas legally accountable for pumping bad fuel into that aircraft."

Even my addled brain can process how dire the implications of that news might be for our clients. Without tainted fuel to hold out as a cause for the crash, the lawyers for the plaintiff will almost surely turn to an argument pointing a finger at faulty maintenance. Penelope sags back in her chair and stares up at the ceiling, deep in thought. Larose sits quietly, as do I. Thoughts of my daughter quickly flood into the temporary vacuum in the discussion.

Where is she? Is she still alive? If so, how do I keep her that way? Answers are just as elusive as they were the other ten thousand times I've posed those questions to myself since Saturday night.

"Tony?" Penelope says softly, breaking into my reverie.

Without quite knowing when I assumed the position, I find my forehead resting on my crossed arms on Penelope's desk. "Sorry," I murmur as I look up.

She waves the apology aside before her eyes slide over to Larose. "The insurance company has the aircraft, right?"

"They should still have it," he replies. "The NTSB turned it over to them some time ago, though. If they're done with it, they'll probably sell it for scrap."

"We need to file an injunction to preserve any additional fuel trapped in the engine block," Penelope says. "Actually, to preserve the entire aircraft."

"I agree about the wreckage, but there are two problems with the fuel angle," Larose says. Penelope's brow furrows in disappointment as he continues, "Even if there is more recoverable fuel in the engine block and it's contaminated, there's no way to prove it didn't happen sometime during the past couple of months."

A great weariness settles over me. Are we ever going to catch a break in this damned case? And if we do, will it cost my daughter her life?

"Rumor has it that Windy City and their insurance company have reached a settlement in their lawsuit," Larose says next.

"What does that mean to us?" I ask.

His shoulders sag. "I'm told the settlement stipulates that all details and materials amassed by the insurance company are to be considered confidential and privileged information."

Penelope groans and swears for the first time in my experience. "Damn!" she mutters while slapping a hand on her armrest in frustration.

"We can sue for release of the information," I suggest.

"I wouldn't bet on winning," she says thoughtfully. "That

wreckage is starting to look like the only thing we'll have to work with. We need to get our hands on it."

"If the FBI charges Billy and Rick, how are we supposed to defend them?" I wonder in horror.

"Good question," my partner replies. Then, as she usually does, Penelope unearths a silver lining. "Mind you, in that case we'd have the urgency of a criminal trial to argue for overturning the confidentiality provision of the settlement between Windy City and their insurance company."

So, I'm supposed to be excited about the prospect of criminal charges being laid against our client? How in hell did things come to this?

Penelope squares her shoulders as if she's gearing up for battle. "We'll start by suing AAA Avgas for all their records from the week before and after the crash. Heck, we'll countersue Windy City to make sure that we get our hands on everything they have when they turn over discovery."

"Go after every scrap of paper you can lay your hands on about Megan Walton and the rest of their pilots," Larose suggests.

I'm stricken with horror over the potential ramifications from us going after AAA Avgas and Windy City. Joe was pretty clear that he was looking out for their interests. Not for the first time in the past few days, I feel as if I may buckle beneath the weight of the competing interests at war within me. The lives of multiple people—Brittany, Papa, Billy Likens, Rick Hogan, and Bobby Harland—will potentially be put at risk or devastated by whatever we do.

Penelope is again staring at me with open concern, which fills me with guilt and remorse. It's hardly fair that her partner is withholding pertinent information. But she can't know everything. Or can she?

I throw my hands up and stand. "I don't know what the hell to do!" I exclaim before I turn away and stalk out the door. Which is a massive mistake. I should have sat Penelope down and told her all about Joe. But I didn't.

Thinking we're in agreement, Penelope goes ahead and files suit against AAA Avgas and serves Windy City Sky Tours with a court order for all records pertaining to the hiring and training of their pilots, including Megan Walton. She also files a motion to have the plane wreckage preserved and turned over to us. Moving with her usual efficiency, she files all the actions the following morning.

The blowback isn't long in coming.

CHAPTER TWENTY-FIVE

Jake Plummer calls after dinner Wednesday evening, almost a full day beyond Joe's two-day deadline, and a day after Penelope filed her new motions.

"I need to see you right away," he says tersely.

My stomach twists into a tight, painful knot. "Why? Is Brittany okay?"

"As far as I know."

I'm overcome with relief for a nanosecond before his answer fully registers. "So far as he knows" means he doesn't know a damned thing more than he did yesterday. Or the day before that... or any of the days before that.

"Where are you?" he asks.

"I'm at home."

"Be right there."

"No!" I shout before he can sign off. If Joe's watching the house and a cop shows up, we're screwed. Not that I've gotten a whiff of anyone watching the house, despite continually looking over my shoulder and compulsively peeking out windows at all hours. Still, my fear of Joe's omnipresence is such that I assume someone *is* out there. Always.

There's a long silence before Jake asks, "What's up?"

"Long story, but can you sneak in through the alley and back door?"

"Seriously?"

"Please."

This is greeted by another prolonged silence. "Why?" he finally asks.

"I'll explain when you get here."

He sighs and grumbles "All right" before he signs off.

I've been home for most of the last couple of days. Putting Pat and Deano at risk with my presence at Pat's doesn't sit well with me, and the truth is that I'm not feeling as comfortable there as I had been when Brittany was there. Then there's the possibility, however remote, that Brittany might end up here for some reason. If she does, I need to be here. Trish Pangborne, who has called and texted with her support and managed to do so without being intrusive, has edged into my thoughts surprisingly often, given my preoccupation with Brittany. I'm immensely grateful for all Pat is doing, especially the way she's smothering the dog with love and attention as he recuperates, but things simply feel off when I'm around her. I'm not sure I'd be spending any time at Pat's if I wasn't going by to hang out with Deano as he recovers. There's no way I want him around Forty-Seven Liberty Street with the likes of Joe dropping in every now and then. It doesn't take much imagination to picture the outcome of Deano taking exception to Joe and company waltzing into the house uninvited. As for me, I've brought the danger upon myself, so it's my job—and mine alone—to deal with it.

In a bid to make Jake's visit as stealthy as possible, I turn off the exterior lights and make a quick sprint to the garage to unscrew the bulbs in the motion-detector lights that cover the yard and alley. I spend the next few minutes pacing around the house, pausing only to stare at pictures of my absent family—especially Brittany. Jake sounded upset. Would he have told me over the phone if something had happened to

Brittany? Probably not. That's how cops do it when someone dies; they tell you in person. I collapse into Papa's La-Z-Boy and bury my face in my hands. Has Joe retaliated for Penelope's filings at the courthouse yesterday? If so, he's moved quickly. Then again, I haven't exactly gotten with the program.

The thought of Joe and a mental image of Brittany's lifeless eyes shoots me out of the easy chair and into the kitchen for the bourbon. I'm well into a tumbler of it when pounding on the back door breaks through my stupor. I turn and spy Jake's agitated face in the window.

He steps inside with a look of concern and studies the almost-empty glass sitting on the kitchen table. "You okay?"

I nod.

"I got a little concerned when you didn't answer."

I cock a questioning eyebrow at him.

"The doorbell, Tony. I rang three times, then started pounding on the door before you noticed me."

Oh. "Sorry."

"You look like hell," he says after studying me for a few seconds. "Not sleeping?"

"What's sleep?" I force a smile, or I think I do while he leads me back to my seat at the kitchen table and plunks his ass down on one of the maple chairs. I can't bring myself to ask why he's here.

"I've got some tough news," he says after a beat.

I squeeze my eyes shut and wait for the hammer to fall.

"Bobby Harland's body was discovered this afternoon."

My eyes snap open and lock on Jake's. *"Bobby?"*

"Looks like he was killed sometime today and dumped inside the Independence Park pool change rooms."

Not Brittany! I think with relief. Then I'm immediately overwhelmed by crushing guilt for momentarily being elated that it's someone else's child who has died.

Jake sits patiently while I process the news. Jesus, Bobby's death is going to gut Brittany if she's alive to find out about it. Does Brittany know what happened? Did they make her watch? Dumping Bobby's corpse across the street is a message intended for me—Joe's admonishment for me missing his deadline, and possibly in retaliation for our new court filings that ramp up the heat on Windy City and AAA Avgas. Is it a warning that worse is still to come if I don't get my ass in gear and do something to torpedo our defense in the R & B in the lawsuit?

My thoughts turn to Independence Park. What a god-awful place for Bobby to end up. Recent images of the decrepit building come to mind. The pool and outbuildings I frequented in the summers of my youth have fallen into disrepair in recent years and have become a place for druggies, hookers, and their customers. Condoms, human and animal waste, and all other sorts of filth littered the place last time I saw it. The village has committed to a cleanup; I hope to God it's already underway. My vision narrows while I stare dumbstruck at a cabinet door and recall the few hours I spent with Bobby. Did I cause this? Might I have prevented it?

"Are they sure he was killed today?" I ask Jake.

"Yeah, they are." When I don't respond, he moves on. "The kids were obviously kidnapped. That's FBI turf."

"The FBI?" Won't Joe love that?

"That's right," Jake replies.

I nod dumbly. Is Brittany's lifeless corpse lying somewhere more remote than Independence Park?

"Even though nobody has contacted you with a ransom demand, we're now treating this as a kidnapping," Jake says. "The FBI has been notified and are taking over."

But demands *have* been made.

"They should be by to see you…." Jake's voice trails off as his eyes lock on mine. "That's correct, right?" he asks sharply. "No demands?"

What the hell do I do now? Joe will assume I've called the

FBI despite his warnings not to involve the cops. Then what? Bobby's already dead. If they haven't killed my daughter yet, they will now. "Jesus God," I groan before I pound the table with both fists.

Jake's eyes pop wide open. "Tony?"

My eyes touch on his as my mind careens wildly in search of a solution, seeking anything solid to grasp onto. God, this is all so screwed up! What should I have done differently?

Jake leans across the table and grabs my forearm. "Get a grip, Tony!"

My eyes finally focus on his face. His lips are moving, but no sound seems to be coming out. Should I tell him everything? Jake's proven himself to me time and again, but Joe will surely find out if I talk to him. I know he will. Then he'll kill Brittany if he hasn't already.

"The FBI can throw resources at this that I can only dream about," Jake is explaining when the roaring in my skull abates enough for me to tune him in again. "They have more bodies, more technology, more of everything. If anyone is going to bring Brittany home safely, it's the FBI."

Do I drop everything in Jake's lap?

He inches right up to the edge of the table and stares hard at me until he's sure he has my full attention. "No holding anything back when the FBI get here, Tony," he says firmly. "They'll have a much better shot at bringing her home safely if they know everything."

That's probably true, but.

Jake gets out of his chair and walks around the table to kneel beside me, then grasps my shoulders, turns me square to him, and gets right in my face. "You're making a big mistake holding things back from us, Tony. A *big* mistake."

I stare back into his eyes. So, he's figured me out. Not the details, of course, but he knows I'm keeping secrets. I look away and sigh heavily. He allows me ten seconds to come clean. Then his patience runs dry.

"What the hell's going on?" he asks sharply. "A teenage boy is dead, and you still think you can manage this on your own?"

His outburst is like a slap in the face. My eyes refocus on his. Anger and exasperation are there, yes, but compassion and concern are present, too. And fear. Our eyes remain locked for a few long seconds before my resistance evaporates in a huge, shuddering sigh. Apparently recognizing that he's broken me, Jake walks back around the table and resumes his seat. He folds his hands on the table and listens intently while I tell him about Joe. I leave nothing out.

"That's *everything*?" he asks when I stop talking.

I nod, feeling as if I've just wrestled a massive anvil off my chest. He walks me through it all again with notebook in hand while he takes copious notes.

"Jesus H. Christ," he mutters angrily after we finish. He thinks things through for a minute or two, then visibly relaxes and catches my eye. "I'll make sure the FBI gets this pronto, Tony. This is information we can act on immediately."

"Okay," I mumble.

"Where did this Joe guy sit when he was here?"

"Papa's La-Z-Boy."

"Which you've been sitting on every day since?"

I nod.

"Did he touch anything else? A glass maybe?"

"He had a glass of bourbon the first time he showed up."

"Where's the glass?"

"I ran it through the dishwasher with everything else," I reply sheepishly. "I threw a blanket over his chair after his last visit."

"Which was when?"

"Sunday evening. He didn't touch much of anything that time."

He nods without comment, then his eyes drift to the front door. "Have you seen anyone watching the house?"

I shake my head. "Not for lack of trying."

"How about when you're out and about? Anyone tailing you?"

"Not that I've seen."

"This Joe guy has you spooked, huh?"

"Damned right he does, Jake. He's got my daughter. He killed Bobby, for Christ's sake!"

Jake holds his hands up. "He's a gangster, man. Scum. You *should* be afraid of the guy, Tony, but here's the thing. He's *just* a two-bit gangster. He's not Superman. He can't be everywhere at once, and the Lucianos don't have the manpower to keep watch on *anyone* twenty-four-seven, let alone someone like you."

"So, I shouldn't worry about surveillance?"

Jake sighs. "Yeah, you should, but don't think they've got you staked out around the clock the way cops would."

"Should I have the house checked for bugs?"

He thinks on that a moment, then shakes his head. "That's not really their style. It's a lot tougher to do that effectively than people seem to think, but I'll send someone by to check if it'll make you feel better."

"Thanks."

"I'll send a fingerprint technician out to dust around the La-Z-Boy. You never know... sometimes we get lucky."

Of course, the chances of getting lucky would be far better if I'd had my wits about me that first night.

Jake closes his notebook and stuffs it into an inside pocket of his suit jacket. "Time for me to go to work," he announces as he gets to his feet. Then he levels a finger at me. "And time for you to get some sleep. You're already dead on your feet. You'll be no help to anyone if you don't get some rest."

"I can't sleep while Brittany is somewhere out there," I say weakly while throwing a wave toward the window.

"What you can and will do is get some damned sleep. You're not thinking straight, man. I'll send a uniform to sit on the house and make sure nobody surprises you while you rest."

I doubt I'll sleep a wink, but I'm too tired to argue the point. "What will you be doing?" I ask as he slips his coat on.

"Trying to figure out who the hell this Joe character is."

"How?" I ask doubtfully while trailing him to the door. "It's a great big world out there."

"The Lucianos are behind AAA Avgas," he tells me as he opens the inside door and pauses with his hand resting on the screen-door handle. "We'll pull hard at the Luciano thread. Sooner or later—hopefully *real* soon—that thread will come back to us with a noose around Joe's neck."

I don't have a clue how Jake plans to accomplish that, but he sounds determined and confident that he'll succeed.

"Someone will go through mug shots with you," Jake continues. "If Joe doesn't show up in the pictures, expect a visit from an FBI artist, who will do a composite sketch." A little smile turns up the corners of his lips. "Good call on using the back door. You even killed the motion lights, huh?"

I nod.

"Good thinking. I'll tell anyone else coming over to give you a heads-up and to use the alley. Make sure you power up the motion detectors between visitors."

"Will do."

"One final thing," he says." If Joe shows up here again, don't touch anything he may have touched and let us get a crime scene crew here immediately to look for prints or DNA."

With that, Jake shoves the door open and strides purposefully to the alley. A little kernel of hope stirs in the depths of the blind fear that has consumed me over the past few days.

I close the door and go straight to my daughter's bedroom to feed her goldfish, which I've brought home from Pat's. Brittany will have my ass if she comes home to find Pucker-face floating belly up because I forgot to feed him. Of course,

I'll happily take that outcome in a heartbeat if she comes home. There are more Puckerfaces in the ocean... or at the pet store. After sprinkling flakes of fish food on top of the water, I walk back into the living room, where I see an apparition of Joe sitting in Papa's La-Z-Boy. At least I think it's a mirage. Could this be some sort of psychic message that he already knows what I've just done? I close my eyes and shake my head to clear it, but the specter of Joe remains in the chair, once again warning me, "No cops, Mr. Valenti. We *will* know if you talk to them."

CHAPTER TWENTY-SIX

I t's late Friday morning, and Penelope is at the wheel of her silver Audi A4 sedan as we inch toward downtown on the Eisenhower "Expressway," where it's rush hour all day, every day. Brittany has now been missing for almost a week, and it's been two days since Bobby Harland's body was found. I know the statistics and understand that the odds of Brittany being found alive at this point are slender indeed. Yet there *is* a chance. We won't give up hope, and Jake and the FBI won't quit looking while there's even the slightest prospect of bringing her home safely. Miracles *do* happen— just not very often. One might say we've already experienced a little one in that I haven't yet collapsed from exhaustion. Or despair. I've dipped into Papa's medicine cabinet the past couple of nights and swallowed a few of the sleeping pills that were prescribed for him last year. They still work.

Now that word is out that a pretty white girl is missing, the media have pounced on the story, the city's good Samaritans have sprung into action, and prayers are flowing. I'll take whatever help is on offer, however nonsensical and self-serving some of it seems to be. As for Michelle, I've simply refused to pick up any of her calls. The couple of screeching voicemails she's left attest to the wisdom of that decision. I don't have the time, energy, or emotional reserves to deal with her outrage and maneuvering. Isn't it interesting that she's expressing her outrage and railing about what a shitty father I am while she's still in Brussels? Wouldn't most mothers have hopped on the first plane to Chicago and thrown themselves into the effort to bring their daughter home safely? Perhaps it's a busy week in Human Resources at Coca-Cola Europe.

Penelope is pensive after we exit the parking garage and walk three blocks along Wacker Drive to the modern skyscraper that is our destination. She shoots me a sideways glance. "I wish we knew what this girl has to share with us."

She's referring to an enigmatic phone call to our offices two hours ago from a woman who claims that her daughter has information about Megan Walton's pilot training that "you'll definitely be interested in." We've arranged for a deposition tomorrow. If the girl really does have damaging information about Megan, it would have been nice to have it prior to the confrontation we're heading into.

"So do I," I reply as we arrive and push through a set of revolving doors that spill us into an expansive granite-floored lobby. We don't need to consult the building directory to locate the offices of Butterworth Cole, where Penelope worked as an associate until quitting a year ago. I had briefly been a client before her boss, Herbert C. Cumming, dumped me. We've been summoned here this morning by none other than Cumming himself, who is the lead lawyer representing Senator Evan Milton in his lawsuit against Windy City Sky Tours et al—with one of the et als being our client, R & B Ramp Services.

"How about what Randall Lennox's friend told you about Wisnowski collaborating with Cumming?" I ask Penelope. "Should we go there if Cumming opens the door to it?" Our source claims that he's been seeing a lot of Wisnowski around

Butterworth Cole after hours of late, always in the company of Herbert Cumming. He also claims he saw them with their heads bent close together in a conference room a couple of weeks ago. When he'd slipped in for a peek while they zipped off to the break room for coffee, he'd seen paperwork from both lawsuits spread out on the table. What does it all mean? Undoubtedly, nothing good, but there isn't much we can do about it unless we choose to take Cumming on directly, and we have zero corroborating evidence to back up the claim of our witness. Cumming would eat us alive if we tried.

Penelope meets my eye when a trio of young business types exits the elevator and we find ourselves alone as we're whisked to an upper floor. "Seems odd to be here in an adversarial role."

I wonder if she's feeling intimidated about facing off against her old boss, who I suspect isn't outwardly supportive nor overly appreciative of the work of his underlings.

Her eyes glitter mischievously. "I've often fantasized about beating up on Herbert C. Cumming."

"Figuratively or literally?" I ask with a weak grin.

She bounces her eyebrows and drolly replies, "Both."

I smile absently as my daughter's predicament forces its way back to the forefront of my thoughts. I push the thoughts aside, or at least try to. The distraction of work hasn't been a panacea, but it has provided scattered moments of relief. That's about the best I can hope for over the next thirty minutes. Doing something to help Billy and Rick won't alter Brittany's fate, whatever it turns out to be. That's now in the hands of Jake Plummer and the FBI.

The elevator glides to a stop at the forty-ninth floor, and the doors whoosh open onto the plush reception area of the Law Offices of Butterworth Cole LLC. I recognize the receptionist from my single visit here last September, back when collegiate sports groupie Herbert Cumming fawned over me amid fond memories of my leading our shared alma matter to a national volleyball championship. Things between us had soured quickly, in equal parts because of my affiliation with Sphinx Financial and his subsequent recognition that I wasn't the deep-pocketed potential client he'd hoped I might be. The good news? I was demoted to the status of a client worthy of nothing more than representation by an associate counsel, which turned out to be Penelope. She did a great job then, and look at us now. She beats the hell out of Cumming in every possible way.

The receptionist's eyes widen when she recognizes Penelope exiting the elevator. She might even recognize me, too, though I doubt it.

Penelope's eyes light up and her smile dazzles as she walks straight to the reception counter and reaches across to squeeze the hand of her former colleague. "Hello, Jennifer! It's so nice to see you."

Jennifer's initial grudging half smile widens into something near a genuine smile. "Hello, Miss Brooks. Nice to see you, as well," she whispers. I imagine being seen exchanging pleasantries with turncoat associates who have spurned the hallowed halls of Butterworth Cole is frowned upon.

"We're here to see Mr. Cumming," Penelope says.

Jennifer nods and glances at her computer screen.

"Conference Room B?" Penelope asks.

Jennifer nods again. "I'll have someone escort you."

"I know the way," Penelope replies, tugging at my sleeve before she marches past reception and down a hallway while Jennifer calls after us to wait. My partner smiles over her shoulder and disingenuously waves the offer of assistance away as an unnecessary courtesy. Then she shoots me a sideways smirk. "Let's surprise the old bastard."

She's developing quite a potty mouth.

We spot Cumming through the glass wall of Conference

Room B as we approach. He's standing over a group of seated Butterworth Cole youngsters with his thumbs hooked in the straps of a pair of suspenders that is one of his courtroom props. He seems to be holding court—perhaps regaling them with tales of lawyerly derring-do, perhaps spinning a scintillating preview of how he plans to carve up and humiliate Penelope and me. He's not a big man, maybe five foot eight or thereabouts, with thinning black hair teased into something of a comb-over and a little paunch bubbling over his belt buckle. Aging detracts somewhat from his assured self-image as an imposing legal giant, but he still has something of a presence about him. Cumming looks pretty much as he did a year ago. He's probably just as much of an asshole as he was last year, too. He confirms that as soon as we stride into the room unannounced and interrupt his monologue.

Cumming's eyes widen when he recognizes us. His gaze quickly morphs into annoyance as he looks beyond us, probably wondering how a disreputable pair of ambulance chasers such as us have waltzed into the inner sanctum unannounced and unescorted. The flash of anger passes quickly, replaced by a transparently false welcoming smile as he advances on us with a hand extended and exclaims, "Tony! Good to see you."

I nod and shake hands with the phony bastard, making sure to crush his pudgy little hand in my big paw as I do so. He can pretend last year didn't happen all he wants. We Italians have long memories.

"Penelope," he says while wrapping her hand in both of his in what's probably an even less authentic welcome.

It's a paternalistic, condescending display, delivered as if she were still a flunky of his. Is he attempting to put her on her back foot by treating her shabbily, or is this simply a display of unconscious misogyny? I bristle on her behalf but am well aware that Penelope doesn't need anyone's protection. Her game face is set firmly in place.

"Herbert," she replies curtly with a disdainful expression that says, "Screw you."

I step back and lock eyes with Cumming. "What can we do for you?"

He casts his eyes toward his acolytes with a bemused smile. "I believe the correct question is 'What can *we* do for *you*?'" His flunkies smile and chuckle in sycophantic admiration of their leader's rapier wit.

And so the dance begins. The table is laid out with several pads of paper and glasses of water ranged along one side. This is where the assembled Butterworth Cole host will sit. A lonely pair of water glasses awaits us on the opposite side of the table.

"You asked us here," I remind him as I bypass our assigned seats, snag a water carafe and two glasses, and pull out a chair at the head of the table. I drop into it while I await his answer. Penelope slides into the seat beside mine and works it around until we're sharing the end of the table.

Cumming's minions scramble to rearrange themselves around the far end of the room while I pour myself a glass of ice water from the sweating carafe. He remains standing. Some sort of power move, I suppose—the Big Man lecturing the Lesser Beings.

"Let's recap where things stand," he begins. Then he starts to pace while he explains the state of the case from his exalted perspective. "My client will win this lawsuit, of course. We all know that. So the question becomes who will pay and how much." He slows to a stop and looks at me. Then his eyes shift to Penelope. "Agreed?"

Penelope doesn't agree or disagree. She simply stares back at her former boss.

Cumming purses his lips in a look of disapproval before he turns his attention to me. "Mr. Valenti?"

Following Penelope's lead, I don a neutral expression. "Yes?"

"So, you plan to make this difficult," he mutters with a rueful shake of his head while he slides a chair out and settles into it. "So be it."

What the hell is he up to? He clearly intended to put us on the defensive and is annoyed that we didn't take the bait.

Cumming sighs theatrically and looks to the young lawyer seated to his right. "Lay it out for them, Mr. Daniels." Cumming then pushes his chair back, crosses an ankle over his knee, and feigns a Jonathan Walton-worthy look of disinterest. Interesting that the two of them share the same dismissive pose. I mentally dub it "The Asshole Move."

I resist the urge to mimic Cumming and settle for a display of mild interest by resting my arms on the table, then loosely clasp my hands together with fingers interlaced and settle my gaze on young Mr. Daniels. The guy is a cookie-cutter vanilla baby lawyer so common to big firms. I doubt I'd be able to tell him apart from his junior colleagues in a lineup five minutes after we walk out of here.

"We assume you've been following the progress of the NTSB investigation?" Daniels asks us.

I reach for a confused look. "Are you referring to Sandy Irving's stories in the *Sun-Times*?"

"In part," he replies.

"What else is there?" Penelope asks.

"We've heard from other sources."

"Heard what from whom?" she presses.

The look of contempt Daniels turns on my partner suggests that these two have a history. "We're not about to share information with you, Penny," he replies with a smirk. "Do your own research. If you can afford to."

So, there is a history here. Penelope *hates* to be called Penny, a fact Daniels seems to be well aware of. He's trying to push her buttons. The slow smile that curls her lips while she pours herself some water signals that she's got this.

"My, my, Matty," she says to Daniels in a syrupy voice I

would never in a million years have expected to hear coming out of her mouth, "you really need to get over your schoolboy infatuation with me. Does that little snub still smart after all this time, poor boy?"

Daniels reddens while he glares at Penelope. She smiles back sweetly before she sips her water, but there's ice in her eyes.

I tap my finger on the table to get everyone's attention, then lock eyes with Daniels and riff off Penelope's schoolboy taunt. "Perhaps we can dispense with the infantile posturing so you can say whatever you've dragged us down here to tell us?"

Daniels's poisonous glower lingers on Penelope for a second longer before he shifts his attention to me. "The point we wish to impress upon you is that culpability for the accident on September eighth is settling squarely on your clients."

I make a minuscule wave-off motion when I sense Penelope gearing up to argue the point. We're not here to squabble about blame. I want these guys to lay their cards on the table without telegraphing any sense of where our heads are. Penelope shoots me a sideways glance and settles back, signaling that it's my show for the moment.

"Go on," I tell Daniels while idly spinning my water glass with my fingertips.

"We all know that the left-wing strut on the Cessna failed," he states is if it's an acknowledged fact, then expands upon his point when we don't respond. "The FBI has determined that the hundred-hour inspection due in August was not completed by your client."

That's news to me. Scary news. I do my best to tamp down my burgeoning fear while I continue to wait him out, interested to hear what other news Daniels has for us.

"There's no evidence of fuel contamination," he adds.

"No *surviving* evidence," I note.

Cumming's eyes rise to mine. He shoots a satisfied little smirk my way.

"You're suggesting that the fix is in?" I ask Daniels.

He turns a smarmy smile on me and replies with a curt nod.

"I see," I murmur. Penelope is tensing at my side, anxious to shoot back. I don't think it's time to do so. Not just yet. "You've asked us here to tell us how this should play out?"

Cumming drops his foot to the floor, pulls his chair in, and squares his shoulders. "That's right."

"And?" Penelope asks.

Cumming tents his hands and rests his chin on the tips of his thumbs. I sense that he's about to tell us precisely why we're here, so I settle back and nonchalantly roll a pen between my fingers. It would be poor form to appear as if we're eager to hear his offer.

"Senator Milton realizes that no amount of money can bring back his loved ones," Cumming begins with the air of a college professor addressing a particularly dim-witted class. He pauses to foreshadow the gravity of his next words, then solemnly announces, "We're proposing a settlement of ten million dollars."

Ten million? The original claim was for twice that. What's going on?

Penelope goes straight to the heart of the matter. "How do you propose to apportion that settlement?"

Cumming shifts his gaze to her. "Five million from Windy City Sky Tours, two point five million each from AAA Avgas and R & B Ramp Services."

Hmmm. Billy and Rick carry exactly that much liability insurance. Coincidence? Probably not, but the point is moot if R & B's insurer gets away with dropping its policy retroactively. How should we play this?

"So?" Cumming asks while we contemplate the offer.

I hold up a hand and mutter, "Thinking." A look at Penelope confirms that she's doing the same, arms crossed while she stares up at the ceiling. The big question to me is why they're proposing a settlement at fifty cents on the dollar. What's changed? The rich shits at Windy City will hardly miss five million, ditto for AAA Avgas's two and a half mil or, to put it properly, two point five million from the pockets of the Luciano crime family. They probably launder that much cash every day or two. R & B could scrape through this settlement *if* their insurance pays up. Of course, if Windy City and AAA Avgas manage to pin all the blame on Billy and Rick by winning the lawsuit they've brought against R & B, this entire discussion is moot. Surely Cumming knows that. What's going on beneath the surface here that we don't understand?

"Does anyone accept responsibility?" Penelope asks.

Good question. Whoever takes the rap can probably say good-bye to a future in the aviation industry.

Cumming shrugs. "Given the mountain of evidence that is coming to light against them, it's clear that R & B has to."

Well, that explains what this is all about. AAA Avgas stays in business. Windy City, too... assuming the rich pricks want to keep playing around in the air-tourism business. Rick and Billy—the only defendants in the case who need the work and love aviation—will find themselves cast into the wilderness without a pot to piss in.

"So, you want to pin the whole mess on our client," I say.

"Our clients can't be shown to be liable," Daniels blurts.

The implications of his statement escape me, at least until I sense Penelope tense at my side.

"*Your* clients?" she asks sharply while Cumming glares at Daniels. Then, with barely constrained venom, she adds, "and here we thought Senator Milton was your client in this matter. You're representing the interests of AAA Avgas, as well? Or is it Windy City? Maybe both?"

Daniels is wearing a deer-in-the-headlights expression.

"Can we say conflict of interest?" Penelope asks sharply.

"We heard you were spending a lot of time with Wisnowski. Now we know why."

"Does the good senator even know about this conversation?" I ask Cumming. I'm having difficulty coming to terms with the notion that a firm as storied as Butterworth Cole could be involved in something so slimy—and I've developed a decidedly jaundiced view of the state of business ethics.

"Of course, he does!" Cumming splutters unconvincingly.

The snake!

Penelope wags an admonishing finger at the other end of the conference table while her eyes settle on Daniels. "I think that's going to turn out to be a very damaging gaffe, Matty."

I sense Daniels's career flashing before his eyes as he reddens and shoots a terrified sideways glance at his boss. The murderous expression on Herbert Cumming's face suggests that those fears are well placed. Daniels's young colleagues look almost as frightened as he does. I meet his gaze and lift my water glass in a little toast before taking a sip.

Penelope slowly rises to her feet and, in a parody of Herbert Cumming's earlier pretentious professorial performance, begins to pace slowly around our end of the table. "Another mistake you folks seem to be making is to assume that you're the only people with sources inside the NTSB investigation and law enforcement." Her eyes settle on Cumming. "Of course, to those of us who are familiar with Butterworth Cole's leadership, that level of hubris isn't unexpected."

To my surprise, the possibility that we might have our own conduits of information seems to blindside Cumming and company. Although it might be working to our benefit at the moment, their lack of regard for the legal juggernaut known as Brooks and Valenti rankles. Penelope has stopped pacing and is glaring at Cumming as if she's having the same thought.

I slap both palms down on the tabletop and fix what I hope is a shrewd smile on my face. "You'd just love to wish away any questions about how a novice pilot named Megan Walton happened to be at the controls of that aircraft on September eighth, wouldn't you?"

Cumming looks as if he's about to wet his pants, not exactly the expression one expects from an arrogant senior partner of a prestigious Chicago law firm.

I channel Ben Larose. "Poor Megan was marginally rated in that aircraft—perhaps not even that. Her instructor is a pretty sketchy guy, so who knows how that rating came about, huh? Then there's the apparent nepotism involved in her landing the gig at Uncle Jonathan's company to consider. What does Senator Milton make of that?"

"Probably nothing," Penelope sneers. "His attorneys probably haven't told him about any of this."

"Unless *he* has sources that are keeping him apprised of the NTSB investigation," I say, tag teaming with my partner while my eyes bore into Cumming. "Think that's a possibility, what with him being a senator and all?"

Penelope fixes Cumming in her sights and once again demonstrates a mastery of the law and legal research that I can only aspire to. "Did you put in the time and effort to do a deep dive into the corporate structure of your client?" Before he can answer, she adds, with exquisite sarcasm, "Oh, I'm sorry, I should have specified that I was talking about Windy City Sky Tours, which is purportedly Wisnowski's client. How does that work, Herbert—she sets up shop apart from Butterworth Cole so you can work both sides of cases and share a percentage of billings and settlements?"

Cumming seems to have recovered his poker face as he stares back at her without uttering a word. His young flunkies are going to have to work on perfecting their poker faces. With the exception of Matty Daniels, their wide eyes and surprised little O-shaped mouths suggest they can't believe what their fearless leader has been up to. Daniels appears to be the only one who knew.

"There's that hubris again, Herbert," Penelope scoffs with a smile that is anything but a pleasant expression. Her eyes track between him and his acolytes. "*None* of you remembers the dangers of hubris from Greek mythology?"

Nobody replies. Cumming is staring at her with open hostility. The others are simply afraid. I stifle a chuckle. She is so kicking their asses.

Penelope braces her hands on the edge of the conference table and stares hard at our cowed adversaries. "Your friends, clients, or whatever they are—Jonathan Walton, Caitlyn Tyson, and Oliver Franklin—were pretty clever in their bid to shield their personal assets from any legal jeopardy arising out of the operations of Windy City. I imagine that's why Walton is cocky enough to trust that his lawyers have succeeded in erecting an impenetrable force shield around him and his pals, huh?" She pauses while a thought seems to occur to her. "There's that hubris thing *again.* Hmmm. Maybe that's why you're all in bed together? Shared hubris."

I'm not sure exactly where she's headed with her little lecture, but I'm enjoying the ride. Our Butterworth Cole friends are not. My partner's IQ may well exceed that of everyone else in this room. Combined.

"Tony was right about Megan Walton being the key to understanding your settlement offer," Penelope says directly to Cumming. She waits for him to respond. He doesn't. She straightens up, braces her right elbow in her left palm, rests her chin in her other palm, and taps the end of her index finger on the tip of her nose. I know the move but realize that she's not *really* pondering the problem; she's just playing with her audience.

"It seems to me that your Windy City friends are in deep doo-doo if Megan Walton is found to be at fault for the crash, gentlemen," she continues. "Especially if it comes out that she was underqualified to be flying paying customers in an aircraft like the Cessna 210. Hmmm?"

"There's been *no* suggestion of that," Cumming shoots back.

Penelope arches her eyebrows as if she's surprised to hear so silly a thing. "Maybe not that *you've* heard about."

I finally twig onto where Penelope is going. "That would suggest stunning negligence on the part of Windy City Sky Tours, wouldn't it?" I ask Cumming.

He doesn't bother to respond.

Penelope fixes another laser stare on Cumming and agrees with my assessment. "Yes, it would. A clear case of gross negligence and willful misconduct of that magnitude would almost certainly pierce the veil of liability that Windy City's owners are trying to hide their assets behind."

Meaning that Senator Milton would have a clear shot at the personal fortunes of Jonathan Walton, Caitlyn Tyson, and Oliver Franklin, in addition to the assets and liability insurance of Windy City and the estate of Megan Walton. That's some serious coin. I turn an admiring look on Penelope. As usual, even when I thought I'd worked out where her head is, my partner was already a step or two beyond the rest of us. The junior Butterworth Cole attorneys seem to be as surprised as I am. Cumming doesn't. If he knew this, shouldn't he have been pushing to prove the Windy City gross negligence and willful misconduct that Penelope is postulating?

The disdain dripping from her words and the malice in her eyes telegraph Penelope's belief that that's precisely the outcome Cumming is seeking to prevent with today's settlement offer. "So, Herbert, what client are you acting on behalf of this morning? The Walton family? The Tysons? The Franklins? I know that each of those families are Butterworth Cole clients, and you're clearly not protecting the interests of Senator Milton here."

Cumming stares imperiously down his nose at Penelope

as if she's a fly on a hot dog that he's about to shoo away. It strikes me as a stunning display of arrogance in the face of such a devastating accusation.

"Actually, never mind," Penelope says with a dismissive wave of her hand. "I'm sure the Illinois Bar Association will get to the bottom of it." She gathers up her purse and portfolio before she leads me to the door leading out of the conference room. Then she pauses and looks back. "As for how deeply you're in bed with the Lucianos and their lawyers, I guess we'll just put a bug in the FBI's ear and let them muck around in that mess."

Cumming's arrogant expression disintegrates into dust the moment Penelope mentions making a referral to the FBI.

"I think you know where you can stick your settlement offer," I say in a snide aside.

Penelope shoots a surprised, unreadable look my way. "We'll show ourselves out."

"They can stick their settlement offer? What was that?" she asks hotly when we're in the elevator. I know I'm in trouble but don't know why until she adds, "If we can get Rick and Billy's insurance company on the hook for the two and a half million *and* R & B doesn't admit to any wrongdoing, I'll take the deal in a heartbeat."

Oh. Sorry, Billy. Sorry, Rick. Sorry, Mel.

Penelope's gaze softens by the time the elevator reaches the lobby. She punches my shoulder as we step outside, winks, and warns me, "I'll beat you up next time you tell anyone that we'll do something without talking to me first. Understand?"

Properly chastened, I nod.

She meets my gaze. "I'll touch base with Cumming this afternoon to let him know that we'll take the settlement offer under advisement and discuss it with our client."

What if Cumming spurns Penelope's olive branch because of my asinine outburst? "I'm sorry," I mutter.

She waves my apology aside and sets off down Wacker Avenue with me following meekly in her wake. By the time we reach the parking garage, my mind is once again fully occupied with my missing daughter. Having allowed myself to get caught up in the intrigue and fun of sticking it to Cumming, I haven't given a thought to how Joe will react to what just happened. I put my head in my hands and sob silently after we get in the car.

Penelope reaches across the seat to touch my shoulder. "Brittany?" she asks softly.

I shrug and nod. *More than you know.*

CHAPTER TWENTY-SEVEN

After Penelope dropped me off, I endured yet another afternoon where no progress was made in the search for Brittany. I microwave my third consecutive dinner of penne pasta, wash it down with a beer, break out the bourbon, and glumly settle into Papa's La-Z-Boy. Jake sent some technicians by earlier to sweep the house. No cameras. No listening devices. So, that's a bit of a relief. His print guy left a mess on and around the La-Z-Boy that took me twenty minutes to clean up. No word yet whether or not the exercise proved fruitful. I'm sure Jake will tell me when he knows something. There's also promising news on the R & B front, however. Penelope calls to inform me that Butterworth Cole will await the results of our consultation with Billy and Rick regarding the settlement offer. Which leaves the matter of Billy and Rick finding the means to pay their portion. To that end, we have an affidavit from Rick's hepatologist stating that Rick's liver issues and transplant were the result of a genetic condition, not alcohol abuse.

"You've been busy," I say. "Still in the office?"

"Afraid so," she replies. "I just scheduled a face-to-face meeting with a lawyer and senior claims executive of R & B's insurance company. With the hepatologist's report, they'll have to reinstate Rick and Billy's policy."

"And if they don't?" I ask, suspecting the insurer won't give in without a fight. In all likelihood, it will produce a hired gun or two who are willing to dispute the testimony of Rick's doctor.

I can hear the smile in Penelope's voice when she replies, "I'll threaten them with a massive lawsuit to not only reinstate the policy but to pay damages. I've done a little research for precedents."

"And you like our chances?" I ask.

"I do."

"Well, then, so do I. Did you have a nice chat with your pal Herbert?"

She laughs. "A nice chat? With Herbert Cumming? No, but it was productive."

"I'm a little surprised he was willing to wait on us regarding the settlement."

"We shook him up earlier today, partner. He's running a little scared right now."

"He *should* be," I grumble, thinking about the crooked bastard screwing his client.

"He's prepared to withdraw his insistence that R & B accept responsibility for the crash."

"You're a magician," I say. "How did you manage that?"

"I believe he's come to the erroneous conclusion that I won't file a complaint about him playing both sides of the client fence if he makes that concession."

It's hard to believe the guy worked with Penelope all that time without learning a thing about her. If he's counting on her doing anything other than the right thing, he's a damned fool. Cumming is an arrogant asshole, but he's not a fool, so something must have led him to make that error in judgment.

"Why do I suspect there's more to the story?" I ask.

"One might say that I didn't forcefully disabuse him of the

notion when he pitched it," she replies with a trace of humor in her voice.

"Didn't forcefully disabuse him, huh?" I say with a chuckle.

"Well, I didn't disagree, but I certainly didn't agree. I had Mom sit in on the call as a witness."

"Well done, partner. Next steps?"

"I'll draft a complaint to the Illinois bar over the weekend and tuck it away in my desk drawer until we get what we're after," she replies. "If anyone questions the delay, I'll just say that it took me several days to put it together."

I chuckle again. Penelope can draft a complete brief and craft complicated trial motions in the time it takes most of us to have a cup of coffee. "Sounds like you've had a productive day," I say. "Why don't you go relax for the rest of the evening? Hell, take the weekend off, too!"

She laughs softly. "I just may take you up on that generous offer, partner. Have yourself a good weekend."

I pour myself a glass of bourbon, plop my ass back into the La-Z-Boy, and take stock of the R & B case. Penelope, as always, has done outstanding work. We might actually be on the way to justifying the trust Billy showed in us when he put this in our hands. Wouldn't that be nice?

Yes, but it won't bring Brittany home. It might even ensure that she never does. I wonder if there's a way to leverage the Cumming situation against Joe. Not likely, but it's something to think about.

The doorbell rings. I don't think I'm expecting anyone, but my muddled mind wonders if I'm wrong as I peer through the peep hole and see an urbane man standing on the front porch. I initially mistake him for Mr. Rosetti, a retired community bank manager who was a fixture on Liberty Street until recently moving to Florida. Perhaps the resemblance to Mr. Rosetti causes me to let down my guard, or maybe it's just my incomprehensible level of emotional and mental exhaustion that leads me to crack open the door. The man already has the screen door open and pushes past me into the house. I catch a whiff of cologne while I try to process what is happening. When I turn to look at him, the stranger lifts the butt of a handgun an inch or so out of a shoulder holster inside a perfectly tailored, gray pinstriped suit jacket, holds a finger to his lips, and reaches past me to close the door.

"Sorry to invite myself in so rudely, Mr. Valenti," he says in an odd mixture of Italian- and British-accented English. "I have not come to harm you, but to discuss matters of mutual interest."

Anger is stirring within me as I realize that I'm probably speaking to another mobster who feels welcome in my home. "Who the hell are you?"

"All in good time," my visitor assures me as he walks into the living room. "It may be that I am a friend and ally. Perhaps not. Please, let us sit and discover which it will be, no?"

He sounds so reasonable and I'm so weary that I simply shrug and fall into Papa's La-Z-Boy. He settles into Mama's easy chair, sitting very straight and proper while he crosses his legs primly and straightens the blue ascot at his throat. He's a handsome man I guess to be in his late fifties or early sixties, with a full head of immaculately styled gray hair. His nails are impeccably manicured. When he smiles at me, his snowy-white teeth are straight and even. I hope to hell I look this good at his age.

"Who are you?" I repeat.

He steeples his fingers and studies me for a long, unsettling minute before he speaks. "I have come all the way from Italy to speak with you, Mr. Valenti. I hope we can come to a mutually beneficial arrangement."

"Will it bring my daughter home?" I ask harshly.

He appears genuinely distressed when he softly says, "I pray for the safe return of your daughter, Mr. Valenti. Please understand that I am not involved in that unfortunate situation."

Damned if I don't believe him.

"The situation with Brittany is, however, indirectly related to my visit this evening."

My patience, never the greatest at the best of times, is sorely lacking tonight. "Get to the point," I direct Mr.—did he even give me a name? "What's your name?" I ask in a tone meant to discourage argument or dissembling.

His eyes settle on my glass of bourbon. "What are you drinking, Mr. Valenti?"

Is this guy for real? Yet his manner is so studiously courteous that it's hard to take offense. I give him a tired smile. "I'll tell you as soon as you give me your name."

His smile widens as a full-throated chuckle escapes him. "And so *you* open the negotiations. My name is Matteo Giordano."

I nod and raise my glass an inch off the armrest. "Bourbon."

He tilts his head sideways an inch or two in. "This is an American whiskey, no?"

I nod again. This guy really isn't from around these parts. Too urbane. Too gentlemanly. Doesn't know his whiskey. Then there's the ascot. Yeah, I can see him at home in an Italian villa on the shores of the Mediterranean.

"Would you be so kind as to offer me a glass?" he asks. "I should like to try it. I have heard it is a sweet variation on Scotch whisky. Which sounds just about exactly how I would set about making Scotch potable," he adds with a smile.

Potable whisky? I laugh and hoist myself out of my seat. "Where the hell did you go to school?" I ask him as I make my way to the side table where we keep the booze. Am I really joshing with an Italian mobster? I am. Christ, I must be tired.

"I assume you are really asking where I learned to speak English?"

I nod while unscrewing the top from a bottle of Maker's Mark. *Didn't I just open this last night?* I wonder as I upend it and realize it's already three-quarters empty. "I guess I am asking that. Somewhere in the UK?"

"University of Rome and Cambridge," he replies, then adds with a chuckle, "which is where I learned terms such as potable."

I hand him his bourbon and take mine—which I topped off, of course—back to my seat. I settle back and study my guest as he samples my whiskey, swishing it around his mouth with a thoughtful look on his face. Perhaps I was overly hasty in concluding that Matteo Giordano is a gangster. He looks across at me as he swallows, then delivers his verdict on the booze.

"Quite nice." He rests his glass on the armrest with his long, elegant fingers wrapped around it and says, "So."

"You came to me," I remind him. "What's this about?"

"Your FBI is making certain inquiries in my country concerning matters we prefer not to have attention drawn to."

I stare back at him without comment. He'll have to get a touch more specific if he hopes to enlighten me.

"I am a businessman, Mr. Valenti. A portion of my business is done somewhat outside the law, if you will."

A spark of anger flares to life deep within me. So, he's a damned gangster, after all, one who fancies himself a businessman. The guy has apparently gotten his hands on a legitimate business venture or two and thinks he's civilized. Bullshit. He's just a sanitized version of Joe. I ease forward in my chair and growl, "Have you come here to threaten my family?"

He actually looks a little pained at the harshness of my outburst. "Perhaps you will allow me a few minutes to explain myself?"

I decide to accommodate him. After all, the guy forced his way into my house with a gun, which he still has. I managed to lose sight of that while we were talking whiskey a minute ago.

"If it will make sense out of your visit, what the hell?" I mutter.

"Thank you," he says courteously, then sips at his whisky again.

With this demeanor, the guy can't be much of a gangster. He proves me wrong within seconds.

"My brother is a senior leader of *Ndrangheta* in Italy, Mr. Valenti. I have come to see you at his request. Have you heard of us?"

I nod. After learning last year of Papa's run-in with a local offshoot of *Ndrangheta* when he was a young man in Italy, I did a little research. "You're the even more murderous group of thugs that oversees the *Cosche* bastards who kidnapped and raped my aunt in Calabria, right?"

"That unfortunate incident is the basis for your father's recent difficulties," Giordano says without responding to my insult. "Rest assured that the rape of your aunt is unacceptable to us."

"But kidnapping her and holding her for ransom was just business?"

I catch my first glance of the gangster lurking beneath the urbane veneer. "We will make no progress if you insist on being argumentative, Mr. Valenti."

I stare back at him, wondering about the difference between business and criminality in his world. Kidnapping a young teenage girl for ransom is merely "business," but brutally raping her for the gratification of some horny bastard is criminal. Granted, the second is more reprehensible than the first, but how am I supposed to deal with someone whose moral code is this twisted? But deal with him I must, or so it appears. "So, your people wish to kill my father?"

He shakes his head. "Not at all, Mr. Valenti. The truth is that a small circle of us knows that Francesco is staying with his sister in Penne. We do not wish him harm and will not share his whereabouts with his hunters at this time."

I feel the blood drain from my face as my heart rate skyrockets. These people know where Papa is? And what does "at this time" mean?

"I tell you this to demonstrate that I am not your enemy, Mr. Valenti," Giordano says in a reassuring tone while I revisit the bourbon bottle. He waves off my offer of a refill. "We would like the attention of American law enforcement diverted away from our affairs. Things have been somewhat difficult for us of late. Too much police scrutiny, if you will. Some of our associates have become, shall we say, too greedy. Too bold. Perhaps not unlike your former colleague at Sphinx Financial, Mr. Hank Fraser."

I can't even begin to imagine where this is leading, although the suggestion that the practices of my old employer are in any way akin to how the Mafia goes about business hits a little too close to home. I lift my glass to my lips with one hand and circle my other in a "go on" gesture.

"Let us speak of Francesco first," he says after adjusting himself in his seat. He takes another tiny sip of bourbon, all but smacks his lips in approval, and settles his gaze on mine. "When we first began to hear rumblings that American police were making inquiries via Interpol about old events in Orso-marso, we were concerned enough to do a little research. This is how I learned about the kidnapping and rape of Francesco's sister and the retribution he took."

I recall Jake telling me that he was exploring the Italian angle through Interpol. I assume that's what Giordano is referring to.

He continues, "In one respect, the killing of the rapist is honorable and admirable."

"In one respect?"

Giordano nods. "On a personal level, very much so. On an organizational level, it is not helpful for people to believe they can defy us and prosper from doing so. In Francesco's case, the brother of the man he killed is now determined to avenge his long-lost sibling."

"So, killing my father for an incident fifty years ago is an organizational imperative?"

He shakes his head. "I'm afraid you misunderstand what I wish to convey. I'm sorry to be unclear."

Jesus, it's all I can do not to apologize for misunderstanding. "Try again," I mutter.

"We would prefer that this man not pursue his personal vendetta and are prepared to take the necessary steps to ensure that he stops."

I like the sound of that but suspect there's a catch.

"As I say, we are businessmen, Mr. Valenti. So there is a cost to all things."

And there's the catch. "And what is the price of my father's life, Mr. Giordano?"

"The whereabouts of your father is information of value, don't you agree?"

I stare back at him with a face of stone.

"Someone will prove willing to pay for that information, Mr. Valenti... either to harm your father or to put an end to the contract hanging over his head. Will it be you who pays or the man who seeks vengeance?"

In my current state, I have limited tolerance for bullshit, apparently even when it comes from an armed gangster. I blow out an exasperated sigh. "Jesus Christ, just name your price, will you?"

Giordano's eyes widen and an ember of flame flares in them but quickly dies. "We can make that problem go away and guarantee your father's safety for two hundred and fifty thousand American dollars."

In other words, it's going to cost *me* $250,000 to have

Giordano and his people do whatever they are planning to do in order to end an inconvenience to themselves. I sag back in my seat and drink off a healthy slug of booze. Where do they expect me to find a quarter million dollars?

"We know you can raise those funds, Mr. Valenti."

You do, do you? Maybe I can, but I have neither the time nor inclination to work that out just now. I'll find the bloody money somewhere. Somehow. Of course, there's the minor detail of whether Papa is even alive.

"How do I know you haven't already killed Papa?"

"His sister would tell you of his death, no?"

"We're not in touch."

Giordano seems surprised by the answer. He studies me for a moment. "Operational security, I assume?"

I nod.

"Perhaps a wise precaution," he allows. "You have no way to contact him?"

"No."

"Interesting," he muses. "Would I be here to guarantee his safety if he were dead?"

How would I know? He's a gangster, for God's sake. I stare back and counter with, "You want me to accept the word of an extortionist?"

He sighs. "We do have honor, Mr. Valenti."

"Can you send me a picture or something?"

He shakes his head. "We know where he is. We don't have him under surveillance. You will simply have to take my word that he is safe."

I guess I don't have much choice. I'm hardly going to throw Papa to the wolves for the sake of playing a weak hand. Oddly enough, I believe the man. Then again, I'm emotionally and physically exhausted. I nod, then decide to push the conversation in another direction. "What about my daughter? Can you help me with that?"

"As I said before, Mr. Valenti, kidnapping for ransom is a business transaction."

"She's fifteen years old!"

He nods sympathetically. "Were it my daughter, I would feel as you do. I must tell you, however, that your daughter is not our concern."

I glare at him. There's really nothing I can say to that.

He tilts his head an inch or two to the side and studies me. "Unless you're a reasonable man, Mr. Valenti?"

A jolt of adrenaline surges through me. Is he suggesting he can help? If so, it will definitely come at a cost. I'm willing to pay anything to get my daughter back. Unfortunately, the $250,000 demand for Papa's safety will undoubtedly tap me out—assuming I can raise even that much. Then again, we're talking about my daughter. Who takes priority? Her or Papa? What an impossible situation.

Giordano continues to study me as I wrestle with the problem of how to prioritize the survival of the most important people in my life. We both know I have limited options and few cards to play. The bastard looks as if he's intrigued by my quandary and is curious to see which way I'll jump. Desperate I may be, but I succeed in clearing my head long enough to recall a primary tenet of Negotiating 101: Don't appear overeager to accept what's on offer.

"What the hell does that mean?" I shoot back.

"I may, perhaps, be in a position to assist in the safe return of your daughter."

I feel a surge of hope as he ponders whatever thought has occurred to him.

"Of course, I am a businessman," he reminds me.

I know he's a respectable "businessman," so long as one accepts the premise that extortion is properly classified as business. "How much?" I ask impatiently.

He tents his fingers and smiles. The jerk seems to take

perverse pleasure in placing a price on lives. "I have a healthy cash flow, Mr. Valenti. You do not."

Tell me something I don't know, asshole.

"The truth is that you don't have enough money to be of interest to us," he says thoughtfully. "No, I think perhaps a favor is best."

"A favor," I say flatly. What kind of favor can *I* do for this guy?

He nods and uncrosses his legs to sit forward. "While most of my business is in Italy, I do have some interests here in America. Perhaps a day will come when I encounter a problem that can be resolved only by someone with your talents and status as a lawyer. Having you on standby to assist in resolving such a problem would be of value to me, Mr. Valenti."

I can't believe I'm entering into a negotiation with a mobster about how I might be of future service, but here I am. I set my glass aside. I'm starting to feel the booze and can't afford impaired judgment while dealing with this man.

"A question?" I ask.

He nods.

"I know the Luciano family is mixed up in all this. I'm also at least somewhat aware of what their 'business interests' entail. To put it mildly, these are not people I wish to be associated with in any way, at any time."

He listens with interest but doesn't betray the slightest hint of what he might be thinking.

"How closely are you related to the Luciano family?" I ask.

The hint of a smile touches his lips while he considers his reply. "I'm not, Mr. Valenti. At least not directly."

"What does that mean?"

"It means I have no formal relationship with them."

My skin crawls at the prospect of what this "favor" might entail. Defend some goombah in court against charges for crimes that harm innocent people? Murder? Human trafficking? Kidnapping? Prostitution? Drug dealing? I might be able to live with my conscience if I did some work for this guy that involved more or less legitimate business such as tax avoidance or financial fraud: white-collar crime in which people aren't physically harmed. Yeah, I'm rationalizing—*everything* these people do hurts someone, somewhere, somehow. On the other hand, we're negotiating for Brittany's safety. Is there any depth to which I won't sink to that end?

My eyes stray to my almost-empty glass. I force myself to look away. "I don't suppose you can be more specific about this favor?"

He considers the question but doesn't immediately reply.

"Perhaps we can negotiate some exclusions?" I ask hopefully.

"Let's set that aside while I give it some thought," he finally says as he sits back and casually recrosses his legs. "We should clarify our existing arrangements before we consider another."

"How so?"

He looks me squarely in the eye. "There can be no ambiguity about the specific terms of any arrangements we may come to, Mr. Valenti. None. As I'm sure you can imagine, the consequences should you fail to deliver on a commitment will be unpleasant."

Unpleasant? Loved ones maimed, kidnapped, or murdered? Maybe a limb lopped off? An acid bath? "Yeah, let's be clear."

"For two hundred and fifty thousand dollars, the contract that is currently on your father's head will be canceled."

The contract *currently* on his head? "That sounds considerably more limited than your promise to make the contract go away *and* to guarantee my father's safety," I counter. "Perhaps you can clarify your offer?"

"The brother of your father's victim has contracted with

the Lucianos to eliminate your father. That contract will be terminated."

"That's it?" I ask in stunned disbelief before a wave of outrage washes over me. "Leaving that *Cosche* piece of shit free to put out another contract or come after Papa himself?"

Giordano arches an eyebrow.

I think back on our conversation about the $250,000. "To hell with that. You promised that two hundred and fifty thousand dollars would *guarantee* my father's safety, not buy him an extra few days or weeks and leave him looking over his shoulder every day."

Giordano purses his lips thoughtfully, stares off into the fireplace for a long moment, and then nods. "I believe you are correct, Mr. Valenti. I can see how my words might be interpreted that way. My apologies for not being clear."

I stare back at him and wait for more.

"I am a man of my word," he adds. "We are agreed, then. You have my promise that the matter of your father's safety will be resolved."

"Good. Thank you," I say as a wave of relief washes over me. As he dips his chin and nods, it occurs to me that I may have just issued a hit of my own. How do I feel about that? Not so good, even as I rationalize it as trading some nameless gangster's life for Papa's.

"There is more to this matter," he continues.

I sigh. "What?"

"You'll recall that our primary motivation in approaching you is to prompt an end to the interest your police have in our business."

"I don't see how accomplishing that is within my power."

He smiles. "Oh, but I think it is. The inquiries through Interpol were in regard to your father's problems from Orsomarso. If you pass the word to the police here that the danger to your father has been removed, there should be no reason

265

for the American authorities to continue poking their noses into our affairs. Business can then return to normal."

He makes it sound so simple. Maybe it is. "I can certainly pass that along."

"I assume you will speak to your friend, Detective Plummer."

Is there anything about my life this guy doesn't know? It's unnerving as hell to realize how closely these people have been watching me and how deeply they've probed into my life. He knows this, of course, and is using the knowledge to keep me off-balance. And compliant, I suppose. Well, he's going to have to work a little harder to make me that malleable.

He leans forward and gives me a look signaling that I should listen very carefully to what follows. "It would be best not to disclose my visit when you speak with Detective Plummer, Mr. Valenti. The police in America would not consider me a welcome visitor."

Meaning he's wanted by law enforcement. Great. At the moment, I'm probably guilty of harboring a wanted criminal.

"Should the police learn of my presence here and detain me, it could prove to be more than a simple inconvenience, Mr. Valenti. It would needlessly complicate or even preclude our business together."

"I'm not sure if that's an explanation or a warning," I mutter.

"Both."

I nod while a fresh tentacle of fear creeps into me. "Understood."

He smiles. "Of course, you understand such things. You are a paisano yourself."

I'm not your bloody paisano. My friends aren't a bunch of murdering thugs. Not that I dare give voice to those thoughts. I screw up the courage to return to the topic of my daughter. "I want Brittany home."

"As I said, Mr. Valenti, that depends on whatever terms we may agree to. The ball is in your court."

And I haven't got a clue how to return his volley.

"I see that this is something of a quandary for you," Giordano says after a moment. "If I may make a suggestion?"

I nod.

"If we are to proceed in the matter of your father, he will be under our protection the minute your funds clear. Not a minute before. *Capisce?*"

"I totally understand," I seethe. Papa's at risk until I pay up.

"A point to consider in that regard, Mr. Valenti. Time is of the essence. Your father's location is an asset we currently possess. It is of value to others, as well."

"I know."

"You are familiar with the expression 'a bird in hand is worth two in the bush?'"

"Yeah."

"The promise that you will raise two hundred and fifty thousand dollars is like a bird in the bush, Mr. Valenti. Your father's hunters would also be happy to compensate us immediately for that information. Perhaps not as much as you have agreed to pay, but they have cash readily available— cash in hand, if you will, whereas your two hundred and fifty thousand dollars is still somewhere in the bush. I suggest you act quickly on our offer."

I take a deep breath as outrage stirs within me.

"Relax, Mr. Valenti. We *do* have a deal, but our patience is finite."

"I already told you that I don't have that kind of cash lying around the house," I shoot back with a mixture of anger and fright.

He smiles. "Because you don't *have* that kind of cash. Here or anywhere. We know this, but we also know that you have the means to raise it. I only suggest that you do so without undue delay. We will be watching."

"It's Friday evening," I remind him.

He nods. "Unfortunate timing, I agree. While you wait for the banks to open on Monday, you will have time to weigh my offer concerning your daughter. That is a matter of perhaps more urgency. I can do nothing to influence events concerning Brittany unless we come to an agreement. It would be a shame were something to befall her while you think things over, wouldn't it?"

I rummage through the kitchen cabinets until I find a couple of old paper sandwich bags, the only kind Mama ever used for lunches. No plastic baggies for Mama. I take one to the living room and tuck Giordano's glass inside. I'm pretty sure he's exactly who he said he is, but I'm not going to screw up again on the chance that he isn't. Of course, I don't know what to do with it. As usual, I'm painted into a corner. Do I tell Jake about the newest gangster in my orbit?

CHAPTER TWENTY-EIGHT

I t's a good thing Penelope called an hour ago to remind me that I'm due in the office by nine o'clock, even though it's Saturday morning. I was already awake, but the work appointment had slipped my mind while I riffled through my latest investment statements, desperately trying to figure out how to raise a quarter of a million dollars in short order. My brain has been scrambled since Matteo Giordano walked out of my home last evening. I polished off the bottle of bourbon I shared with him and made a good start on another while I had an initial look at the investments. In my inebriated state, a solution didn't offer itself. I woke up this morning hoping things would look better in the morning light. They don't.

My thoughts turn to Brittany after I cast the paperwork aside and head for the bathroom. Can Giordano really save her? Does he know if she's still alive? He seems to know a hell of a lot, but does he know that? Why the hell didn't I ask him last night? I'd do so now, but I have no way to contact him.

"We'll be in touch," he had informed me as he let himself out.

After a quick shower and shave, I hop into my Porsche

and arrive at the office only five minutes late. Not a big deal as our appointment is scheduled for ten o'clock. We've come early to prepare for our visitors.

Penelope greets me with a grin. "Good morning, sleepyhead."

"I was awake when you called," I protest.

"You look like heck," she observes after giving me a long look. Then she moves closer and gives me a sniff. "Have a little too much to drink last night?"

I still stink after gargling a gallon of mouthwash? Rather than simply answer the question honestly, I toss out a line I heard somewhere or other. "I might be feeling a little storm-tossed."

"Storm-tossed?" she says with a snort. "You look and smell hungover."

"Well, it's much the same thing, but *storm-tossed* sounds ever so much more romantic, doesn't it?" I ask in a lame effort at levity. I'm embarrassed and a bit ashamed about waking up less than sober. The drinking is becoming a bit of an issue again. It sure as hell isn't going to help me save Brittany, but I reason that losing myself in a fog of alcohol helps maintain my sanity for a few hours at a time.

Penelope smiles the smile of the exasperated.

"Do I smell like a brewery?" I ask.

She ponders the question, then shakes her head and replies, "Maybe like we're a block or two away from one. Have you eaten?"

Meals have become a decidedly hit-or-miss proposition. Most of the normal activities of life have. I shrug. "Forgot, I guess."

Out comes her cell phone. I listen to her side of the conversation while clearing off my desk.

"Mom? Can you stop and pick up a bagel or two on your way in? Tony hasn't eaten. I know… we'll just need to keep harping on him. Thanks, see you shortly." She drops the phone back into her purse. "Mom's bringing you a couple of bagels. They should sop up whatever alcohol is still sloshing around your stomach."

After I tuck the last of my meager desktop accoutrements into a drawer, it's time to complete the transformation of my office into the Brooks and Valenti conference room. Penelope helps me push the desk back into a corner. Then we drape a starched white linen tablecloth over it. Voila! Our conference room has a side table to hold a coffee pot, stainless-steel water carafe, and a dozen of Penelope's scrumptious home-baked muffins. I head for the back hallway, where an oversized walnut folding table sits on a wheeled furniture dolly. I trundle that back to my office, where Penelope helps me wrestle it off the dolly and unfold it. God knows how old the thing is, but it doesn't look too makeshift, not after Papa stripped it down to bare wood and refinished the wood to a museum-grade gloss. This is the Brooks and Valenti conference room table. We place the little visitor chairs from our offices around it somewhat self-consciously—we're well aware that the result is a far cry from a typical law office conference room. We considered buying more appropriate chairs, but they wouldn't fit in our offices. There's nowhere to store full-size chairs in our sprawling premises, anyway. We make do.

All the while, through chatter about the Netflix movie Penelope watched last night and speculation about what we will discover at ten o'clock, the fallout from Giordano's visit percolates through my mind. The $250,000. The "favor." How do Giordano's directives square with those laid down by Joe? How the hell do I balance the competing demands? Who do I involve?

"Ah, here's Mom," Penelope says when we hear the front door crash closed at nine forty-four. She heads out to reception and is back within seconds to launch a paper bag from Daigle's Deli at me. "Breakfast!"

I snag the bag in midair and dig out the first of two plain bagels. I prefer sesame seed, but Penelope banned them during our second month of operation after I'd strewn seeds all over the conference room table just before a client meeting.

"Be quick about it, partner," she orders.

Joan Brooks, jack of all trades, plays the role of transcriptionist at Brooks and Valenti, Discount Attorneys at Law. She walks in pushing a little cart holding a court-reporter-typewriter-like thingamajig and a tape recorder.

I hold up my bagel and mutter thanks around a mouthful.

She nods while she plugs in her thingamajig and sets it up. Then she retires to her desk to play receptionist, leaving me alone with Penelope. I collapse into a chair while my partner eases the door closed and comes back to stand nearby as I polish off bagel number two.

"Anything new?" she asks with quiet concern.

I assume she's referring to Brittany, although it could be Papa, or maybe even the R & B file. I look back at her for a long moment. Where in hell to begin?

"Tony?" she prompts softy before she reaches up and holds a finger to my temple. "I can hear the wheels grinding in there, partner. Please let me help."

I'm surprised to feel my scratchy eyes well up like a fire hydrant being cranked open.

"Oh, Tony," Penelope says as she pulls my head to her shoulder.

The urge to tell her everything is overwhelming. From a strictly professional perspective, she absolutely deserves to know of the connection between Brittany's kidnappers and our case representing Billy and Rick. Not that we have time to get into that now. Maybe after the deposition.

As if on cue, the door opens, and Joan announces the arrival of our guests.

"Let them know that we're almost ready for them, Mom," Penelope says. Then she hands me a clutch of Kleenex to dry my eyes and blow my nose. I nod in appreciation and then, in a superhuman feat of pulling one's shit together, turn off the tear ducts.

Penelope pauses with her hand on the doorknob and meets my gaze. "Ready?"

"Ready."

She's back within the minute, trailed by an exquisitely groomed woman in a plum knee-length dress who looks like something out of a fashion magazine. In her wake follows a young woman wearing jeans and an orange sweater. She falls just short of beautiful and is clearly the woman's daughter. The fragrance of expensive perfume wafts off one or both of them, hopefully masking any residual hangover odor coming from me. Mother walks straight to me with her hand extended, drooping "just so" as a badge of her femininity. I almost feel as if I should dip to one knee and kiss the back of her hand. Everything about this woman's appearance and demeanor spells one word: Money.

"September Larkin," she announces by way of introduction.

September?

She notes my surprise and titters in a coquettish laugh just short of a giggle. "Mother named me after my birth month."

I paste a smile on my face and nod. September Larkin seems to be cut from the same cloth as the Rice family and the assholes at Windy City Sky Tours... not exactly my favorite type of people.

She reaches back to clutch the hand of her daughter and drags her forward. "This is my daughter, Sapphire," she announces proudly, feeling the need to add, "Sapphire, of course, is September's birthstone."

Oh, isn't that just precious? I'm taking time away from the search for my daughter for this? The poor girl looks as if she wants to die. Penelope's and my eyes meet in a sardonic echo of my initial reaction.

Penelope, whom September has so far chosen to ignore, steps forward and forthrightly extends her hand. "I'm Penelope Brooks, Mrs. Larkin."

"Senior partner of Brooks and Valenti," I add, earning myself a wry smile from Penelope. What the hell, September's misogyny shouldn't go unpunished.

September nods curtly at Penelope and turns back to me. "Sapphire was well acquainted with Megan Walton."

Penelope nods, then settles into a seat at the table, motioning for our guests to do likewise. September is informing us about her family's social standing when Joan bustles in to extend September and Sapphire the courtesy of our beverage service. Sapphire accepts a bottle of chilled spring water. September takes a horrified look at the Mr. Coffee brewer on our side table and waves the offer away.

Penelope smiles at the girl. "You were friends with Megan?"

Sapphire nods.

"I'm sorry for your loss," Penelope says softly.

September, apparently unhappy to be shunted aside, leans in and injects herself back into the proceedings. "Was Megan Walton's cell phone recovered?"

"You'd have to ask the NTSB about that," Penelope replies.

September isn't pleased with the answer. She turns to me and demands to know where Megan's cell phone is.

I shrug. "If it wasn't recovered with her body, it's probably at the bottom of Lake Michigan."

She's either bewildered or scandalized by the possibility. "How can that be? Why wouldn't they try to find it?"

I'm tempted to reply, "Plane crash. Little object. Big lake," but simply offer up another shrug instead.

"The aircraft wasn't intact when they found it," Penelope says.

"But surely they looked?" September presses.

Penelope ignores the question and focuses on Sapphire. "As I explained to your mother over the phone, we will be treating this as a legal deposition, complete with a stenographer and a digital recording of our conversation."

Sapphire seems a little startled.

Penelope sits back, carelessly throws one leg over the other, smiles, and says reassuringly, "It helps us capture the information accurately. No need to be nervous. Okay?"

Sapphire smiles tentatively and nods.

"Are you ready?" Penelope asks Joan, who presses the Record button on the digital recorder and positions her fingers over her court reporter thingamajig.

"When did you last see or speak with Megan Walton?" Penelope asks once the preliminaries such as date, time, and names are out of the way.

"The July Fourth weekend."

A teeny lifting of Penelope's eyebrow mirrors my own surprise. September had intimated that her daughter and Megan Walton were BFFs. How likely is it that best friends, especially best girlfriends, wouldn't see each other for over two months?

Penelope is on my wavelength. "Were you both in Chicago over the summer?"

"I think so."

Penelope leaves it there and asks, "What did you wish to share with us about Megan?"

September steps in. "Would Megan's phone be usable if they found it?"

Sapphire rolls her eyes. "For God's sake, Mother, I *told* you they don't need Megan's phone to see her social media feeds."

September shoots her daughter an indulgent smile and then looks from me to Penelope and back again. "Everything these kids say or do or even breathes is on social media nowadays. Did you know?"

I nod. Hell, even *I* know that.

Penelope refocuses on Sapphire. "What did you want to tell us about Megan?"

"Have you seen her social media accounts?" Sapphire asks back.

Penelope shakes her head. "Megan's accounts were shut down immediately after the accident."

"That's not surprising," September says with her mouth twisting into a spiteful grimace. "That girl was the epitome of the spoiled high school rich bitch who grows into an irresponsible party girl. Megan didn't give a damn about other people. You have no idea how that little witch simply *brutalized* poor Sapphire during high school. It's just like her mother to hide the evidence by shutting her social media accounts down."

This is some sort of high school Mean Girls vendetta? Please, God. Spare me.

September's face morphs from spiteful to hateful with her next outburst. "If someone had put that girl and her bitch of a mother into their places years ago, perhaps none of this would have happened."

This dates back to Mommy's high school trauma? There better be more to this than September hoping to stick a knife in an old rival.

Sapphire seems to be embarrassed by her mother's bullshit. She ignores September and leans in to say, "There's something from last spring you probably need to see."

"What's that?" Penelope asks.

"Megan was bragging about bribing her way into whatever she needed—a qualification or something—to fly the planes her uncle's tour company uses."

Even sleepy-headed, hungover me is electrified by this revelation.

Penelope sits up straighter and asks, "Megan said she paid a flight instructor to get her rating for the Cessna 210?"

"Is that the kind of airplane Megan was flying when she... she crashed?" Sapphire asks.

"Yes, it is," Penelope replies softly.

A veil of sadness washes over Sapphire's face.

"Do you remember who else might have heard Megan talk about that?" I ask.

"Oh, everyone," she replies.

"Was this at a party or something?"

Sapphire shakes her head at me. "Megan posted about it on social media."

My spirits sink. All record of Megan's social media has long since been scrubbed by her family. Sapphire leans across the table to Penelope with her cell phone in hand, taps the screen a few times, does a finger swipe or two, and presents the screen for inspection. I inch sideways to look. Apparently, not even the Walton family has the clout to erase all record of their daughter's social media presence.

"I'm in!" exclaims a social media post under a photo of a smiling Megan Walton. "Uncle Jonathan had to pay the asshole instructor a boatload of money to get him to pass me, but I'm rated on Cessna 210s! Yay! Come fly with me on Windy City Sky Tours starting next Thursday!"

Penelope gets Sapphire to text screen shots of a couple of dozen pertinent posts, befriends her or whatever they call it on this year's hot social media app, and thanks her for coming in. I'm happy to usher September and her daughter out of the office.

My good spirits evaporate by the time we set about returning my office to a respectable executive suite.

Penelope claps her hands and smiles. "This is great! It totally changes the landscape of this case."

Does it? I wonder. Bobby is still dead. Is Brittany? What it doesn't change is Joe's demand that we betray our clients. When I don't hop onto the happy dance wagon, Penelope's brow furrows with concern.

"What's up, partner?" she asks. "You look like a ghost just walked over your grave."

Penelope's mention of ghosts and graves is distressingly apt for the realization that just blindsided me. What will Joe do if Billy and Rick win? Would their victory be a death sentence for my daughter? My mind swirls from one depressing thought to another while I imagine a slew of frightening possibilities. I take Penelope's hand and lead her to my desk after we finish putting my office back together. After she settles into a guest chair, I lean my butt against the desk and look down at her. "We need to talk."

"About?"

I walk around the desk and drop into my office chair, then dip my head and rub my temples while I search for the words to tell my partner that we can't win the case against Windy City and Avgas … at least not yet. Do I tell her everything? Does she need to know about Matteo Giordano? In the end, I realize there's no way to dance around the crux of the problem, which is Joe's demand that we throw Billy and Rick under the bus. I draw a deep breath, cast my eyes to the ceiling in what might be an actual prayer for mercy, and then drop them to study Penelope while I launch into the story of Joe. Once I start spilling my guts, I don't stop until she knows everything, right through to Matteo Giordano's parting words last night.

By the time I finish, her facial expression passes from initial shock and disbelief to bewilderment and finally hurt. "I can't believe you haven't shared a word of this with me, Tony. I'm your partner. I'm your *friend*."

I repeat the parts about Joe threatening me if word of his visits got out.

"Joe warned you not to speak with the police, so I understand why you didn't tell them right away. But me, Tony? You don't trust *me?*"

I apologize, rationalize, and make every excuse I can think

of, but I know damned well I should have spoken with Penelope the morning after Joe first appeared in my living room. She deserved that. Billy and Rick deserved it, too. I get up and fix myself a coffee. Penelope declines my offer to get her one as well. I snag a couple of muffins before I sit down again.

Penelope leans back in her chair, crosses her legs, and runs her hands through her hair several times while she thinks. Is she going to throw my ass out and terminate our partnership right here and now? I sample my coffee while I await my punishment.

Penelope finally meets my gaze and surprises me by asking, "Have you got access to two hundred and fifty thousand dollars?"

She's not throwing me out? I shake my head. "Not in cash, no."

"Liquid investments?"

Again, I shake my head. "I'll call my investment guys on Monday morning to see what I can get my hands on quickly."

She gives me a long look. "What about the Titan settlement?" She's referring to the million dollars she'd extracted from Titan Developments in a lawsuit over the harassment and other skulduggery that had been employed in the effort to drive my parents and their neighbors out of their Liberty Street homes.

"All Papa's," I reply.

"All of it?"

"His house. His money."

She shakes her head softly and gives me a gentle smile. "I suppose that shouldn't surprise me. It was the decent thing to do."

Have I just been called decent? By someone I've just betrayed?

"What about the Fleiss Lansky settlement?" she asks next, referring to my payout from the wrongful-dismissal suit.

While satisfying and nothing to sneeze at, the settlement hadn't produced anywhere near as big a payoff as the Titan action did. A good portion of the Fleiss Lansky windfall was gobbled up by legal fees and a mountain of credit card debt I'd run up while unemployed. More was invested in our legal partnership.

"What's left is invested," I tell her. "I'll find out how much of it is accessible—and how quickly—on Monday."

She nods, then strikes her thinking pose. "You know, that quarter million this Giordano guy demanded is really for Francesco's benefit."

I nod.

"Francesco has all that Titan money, plus the house. At the risk of sticking my nose somewhere it doesn't belong, this is really *his* issue. He's the guy who shot the man in Italy way back when. He's who the killers are after now. Right?"

I nod again.

"Seems to me that Francesco should be the guy footing the bill for his own safety, Tony."

"I don't disagree."

"Then that problem is solved?"

"You'd think so, right? He's got the money in CDs at a few different banks."

Penelope looks relieved while she mimics ticking an item off an imaginary list. "Perfect. One down."

"I wish it were that simple," I mutter. "In the rush to sneak Papa out of the country, I didn't get him to execute a financial power of attorney."

She groans. "So, all that ready cash and no way to get at it."

"Right," I confirm before getting up to score another couple of muffins.

"Can you send the paperwork to him wherever he is now?" she asks.

I haven't told her that Papa landed in Penne, Italy. I do now. "We're not in contact, though. Too risky."

She slumps lower in her seat and mutters, "Darn it." Then she brightens. "I've got some money in IRAs and a few other investments. I'll round up what I can if you're short."

I feel like even more of a heel now than I did five minutes ago. How the hell did I not realize that I could trust Penelope with anything and that she'd be solidly in my corner come what may?

"Okay, I think we've taken that talk as far as we can at the moment," she announces while reaching across my desk to snag a muffin. "What about this Joe guy? How do we balance Brittany's safety against Billy and Rick's interests?"

I turn my palms up, collapse back into my seat, and brush muffin crumbs off my shirt. "I haven't got a damned clue. I've been thinking about it for days and haven't come up with anything workable."

"I can't believe you've been shouldering all this alone, Tony. You should have come to me."

I nod gratefully. "I know that. Now."

"What do the police say?"

"They're still investigating. They haven't gotten anywhere."

"That's frustrating," she mutters in disappointment. "They're usually all over missing kid cases and, well, after what happened to Bobby, you'd think they'd have a little more sense of urgency."

"They don't know everything," I tell her softly.

Her eyes narrow. "Pardon me? What haven't you told them about?"

"Giordano."

She dips her head and rubs her forehead between her thumb and fingers. "But he explained quite a bit you didn't know, didn't he? Put some things in proper perspective?"

"True."

"You need to tell Jake Plummer about him, Tony."

"What if Joe really does have eyes and ears in the police department?" I counter. "He knows Pat and Bobby's parents filed missing person reports, so he doesn't blame me for Jake knowing that the kids are missing. If Jake gets wind of Giordano and Joe finds out, though, things could get dicey."

"Assuming Joe even knows about Giordano."

"Of course, he does!"

Penelope looks at me in pity. "This guy's really gotten to you, hasn't he?"

One might say so. I think back to Jake telling me that Joe is hardly Superman. Maybe Penelope has a point.

"You're not thinking straight, Tony," she continues. "The police are the guys to trust here, not this Joe character. You're playing right into his hands."

"I don't want her to get hurt."

She gets up and comes around the desk and rubs a hand in soothing circles around my back. "Then you need to get the police involved with everything, partner. Trust them to play their cards close to the vest."

"And if they don't?"

"They will," she assures me. "A final thought?"

"What's that?"

"We can't leave Billy and Rick twisting in the wind. We have a responsibility to them that we can't put off indefinitely."

"Brittany's safety comes first!"

She nods sympathetically and lays a hand on my shoulder. "Agreed, but we don't know how things really stand with Brittany."

"What's that supposed to mean?"

"As much as I, or anyone, hates to consider it, we need to be alive to the possibility that Joe may have already killed her."

I can tell how much it pains her to have this conversation, but I'm still pissed at her for giving voice to the unspeakable.

"It's possible that Joe plans to use the time he's bought to make a play to put the screws to our client, Tony. We can't give him the opportunity to do so."

I can't believe she's prioritizing a civil lawsuit over the safety of my daughter. "We've got Sapphire's deposition."

Penelope settles her hands on my shoulders and gazes into my eyes. "And if Joe knows about that?"

The possible answers are all varying shades of disaster. "We're giving him time to eliminate Sapphire."

She nods.

I head home to spend the rest of Saturday searching for a quarter million dollars I'm not sure I have.

CHAPTER TWENTY-NINE

I'm still counting pennies when Jake calls to tell me that we need to talk.

"We know who Joe is," Jake announces triumphantly an hour later as he settles into a seat in the cramped office at Zack's Used Books. We figured meeting here would be safe, with me coming in the front and him slipping in the back door from the alley. Zack Menzies runs his bookstore from a small steel desk wedged into a tiny office that also holds a trio of four-drawer file cabinets. The building has the peculiar smell of burnt dust caused by ductwork in dire need of cleaning.

"What's his real name?" I ask.

"Giuseppe Vitale."

"So, he really is an asshole named Joe," I mutter, Giuseppe being the Italian equivalent of *Joseph*.

"Yeah," Jake mutters with a wry smile. "Right on both counts."

"Are you picking him up?" I ask tentatively. My initial burst of excitement was immediately tempered by the realization that this could be a bad thing. Like the dog that finally chases down that elusive car, the outcome of the encounter may prove tragic for the pursuer. In this case, Brittany's death could well be an unintended side effect of catching up to Joe. Which is backward thinking, I suppose. How else will we get her back?

Jake shakes his head. "We know who he is but not where he is. We're looking, though. So is the FBI. The question is: Now what? Even if we do locate him, do we move in on him? That could put Brittany in mortal danger if…."

I have no difficulty surmising the unspoken next three words: *she's still alive.*

"Then there's your father to consider. A lot of moving parts in this thing, all interconnected in some way."

I nod.

"Makes it hard to know what to do," he says unhappily.

"I know." I relate the story of Sapphire Larkin's visit. "Penelope and I don't know what to do next."

Jake shakes his head and frowns. "Ain't that a bitch? You've finally got the bastards by the balls, and you're scared to squeeze."

"Penelope raised the possibility that waiting might put Sapphire at risk."

"How so?"

"Gives Joe time to track her down if he gets wind of her story."

Jake blows out a long sigh. "Your partner has a point. Then again, Joe probably doesn't know anything about Sapphire."

"But he might. Can't you take her into protective custody or something?"

Jake dips his chin and rubs his hands over his face. "I'll look into it."

"If we sit on the information and we lose her, we're doing Billy and Rick a disservice for nothing," I continue. "Especially if Joe already killed Brittany."

Jake winces. "We've been kicking options around with the

FBI. It's hard to know what to do, you know? Do we push harder and risk tipping off Joe and his pals to their peril? Nobody wants to put Brittany at risk, but the longer she's gone, the better the odds become that something bad will happen."

"Or has happened," I add morosely.

He nods. "We wish we had more information to work with."

I can't hold his gaze and drop my head to study the floor. There's still Matteo Giordano to discuss.

Jake stirs, and an edge creeps into his voice when he says, "*Now* is the time to come clean if there's anything else you haven't told me, Mr. Valenti."

The use of my surname brings my eyes up to his. He's angry.

"Your daughter's well-being may well depend on us knowing everything there is to know."

"There *is* one other thing."

"Damn it!" he exclaims with disgust before I get another word out, which kind of pisses me off.

"It just happened on Friday night," I say defensively.

He throws his hands up in the air. "Today is Sunday!"

"When were you planning on returning my call from yesterday?" I retort. I'd heeded Penelope's plea and called Cedar Heights PD, leaving a message for Jake to call me ASAP.

He looks confused. "Yesterday?"

"Yesterday. I left a message for you at work."

Anger flashes across his face. "Sorry, then. Mind you, you could have called my cell."

"I don't have the number."

That surprises him. He scribbles it on a notebook page, rips it out, and pushes it across the desk. "You also could have called the feds. I gave you a name and number."

I shake my head. "Don't know them, don't necessarily trust them, suspect they might have balled things up."

Jake takes my little diatribe in stride, then asks, "What's this other thing you forgot to mention?"

"Grab your notebook so we only have to do this once," I suggest. He does so with a wry smile. Then I tell him about Matteo Giordano's visit.

Predictably, he blows up. "Another mobster?"

I suspect he's angrier about gangsters crawling out of the woodwork than he is about me speaking with them. Still. "It's not like I'm inviting these guys over!"

Jake sighs and nods. "Fair enough."

"The feds would have gone after Giordano if they'd known he was here, wouldn't they?" I ask. "Even if it put Papa and Brittany at risk."

"Probably so," Jake allows.

My interests aren't aligned with the FBI's interests. Something to keep in mind. "Anyway," I say, "Giordano called me this morning to follow up."

"Did you get a number?"

"Blocked, of course. He's probably back in Italy by now."

Jake nods in agreement. "Probably so."

"Anyway, I told him I'll do everything I can to raise the 250K tomorrow when the banks and markets open."

"And until then?"

I shrug. "He reminded me that Papa's safety isn't guaranteed until I pay up and they take care of the situation."

"Speaking of which, any mention of what 'taking care of the situation' entails?"

I swallow and shake my head. "No, and that's been bothering me."

"How so?"

"What *does* taking care of the situation mean?"

He shrugs his shoulders in a "don't ask me" gesture.

"They won't kill him, will they?" I ask anxiously.

"They might. I doubt they'll want to keep eyeballs on him for any length of time."

"I'm not sure I can live with paying for a hit."

"Then don't think about it, Tony. Remember Ed Stankowski?"

I swallow and nod.

"All right, then. To hell with this guy. He's got it coming to him."

He's right, I suppose, but it's going to take some time for me to process things. In the meantime, there are more pressing concerns. "Giordano knows where Papa is."

The detective's eyes widen. "He has the address?"

"He didn't mention an address, but he knows Papa's in Penne with his sister."

Jake is clearly shaken by the news. "How the hell can he know that?"

Like I know.

"Jesus H. Christ," he explodes. "I played that close to the vest. Real close."

I shrug again. If Jake doesn't know, I sure as hell haven't got a clue.

"So, what next?" he mutters.

I feel as if I'm lost in a fun house maze of mirrors. "I don't know! My daughter is probably dead, and we're trying to figure out how to bring in Joe without putting her in danger. What do we do about a gangster from Italy who knows where Papa is hiding? Hell, the bastard might have already popped Papa. Either way, he's going to walk away with two hundred and fifty thousand dollars of my money that maybe I could have used to free Brittany." I push my chair back so hard that it topples over. "The hell of it is, there's no way to know!"

Jake watches my blowup without comment. After I pluck the chair off the floor, drag it back to the table, and sit down, he meets my gaze. "There *is* a way to check on Francesco."

There is? Why the hell hasn't anyone told me? Not trusting myself to speak civilly, I gesture at him to continue.

We're interrupted by a knock on the door. Zack Menzies pokes his head in. "Everything okay in here?"

Jake nods and gestures at me. "Yeah, this clumsy ass fell off his chair."

Menzies smirks at me and backs out.

"The kid who picked up Francesco and Max in Austria… your nephew, isn't he?" Jake asks.

I nod. "Beppe."

"Odd name, but he sounds like a good kid. Max and Beppe worked out a backdoor channel just in case one of them needed to reach the other."

"And?"

"Beppe's girlfriend's sister runs a café that he frequents. Max has a sister who lives somewhere north of Bumfuck, Maine. He and Beppe exchanged burner phones and worked out some kind of code to get messages back and forth. If Beppe needs to talk, he'll call Maine, Max's sister will get word to Max, and he'll call the café in Penne. If Max needs to talk, same routine in reverse."

"Great. Let's find out if Papa's okay."

"My initial thought, as well," Jake says. "But don't you think Beppe would have tried to reach Max if anything was wrong?"

There's a certain logic in that, but. "What if something happened to Beppe, too?"

Jake sighs. "Yeah, there's always that possibility."

"There are altogether too many possibilities, almost all of them with shitty endings," I grumble, then ask, "Why the burner phones? Why not just call her house?"

"Couple of things. Max had the same question. Francesco's sister doesn't have a phone. Phone directories, mobsters bribing phone company employees, just too many ways for that to go wrong. When this all began way back when, they decided that sending letters was too risky. Someone peeks in a mailbox and sees a return address, you know. Anyway, they applied the same principal to phones."

"Almost sounds a little overly paranoid," I say.

Jake shakes his head no. "We're talking about some nasty bastards, Tony. Your dad and his sister might have done the right thing. Worked well enough for fifty years, didn't it?"

"True."

Jake sits back and plants his palms on the desk. "The Giordano angle gives us another avenue to explore. I'm going to sit down with my FBI friends to see what they know about him and pick their brains on next steps."

"Will they be pissed that it's taken me a day to reach out to you?"

He chuckles. "Probably, but I think you hit the nail on the head about their knee-jerk reaction. Giordano's probably wanted in the US, and that would override whatever concern the feds might have about the safety of Brittany and Francesco. The missed phone message may turn out to have been a blessing in disguise."

Sounds like I've done something right. Inadvertently, of course. "So, you'll talk to the FBI."

He nods.

I twist in my seat in a bid to get comfortable behind the desk, but there isn't enough room to stretch, so I stand and push my arms straight up above my head. My fingers touch the ceiling when I do so. How in hell does Menzies work in this cubbyhole?

I hope to God Joe doesn't get wind of the FBI's involvement. "The FBI is being careful, right?" I ask.

"Sure. This isn't their first go round with these people."

"Will I have any idea what's going on?"

Jake thinks that over for a long minute before he replies, "I'll keep you in the loop as much as I can."

I slap my hands down on the desktop and lean over to

hover above Jake before asking, "Meaning?"

"What you need to know, you'll know," he replies curtly.

"Where will you draw the line on that?"

"Need to know. Any plans need to be tightly held for operational security."

I think I know what that means. I won't be told a thing.

He gives me a tight smile. "Yeah, just what you're thinking. I'm not telling you a damned thing about whatever operational plans we decide upon."

Probably a wise idea. I resist the instinct to challenge his decision. He's not going to bow to whatever pressure I try to exert. Nor will he respond to a heartfelt plea from a worried father. He'll stand his ground and do whatever he thinks best. It's a quality I've come to admire—even when it doesn't get me what I want.

"One more thing about Giordano," I say.

"Jesus, Tony. I thought you already told me everything."

I shrug. "This is a little vague. He said he might be able to help out with Brittany."

"How?"

"I'm not really sure. The *Ndrangheta* is a bigger outfit than the Lucianos, right?"

"Oh yeah."

"Would the Lucianos follow an order from Italy?"

Jake thinks on that for a long moment. "I don't know. Maybe."

"What if Giordano threatened them?"

"I don't see it, Tony. I doubt the *Ndrangheta* is willing to put that much effort and risk their prestige over a matter as minor as this is. At least to them."

"What if they get something in return?"

"You've got more money tucked away somewhere?"

I shake my head. "No. Giordano mentioned me owing him a favor if he intervened."

"What did you say?"

"Nothing, really. He caught me off guard."

"What can you possibly do for him besides pay ransom?"

"Helping him out if he ever needs legal work done here."

"Jesus," Jake murmurs while he runs a hand through his hair. "Whatever he asks won't be legal. You know that?"

I nod.

"But if it gets Brittany back," he muses.

"Exactly."

"Cross that bridge when you get to it?"

"I'm kinda thinking that way," I agree.

"I don't know what to tell you. These are dangerous people, Tony. Cross them, well…"

"I'm not even sure he *can* help," I mutter. "Hell, he might just pocket my two hundred and fifty grand and walk away with it, leaving Papa to twist in the wind."

"Yeah, that's possible," Jake says unhappily. "Guess you need to decide how to play the favor conundrum."

I nod. "If it will get Brittany back, what choice do I have?"

"Helluva spot to be in, pal. I wouldn't presume to tell you what to do. Detective Plummer says that you should tell him to go to hell. Your pal Jake says you gotta look out for your daughter's safety. Whatever you decide, be careful with these people."

"I will."

"I need to get to work, Tony. You go out first in case this Joe character has eyes on the place. I'll visit with Zack for a bit and then slip out the back door."

I'm fully immersed in desperation and melancholy by the time I get home. Commiserating with Puckerface after I feed him underscores Brittany's absence. I wonder if—just like Mama's roses—nursing Puckerface along will end up being my way of trying to hang on to a piece of my daughter. I try to drown my sorrows in a fresh bottle of Maker's Mark that takes me through the afternoon and into the evening.

I stir in fuzzy bewilderment when the ringer on my phone

wakes me up. My neck is bent into some sort of pretzel shape that refuses to yield to my attempts to roll or straighten it, my leg is asleep, and it's pitch dark in the living room as I fumble about for the phone.

"Hello?" I ask sleepily when I finally find it and connect the call.

"It's me," Trish says in a tone that is equal parts concern and annoyance. "I haven't heard from you in a couple of days."

"Sorry," I mumble. She's been so sweet and discreet, touching base now and again, not pressing for details, just letting me know she's thinking about me and hoping for the best.

"Have you been drinking?" she asks.

"Maybe."

Her voice softens. "Maybe? You're an adult, Tony. It's legal. Can't say I blame you."

Misery loves company. Should I ask her over?

"No news about Brittany?" she asks, throwing a damper on whatever carnal thoughts are stirring.

"No news," I mumble. Mafia visitors notwithstanding.

"Okay, then. Please keep in touch."

"I will."

"Now, go sleep it off," she suggests with a trace of humor in her voice.

If only I could sleep this nightmare away. Instead, despair burrows into me like a living thing creeping into the very center of my being. I wander the family home alone while I tumble deeper and deeper into a bourbon-fueled waking nightmare in which I'm faced with a life empty of the people I value most. Mama. Amy. Mel. Papa. Brittany. Fate seems to be squeezing me dry... using me up. Swallowing a bottle of pills or taking a long one-way swim in Lake Michigan might be the only way I'll find peace if things go all to hell. That's the bourbon talking, I know... but I'm starting to listen.

CHAPTER THIRTY

I t's now Tuesday, three days after my chat with Jake about Joe. Hard to believe it's only been eight days since Brittany vanished. I'm at work again. Thoroughly exhausted again. Thoroughly discouraged. Again. Why am I even bothering to come to the office? It's not as if it's keeping my mind off my daughter. I'm drinking my first cup of coffee and thinking I should probably pack it in and go home when Penelope knocks on my door.

"Are you okay?" she asks.

"I suppose," I murmur before I drain the rest of my coffee. I'm about to get up to leave when she walks in and sits down in one of my guest chairs.

"I have a meeting in a few minutes that I'd like you to sit on, if you don't mind."

Why not? And who am I to say no to Penelope. "Sure. What's it about?"

"It's with the attorney from the insurance company that carries the R & B policies," she replies. "He insisted on coming."

"Why?" I ask. As far as I know, everything has been worked out and R & B's policy has been reinstated.

"I know, right?" she replies. "This hardly needs to be handled in person, so I'm a little concerned that he might be coming to throw us a curveball. I'd like you with me in case this turns out to be trouble. I don't want to end up in a he said, she said pickle."

Now I'm curious about the purpose for the meeting, too. "What time is he coming?"

She glances at her watch. "Any minute now."

Like magic, Joan appears in my doorway and looks at Penelope. "Mr. Lennox is here, honey."

Penelope smiles. "Thanks, Mom. Tony will sit in."

Joan looks a little uncertain about that, but nods. I don't blame her—especially if I look anywhere near as burned out as I feel.

Randall Lennox smiles at Penelope with a gleam in his eye when we walk into the reception area to introduce ourselves.

"So, your name is Penelope Brooks, huh?" he says with a chuckle,

"And you're Randall Lennox," Penelope replies with a soft laugh. "Now we know."

I shake hands with Lennox as my eyes travel between him and my partner. "Anyone care to let me in on the joke?"

"We were both at Butterworth Cole at the same time," Penelope tells me.

"Never met, never even knew her name," Lennox adds.

"Same," Penelope says with a laugh.

"Two ships passing in the night, as it were," he says.

Penelope does an eye roll. "How sad is that?"

After a little reminiscing on their lives post-Butterworth Cole, we collect beverages—coffee for Lennox and me, tea for Penelope—and settle in the conference room.

"So, you wanted to do this in person to reconnect with Penelope," I say to Lennox.

He shakes his head. "I had no idea she was here."

"Then why are you here in person?" Penelope asks.

"Maybe I'll explain when we finish up," he replies enigmatically.

What's that about? I wonder warily.

Finishing our business takes all of ten minutes before he hands us the official reinstatement letter, a copy of the policies, and asks us to relay his firm's apology to Rick and Billy for the "unfortunate misunderstanding."

"Unofficially, can you tell us where the information came from that prompted your company to cancel the policy?" I ask.

Lennox frowns. "I don't know for certain."

"Can you ask around?" Penelope asks.

He responds with a rueful smile. "I made a discreet inquiry or two about that and was rebuffed. Quite firmly, considering that I was only displaying a little curiosity about a matter I was litigating."

"Doesn't add up," I say.

Penelope's brow furrows. "No, it doesn't."

"I assumed it had to do with alienating a client or something along those lines, but that didn't quite feel right," Lennox says.

"Maybe they were afraid of someone," I say. "As in physically frightened."

"You might have it right," Lennox says as we start to pack up. "The guy who warned me off near wet his pants when I broached the topic."

Penelope gives him a searching look. "And that's why you're here, Randall? To warn us?"

"Partially," he replies. "Here's another interesting tidbit. Rumor has it that none other than Herbert Cumming himself paid a visit to one of our executive VPs, only hours before we started to take an interest in Rick Hogan's liver transplant."

"Really?" Penelope asks in disbelief.

He nods "You shouldn't be surprised. You worked there—you saw how Cumming operates."

"I suppose," she murmurs.

"Anyway," Lennox continues, "now that I know who you are and that we're fellow Butterworth Cole escapees, there's something else I should pass along."

"What's that?" I ask.

A slow smile crosses Lennox's face as he digs a Butterworth Cole business card out of his pocket and hands it to me. "You might want to talk to this guy. He's a pal of mine from law school with a thing or two to get off his chest. He tells me that our Butterworth Cole friends are playing both sides of the fence on your case."

"Sleazy, but hardly surprising," Penelope says with a snort of disgust. "I'd like to nail Cumming's butt someday, but we both know how well he covers his tail."

Lennox winks at her. "Maybe you're about to get your chance."

I give him an appraising look. "You almost left without giving that to us. Why?"

He shrugs. "I wanted to take the measure of you folks before I slipped you the card. I'm not about to throw my pal to the wolves."

I nod. "Fair enough. He's still with Butterworth Cole?"

"For now," he says as he reaches the door. "What you do with this from here on is your call. Hell, I'm not sure if it will help. Good luck."

After we say goodbye to Randall Lennox, a grin turns up the corners of Penelope's mouth as she plucks the card from my fingers. "This could be sweet, partner."

I'm not convinced that we've been handled a cudgel we can wield in court, but Penelope may figure out a way to use it to bludgeon Cumming's professional standing. My thoughts turn to my missing daughter as we enter my office. Brooks and Valenti are doing a very poor job of meeting Joe's demand to throw the case. I relay my worry to Penelope.

She frowns. "Ideas?"

I drop into my chair and stare out the window. "I don't think there's a thing I can do for Brittany at this point. Her fate is in the hands of Jake and the FBI."

Penelope nods solemnly, sets her chin in her hand, and does the tapping on the tip of her nose thing.

"The thinker," I say wryly as I watch, but it's me that comes up with an idea.

"Let's ask for an emergency meeting with Judge Ngo and make a big deal about wanting to discuss a settlement," I suggest.

Penelope looks startled for a moment before a smile teases her lips. "Good thinking, partner."

"Might buy us a few days if Joe gets wind of it."

"Oh, he'll get wind of it," she says as a smile blossoms on her face. "Wisnowski and Luigi, Cumming—someone has a direct line to Joe. In the meantime, I'll reach out to Randall Lennox's law school friend.

CHAPTER THIRTY-ONE

J ake Plummer calls me an hour later. "Where are you?"

"At the office."

"I need to see you. Right now."

"Not here. Joe may be watching."

"Where, then?" he asks impatiently. His urgency is spooking me.

"Go to our new office," I reply after a moment's thought. "It's not unusual for me to stop by over the lunch hour to see how the work is going."

"What's the address?"

I give it to him and add, "If you get there before me, just go on in."

"Give me and Max ten minutes to get there before you leave. If Joe is watching, we'll already be inside when you arrive."

The ten-minute wait to be on my way is torture. What's up? Is Brittany okay? Is Papa? What other calamities might they be coming to tell me about?

"What's up, partner?" Penelope asks as I pace around the office like a zoo animal looking for a way out.

"Detective Plummer needs to see me."

"Everything's cool?"

"Nothing's cool," I snap.

She touches my arm gently. "Just checking that there's no bad news, Tony."

"I know. I'm sorry."

"No worries." We stare at each other for an awkward moment.

"Good luck with Plummer," she says before retreating to her office.

I linger for five more slow-moving minutes before setting out for our future workplace. The building itself is a definite step up from the strip mall. We're on the second floor, up a narrow staircase or a slow elevator ride from street level. The smell of fresh paint grows stronger as I take the steps two at a time before stepping into a bright space that will be Joan Brooks's greatly expanded reception area.

Jake and Max stare at me from the open doorframe leading into my new office. The wooden interior doors are all off somewhere to be stained. The place actually looks substantially complete. The painting is underway, only a couple of electrical fixtures remain to be installed, and the IT connections are mostly in place. The furniture is still to come. A pair of five-gallon paint containers sits beside freshly painted walls. Ladders are scattered about, drop cloths cover the floor, and paint rollers and brushes lie here and there.

Jake waves a hand around. "Pretty nice place."

"Great windows," Max adds.

Both Penelope's and my offices feature tall, wide windows. "One of the things I like best."

"When do you move in?" Jake asks.

"Supposedly for Christmas," I reply, parroting our contractor's promise. He might actually keep this one. "That's not why we're here, guys. What's up? Did you find Joe?"

Jake nods. "Yeah. We'll come back to that in a minute."

What's more pressing than that? The obvious answer slams into my brain like a sledgehammer. Brittany.

"Got a note this morning from the Italian police via Interpol to say that the problem in Orsomarso has been resolved," Jake continues. "Guess you paid up?"

I nod. With Penelope's help and a margin loan against my investments, I scraped together Papa's $250,000 ransom by noon Monday and promptly wired it to a bank in the Cayman Islands. The news from the Italian police confirms that it made its way to an account belonging to my latest Mafia buddy. Speaking of which, Giordano called earlier today regarding Brittany and the favor. I told him that I'll do whatever the hell he wants if he can get her home. He was going to check into it and get back to me in the next day or two. He closed by reminding me that I'm agreeing to an open-ended favor, collectible at any time on his terms. I reluctantly agreed. With any luck, someone will blow him away before he comes to collect.

"Giordano's work, I imagine," Jake says about the news from Italy. "Maybe a quiet word to cease and desist."

"A bullet in the head is a hell of a lot more likely," Max adds from his perch on an upended empty five-gallon paint pail.

Jake nods. "Yeah. Could be. Anyway, problem solved one way or another."

I feel sick deep in the pit of my stomach at the thought of the bullet-to-the-head solution, which would make my $250,000 blood money. Jake is studying me, perhaps intuiting where my thoughts have gone.

"So, Joe," he says.

I'm happy to turn my thoughts elsewhere. "You found him?"

"Yeah."

"And?"

"The FBI still isn't sure where Brittany is, and moving on

Joe is too risky without knowing. They'll act fast if they locate her."

"*If,*" I mutter.

"Afraid so," Jake says sympathetically. "They've got a few wiretaps in place and are tailing Joe as best they can."

"As best they can?"

"He's Mafia, Tony. Most of them know how to shake a tail. There's also the little matter of not spooking him, so the feds lose him now and then. They hope he'll lead them to Brittany."

"How likely is that?" I ask skeptically. The FBI has known about Joe for four days. Nothing in their vaunted bag of tricks has helped us one whit to this point.

Jake steps across to lay a hand on my shoulder. "Don't despair. They've been picking up cryptic communications they think might be about Brittany. If so, that suggests she's still being held."

Which suggests she's still alive! "Held where?" I ask.

"There's the rub," Jake mutters unhappily.

"No ideas?"

"Some. The feds are leery of poking around too closely for fear of showing their hand. That's too risky for Brittany unless there's a location to move on."

"Yet the clock is ticking," Max mutters.

Jake's been pacing throughout the conversation, which makes me nervous. He's usually a pretty calm guy, so the display of nerves is unsettling. He takes a deep breath and meets my gaze. "Me and Max have a bad feeling about where this is going and are worried as hell about Brittany. We think something is brewing."

"Why?"

"The pattern of communication between the goombahs has changed," Max answers. "New voices, more frequent chatter. Same code words but more urgency."

"The usual signs that something is developing," Jake adds.

"We're wondering why," Max mutters. "What triggered the new activity? Maybe word of what this Diamond chick told you got out somehow."

"Sapphire," I clarify.

Max shrugs impatiently. "Yeah, her. Did you send her to the NTSB? If not, how long can you hold off?"

My shoulders sag. "Penelope and I got our wires crossed. She already filed against AAA and Windy City. She's chomping at the bit to get moving with Sapphire."

Jake looks annoyed. "Maybe the court filings set Joe off."

"This Sapphire shit can't wait a few days?" Max asks tersely.

"Not long, if at all." I explain Penelope's fear that delaying may prove fatal to Sapphire *and* our case.

"That's a good point," Max says.

Jake tosses an unused paint-roller sleeve in the air and catches it. "Yeah, it is. The FBI was supposed to pick up Sapphire for safekeeping. Let's hope they did. Anyway, what's done is done. Maybe the court filings pissed off Joe, maybe it was something we don't even know about. The important thing is that something is afoot."

"What does the FBI think?" I ask.

Jake frowns while he continues tossing the roller sleeve. "We're not all on the same page at the moment."

"How so?" I ask in alarm.

"They don't share our sense of urgency."

"We're pretty sure Joe and his people are gearing up to make a move," Max says. "If we're right, we need to act now. The FBI isn't so sure."

"But I think J.P. is moving our way," Jake says.

"J.P.?" I ask.

"The FBI agent in charge," he explains. "J.P. Duclos."

We fall silent, with Jake and Max presumably thinking next steps and me worrying that they're moving too quickly. Or the FBI is going too slowly. Hell, I don't know what I think. I only know that I'm worried sick. I tell them about the meeting with Lennox and our plan to seek an emergency hearing, and conclude, "We hope it buys us a couple of days with Joe."

Max nods in approval. "Two or three days may be all we need."

Jake misses catching the paint roller, which rolls under a ladder. He leaves it there. "Let me call J.P. to get the FBI take on things. If something's going to happen, it's probably going to happen soon."

"Like tonight," Max grumbles.

Tonight? "Then what?"

"We'll let you know," Jake replies.

"When?" I ask anxiously. "*Not* after the fact, Jake. Please."

He gives me a long look and answers with a noncommittal, "We'll see. In the meantime, speak to your partner. No more new motions that might set Joe off. Keep this Sapphire news under wraps if you can."

"I'll talk to her." Whether it will make any difference, I don't know.

Max slaps his hands on his thighs and pushes himself up off the paint bucket. "Probably won't matter, anyway. Dollars to doughnuts, something is going down tonight. We need to get our asses in gear," he tells Jake as he heads for the door.

"We'll be in touch," Jake assures me as he turns to follow.

"Wait!" I exclaim. "Don't I leave first?"

Jake nods. "Jesus. I've gotta get my head out of my ass."

I touch his arm as I pass by on my way out. "No harm done."

As much as the days of uncertainty have been eating me alive, the idea of everything coming to a head as soon as tonight is even more frightening. The finality of that stirs up every fear in my being. I break into a cold sweat. *If* Brittany is still alive somewhere out there, she may not be by morning.

Thoughts of her pour through my mind as I walk back to the office. Brittany the toothless baby gumming my fingers and then smiling up at me with her little pink tongue lolling about in her mouth. The precocious toddler toddling all about. My little girl, doting on Daddy before it became unfashionable to do so. The self-assured teen she grew into. The damaged teen she became after Michelle abandoned us. The memory of losing her to Michelle and Europe last year still bites hard, as does the fear of losing her again if Michelle and her father get their way.

Those thoughts take me back to Gadsby's—was it really only a little more than a week ago?—and the happy memory of Brittany going toe to toe with her mother and grandfather on my behalf. Not to mention Pat's revelation about Brittany wanting to stay in Cedar Heights. The notion of another human being wanting to be with me is almost foreign. Thoughts of my brother's assessment of me surface but don't quite take hold, pushed aside by thoughts of Brittany's support and Trish's seeming approval. The years of being conditioned—or conditioning myself?—to feel inadequate are proving tough to overcome, but Brittany needs me to be strong for however long she has… be it hours, days, weeks, or hopefully decades to come. I feel so damned powerless. I don't know what, but there has to be *something* I can do to help.

CHAPTER THIRTY-TWO

After a restless afternoon at the office following my lunch hour meeting with Jake and Max, I've dropped by Pat's to feed Deano and take him for a trek around the block. He's still slower than hell as he hobbles along in the rain, but at least he's up and around and doesn't seem as tender when I towel him off. He's making progress. Physically, anyway, but the poor old guy seems to be down in the dumps. Deano's probably wondering if he has a family anymore. He's lapping up water from his bowl when my cell phone rings.

"Where are you?", Jake asks without preamble.

"Pat O'Toole's house," I reply as I rip a handful of paper towels off a roll mounted on a counter spike. Deano has left muddy paw prints on the floor.

After a pause during which I hear muffled conversation on the other end of the line, Jake says, "We'll be along in a few minutes."

"Sure."

"Is there parking in back?"

"Yeah."

"Good. We'll come to the back door."

I stuff the phone back in my pocket and stare aimlessly out the window as my head spins out possible explanations for the impending visit. None of the scenarios I imagine ends happily. Jake's going to give me a heart attack one of these days with his calls about needing to see me right away.

"What's going on, Tony? Has something happened to Brittany?"

I look up to find Pat studying me with concern from the bottom of the stairs. She's wearing faded jeans, a gray, long-sleeve T-shirt, and fuzzy Dumbo slippers that were a gift from her niece.

"I'm not sure," I reply. "Jake and Max are on their way here."

"You look scared."

I shrug and squat down to clean Deano's paws, and then start in on a tummy rub. "Maybe a little. I'm a little frazzled in general."

She frowns and changes the subject. "I had a chat with Ben Larose today. The NTSB people were drafting their final report when they received some sort of bombshell information that put things on hold."

I think I can guess what that is. Penelope sent Sapphire Larkin to the NTSB with her Megan Walton story, but it's not for public consumption. Not yet, anyway, so I can't tell Pat about it.

"Does Ben have any insight into the FBI's plans regarding Billy and Rick?" I ask.

"He thinks that can still go either way."

I guess there's still room for hope on that score. Temporarily distracted, my hand has gone still on Deano's tummy. His wet nose nudges my derelict fingers back into action.

"Ben's sources suggest the investigation is leaning toward a finding of pilot error, although they're considering other contributing factors," Pat continues. "Whatever new information they received supports the pilot-error theory."

Damned right it does.

"Anyway," Pat says, "the report will be delayed for another couple of weeks."

After I discussed Sapphire's situation and our fears with Jake and Max, they spoke to their FBI contacts. The Feds agreed that the information should be held closely and have taken Sapphire into protective custody until Joe is rounded up. I hope they can keep her safe.

Two car doors slam out back. Pat glances out the window while she stirs cream into a cup of tea. "Here they come."

I wait with my heart pounding against my ribs. I *know* something momentous is coming. Jake sounded on edge over the phone, and he and Max are stone-faced when they step inside. I give Deano's tummy a final rub and get to my feet. The dog sighs in disgust, then turns his head away and rolls onto his side.

"Tony," Jake says curtly as he peels off his dripping jacket. Max merely nods a greeting.

My flagging spirits revive a little when I recognize grim determination in their demeanors. They don't look like a couple of guys resigned to delivering catastrophic news.

Jake grabs Deano's damp towel off the floor and starts to wipe his face, wrinkles his nose in distaste, then holds it away and studies it with disgust. I stifle a chuckle. Ah, the smell of wet dog. There's nothing quite like it.

"Can we speak with Tony alone?" Jake asks Pat after he drops the towel and reaches for the paper towels.

Pat's a little surprised, maybe even a little miffed to be kicked out of her own kitchen, but she recovers quickly. After shooting me a look filled with fear, she collects her tea mug and trudges up the stairs as if she's ascending a hangman's gallows.

"Got any coffee?" Max asks.

I put on a pot of coffee and dig three mugs out of the cupboard while he and Jake settle in around Pat's kitchen table.

"So?" I ask when I join them.

"The FBI is moving in tonight."

My heart skips a beat. "They know where Brittany is?"

"Not exactly," Jake mutters.

What in hell does that mean? "Is she okay?"

Jake waves me off and says, "Sorry. Let me back up a bit."

"Okay," I mutter impatiently while Max pulls a plate of cookies close and snags a few.

"The FBI has come around to our thinking that something is going down tonight," Jake says. "A move, maybe some-thing more."

The words "something more" send a chill through me.

"J.P. is pretty confident that they've narrowed Brittany's whereabouts down to two possible locations."

"Where?" I ask.

"Both are more or less local," Jake replies.

Whatever more or less local means. Probably not impor-tant. "They'll hit both places at the same time?"

Jake shakes his head.

"What?" I ask in alarm. "Why the hell not? Those bastards will kill her the minute they know the FBI is after them!"

Jake frowns. "Have you been following the news this afternoon?"

"No." As if I have time for that these days, or an inclina-tion to watch some stranger kvetching about his or her fears for my daughter's well-being—as if Brittany is something more than a vehicle to boost viewer ratings. "What did I miss?"

"There's a celebrity kidnapping and hostage situation in California."

I get up to pour three mugs of coffee and carry them back while Jake fills me in on the irrelevant details of events in

California. As if I care. There are already sugar, sweetener, and creamers nestled in a basket in the center of the table. I peel two sweeteners open and empty them into my mug, dump in a couple of creamers, and wait while Jake fixes his coffee.

"What does the BS in California have to do with us?" I ask.

"J.P. was supposed to have two HRT teams on hand tonight," Jake replies. "One is now on its way to Los Angeles."

"HRT teams?" I ask.

"Hostage Rescue Teams," Max explains.

"What does this mean to us?"

Jake eyes me steadily and says, "The FBI has only one team to hit two sites tonight."

Now I'm totally confused. One team. Two raids. "So, they're going to hold off, right?"

"J.P. is pretty confident that something's going down tonight. You already know we agree with that. They aren't going to wait."

"How in hell does this make any kind of sense?" I ask. "What if they target the wrong place?"

"That would be a problem," Max mutters. Jake nods in agreement.

I try to wrap my head around the FBI's logic. "They'll hit one and then move on to the other if Brittany isn't at the first place?"

"It's not quite that simple," Jake replies. "Both locations are Luciano family safe houses. There appear to be people at both."

After pondering this for a long moment, the implications of it scare the shit out of me. "If they target the wrong location, word will reach the other place before the FBI can get there, right?"

They nod soberly.

"The goal is to pick the right spot," Jake says.

Why not just state the obvious?

"The FBI has quite a bag of tricks in its arsenal," Max says in a nakedly transparent attempt to soothe me.

"They'll try to jam communications into or out of the property they hit to prevent the other safe house," Jake says. "With any luck, nobody will be able to sound the alarm."

With luck. Jesus. "And if they don't get lucky?"

"That could be very bad," Max admits glumly.

"The mob isn't exactly in the Stone Age when it comes to technology, either," Jake adds with downcast eyes. "Shutting down their communications isn't a slam dunk."

This all sounds much too risky to me. What the hell became of the movie and television cops who have all the right tricks and tools to consistently clobber the bad guys inside of an hour or two? "Use a local SWAT team for one site?" I suggest.

Max shakes his head. "The risk of a leak is too great."

"Then maybe they should wait," I argue.

"I don't think so," Jake says unhappily, underscoring the reality that they and the FBI feel compelled to play a hand they'd just as soon fold on.

"But," I murmur while knowing full well that there's really nowhere to go with the thought. What's about to happen is out of my hands. These two and the FBI probably know best, but that just builds on my feelings of impotency in the matter of saving my daughter. My idle hands reach for a peanut butter cookie. I chew and wash one down with coffee while battling to steady my nerves.

Jake looks at me levelly. "Look, Tony, there's no guarantee HRT can get her out safely even if they get the location right the first time."

It's a sobering realization. I plant my hands on the edge of the table and push my chair back a couple of feet so I can rest my elbows on my knees. "They'll go in sometime after midnight?" I ask. That's how it's always done on TV and in the movies, hitting the bad guys hard while they sleep, doze, or otherwise go comatose at just the right moment.

"Normally, yes," Jake replies. "Doctrine is to go during the wee hours."

"But maybe not tonight," Max interjects. "We're not sure we have that kind of time on our hands."

Jake nods. "That's right. If the bastards have something planned for tonight, they won't wait until the wee hours to do it."

We sit in silence for a long minute while I study my shoelaces. I suspect we're all consumed with the same thoughts and fears.

Jake and Max are studying me intently when I look up. A silent signal passes between them before they exchange a nod.

Jake slides his chair back, slaps his knees, and stands up. "So, against an explicit FBI directive, we're thinking that we'll quietly stake out the second target location."

"Who's we?" I ask.

"Me and Max."

"Just the two of you?" Are they crazy? What the hell can two old cops accomplish alone against a nest of gangsters?

"Maybe with one or two of Ed's fossils, if we can arrange it," Jake replies.

"If we can find any of the candy-assed old bastards who haven't already bugged out to Florida for the winter," Max adds with the trace of a smile. Despite the direness of the situation, the old bugger is relishing the prospect of chasing after bad guys.

The more I think about them going in on their own, the more aghast I am at the risk they'll be taking. "Why don't you take some regular cops with you?"

Jake shrugs uncertainly. "Same security issue as involving

a second SWAT team. I'm still smarting over Giordano knowing where we stashed Francesco."

"Can't take a chance that Jake's got a Mafia mole in his backyard," Max mutters in quiet fury. "If I ever catch the bastard, he'll get the same treatment the Mafia doles out to snitches. Throat slit and his balls stuffed down his throat."

I cringe at the visual. The vehemence of the statement and the look of rage on Max's face startle me. I don't think it's an idle threat.

"So, maybe just the two of us," Jake says softly. The prospect doesn't seem to sit well with him, yet he and Max are prepared to risk it all on behalf of my daughter.

"I'm coming," I blurt.

"No!" they reply in unison.

"Yes," I retort.

Jake settles his hands on the back of his chair and smiles grimly while he stares down at me. "What the hell would you do?"

"I don't know. Drive? Be an extra set of eyes and ears? Something, damn it!"

They exchange another of their telepathic looks. Max nods. Jake nods back.

"You any good with a gun?" Max asks me.

"Remember Papa's position on guns?" I ask.

"Right," Jake says with a snort. "So, the answer is no."

"That's right," I admit in frustration.

Max watches the exchange, then turns to Jake. "Shotgun."

Jake thinks for a long moment before he nods and turns to me with a look of reluctant resignation. "I don't like this *at all*."

"No choice," Max says.

Jake doesn't look convinced as he continues to study me. "Involving you may turn out to be the biggest mistake I ever make, but we *could* use an extra body. If we can't get a fossil or two organized, I guess you're in."

Max reaches over and clasps my forearm in an iron grip while he stares hard into my eyes. "You'll do *exactly* what we tell you to do. That shotgun will be for self-defense and *only* for self-defense."

Jake nods in agreement. "Understood?"

I lick my suddenly dry lips and nod. "Understood."

Jake stares me down for a long moment, as if he's assessing my response and deciding if I can be counted on in a pinch. Whatever he sees in my eyes seems to satisfy him.

"We'll need wheels to get Brittany away in a hurry if we end up springing her," he tells me.

"We'll leave you with the car and the shotgun," Max adds.

I swallow. Mama always warned me to be careful about what I volunteered for. This certainly fits the bill, yet I don't regret my impulsive offer to go along, no matter how much the prospect of what may lie ahead terrifies me.

Jake steps back from the chair and mutters, "We need our heads examined."

Max shoots him a sardonic look before he finally releases my arm. "Just point and shoot that thing if you need to," he tells me matter-of-factly.

I nod slowly. "As long as Brittany isn't around."

They exchange a concerned look. At the mere thought of me with a gun, or at the idea that I might end up in a situation in which Brittany is nearby and I have to shoot?

"Right," Jake finally says. "But if Brittany is there, she should be coming out with us."

"And if you're not with her?" I ask.

They stare back at me without comment.

I realize that will only happen if Jake and Max have been taken out or are otherwise occupied, leaving me alone to face one or more armed gangsters.

"That shouldn't happen," Jake assures me.

Shouldn't.

CHAPTER THIRTY-THREE

I t hasn't taken me long to disregard my first directive of the night. It's been almost an hour since I dropped off Jake and Max on the shoulder of a secondary road. They are now making their way through several hundred yards of forest to our target, an old country farmhouse a few miles into Wisconsin. My instructions were to drive around the back roads while they crept through the woods. I did so for about ten minutes before my nerves got the better of me. What if I got into an accident or attracted attention from the local cops? What if the beaten-up old 2009 Dodge Journey Max had requisitioned from his son broke down? Max assures me it runs much better than it looks, but the rust spots, dents, and scrapes adorning its oxidized black paint don't inspire much confidence. Looking on the bright side, aside from the Illinois plates, it fits right into the neighborhood.

I've pulled into a little stand of bushes off the side of the road about three miles from our target. From here, the Journey should be pretty much invisible from the crumbling asphalt road—not that there's much traffic. The evening air is cool and heavy with humidity. The rain has stopped for now and the sky is clearing, but the ground is still damp. Water drips from the trees, and there's a little haze hanging ten or twelve feet in the air. It will develop into ground fog in the coming hours. I've stopped obsessively checking my watch. What's the point in tracking every single minute that crawls by? For maybe the fiftieth time, I heft the shotgun and mimic aiming and shooting until the motion feels somewhat familiar —or at least not totally foreign.

It's eleven thirty-seven when the tip of what will be a full moon finally edges above the trees. Jake and Max should be in position; they'd timed their excursion through the woods to arrive just before moonrise so they'd have darkness for their approach and moonlight to operate with after arriving. As we were on the evening when we spirited Papa out of the country, we're dressed head to toe in black, complete with ski caps pulled low over our foreheads and ears. Just like any other self-respecting SWAT team, we're outfitted with the latest personal cell phones to coordinate our stealth mission. As if on cue, mine vibrates in my jacket pocket.

The text from Jake is a simple letter *A*. I don't respond. I'm to keep off the phone unless some sort of emergency arises that Jake and Max absolutely *have* to know about—bad guys coming, tanks, the plague, that sort of thing. The text notifies me that Jake and Max are in position at the farmhouse. It also signifies that I'm to move to my initial post, which is a stand of trees in a turnout about two miles from the farmhouse. Our plan is a little threadbare from this point forward. Jake is carrying our one piece of technology, a compact directional listening device they hope will give them an idea of what's happening in and around the farmhouse. We'll see. Jake browbeat J.P. Duclos of the FBI into agreeing to give him a heads-up if the FBI Hostage Rescue Team deviates from its scheduled assault on Target One, with the understanding that the information was for his ears only.

"She's gonna have my ass if she finds out you're with us," Jake had warned me in the car on our way here.

"J.P. is a woman?" I asked.

Jake nodded. "Yup."

"I've never heard a woman called J.P. before," I said. Rather stupidly, now that I think about it.

Jake smiled. "Exactly. She claims it helps the troglodytes to accept her bio and reputation without having to sort through their sexist baggage. Seems to work most of the time."

Max had chuckled and told Jake, "When she finds out that we're out *here*, she'll have your balls, too."

"If so, she'll be the first woman to show any interest in them in years," Jake retorted with a laugh.

The exchange had loosened the tension in the car for an instant, but not by much. I could use another break in the stress that begins to squeeze my chest when text *B* arrives a few minutes later, signaling that they're ready to move. Time to relocate closer to the target property. With all lights off, including the interior and dashboard lighting—Max had gone so far as to pull a few fuses to make sure I couldn't screw things up—I carefully back out of my hiding spot and drive to another turnout screened by trees. This one is within 400 yards of a gravel drive that leads to the farmhouse. Max also seems to have pulled the fuse for the rear-window defroster, so I've opened all the windows to keep the window clear and have the heater cranked up to keep me warm. I turn it off now so I can hear better. Once parked, I've been tasked with a quick recon to ensure there are no other vehicles lurking nearby and that no guards have been posted at the entrance to the property. I'm concerned there will be and that they'll spot me. Then what?

After I maneuver the Journey into position, I can't see a damned thing through the branches and bushes. My fingers snake across to the shotgun that rests on the passenger seat and close around it as I ease the driver's-side door open. Max gave me a ten-minute lesson on how to load and fire the thing. It all seemed simple enough when there were no distractions, no sweaty palms, no shaking hands, and nobody pointing a weapon back at me. It doesn't seem simple now. I work my way deeper into the trees and part some branches to have a look up the visible portion of the driveway leading to the house. All clear. Same for the intersection where the driveway meets the road. Aside from soaking my head in the bushes, so far, so good. No call to inform my partners is required. We're operating on the principle that no news is good news. I exhale a breath I didn't realize I'd been holding, creep back to the van, slip inside, towel off, and peek at my watch.

Eleven fifty.

If all is well and the FBI team is on schedule, show time will be in five minutes. I'll make my next move if and when Jake sends prearranged text C.

Jake Plummer is sweating in the damp, cool night air, despite being soaked from the waist down after the trek through the woods. He's hunkered down behind a low stone wall about sixty feet from a back door that's nestled under the rear porch of a white farmhouse. A single, bare incandescent light bulb casts a pool of light around the entrance. With his night vision fully engaged and moonlight filtering through the thin cloud cover, Jake has a decent view of the target building through a small pair of binoculars. The house isn't particularly well kept up. The white clapboard siding is coated with a layer of grime. The aluminum-framed windows and standard steel door with a glass upper panel look to be at least a couple of decades old. The earpiece from a parabolic directional microphone is tucked into his right ear. It's capable of picking up sound from as much as 500 feet away. Jake slips the binoculars back into one of the generous leg pockets of his black tactical pants, then picks up the microphone and aims it across a cracked and chipped concrete patio at a sliding kitchen window. It's cracked open an inch or two. He can hear men's voices, but not clearly enough to make out what they're saying or even to be certain how many voices there are. To add to the confusion, the flickering light behind the red-and-white-checkered kitchen curtains is almost certainly from a television, which may account for the voices.

At least we know someone's in there, he thinks.

Max is in position covering the front door and a black, late-model Ford F-150 pickup truck that is parked about fifteen feet away from it. He and Jake are wearing earpieces that are attached to their cell phones. They've dimmed their screens to almost nothing by using settings Jake wasn't aware of before Max showed him. Who would have guessed Max was a techie?

I hope to hell J.P. remembers to clue us in when they move on Target One, Jake thinks anxiously. That farmhouse is several miles outside Rockford, Illinois, about an hour west of Chicago. Even a few seconds' advance knowledge might make all the difference if and when the shit hits the fan here. His thoughts then turn, as they often have tonight, to the third member of their team. Or, more accurately, he once again begins to worry about Tony Valenti, operationally and as a matter of conscience. Agreeing to include Tony on the operation went against all of Jake's instincts. What the hell was he doing putting a civilian in harm's way?

"Tony's got more skin in the game than anyone," Max had told him when he prevaricated over bringing Tony along. "He knows the risks."

But does Tony really understand them?

"We need him, and I get the sense that he'll rise to the occasion if he needs to," Max had concluded.

Jake, thinking back to a year ago when Tony helped his father beat a murder rap, is confident Tony will try to. But going head-to-head against Luciano family soldiers in the wild isn't quite the same thing as kicking the asses of a prosecutor or two in a courtroom.

Jake's phone buzzes with a text from J.P. Duclos of the FBI: *Moving now.* Jake is in the process of forwarding it to Max and Tony when the directional mic feed erupts in his ear.

"The cops are raiding Rockford!" a guttural voice exclaims from inside the house. So much for the FBI's ability to jam mob communications.

"Let's get outta here!" another man shouts.

"Fuckin' right!"

"People inside," Jake whispers into the microphone attached to the cord of his cell-phone earpiece. "At least two males. They know about the Rockford raid."

"What about the girl?" the second and younger-sounding voice calls out.

"You know," comes the reply.

What the hell does that mean? Jake wonders in frustration. He wedges the parabolic antennae between a pair of rocks to free his right hand and pulls a Glock pistol out of its shoulder holster. Against every impulse he has, he holds fast and waits, desperately hoping that he didn't just hear an order to do away with "the girl," who is almost certainly Brittany Valenti.

No joy, reads a new text from J.P. Duclos.

Jake thinks for only a fraction of a second before deciding to send a request for help. *Am at Target Two,* he texts. *Joy here.* He hopes that J.P., who Jake suspected and hoped was wise to his and Max's plans, earmarked some assets to send to their aid if need be.

Jake ponders his next move. The bad guys already know they have company, so things will start hopping any minute. If he and Max get into a firefight trying to get Brittany out, they'll probably need the Journey on short notice to make their escape, so it makes sense to move Tony closer. Doing so is a risk, but seconds saved could prove critical. If Tony goes where he's supposed to and does what he's been told to, he shouldn't become a target.

Jake sends text C.

"Hey!" comes a voice from inside, "I got a guy on camera hiding behind the rock wall out back!"

That would be me, Jake realizes as a rush of adrenaline surges through him.

"How did that happen, asshole?" the deeper, older voice roars. "You watching porn again instead of monitoring the damn cameras?"

Thank God for porn, Jake thinks dryly while he calls Max and tries to tuck himself more tightly behind the meager protection of the two-foot-tall stone wall. Nobody inside is going to hear him and Max amid their bickering. "They know I'm out here," he whispers to his partner. "Expect them to bug out any moment, probably shooting when they do. They mentioned a girl."

"Is she going with them?"

"I don't know. One said to the other, 'You know what to do,' whatever that means."

"Shit!" Max hisses, sounding every bit as impotent as Jake feels. "What's our play?"

A very good question, Jake thinks. Go in? Let the bad guys get to the pickup truck if they try to move Brittany, then follow? Keep them from getting to the vehicle at all? Should he plan for FBI support?

"Jake?" Max whispers impatiently.

"Thinking."

"Think faster."

"They're not taking that girl anywhere if I can help it," Jake decides aloud. With the FBI now in play, he wouldn't give a plug nickel for Brittany's safety if these bastards get away again. "Don't let them get in the car if you can stop them without hitting the girl."

"Copy that."

The night falls still for an interminable moment, during which Jake weighs the pros and cons of making a move of their own. Go? Don't go? The decision is promptly taken out of his hands.

Gunfire erupts from the front of the house. Semiautomatic. Big bore. Max is outgunned, but the sharp crack of his Glock assures Jake that his partner is still in the fight. Jake begins to scurry toward the front of the house to support Max, trying his best to keep low behind the wall as he does. He's only moved ten feet when the back door explodes open and a man bursts out with an assault rifle, cuts sideways a few steps, and starts firing on full automatic. While he sprays rounds along the wall and into the spot where Jake had been only seconds ago, Jake ducks behind a bush and grips his Glock in both hands. His enemy's magazine clicks empty within seconds.

Undisciplined bastard, Jake thinks with a sliver of hope while the shooter slaps a fresh magazine into his weapon. *I'm only gonna get one shot at this guy before he turns that thing on me. Do I warn him before taking him out?*

Jake's in a millisecond of indecision when a second man wearing jeans and a T-shirt barges out the back door with someone slung over his shoulders in a fireman carry. He runs toward the south side of the house and disappears around the corner. Jake's eyes snap back when the shooter unleashes a fusillade into the bushes, walking the stream of lead toward his hiding spot. Jake shouts "Police!" and squeezes the trigger just before the heavy-caliber bullets shred the shrubbery he's sheltering behind.

Max has just put his target down beside the pickup and shot out the truck tires when automatic gunfire erupts from the rear of the house. He breaks cover and races toward the action. The gunfire stops after a few seconds.

"Police!" Jake shouts.

What the hell? This is no time to give the scum balls a break! "Put him down, Jake!" Max hollers as he sprints along the north side of the house. The crack of Jake's Glock is all but drowned out by the roar of the heavier automatic gunfire. The shooting stops within seconds. Max recklessly turns the corner onto the back patio with his gun thrust ahead of him and slides to a stop. A groaning man he doesn't recognize is sprawled on his back. An assault rifle lies on the ground a foot away from his twitching hand.

"Jake!" Max shouts. He kicks the gun farther away from the gangster while his eyes roam the back of the house and yard for additional threats. The only human sound is the labored breathing of the mobster at his feet. Max glares down at him and snarls, "Where's the girl?"

The unmistakable death rattle of the bastard's last breath is all the answer Max gets.

His attention shifts when he hears footsteps running down the driveway. *Gotta be Jake,* he thinks with relief when he spies someone sprinting away with a person draped over his shoulders. *And he's got Brittany!* "Yippee ki yay!" Max whoops as he bends down to collect the assault rifle.

He's about to set out after Jake and Brittany when he hears a low moan from the bushes lining the back patio. He studies the runner a moment longer. Big bastard, running a hell of a lot faster than Jake can—especially while carrying dead weight. So, where the hell is Max's partner?

"Jake?" he calls as he hurries across the patio toward the moaning and spies his partner's bloodied face peering up at him from the bushes. Max kneels beside Jake and rests a hand on his shoulder. "Who's the runner?" he asks as his eyes stray back to the driveway.

"No idea," Jake whispers hoarsely. "Carrying someone. Brittany? Warn Tony."

Max pulls out his cell phone and calls Tony. "You're about to have company. Bad guy carrying a girl coming your way."

"Brittany?" Tony asks.

"Could be. Keep your head down!"

Tony's reply is unintelligible. "Got it?" Max asks impatiently. Tony's whispered reply sends a chill through Max before he tucks the phone back into his pocket. Then he leans in closer to get a good look at Jake. Blood glistens on his partner's ashen face and coats his chest.

Jake holds up his cell phone and waves Max away. "I'm calling 911," he mutters. "Go!"

Max takes off after the guy carrying the girl. The man has a healthy head start. *I wish to hell I hadn't shot the tires out,* Max thinks bitterly as he runs past the pickup truck and spies his prey a couple of hundred yards ahead. *Son of a bitch is probably twenty years younger than me.*

I pull into position C, as instructed by Jake. I tuck the Journey into yet another little grove of trees and bushes, this one a dozen or so yards up the lengthy driveway leading from the road to the farmhouse. My instructions are to keep my head down and duck low beneath the dashboard to use the van's engine for protection if shots come from up the road. I have no role to play until Jake and Max need the vehicle brought up to the house or they meet me here.

Gunfire erupts from the direction of the farmhouse—booming explosions with a string of sharper little pops mixed in. Jake's and Max's shots would be the little pops. Handgun pops. The majority of the gunfire is from the bigger guns. It's heavier. Faster. Even from here, I can feel the damned blasts. It's all over in twenty or thirty seconds.

A quick glance at my phone shows no new messages from Jake. Or Max.

Now that whatever mayhem was taking place up there has ended, a message from one of them would be welcome. Are they okay? I sit still for a couple of seconds, mindful of Jake's orders to keep my head down while I await instructions. None come. We didn't discuss this possibility. I lift my head above the dashboard and look in the direction of the house, but can't see a damned thing through the tree branches and surrounding shrubbery. I ease the door open, step out, and rise to my full height to peer above the foliage. The vegetation still hampers the view, so I push deeper into the bushes and part a few branches. The roof of the house is visible in the moonlight above a rise in the driveway that obscures a view of the rest of the house and its surroundings.

The phone in my pocket finally vibrates. I duck down and pull it free, fully expecting to find a text letting me know that the excitement is over and it's time to bring the Journey. Instead, it's a voice call from Max.

He's talking rapidly before I get the phone all the way up to my ear. He sounds agitated, saying something about a bad guy and a girl headed my way.

"Brittany?" I ask stupidly.

"Could be," Max mutters. He's out of breath.

What the hell is going on? I wonder in the same moment that I hear footsteps approaching, crunching on the gravel. Whoever it is, he's coming fast. I don't hear what Max says next as I duck back into the van and pull out the shotgun.

"Got it?" Max asks when I put the phone back to my ear.

"He's coming," I whisper before cutting the connection and dropping the phone into a pocket. I hold the gun awkwardly across my body and take a sideways step closer to the drive as the pounding footsteps move steadily closer.

Only one set of footsteps? Didn't Max say that a guy and a girl were coming? The footfalls I hear are heavy. The guy, then. Where's the girl?

I duck down when a bobbing head appears above the rise

in the road. I'm confused by the silhouette for several seconds. Then I work out that I'm watching a man—an extremely large man—sprinting right at me with someone draped over his shoulders. One hand is wrapped around the legs of the person he's carrying. The other is holding an arm that dangles across his chest.

Which means his stomach is unprotected when I step into the drive and bury the muzzle of the shotgun in his midriff. I hope I've run the shotgun barrel clean through the son of a bitch. Air explodes out of his lungs as he slams into me. I realize it's Joe just before his forehead slams into my face. As we rocket backward in a tangle of bodies and limbs, I inadvertently squeeze the trigger. The blast of the shotgun is deafening. Then the back of my head slams into the packed rock of the driveway and the world goes black.

BOOM!!!

"Jesus God, no!" Max exclaims as he drives one foot after the other in the wake of whoever was bearing down on Tony's location. Silence replaces the startling explosion, save for the sound of Max's footsteps and his wheezing while he struggles to suck in enough oxygen to keep propelling himself forward.

Shotgun for sure. Did the mob bastard have one? Max has no idea. Surely, Tony didn't open fire. *I told him the bad guy was carrying a girl! Possibly Brittany, for Christ's sake.*

Max finally clears the rise that leads down to the road. Three bodies are strewn across the drive. All still. All silent. Oh God, what had they done? Maybe Jake was right when he wanted to leave Tony behind.

As he closes the distance, Max gets a better look at the bodies lying still in the moonlight. The smell of cordite hangs in the air. The girl is easy to pick out with her slender limbs all akimbo. She's tiny in comparison to the big figures sprawled on either side of her.

Secure the scene is his first thought when he reaches the bodies. *Where's the gun?*

Oh shit, that's Tony, he realizes when he looks down on the man lying face up. Tony's face is drenched in blood that is flowing freely and pooling on the gravel beneath his head.

"There it is," Max mutters when he spies a rifle butt sticking out from beneath the corpse that is face down—definitely a corpse, judging from a hole the size of a dinner plate that has been blown out of the back of the man's T-shirt. It takes Max the better part of a minute to wrestle the gun out from beneath the deadweight pinning it to the ground. He works the gun free and angrily flings it aside, then yanks out his cell phone to call Jake. No answer.

"Shit!" he howls at the indifferent moon before he calls 911 and unleashes a flurry of information.

"We've already received a call from that location. Units are on the way," the emergency operator says.

"Jake," Max mutters in relief. Maybe he's still okay.

"Pardon?" the operator asks.

"My partner. Jake Plummer. He called you?"

"Someone called," she replies. "An unidentified male. We're not sure what's going on, sir. What's your name and interest in the situation?"

"Maxwell," he replies impatiently. "Retired cop. My partner, Jake Plummer, called you. Is he still on the line?"

"No," the operator replies after a beat. "We received a call about gunshots with an officer and others down. That's all we got before the caller stopped speaking."

Max sags down on his haunches and rests his forehead in his palms while his phone dangles between two fingers.

"Sir?"

Max blows out his frustration in a long exhalation and lifts the phone to his lips. "You've got the location here?"

"Yes," the operator replies. "I need—"

"There are at least six victims out here," Max interjects. "There may be more in the house. Send multiple units. The scene seems to be secure."

"Sir!" the operator exclaims in frustration.

Max's eyes are on the still body of the girl when he snaps back, "I'm checking on people here, madam. Some of the good guys are down, okay? Make sure you get some cops and ambulances out here right now."

Max plunges the phone deep in his pocket as he pushes himself upright and reluctantly walks over to take a closer look at the girl. His first aid training warns him not to move her to take a closer look, but the sliver of face peeking out from under a hoodie confirms it's Brittany Valenti. Her right hand is tucked beneath her. The fabric covering her upper arm is speckled with the type of shredded tearing that comes from buckshot. Max's eyes stray to Tony while he softly asks the prostrate father, "What have you done to your girl?"

CHAPTER THIRTY-FOUR

I come to in an ambulance, groggy and disoriented as hell. Once my head begins to clear, I rip a pile of gauze off my face and reach for the paramedic who is perched beside me.

"My daughter?"

I startle the poor woman, who recovers quickly. "The girl who was with you?"

"Yes," I reply hoarsely.

She rests a hand on mine, meets my gaze, and smiles reassuringly. "She's fine. Bump on the head, a little buckshot in the arm. Nothing serious."

I let out a deep sigh of relief. "When can I see her?"

"At the hospital. Her ambulance is right behind us."

I start to sit up to look out the back window and am overcome by dizziness and nausea. The paramedic reaches for me and pushes me back down. "Whoa, Daddy. You fared a lot worse than she did."

"She's okay?" I ask when the world stops spinning.

She nods.

"She's been through hell."

"I heard a little. Poor girl."

"What did they do to her?"

She shrugs. "Can't say, but I can tell you that she's one tough little gal. Whatever she's been through hasn't broken her spirit."

"Does she know about Bobby?"

The paramedic gives me a blank look. "Was Bobby one of the people who got shot out there?"

"No. Her boyfriend. They killed him."

The paramedic's eyes widen. "I didn't hear anything along those lines, but we were kinda busy with you."

I retreat into dark thoughts about what Brittany has been through. Then the blackness closes in again. When I resurface, I'm being wheeled through an emergency room entrance.

"Dad!" Brittany cries out from behind us. "Wait!"

The stretcher slows before Brittany's tear-streaked face appears above me. She looks terrified.

"Hey," I manage to croak.

"Oh my God, Dad! What have they done to you?"

"I'm fine," I tell her.

Her eyes cut to my paramedic friend, who nods. "He'll be okay. It looks worse than it is."

A manic little laugh of relief escapes Brittany as she throws her arms around me.

The paramedic gently tugs her away after a few seconds. "You might want to hold off on the hugs for a bit, honey. He's probably a little tender."

I try to wave the paramedic aside, but she shoves my arm back to my side and starts wheeling me away. Brittany jogs along beside us. Once we reach the counter, my paramedic tugs her away.

"He needs to see the doctor now, sweetheart. So do you."

Brittany breaks away long enough to lean in and plant a kiss on my cheek. "Hurry up in there, okay?"

I manage a smile and nod.

I check out of the hospital after a few hours in the emergency room. Brittany is with me as we emerge into the lobby.

We've both suffered concussions, plus various scrapes and bruises. I've got a broken nose. If it weren't for the haunted, faraway look in Brittany's eyes and a gauze bandage on her arm, you'd be hard-pressed to see any sign of her ordeal. She caught a few bits of buckshot in her arm when the shotgun went off, but the wounds are minor—especially considering what happened to Joe. Jake Plummer is a different matter. He was still in surgery when I checked out. Max says things are touch and go. Fucking Joe. I'm glad I blew the sonofabitch away.

I call a cab to pick us up.

"Bobby?" I ask Brittany.

Her face crumples. "One of the paramedics mentioned him," she says through a torrent of tears. "I didn't know he was dead until then. Why, Dad? Why?"

I gather her into my arms and stroke the back of her head. "I'm so sorry."

She pulls back after a minute or two and turns her tear-streaked face up to mine. "I suspected the worst after they took Bobby away, but they wouldn't tell me anything about what they planned to do with him. When I asked if they were bringing him back, Joe just smirked."

The bastard.

"I'm glad you killed him, Dad."

I nod. I'm certainly not lamenting the end of Joe, but being the instrument of anyone's death isn't sitting well with me.

"You want to talk about Bobby?" I ask.

She winces and swallows, then shakes her head. "Later, Dad. I'm still having a hard time believing that he's really gone. Besides, you can barely talk."

It's true. My shattered nose has been wrestled back into place and is being held there by some sort of cast, supplemented with a swath of gauze and surgical tape. My nostrils are packed with cotton or something. Speaking is a chore.

We sit quietly for a minute or two before a couple of

people approach. FBI, judging from their demeanor and the cut of their suits.

"Mr. Valenti?" a middle-aged woman asks.

I nod. "FBI?"

She nods, then introduces herself and her partner. "You feel up to talking to us?"

I cut my eyes to Brittany, who is curled up against my side, then shake my head. "Not now?"

She nods as her sorrowful eyes linger on Brittany, then hands me a business card. "We'll need to speak with both of you. Soon."

I nod and pocket the card. "We'll come by tomorrow, if that's okay?"

"Tomorrow is good," she says. "For what it's worth, I'm sorry we'll have to put you through more grief. You've been through more than enough already."

"Yeah," I reply.

"You're free to go," she says with a final sympathetic glance at Brittany. A mother, no doubt.

I thank her, wondering if she would have sprung me if she'd known I have murder on my mind. Good thing I didn't mention it. With my common sense a little scrambled by the drugs from the hospital and maybe the knock on the head, I have decided that I have business to take care of. I have the cab drop Brittany at Pat's house.

When I don't get out of the cab, Brittany turns a surprised look on me. "Where are you going, Dad?"

"I hab a little business to take care of."

Pat, who has come out to greet us, leans down to meet my gaze. "Hab?"

I shrug. The letter V is going to be absent from my vocabulary for the foreseeable future.

Pat eyes me suspiciously. "Business, Valenti? Whatever it is can wait. You should be in bed."

"Soon," I mutter.

When I call to check in with Penelope and tell her where I'm heading next, she demands that I stop in the office first. I do, and when she fails to dissuade me from what she proclaims to be "your crazy idea," insists that she'll drive. I down a couple of extra painkillers before we leave.

"I can't talk you out of this?" she asks a final time when she parks at our destination.

I reply by pushing the car door open and climbing out.

We barge through the doorway of Jonathan Walton's Willis Tower office five minutes later. Walton's eyes widen for a second when he sees us. My blackened eyes are swollen almost shut, but I can see enough to enjoy the moment of fear in his eyes when he recognizes us. I hope the sight of me scares him as much as it frightened Penelope when I walked into the Law Offices of Brooks and Crooked Nose Valenti a short while ago. If my appearance doesn't terrify the jerk, the erupting volcano of my fury ought to do the trick.

"Walton," I growl.

Walton's smug smile drops back into place after he absorbs my appearance. He immediately presses the intercom button on his phone.

"Security," a deep male voice responds.

"Get up here right now."

"Yes, sir!"

Last night's events in Wisconsin haven't yet hit the airwaves. Otherwise, Walton might not look so cocky as he adopts the Asshole Pose by easing his chair back and casually crossing an ankle over a knee. He tilts his head an inch or so and smirks. "You've got maybe a minute to say whatever you're here to say."

Penelope tartly replies, "You'll be seeing plenty of us in the days ahead, Mr. Walton."

"Hopefully in the many nightmares you deserb to hab," I add.

His lips curl up in an amused smile. "Deserb to hab, huh?" he mocks. "Did you take a fall in the shower, Valenti?"

I don't reply. Penelope does.

"Don't be an asshole," she snaps. "The man is hurt."

Walton shrugs. "Whatever. You should have called Herbert Cumming before you came here to bother me."

"Cumming," Penelope mutters in disgust. "He's your lawyer, after all, is he?"

"He's the guy you'll need to speak with about settling the claim against your client."

"So, you really are in bed with Butterworth Cole and the goombahs," I say while a smile tries to form on my face. A picture of Jack Nicholson as the Joker in an old *Batman* movie comes to mind. It scared the hell out of me as a kid. Bet that's how I look. Hope so. "Why doesn't that surprise me?"

A deep voice behind us snaps, "Stay where you are. Don't move!"

Security has arrived. "Is he going to shoot us, Jonathan?" I ask Walton with my eyes locked firmly on his. "If he does, you'll hab to wait for the FBI to show you what we'b brought."

Walton's cocky smile falters at the mention of the FBI. His eyes shoot past us to his security guy. "Let's hear them out for a minute or two."

"Are you sure, Mr. Walton? These people are trespassing. I can have them removed."

I ease the corner of a sheaf of papers out of my shirt pocket and cock an eyebrow at Walton. "Interesting stuff, Jonathan. Sure you don't want to hab a look-see?"

A big hand grabs my biceps and jerks me back a step. "I told you not to move!"

Penelope reacts before I can. "Get your hands off him!" she snarls while ripping Mr. Security Guard's hand off my arm.

Walton holds his hands up. "Stand down, Jones. You can turn them over to the cops after I hear what they have to say."

"If anyone is about to get handed over to the police, my money is on it being you," Penelope snaps.

"You sure you want Jones here to listen to this kind of talk?" I ask Walton. "You might want to get Oliver and Caitlyn in here instead. Jones's ass isn't on the line. Theirs are."

"Along with yours," Penelope adds sweetly, lest Walton feel left out.

When Walton hesitates, I turn on Jones, whose eyes widen when he takes in my battered face. He's a big boy, though not Joe and his goombahs big. Not as tough, either, I'd wager. I lean in just a bit and say, "Miss Brooks is right. If anyone's getting frog-marched out of here today in cuffs, it's probably gonna be your boss. I suggest you go back whereber you came from and keep your head down."

Walton goes pale at the mention of handcuffs.

"That's right," Penelope says with anger bleeding into her voice. "It hasn't hit the news yet, but Tony helped rescue his daughter last night." As Walton's eyes widen in surprise, Penelope's voice turns glacial. "Your Luciano family friends kidnapped a couple of kids and murdered one of them to put pressure on Tony to lose the case against R & B Ramp Services, Mr. Walton. I'm betting you knew it. Expect a visit from the FBI sometime today."

I can tell Walton is wondering how to play this as his eyes flit about the room and his tapping foot goes into overdrive. There's always someone else to blame, some flunky to take the fall.

Not this time, asshole.

"Better call Caitlyn and Oliver," Penelope reminds him.

Walton nods at Jones. "Go ask Miss Tyson and Mr. Franklin to join us, then wait in your office until I call."

Jones shoots a final glance my way before he turns to go.

He looks unnerved, as he should be, working for an asshole like Walton. Who knows what mischief Jones has been up to at this dick's behest?

I pull a copy of Sapphire Larkin's deposition out of my pocket and toss the papers on Walton's desk after Jones leaves. Select screenshots from Megan's social media account are attached. "Interesting interbiew, Jonathan. Give it a read. Then we'll talk."

Oliver Franklin and Caitlyn Tyson file in a moment later. Penelope hands both their very own copies of Sapphire's deposition. Then we step back, rest our butts against a side table, and let them read. Franklin is as white as a grand wizard of the Ku Klux Klan when he finishes. He sits and fidgets while the others continue reading. Tyson finishes last, slams the papers down on Walton's desk, and turns a look of hatred on me. Maybe she's still miffed about my showing up to dash their hopes of setting Billy and Rick up a couple of months back? It's the only time we've met, after all. The loathing in her fiery eyes deepens when her gaze shifts to Walton.

"Is this true?"

"That's not all," Penelope pipes up before passing along the news that Walton was in cahoots with the Luciano crime family. "Were you two in on that, too?" she asks Tyson and Franklin.

After Tyson delivers a blistering twenty-second tirade at Walton, I step into the void. "We'll leab you folks to sort this out among yourselves."

"And the FBI," Penelope adds.

"Yes, them, too," I agree before I walk to the door and look back. "You know how to reach us."

"I think we can safely say that Rick and Billy are in the clear now," I mutter to Penelope as the Willis Tower elevator whisks us back to ground level. "Those shits are going to chew each other up trying to save their sorry asses."

She nods and says, "It seems so much longer ago than six or seven weeks since Billy first walked into our office with this mess."

And only five since the worst of this bloody nightmare started the first time Ed Stankowski was shot. Things got steadily worse from that point on.

Penelope helps me back into the car and shakes her head.

"I hope that made you feel better," she says.

"Maybe a little," I reply. "I'm just so furious at that bastard for putting Brittany at risk!"

"I get it," she says, then adds with a hint of a grin. "And you're stoned out of your mind."

She's got that right.

"You should be home resting with her," Penelope says firmly.

She's right.

CHAPTER THIRTY-FIVE

It's been a week since Brittany's rescue when Penelope and I enter Judge Ngo's courtroom to attend the emergency hearing that we requested last week. Andrea Wisnowski and Luigi the knuckle dragger are here to represent Windy City and AAA Avgas in their action against Billy and Rick. Herbert Cumming is also present, summoned to personally appear by Ngo after Penelope shared a copy of the complaint she filed with the state bar association alleging that Cumming was double dealing his client, Senator Mitton. Someone from Butterworth Cole must be present to keep today's proceedings from proceeding *ex parte*—that is, excluding any of the interested parties to the action—but this is not the sort of thing a senior partner at a large firm would bother coming to. So, Ngo is either making a point, or—and I dearly hope this is the case—he plans to punish or humiliate Cumming in some way.

Ngo peers down, his gaze roaming across all of us before it settles on Cumming for a long moment. He shakes his head sadly.

"All parties to this hearing seem to be present," he says. "Are we missing anyone?" After we shake our heads no, he straightens his shoulders and settles his gaze on Penelope. "You'll be speaking on behalf of your client, Miss Brooks?"

Duh. I'm still an unsightly mess. Better than a few days ago, for sure, but I still can't speak clearly. I'm here to offer Penelope a little moral support.

Penelope nods up at the bench. "That's correct, Your Honor."

Ngo studies the papers spread in front of him. "I hardly know where to begin," he grumbles with an icy stare at Cumming. "I've never seen a situation quite like this."

"May I address the court?" Penelope asks.

"Go ahead, counselor."

"Thank you, Your Honor. My request for a hearing is in regard to the lawsuit filed against our client by Windy City Sky Tours and AAA Avgas. We'd like to restrict this hearing to that matter."

"So be it," Ngo replies. "Although I may go beyond that topic after we finish addressing your original motion."

Penelope smiles up at him. "Thank you, Your Honor. In light of recent developments, we have been in communication with Miss Wisnowski. While we've presumably all seen the preliminary report of the NTSB concerning the September eighth crash of a Windy City aircraft, we also know that the report itself is not admissible as evidence in a courtroom. Nonetheless, we have taken steps to prove that the preliminary finding that the cause of the crash was due to gross negligence on the part of Windy City Sky Tours and their pilot, and that no fault accrues to our client, R & B Ramp Services. Given the facts of the matter, we have proposed that this action be withdrawn. Miss Wisnowski has indicated a willingness to do so."

Ngo's eyes cut to Wisnowski. "Is that so?"

"To some extent, Judge," she replies. "Opposing counsel has also proposed that we concurrently negotiate a financial settlement in favor of their client to conclude the matter of their countersuit against our clients."

"And your client rejects that proposal?" Ngo asks with a note of disbelief.

Wisnowski shrugs. "There are a lot of moving parts in play here, Your Honor."

Ngo's eyes stray to Cumming for a moment before he leans back in his seat. "I'll say. Multiple lawsuits, FBI involvement, a formal complaint to the bar association. Still, we're here to discuss the cases between R & B and your clients. In all fairness to defense counsel, the other matters in play—while fascinating—are extraneous to the matter at hand."

The judge turns to Penelope. "Anything to add, counselor?"

"Given the position Miss Wisnowski finds herself in, perhaps a continuance for a few weeks is in order," Penelope replies. "I would like to conclude this matter before the new year. It doesn't appear as if the outcome is in doubt—it's only the dollars and cents that need to be worked out."

Ngo has been nodding along as he listened. His eyes swing to Wisnowski, flicker to Cumming, then settle again on Wisnowski. "I think Miss Brooks has summed things up nicely. I'm going to grant a continuance to the first week of January, and I strongly urge you to arrive at a settlement before the end of this month. I will be disappointed if we find ourselves back in this courtroom in the new year. Are we all in agreement with that?"

"Yes, Your Honor," Penelope quickly replies.

Ngo settles a malevolent eye on Herbert Cumming, who has so far been strangely quiet. "It is my hope that other matters surrounding this case, but not germane to it, will not be permitted to delay a resolution, Mr. Cumming—no matter how much more important or pressing they may seem to you."

Cumming merely nods.

Ngo leans a little further across the bench with his arms crossed in front of him. "If I may make a suggestion, Mr. Cumming, it may behoove your firm to withdraw as counsel in all other matters pertaining to the accident on September eighth."

The look of defiance on Cumming's face suggests that he doesn't appreciate the judge daring to offer him advice. I can't imagine Cumming's legal career surviving the fallout from the debacle he's brought upon himself—especially given that Randall Lennox's buddy at Butterworth Cole has offered testimony about Cumming's misconduct to both the FBI and the disciplinary board—yet he seems to be gearing up for a fight. Doesn't the fool realize that his law firm partners won't think twice about making a clean break with him in an effort to salvage some shred of their firm's reputation? Well, as Penelope has pointed out over and over again, Cumming is blessed with more than his fair share of hubris.

Penelope leans close as we leave the courtroom five minutes later. "Looks like Herbert is determined to go down fighting."

I snort. "If there's any justice in this world, he'll meet his fate at the hands of his Mafia buddies."

Penelope gives me a sideways look. "I worry about you a bit, partner. I want you to take a few weeks off, maybe until after New Year's. Spend time with Brittany and Deano. Chill."

"Not the worst suggestion," I say. "But, really, there's nothing to worry about. I'm okay now."

She shakes her head gently and slows as we approach our cars. "This ordeal has changed something in you, partner."

"How so?"

She stops and studies me for a long moment. "You radiate anger, even a mean streak at times. Justifiably so, but I hope the rage is about burnt out. Maybe a quiet month of recuperating will turn you back into the partner I had a couple of months ago."

"That bad?" I ask in surprise.

She pulls a sad face and nods.

So, the nightmare didn't end on a driveway in Wisconsin, after all. I pull Penelope into a hug. "Thanks for being straight with me, partner. I'll work on it."

CHAPTER THIRTY-SIX

W e're well into our open house at Forty-Seven Liberty Street the day after Christmas when Penelope and her roommate, Becky Seguin, arrive.

"Hi, handsome!" Becky says while she pinches my cheek, pats it affectionately, and plants a chaste kiss on my lips. We've always gotten along but have ramped it up a notch since I inadvertently walked in on her and Penelope sharing an intimate moment at the office a few weeks ago. It had happened on the occasion of the grand opening and christening of the new Executive Offices and World Headquarters of Brooks and Valenti, Attorneys No Longer Shoehorned into a Strip Mall Shithole.

Penelope had blushed in embarrassment but thankfully hadn't felt any shame. I was glad to finally solve the riddle of why she wasn't attached. If anyone deserves to be loved and happy, it's got to be her. I've always liked Becky, and now that she's totally free to be herself with me, we're getting along like gangbusters.

"Sometimes I'm jealous when I have to listen to her rave about you," Becky had admitted with a grin an hour or so after I walked in on them. "If she's ever gonna do it with a guy, it might be you."

"Nah, I hear we're all assholes."

"That's true," she agreed with a sly smile. She says the nicest things.

Trish, who's been spending quite a bit of time nursing me back to health, hugs my arm close to her and shoots Penelope a mock scowl. "Hands off."

They share a chuckle before Becky stands back to give me an appraising look. "You're looking almost back to normal."

It's true. Joe's head left me with a couple of horrific black eyes that had morphed through almost every color of the rainbow over the following weeks. I can now breathe, pronounce the letter *V* properly, and am recovering from the concussion I suffered from either the head slam with Joe, smashing my head into the driveway, or both. "At least now you've got an excuse for being a doofus," Brittany tells me from time to time.

The Luciano family has taken a few good blows from law enforcement in the wake of Brittany's kidnapping and the murders of Ed Stankowski and Bobby Harland. I've been looking over my shoulder, but Jake and Max assure me that the mobsters currently have their hands full just trying keep their asses out of jail. If Jake and Max are to be believed, the thugs are either lying low or lying on beaches somewhere far from Cedar Heights. It's comforting to think so, yet I worry that they'll circle back to take vengeance on me when the dust settles.

But today isn't the time to think about that.

As for my other Mafia *paisano*, I haven't heard from Matteo Giordano. I wonder if he still feels as if I owe him a favor. He had nothing to do with rescuing Brittany, so trying to hold me to that nebulous agreement is ridiculous on its face. Then again, he's a Mafioso.

Billy and Rick used the occasion of our office opening to treat the entire firm to beer and pizza in a show of appreciation. There's been plenty to celebrate on the R & B front over the past few weeks. The NTSB finally issued its official report on the investigation into the September eighth crash. They laid primary blame for the tragedy on the doorstep of pilot Megan Walton. It turns out that Megan had been drinking the night before, in contravention of FAA rules, and had made at least three critical errors after she got into trouble over Lake Michigan. She hadn't feathered the prop, hadn't raised the landing gear, and had sealed their fate by attempting a tight turn back to shore when she should have made a wide, sweeping turn. The Cessna engine hadn't been running at the time of the crash, which suggested fuel starvation as the inciting cause of the accident. The NTSB noted Billy's and Rick's testimony suggesting Megan may not have bled the fuel tanks that fateful morning. Because of the missing fuel samples, AAA Avgas is off the hook for the accident, although fuel samples collected from their supplies the next day proved to be tainted, so at least they haven't gotten away scot free. Windy City and its preferred flight instructor also came in for brutal criticism. The tour company lost its license to operate aircraft after Megan's flight instructor cut a deal with prosecutors, admitting to the bribe from Jonathan Walton and agreeing to testify against him. The scuzzball escaped jail time by rolling over on Walton, but he won't be doing any more flight training. Walton, of course, has a battery of high-priced lawyers trying to get his sorry ass out of the crack it's in.

The best news is that R & B has been absolved of any responsibility by the NTSB and FBI. Senator Evan Milton has removed them as a defendant in the lawsuit filed against those responsible for the death of his wife, child, and parents. He was even gracious enough to stop by their little airport office to unnecessarily apologize for initially including R & B in the action Penelope made the wreckage of the Cessna available for him to use in his case against Windy City. Penelope has arranged to sell Milton what's left of the plane. I hope it happens soon. We can't afford to have money invested in the damned aircraft.

Actually, now that I think of it, perhaps the fate of Herbert Cumming vies for the best news crown. His co-conspirator, Andrea Wisnowski, was quick to turn state's evidence against him, which sealed his fate. As I predicted, his partners kicked his ass to the curb in a New York minute when the scandal broke, his law license was suspended pending a hearing that will most likely revoke it for life, and he's facing criminal charges and a massive civil suit filed by Senator Mitton. I wish him only the worst. Penelope has put him out of her mind and moved on.

I, on the other hand, must be a miserably vindictive SOB, because I'm reveling in every new snippet of misfortune that befalls Cumming the rancid owners of Windy City Sky Tours. I've especially enjoyed the FBI rolling out a string of charges against them. The cherry on top was a court ruling that opened them up to personal civil liability based on Jonathan Walton's machinations to put Megan in a Windy City cockpit. Predictably, they've turned on one another with a vengeance as they try to limit the hit on their personal fortunes. As for the self-evident truth that Walton was in bed with the Luciano family in the campaign against Billy and Rick—including the kidnapping of my daughter—the FBI has so far been unable to turn up evidence or a single witness to buttress that case. I hope the Windy City assholes end up slitting one another's throats. Maybe Franklin and Tyson can both take a turn on Walton.

After I fetch drinks and snacks for Penelope and Becky, I settle back in a corner and observe the festivities as people drift back and forth between the kitchen and living room. It's nice to have this intimate group of family and friends together after the hell of October and November. The deaths of Ed Stankowski and Bobby Harland hover on the edge of everyone's thoughts, threatening to cast a pall over the party, but there are other lives to celebrate—some of which were almost cut short, as well.

Deano is doing that Deano thing where he presses his snout into Papa's lap to demand attention. Papa flew home within a week of Jake Plummer getting word to him that his old nemesis from Orsomarso was no longer a concern. The dog abandons my father without so much as a glance back when Brittany settles onto the corner of his doggy bed. He may have lost a step since his Mafia encounter, but he's on his back in tummy-rub position within seconds. Deano remembers who nursed him back to health. Given the price of his treatment and rehab, I suspect that his vet and her family found lots and lots of goodies under the Christmas tree yesterday. BMWs. Mercedes-Benzes. Diamonds. That sort of thing. Deano's worth it. Right?

My eyes shift from Deano to Brittany. I'm relieved that she seems to have come through her ordeal in reasonably good shape. She catches me looking, gives me a teasing smile, and rubs her shirt sleeve just about where a couple of buckshot pellets nicked her when the shotgun discharged during the collision with Joe.

"I wonder if anyone would care to make me a cup of hot chocolate?" she wonders aloud. When nobody leaps at the opportunity, she turns her big drama-class eyes on me. "Not even the father who shot me? I might forgive him if he made me some nice hot chocolate."

As I laugh and get up, she says to the room at large, "My therapist thinks I may eventually get past the trauma of attempted filicide if Dad makes me at least one cup of hot chocolate every day."

"I had to look filicide up, too," I say when I notice some

blank looks. "Think infanticide for kids and teenagers. Think mercy killing for parents."

My thoughts stay on Brittany after I put the kettle on to boil. To my immense relief, she's rebuffed Michelle's attempts to convince her that she would be better off living in Europe with her mother. Brittany refuses to even visit unless Michelle withdraws her legal effort to win custody. While I stand in the kitchen doorway watching, I notice her drifting away with a pained longing on her face that suggests her thoughts have turned to Bobby. She's pretty much quit mentioning him over the last week or two, but I sense that the loss remains acute and that my daughter is in more emotional pain than she lets on. At least she's not consumed by guilt, which was a distinct possibility given that the kidnapping was related to our family and that she survived while Bobby did not. The idea that she is in any way responsible for what befell Bobby is ridiculous, of course, but the unfathomable twists and turns that guilt and grief follow are often beyond understanding.

Papa, for instance, was utterly devastated and inconsolable after the death of his newfound friend, Ed Stankowski. My father blamed himself for Ed's murder and yet, since his return from Italy, he hasn't seemed to have given his deceased friend a thought. I hope that's not the case, but sometimes I wonder. Papa is a bit of an enigma to me these days, distant and preoccupied. I've seen glimpses this melancholy in him ever since the dramas he went through last year, which left him shaken and scarred. Now that he's finally free of the specter of retribution for his long-ago crime in Italy, I have a sneaking suspicion that he's on the verge of decamping to Italy permanently to make up for lost time with his sister and her family. It will do him good to escape the Liberty Street memories that haunt him: the murder, Mama's death, and the trauma we've been through over the past few months.

The doorbell rings, attracting a lazy sideways glance from

our watchdog, who promptly nudges Brittany, gives her hand a quick little lick, and sighs in contentment when his tummy rub resumes.

I find Jake Plummer and Max Maxwell on the doorstep. Max holds the screen door open wide while Jake maneuvers a walker over the threshold and shuffles inside. He's dressed in shiny maroon sweatpants, a matching zip-up hoodie, and a pair of unlaced black sneakers. Nothing difficult to get on and off. There's even a little stubble on his chin.

"Is that a nascent goatee or a shaving oversight?" I ask while touching a fingertip to the whiskers.

"One or the other," he replies irritably.

We exchange a handshake and hello before Max pushes inside, flicks a thumb toward the walker, rolls his eyes, and mutters, "Big production for a fuckin' flesh wound, ain't it?"

"Screw you, Max," Jake answers softly, then lowers his voice barely above a whisper to add, "and watch your god damned language, will you? There's ladies and a teenager present."

We all chuckle, and then Max and I follow Jake into the kitchen. Jake suffered considerably more than a flesh wound during the shootout at the farmhouse the night we rescued Brittany. His survival had been touch and go for several hours after he'd caught a couple of slugs. Fortunately, the bullets had missed vital organs and arteries when they tore into him, but Jake is facing a long, painful stretch in rehab and is being pensioned off his detective job with the Cedar Heights PD. Unlike my daughter, who *did* suffer a flesh wound, Jake doesn't demand a beverage, so I pour him a nice glass of his favorite Glenfiddich 21-Year-Old Scotch without making him play the guilt card to be served. Brittany slides a plate of Joan Brooks's terrific chocolate chip cookies under his nose and plants a kiss on his cheek.

"How are you doing?" I ask after setting his drink in front of him at the kitchen table.

"Can't complain," he replies.

I shoot a sideways glance at my daughter and bounce an eyebrow. "Nobody would blame *you* for doing a little complaining, Jake."

"You don't have to listen to all his damned griping and moaning and groaning the way some of us do," Max grumbles. Jake is in good if not sentimental hands. The first time we'd gotten together after Jake was released from the hospital, it was clear that Mrs. Plummer was going to need help. Max had immediately volunteered, but had laid out the ground rules for Max Care. "There ain't gonna be an any schmaltzy bullshit, pal. Don't get used to being waited on hand and foot, you old bastard. I ain't your babysitter or a damn nurse." From what I've seen over the last few weeks, Max is doing a surprisingly good imitation of both.

My cop buddies add considerable spice and humor to the proceedings for the next little while as I bask in the camaraderie and, yes, the love that permeates these relationships. In one way or another, everyone here has been through his or her own version of hell over the past few months and understands that we've all played a part in seeing one another through. We share a bond that I hope doesn't diminish as events recede into the rearview mirrors of our lives. Somehow, I just can't see that happening.

Penelope and Becky are the first ones to call it a night.

"I need to get a good night's sleep for a big meeting in the morning," Penelope says before she deposits her glass in the dishwasher and circles the room to dole out kisses and hugs.

"What about you?" Jake asks me. "Are you going to this meeting, too, or are you still making her do all the work?"

I shrug and say, "She's the brains of the organization."

Max snorts. "I suppose you think you're the brawn after our little escapade in Wisconsin?"

"Hardly," I reply, and mean it. I hope to never again find myself in a situation that even vaguely resembles that night in

Wisconsin. Joe was an asshole and I hated the son of a bitch, yet I still have nightmares about killing him and inexplicably wonder if I couldn't have played those chaotic few seconds differently. I guess that makes me different from guys like him. I can live with that.

"What's this big meeting tomorrow about?" Trish asks Penelope.

"Hopefully, the final settlement negotiation between R & B and the principals of Windy City. I'll be happy to get back to our mom-and-pop cases when this is finally over."

"Amen," I say as I kiss her and Becky goodnight.

"Good luck with that," Jake tells Penelope as he casts a skeptical eye on me. "Trouble seems to follow your partner around."

Dear Reader,

Thank you for taking the time to read *Plane in the Lake*, the second book in the Tony Valenti Thriller series. You'll find links to the books are on the following pages.

Do you wish to be among the first to hear about upcoming releases, giveaways, and contests? If so, please join my exclusive Reader's Club here. Your email address will not be shared or used for any other purpose. Promise! While you're on the website, feel free to poke around a bit to learn a little more about me and the upcoming releases.

If you enjoyed *Plane in the Lake*, I would greatly appreciate you taking a moment to leave a review at your favorite book retailer. You can also leave a Goodreads review here. Reviews are invaluable to authors, particularly those of us who have chosen to publish independently. The review doesn't need to be anything elaborate, just a brief line or two about why you enjoyed the book. It would mean the world to me. A final tip about reviews:

Please don't include spoilers that give anything important away!

My sincerest thanks again!

Take care, be well,

Neil

THE END

BOOK ONE - A HOUSE ON LIBERTY STREET

TONY VALENTI THRILLERS BOOK ONE

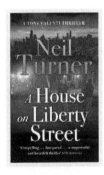

BUY IT HERE

When Tony Valenti's sixty-nine-year-old father inexplicably shoots a sheriff's deputy on their front porch, Tony is thrust into a life and death struggle to discover why his father shot a cop. He enlists the help of a public defender and a local newspaper reporter in a rush to unravel the truth about the night of the shooting, only to become a target himself. His initial bewilderment turns to rage and fuels a gritty determination to get to the bottom of what really happened—regardless of the risks. Can he save his father? The family home? Himself?

BOOK THREE - A CASE OF BETRAYAL

TONY VALENTI THRILLERS BOOK THREE

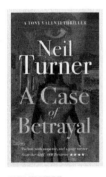

BUY IT HERE

A woman is brutally slain, and suspicion immediately falls upon her ex-husband. But should it? The suspect turns to Tony Valenti for help. The case is a bewildering maze with a mountain of contradictory evidence that points both to *and* away from Tony's client. What *is* the truth? Even Tony isn't sure of his client's innocence in a case where nothing is as it seems. Then a lethal terror from Tony's past surfaces to shake his faith in himself... and to threaten those dearest to him. Is Tony being pulled in too many directions to save anyone?

BOOK FOUR - A TIME FOR RECKONING

TONY VALENTI THRILLERS BOOK FOUR

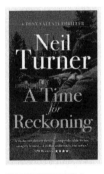

BUY IT HERE (Click on the image)

Tony Valenti and Penelope Brooks are enlisted to come to the aid of a young woman when her marriage turns sour in a remote corner of Wyoming. They don't practice law in Wyoming, but representing vulnerable clients battling impossible odds is what they do. They are quickly embroiled in a fight that may be to the death, with danger coming at Tony from several directions. Ill-equipped to face the battles he's forced to wage, he must rely on his guile and the help of unexpected allies to survive long enough to rescue his client… and himself.

BOOK FIVE - SCARED SILENT

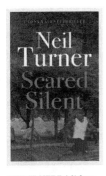

BUY IT HERE (click on cover)

His choices: prison or death. Which scares him more?

When fifteen-year-old Denzel Payton is charged with the murder of a disabled veteran at a homeless camp, he's trapped in a no-win situation: remain silent and risk almost certain conviction, or name the real killer and face the wrath of a monster who terrifies him.

After Denzel's attorney is murdered, lawyers Tony Valenti and Penelope Brooks step up to defend him, despite the risk of becoming the killer's next targets. As the evidence against their client mounts and potential defense witnesses vanish, Tony and Penelope race to unravel a dark secret that may hold the key to the case. They'll need smarts, guts, and a little luck to save Denzel.

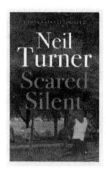

BUY IT HERE (click on cover)

FREE - LAST EXIT ON THE ROAD TO NOWHERE

FREE READER'S CLUB SERIES PREQUEL NOVELLA

CLAIM YOUR FREE COPY

Last Exit on the Road to Nowhere is a prequel novella about the high-stakes dramas at work and home that precipitated Tony Valenti's move to Cedar Heights. These are the events that propel Tony and Brittany into the opening chapter of *A House on Liberty Street,* and will continue to reverberate through Tony's world in the novels that follow. What will ultimately become of Tony's family? His career? His life? It all begins here. Become a Reader's Club member and find out!

ACKNOWLEDGMENTS

As always, there are a great many people to thank for helping to make this book possible. My thanks to Susan Turner, Kyle Turner, Tamara Miller, Monica Furness, Tina Raymond, Mary Ann Tippet, Raymond Huet, and Erin Scothorn, who read and commented on my working files along the way. Your input was invaluable and made the book immeasurably better. As I said in the acknowledgements of *A House on Liberty Street*, while writing can be a solitary endeavor, generous souls such as yourselves ensure that it need not be a lonely journey.

My gratitude also to a pair of amazing professionals who helped to ensure that *A Plane in the Lake* was as good as I could possibly make it. Leighton Wingate did a terrific job proofreading the manuscript so that it reads far better than it did when he took on the arduous task of cleaning up after me. The talented David Prendergast has once again designed a stunning cover. I hope the inside of the book is as good as its cover.

As for the portions of the story pertaining to aircraft, flying, and accident investigations, any mistakes in technical information are my responsibility—as are decisions to take artistic license in crafting events in service to the story. I'm a fiction writer, after all. It's my job to make things up!

ABOUT THE AUTHOR

Neil discovered the thrill of losing himself in the pages of a book as a five- or six-year-old when Beatrix Potter and Thornton Burgess immersed him in the worlds of Jerry Muskrat, Peter Rabbit, and their furry friends. His mother and father had the good grace to indulge his excitement about being able to read *them* stories, which he thought was pretty darned cool. He's been reading and writing one thing or another ever since, but it was many years before the audacious idea of *writing a book* wormed its way into his head. He's lived throughout Canada, spent three years in Europe, and lived in Chicago and Arizona, somehow managing to squeeze a career in banking and finance into his travels. After doing an apprenticeship reading, reading, reading, taking courses, attending seminars and conferences, and churning out some truly atrocious manuscripts, he began writing and stockpiling the Tony Valenti series of thrillers. The series will total four published novels by the end of 2021, plus a free prequel novella for members of my exclusive Reader's Club. There will be more titles to come in 2022 and beyond, probably at the rate of two or three per year. Stay tuned!

Neil lives in Ottawa, Ontario, Canada.

Made in the USA
Middletown, DE
22 December 2022

20214497R00222